Love's
MASQUERADE

Praise for Radclyffe's Fiction

"...well-plotted...lovely romance...I couldn't turn the pages fast enough!" – Ann Bannon, author of *The Beebo Brinker Chronicles*.

"...well-honed storytelling skills...solid prose and sure-handedness of the narrative..." – Elizabeth Flynn, *Lambda Book Report*

"...a thoughtful and thought-provoking tale...deftly handled in nuanced and textured prose that is both intelligent and deeply personal. The sex is exciting, the story is daring, the characters are well-developed and interesting – in short, Radclyffe has once again pulled together all the ingredients of a genuine page-turner..." – Cameron Abbott, author of *To the Edge* and *An Inexpressible State of Grace*

"With ample angst, realistic and exciting medical emergencies, winsome secondary characters, and a sprinkling of humor...a terrific romance...one of the best I have read in the last three years. Highly recommended." – Author Lori L. Lake, Book Reviewer for the *Independent Gay Writer*

"Radclyffe employs...a lean, trim, and tight writing style...rich with meticulously developed characterizations and realistic dialogue..." – Arlene Germain, *Lambda Book Report*

"...one writer who creates believably great characters that are just as strong as mainstream publishing's Kay Scarpetta or Kinsey Milhone...If you're looking for a great romance, read anything by Radclyffe." – Sherry Stinson, editor, *Outlook Press*

Love's
MASQUERADE

by

RADCLYfFE

2005

LOVE'S MASQUERADE

ISBN 1-933110-14-7

THIS TRADE PAPERBACK ORIGINAL IS PUBLISHED BY
BOLD STROKES BOOKS, INC.,
PHILADELPHIA, PA, USA

FIRST EDITION: DECEMBER 2003
SECOND PRINTING: NOVEMBER, 2004 BOLD STROKES BOOKS, INC.
THIRD PRINTING: JUNE, 2005 BOLD STROKES BOOKS, INC.

CREDITS
EDITOR: LANEY ROBERTS
EXECUTIVE EDITOR: STACIA SEAMAN
PRODUCTION DESIGN: STACIA SEAMAN
COVER DESIGN BY SHERI (GRAPHICARTIST2020@HOTMAIL.COM)

By the Author

Romances

Safe Harbor

Beyond the Breakwater

Innocent Hearts

Love's Melody Lost

Love's Tender Warriors

Tomorrow's Promise

Passion's Bright Fury

Love's Masquerade

shadowland

Fated Love

Distant Shores, Silent Thunder

Honor Series

Above All, Honor

Honor Bound

Love & Honor

Honor Guards

Justice Series

A Matter of Trust (prequel)

Shield of Justice

In Pursuit of Justice

Justice in the Shadows

Justice Served

Change Of Pace: *Erotic Interludes*
(A Short Story Collection)

Acknowledgments

Creating a book is a many-faceted and fascinating process. This one began, as all of mine do, with a mental snapshot of two women in a particular setting. When I began the Honor series, I thought, "Oh, it would be fun to write about a secret service agent and the president's daughter," and I pictured them sequestered together in the back of a fortified vehicle. That set the tone for the entire series. When I began *Love's Masquerade*, I imagined a woman leaning across a desk piled high with manuscripts in disorderly piles debating some issue with the woman seated on the other side. The words on those pages that lay between them, and all they revealed about those who wrote and read them, forged their relationship. This book is my homage to the power of the written word and the critical place that writing holds in my life.

I owe special thanks to Katlyn for allowing me to excerpt several scenes from Storm Surge for inclusion in this work.

Thanks to my editors, Laney Roberts and Stacia Seaman, for dealing with the particularly difficult editing challenge presented by the format of this work with good humor and their usual thoroughness; to my beta readers, Athos, Eva, Diane, Denise, JB, and Tomboy, for their review of the early manuscript and proofing of the final one; and to HS and the members of the Radlist for their incredible enthusiasm and inspiration during the posting of the Web version.

The cover presented a challenge in that Sheri, like all artists, had a particular image in her mind of a very specific mask. We finally found the hand-painted Venetian mask—where else—on the Internet, and I purchased it and had it shipped to me. Lee photographed it and from a single image of a mask against a plain white background, Sheri made magic once again.

It was through the written word that Lee and I met, and sharing this passion with her is the joy of my life. Every word is for her. *Amo te.*

Radclyffe 2004

Dedication

For Lee,
For All the Days to Come

CHAPTER ONE

A uden Frost read the form letter again.

```
Dear Ms. Frost:

   Your interview has been scheduled for
Monday, March 17th, at 10:00 a.m. in Suite
4000, the Palmer Building, 1900 Rittenhouse
Square.
   We look forward to the opportunity to
meet with you.

Sincerely,
Abelard H. Pritchard
Director of Operations
Palmer Publishing, Inc.
```

It was eight-thirty. If she walked slowly, stopped at Starbucks, and read the morning *Inquirer*, she'd only be half an hour early. Her destination in one of the elegant stone edifices that bordered the historic square was five blocks from her three-story brownstone on St. James Place.

Early is good. Early shows interest; early shows reliability. Early shows...punctuality. She grimaced. *Early is desperate. And I'm not desperate...yet.*

She still had a few thousand dollars left in her savings account, and she had resumes out to every publishing house, magazine, and press in the tri-state area. Thank God for Great-Aunt Sophie and the long, rain-filled winters.

Soon after Auden had begun her freshman year at Penn, Aunt

Sophie had decided that the Philadelphia climate was bad for her arthritis and had precipitously moved to Florida. She'd declared Auden manager of the apartment house she owned and offered her niece the ground-floor apartment with reduced rent as payment for her newly designated duties. Now, seven years later, the Center City enclave west of Rittenhouse Square was so popular with young professionals that the rents had become ridiculously inflated, and Auden never would have been able to afford to live there under other circumstances.

And I won't be able to stay here much longer unless I get a job soon.

Eight-forty. Before stepping outside, she stopped in front of the walnut-framed, full-length mirror just inside the entranceway and checked her appearance. Medium height, medium build, medium-length golden-blond hair. Ordinary in every respect. The pale green suit was well cut if not terribly expensive and the ochre silk blouse, an admitted extravagance, was both.

The morning news had said unseasonably warm, so she decided to forgo her winter coat, choosing a raincoat instead. Outside on the marble steps, she turned sideways to allow the third-floor tenant to pass on the narrow stoop.

"Hi, Gayle."

"Aud, hi. I was going to ca—Shylock! No!" The petite, tawny-skinned woman in a Temple sweatshirt and baggy blue jeans yanked on the lead of the black and brown mixed-breed terrier by her side.

Laughing, Auden put a hand down to stop the inquisitive nose before it landed unceremoniously between her thighs. "I do *not* need dog smears today, thank you very much."

"Today's the big interview?"

"Yep." Auden agilely circumvented the dog and escaped to the sidewalk. Looking up at her tenant and best friend who lingered on the small landing, one hip braced against the wrought-iron railing, she added, "This is the perfect job. Right location, right division, right... everything. Wish me luck."

"You don't need luck," Gayle stated, juggling leash, a cup of coffee, and a take-out bag as she unlocked the door. "You've got brains. Call me later with all the details."

"Don't you have to work?"

"Just got back. I was the float resident last night."

"Okay. I'll check in this afternoon after you've had a nap."

"Call me," Gayle repeated as she disappeared inside. "I want to hear everything."

Auden took a deep breath and started off. *I just hope there's something to tell.*

❖

Despite every delaying tactic she could devise, Auden was still fifteen minutes early. When the brass-plated doors of the double-wide elevator slid silently open on the top floor of the Palmer Building, she had hoped to find a lobby or hallway where she could loiter a few more moments before entering the appointed office. No such luck.

Directly across the wine-colored, carpeted expanse stood a waist-high, dark wood counter that clearly designated the reception area. The executive suite appeared to occupy the entire top floor. As Auden approached, a perfectly coiffed redhead looked up with a practiced smile from behind the adjoining desk.

"Good morning," the receptionist purred. "May I help you?"

"Yes, I have an appointment with Mr. Pritchard."

The smallest of frowns, quickly extinguished, marred the flawless forehead for a millisecond. "Your name?"

"Auden Frost."

"Just a moment." A half-swivel on the leather chair, a flash of fingers flying across a keyboard, a series of entries scrolling down the computer monitor. Another pleasant smile. "I'm sorry. I don't see your name. Perhaps it's with another division? I doubt that Mr. Pritchard—"

"I have the confirmation here," Auden interrupted smoothly, taking care to keep her voice even. She passed the letter across the wide surface.

A quick scan and yet another smile. "If you'll wait just another moment, please," the redhead said with an inclination of her head toward the sofas and chairs to the right of the reception desk.

"Of course."

Auden settled onto a plush fabric couch, watched as the receptionist made a call, then glanced out the floor-to-ceiling windows opposite her. She'd barely had time to take in the breathtaking view of the downtown skyline and the Delaware River twenty blocks south before the redhead got up and silently approached.

"Please come this way, Ms. Frost."

"Thank you," Auden replied, barely able to keep the relief from her voice.

She followed through a paneled walnut door into a labyrinth of hallways with smaller rooms opening on either side to yet another set of double doors. There was an intercom discreetly set into the wall.

The redhead pressed a button and spoke softly. "I have Ms. Frost, Mr. Pritchard."

"Come in, please, Alana."

After a nearly inaudible click, Alana opened the doors and gestured Auden through ahead of her.

Once inside, Auden crossed the thick carpet, a deep blue this time, toward another enormous wood desk, behind which stood a tall thin man in a fine gray worsted-wool suit, white shirt, and muted navy tie. He looked to be about fifty, with a full head of dark hair and steel blue eyes. She held out her hand.

"Mr. Pritchard? Auden Frost."

"Ms. Frost." His voice was a well-modulated baritone. "Please sit down." Glancing to the door, he said, "Thank you, Alana."

Another second and they were alone. Auden resisted the urge to survey her surroundings and kept her gaze steadfastly on Pritchard's face. It was impossible to read anything behind his studied expression.

"I'm afraid there's been a miscommunication, Ms. Frost," he advised as he settled behind his desk. "Our records indicate that you were initially scheduled to interview for a position in the nonfiction division."

"That's correct." Perplexed, Auden raised an eyebrow. "And I take it there's a problem?"

"An embarrassing one—for me." He folded his hands and leaned forward. "It seems that the positi—"

"Abel?" A door on the far side of the office opened suddenly and a woman walked in. "Have you got—"

Both Auden and Abelard Pritchard turned in the direction of the interruption. The woman who stood in the open doorway was taller than average, with unruly jet black hair and obsidian eyes that appeared fathomless in contrast to her pale complexion. Her gaze locked with Auden's, and for a moment, the silence in the room made the very air seem heavy. Without moving her eyes from Auden's face, she murmured in a throaty tenor, "I'm sorry, Abel. I didn't realize you had an appointment."

"Neither, apparently, did I." Pritchard looked from one woman to the other, startled by the intensity of their expressions. "I'm afraid I failed to inform Ms. Frost that the position for which she was scheduled to interview had already been filled."

"That doesn't sound like you," the woman commented, a frown line forming between her finely drawn brows. She finally released Auden's gaze and looked directly at Pritchard. There was a faint edge to her voice, but it seemed to be one of curiosity rather than censure. "How did that happen?"

"At the moment, I'm not certain."

"What position?"

Auden cleared her throat, more annoyed at being talked about in the third person than she was disappointed to learn that the job for which she had held such hope was no longer available. "An editor in the nonfiction division."

"Editor?" The dark gaze returned to study Auden as the newcomer leaned a shoulder gracefully against the highly polished woodwork of the door frame. "Have you experience?"

The sudden scrutiny from the penetrating eyes was as tangible as a touch, and Auden found her throat unexpectedly tight as she replied. "Yes."

"Perhaps we should talk."

"I'm sorry?" Auden gave a visible start. *Who* is *this woman?*

"Abel, would you please assemble the necessary paperwork and show Ms. Frost into my office?"

"Hays, I'm not certain—"

The woman turned away. "Thank you, Mr. Pritchard."

Pritchard rose stiffly, then quickly regained his professional equanimity. With a slight sweep of his arm, he indicated the doorway through which the dark-haired woman had disappeared. "If you please, Ms. Frost."

Auden had no choice but to follow. A moment later, she found herself in yet another richly appointed office, larger than the one she had just left. The floor was dark hardwood, highly glossed, with a thick Oriental rug in the center of the room. The desk, with several leather chairs facing it, sat in front of another wall of windows; a sitting area complete with sofa, coffee table, and more chairs filled the far corner.

One entire wall was comprised of bookcases, the shelves filled to capacity. The paperbacks interspersed with the hardcovers all appeared to be reader's copies, rather than the standard bound sets that were often little more than decoration. At first glance, Auden didn't recognize many of the titles, but that didn't surprise her. She wasn't much of a fiction reader. And despite the opulent surroundings, it wasn't the décor that interested her.

Mr. Pritchard handed a slim file folder, which Auden presumed held her job application and resume, to the woman standing beside her. After he discreetly left, Auden found herself looking once again into those dark eyes. Up close, she realized that what she had thought initially to be solid dark pupils were actually nearly black irises flecked with bits of silver and gold. Lovely, hypnotically beautiful. Like the woman.

Auden's heart beat loudly in her ears.

"I'm Haydon Palmer, Ms. Frost."

Auden blinked, and the spell was broken. Once again she held out her hand, and the returned grip this time was just as firm as Mr. Pritchard's, but the skin cooler and very soft. "I'm happy to meet you."

"Please, have a seat," Hays said as she gently released Auden's hand. She moved behind her desk and gestured to the file. "If you'll just give me a moment?"

"Of course." Auden tried not to look as shell-shocked as she felt. She hadn't expected an interview with the president of the publishing company, nor had she expected Haydon Palmer to be quite so...well, so...*Young? Commanding? Stunning?*

While the other woman flipped pages, Auden took advantage of the opportunity to study her. She didn't look much older than Auden's twenty-five, although her pale flawless skin, elegantly chiseled cheekbones, and sculpted jaw made it difficult to delve beneath the beauty for the usual clues. From where she sat, Auden could make out a few faint lines at the corners of deep-set eyes, but these could have been from laughter as well as years. Only the barest hint of shadows bruising nearly translucent lower lids marred the otherwise perfect face.

The dark silk jacket and trousers fit the lean and angular frame so well that they had to have been custom made. In surprising contradistinction to the exquisitely expensive suit, the head of Palmer Publishing wore a simple white silk T-shirt beneath the jacket. The hands that held the sheet of paper were long fingered and finely boned. Oddly, Auden could discern a faint tremor in them. For some reason, that unwitting confession of physical vulnerability caused Auden to catch her breath sharply. She found Haydon Palmer infinitely more attractive in the face of this slight hint of human frailty.

Hays glanced up to find Auden's blue-green eyes—made even greener, she'd wager, by the reflection of the fabric the blond wore—riveted on her face. The gently searching look was soft and soothing on her skin. As silence descended once again, Hays allowed her gaze to roam over the woman who watched her.

Reddish highlights glinted in thick golden hair, full red lips parted faintly, and the delicately drawn features, coupled with the glow of honey-tinged complexion, created a visage worthy of a portrait gallery. The suggestion of a strong body tempered by gentle curves completed the picture of an extraordinarily attractive woman.

"What exactly did you edit?" Hays asked, her tone low, almost seductive.

Auden dragged her eyes away from Haydon Palmer's face, hoping to dispel the disquieting distraction the woman's presence created. She cleared her throat and replied in a steady voice. "Miller was a scholarly press. I started out editing art history and literary criticism, and for the last year, I was the education division manager."

An eyebrow quirked. "And that required?"

Auden described her previous duties, an exercise that, in her experience, generally caused a listener's eyes to glaze over. It sounded unbearably dry to most people, but she had enjoyed the order and the predictability of both the work and routine. Haydon Palmer, however, appeared to listen with quiet attention.

"Miller Press was just recently absorbed by the University of Pennsylvania, wasn't it?" Hays remarked when Auden concluded.

"Yes. And, as a result, some positions and personnel became... redundant."

"Redundant."

Auden swallowed, amazed at the intensity Haydon Palmer managed to project with merely a word. "It's not a term I care to apply to myself, but that is, in fact, what I have been deemed."

"Somehow I doubt that." A smile twitched at the corner of Hays's mouth. "Have you ever edited fiction?"

"No," Auden answered carefully. "I won't pretend there are no differences, but the mechanics must surely be the same."

Hays leaned back in the dark leather chair and crossed her ankle over her knee. The suggestion of a smile had become a grin, but it was quickly replaced by an appraising stare. "Who's your favorite romance writer?"

"I'm sorry?"

"Romances. The number one seller in America."

"I...don't read them."

"You *do* read fiction?"

"Uh...occasionally. Well, rarely, actually."

"What do you read for pleasure, then?"

Auden hesitated. If this was an interview, it was the oddest one she had ever encountered. Since she had no idea where the conversation was going, she decided not to worry about the outcome. She had a feeling she had already failed whatever test Haydon Palmer was conducting. "Biographies, social commentary...some history."

"Why not fiction?"

"I don't know..." Auden contemplated the question, surprised that she hadn't a clue to the answer. "I suppose I've never had enough time."

"Light reading doesn't satisfy?"

"Not usually," Auden admitted. "I could never really relate to it. I've always been a little...bored."

Too well grounded for light escapism? Hays passed a hand over her face and straightened slightly, realizing that she shouldn't have even begun this interview. There'd just been something so compelling about the look in Auden Frost's eyes that first moment in Abel's office. Inquisitiveness, intelligence, strength. She sighed, wondering if her weariness showed.

"I'm sorry, Ms. Frost. I apologize that Mr. Pritchard failed to inform you that the advertised position was no longer available. It turns out that the previous editor decided that early retirement wasn't as appealing as it sounded, and she wanted to come back. She'd worked here for many years, and we felt an obligation to her. It made sense for her to simply resume her previous duties."

"I understand. But if I may ask, why am I still here? Mr. Pritchard could have told me this without taking up any more of your time, or mine."

"Because I *am* looking for someone, Ms. Frost," Hays explained, "to fill a very specific position." She paused, uncharacteristically undecided. Then she shook her head, allowing reason to rule instinct. "However, I don't believe the job is well suited to you."

"Or rather, you don't think *I'm* suited to it." Auden was unable to keep the irritation from her voice. It rankled to realize that Haydon Palmer found her lacking. That reaction made no logical sense, but she found herself determined not to be dismissed so easily. "Do you mind telling me why?"

Hays's eyebrows arched in surprise. There was fire beneath that calmly elegant exterior, too, it seemed. "When's the last time you read a work of lesbian fiction?"

Auden stared. After a beat of silence that seemed to last forever, she answered, "I took a women's studies course my junior year in college."

"Let me guess. Allison, Winterson...maybe Lessing?"

"Among several others, yes." Auden leaned forward, intent and curious, forgetting her annoyance. "Why?"

"Because Palmer Publishing just acquired a small independent lesbian publishing company. It was about to go under and I tossed them a net." For an instant, a hint of pleasure glimmered in her eyes. "As part of the takeover, I have acquired all the contracted works in progress as well as right of refusal for the pending submissions under review."

"And you need an editor to evaluate the manuscripts?"

"No," Hays said distinctly. "I need a director for Palmer Publishing's new division of lesbian fiction."

"Well," Auden said, trying not to appear stunned, "I can see where the problem is."

Intrigued, Hays sat forward, her fatigue vanishing. "Oh?"

"Let's look at what you need."

Hays blinked. Auden Frost's face was a study in concentration. She most definitely was not flirting. "All right."

"Unless you intend to run the division yourself, you'll need someone who can oversee its development from the ground up." Auden hoped that she'd be able to think her way through the issues without revealing that she hadn't much of a clue *what* the problem was. The only thing she *did* know was that she wanted the job. Not because she needed the job, which she indeed did, but because she wanted to show Haydon Palmer that she could do it. Why that mattered, she had no idea either.

"I intend to be involved in the formative stages, but I can't run the operation myself," Hays replied regretfully. "I...have other commitments."

"Well, then, you'll want someone who can determine the market value of each submission as well as assess its technical merit, negotiate with the author, and work with your editors."

"Yes, initially, the director may wear many hats."

Auden narrowed her eyes, hearing between the lines. "You expect the director to edit, too?"

"Just temporarily—there are a few works that I'm told are almost ready for press, and I don't want them to get back-burnered in the changeover."

"I have the experience you need."

"Not with what matters most."

Auden's eyes flashed. "You think I'm not suitable because I don't read Nora Roberts?"

"No." Hays smiled at the ire in the woman's voice, impressed by her confidence and passion. "Because you don't read Thane Cutlass or Laura DeHart Young or Susan Smith."

"That can be remedied."

"Why do you want this job?" Hays asked, completely serious. Her head throbbed, but she automatically dismissed the discomfort. She watched instead the fascinating texture of emotions playing across Auden Frost's beautiful face.

"Because it's creative on every level—literally and literarily." Auden surprised herself with what she said next. "Because this division is new, fledgling, and I've been sequestered among the staid and the sheltered for too long."

"Are you adventurous, then?" Hays asked unexpectedly, wondering how the conversation had turned from the professional to the personal so effortlessly. She couldn't remember the last time she had felt so invigorated.

"I hadn't thought so," Auden replied softly. "Until just a few minutes ago."

Hays stood, steadying herself with one hand on the desktop as a faint wave of dizziness passed quickly through her. She extended her other hand as Auden stood to take it. "Welcome to Palmer Publishing, Ms. Frost."

"Thank you, Ms. Palmer." Auden held the cool fingers in hers as she lingered in the depths of dark eyes. "I look forward to working with you."

CHAPTER TWO

H ays?"
Hays gave a start and sat up suddenly, blinking in the bright afternoon sunlight streaming through her office windows. Abel was standing in her doorway, his expression one of thinly disguised concern. Irritably, she rubbed both hands over her face and shook the last remnants of sleep from her consciousness.

"What time is it?"

"Just past one. You didn't answer my knock."

"Late night," she muttered, knowing he probably didn't believe her. "I didn't miss a meeting, did I?"

"No. There's nothing on your schedule until the financial review at four. I suggest you go home for a few hours." *And really sleep.*

"It's okay. I'm fine." She stood and walked to a second door adjacent to the one joining their two offices. He followed as she stepped through and headed down an inner hallway to the coffee room. Without looking at him, she poured herself a cup. "I need to review the authors' contracts from our newest acquisition."

"There's no rush." His tone was mild, almost gentle.

When she turned, her eyes were hot. "Isn't there?"

"Hays—"

She held up her hand, smiling briefly. "Sorry, forget it. There's no problem."

"How did the meeting go with Ms. Frost?" he inquired as they walked side by side back to Hays's office. "I feel bad about that mix-up, and I regret that you had to become involved. I'll offer her another interview as soon as an appropriate position opens up...and send a letter of apology, of course."

"You won't need the letter. You can apologize to her in person tomorrow, if you really think it's necessary." She sat back down behind her desk with a sigh and sipped the rich coffee. The infusion of energy would be short-lived, she knew, but it was welcome nonetheless.

"Tomorrow?" Pritchard stiffened. "What do you mean?"

"I hired her to head the lesbian fiction division."

"Just like that?"

Hays's expression darkened. Brusquely, she said, "I don't need anyone's permission, Abel."

"Yes, I know that. But she's not...qualified."

"She'll do fine."

"Based on what evidence?" His face was red tinged with the effort to curb his temper. The last thing he wanted to do was argue with her, but each day she seemed to grow more impulsive, and more reckless. And it wasn't her business decisions that concerned him. She'd lost weight and clearly wasn't sleeping.

"She's had experience in publishing."

"Editing. Not publishing. When we discussed the acquisition of WomenWords, the plan was to hire someone who could act independently from the outset." *Not for you to take on more work.*

"Auden Frost is capable of running the division." Hays's tone was unyielding as she thought of Auden, clear eyed and unwavering as she outlined a development strategy off the top of her head. And then Hays remembered the spark of excitement in those blue-green eyes and heard again the anticipation in Auden's voice. Her own spirits lifted fleetingly, a rush of pleasure long forgotten. "The only thing she lacks is experience with the genre."

"That's a big deficiency."

Hays grinned and repeated Auden's words. "That can be remedied."

❖

"Run that by me again, slowly," Gayle Dunbar instructed. She wore a faded green scrub shirt and boxers with red hearts, having just gotten up from a nap when Auden called her. Now she sat across from her friend at the small kitchen table in her third-floor apartment. The window was open, admitting a warm breeze that carried the scent of blossoms and the promise of spring.

"I am the new director of the lesbian fiction division at Palmer Publishing." Auden couldn't keep the glee from her voice.

"Uh—I'm ecstatic for you, honey, I really am. But how in the hell did that happen?"

"It's a bit complicated," Auden confided with a grin. She'd changed into jeans and a scoop-neck cotton sweater and sat with one leg curled beneath her as she leaned forward, elbows propped on the table. "I'll just give you the short version."

Gayle listened intently, absently petting Shylock's head as the dog snuggled in her lap. After a few moments, she interrupted. "Wait a minute. Back up. Describe her again."

Blushing unexpectedly as she remembered the way Haydon Palmer had looked leaning against the door, the charismatic intensity she exuded with no effort, Auden struggled to describe her. "She's about my age, very...beautiful. Strong face, sharply sculpted. Black hair, intense dark eyes. Taller then me, tight and lean. Deep voice, kind of...smooth and sultry."

"Jesus," Gayle breathed. "You're making me wet."

"What doesn't?" Auden laughed. "And she *is* gorgeous."

"Don't tease me. I'm in need." Gayle feigned a look of pain.

"What about...who is it? Lillith?"

"She was last week."

"Oh, so you're feeling deprived already?"

"Hey," Gayle protested good-naturedly. "A surgical residency is very demanding. I need to balance all that mental stress with a little fun."

"I don't know that Haydon Palmer could be described as fun." For a moment, Auden pictured the dark-haired woman again. She imagined that the publisher might be many things—driven, demanding, determined. There'd been passion in her eyes, too, when she'd spoken of the new division. But fun? There hadn't seemed room for that. "She seemed so focused, so single-minded."

"Tall, dark, handsome, *and* passionate. Sounds like she made quite an impression on you," Gayle observed, one eyebrow raised. *That's something new. In more ways than one.*

Auden shifted and shrugged, still not quite certain what to make of the feelings the publisher had engendered. She wasn't used to anyone affecting her so strongly after such a brief encounter. "Funny," she mused aloud, "we were only together a few minutes, but I feel as if we talked for hours."

"Mm-hmm." Gayle got up to fetch a soda from the fridge. "Want something?"

"What?" Auden was still lost in the memory of Haydon Palmer. "Oh. No. I'm fine."

"So," Gayle continued as she resettled into her seat and Shylock reclaimed his spot in her lap. "Is she gay?"

"I don't know. How would I know?" Nonplussed, Auden blushed again. "We didn't get personal."

"Well, there's the lesbian fiction thing." Gayle sipped her Fresca and watched her friend carefully. She'd never seen Auden quite so off balance, or quite so excited. Not calm, organized, controlled Auden. "That must mean something."

"That doesn't mean anything. She's a publisher, for heaven's sake—"

Gayle snorted. "Oh, right. And we all know how lucrative lesbian fiction is. Come on, Auden. It's a niche market. I can't imagine anyone gets rich publishing nonmainstream fiction."

"Maybe that's not her intention!" Auden flushed, wondering why in the world she was coming to Haydon Palmer's defense. She didn't even know the woman. In a quieter tone, she added, "Maybe she just wants to publish quality works, no matter what *niche* they fall into."

"Yeah, maybe," Gayle conceded. Casually, she asked, "Does she know you're *not* gay?"

"It was a job interview. She wouldn't ask that," Auden said stiffly. To hide her uncertainty, she busied herself rearranging the salt and pepper shakers on the red and white checked tablecloth, avoiding her friend's too-knowing gaze. *And even if she had asked, what would I have said? "I don't know what I am. Not much of anything, I guess."*

"I just thought she might have hinted at it, considering the area you'll be working in." Sensing her friend's discomfort, Gayle brushed Auden's fingers gently. "I'm sorry. I didn't mean to push."

"That's okay." Auden smiled. "And you did too mean to push. Just because *I'm* not falling into bed with every person I meet—"

"*Any* person."

Auden sighed. "It just hasn't happened yet, okay?"

"If you're waiting for bells or thunderclaps, you'll wait forever." Gayle gave a pained look, genuine this time. "Aud—there just *aren't* any virgins after the age of twenty any longer. You're practically an endangered species."

Embarrassed, Auden looked away. "Stop."

"I just want you to enjoy life, honey," Gayle said quietly. "When you see the things I do, you realize that time is precious."

"I know. But I can't create feelings out of thin air."

"What about that Bernard dude you were seeing?"

"Oh my God. He's last *year's* news," Auden said with a laugh. "Listen, I do need your help and *not* in the dating arena."

"What then?"

"I need to read all of your lesbian fiction."

"All of it?"

"Uh-huh."

"By when?"

"Tomorrow should do it."

"Do you know how many books I have?" Gayle screeched. "I've been collecting them for years."

"No kidding. I've seen the piles of books in your spare room." Suddenly energized, Auden stood and began pacing. Shylock jumped down and followed hopefully on her heels, apparently thinking that food might be in his future. "Seriously, I need a crash course so I can get to know what they're like. What readers want. I need a...feel...for the style, how they read."

"You're going to have to narrow it down a bit," Gayle protested. "Otherwise, you won't leave the house for six months, and when you do, you'll be blind."

"Okay, how about what's the most popular?"

"Come here." Gayle stood abruptly and grabbed Auden's arm. She tugged her into the next room with a disappointed Shylock following. "Let me show you something."

Auden followed her friend into the corner of the L-shaped living room that served as Gayle's study, then leaned down to look over Gayle's shoulder as the other woman sat at the computer.

"You want popular," Gayle muttered, opening Internet Explorer and scrolling down her Favorites list. "Here we go—Amazon's lesbian bestseller list."

"What is this?"

"You've never ordered from Amazon?"

"Not books. A DVD once in a while." Auden scanned the titles. None of them were familiar. "So they...what...rank them somehow?"

"Mmm," Gayle clicked through to the page she wanted. "This will just give you an idea of what's selling. Here—look at the top twenty-five best sellers under lesbian fiction. One, two, three, four..."

Auden waited while Gayle counted, trying to get a sense of the contents of the books scrolling past.

Gayle leaned back in her chair and tilted her head. "Eighteen of the top twenty-five are romances or erotica. There's a mystery or two thrown in, but those are strong on romance, too. No matter when you check this list, and it changes daily, you'll find the same thing. Romance sells."

"Romance." Auden groaned inwardly. "Like Nora Roberts. Or Jackie Collins."

"Well, the dyke equivalent, yeah." Gayle rose and turned to face her friend, leaning her slim hips against the edge of the desk. "But don't knock it 'til you've tried it. Just because it's not *serious* literature doesn't mean it can't be good."

"So—tell me where to start."

Gayle shrugged. "You asked for it. Come on."

An hour later, Auden stretched out on her bed with a dozen books spanning almost twice as many years arrayed around her, all of which Gayle had recommended as popular examples of the type of book she would soon be expected to evaluate and publish. For the first time, the task seemed daunting.

"Lord."

She perused the pile and settled on one because she liked the cover. It depicted a windswept coast, wild and dangerous looking. *Secret Storm.*

"All right," she murmured aloud, "let's see how long I last."

The wind blew softly in the darkness, caressing her skin with gentle fingers. It was soothing, reassuring, and hopefully, would be healing. The air still held the heat of the day, as did the sand sifting between her toes as she walked along the deserted beach. It was after midnight, and all the tourists had long since retired for the night. This was the time of day she liked to walk the beach. There was something about the darkness and the unending roar of the surf that calmed her. Maybe it was the simple fact that the ocean never slept, never tired. Or maybe it was because she felt so comfortable in the darkness. Who knew, who cared, as long as the peace came?

Sentences streamed before Auden's eyes, but she wasn't thinking about structure or narrative style. With the first words, with the first hint of the wind's subtle caress, she had done nothing but feel. The loneliness of walking alone, waking alone, *being* alone ambushed her, and distantly, she ached.

She read on, unmindful of the time or her missed dinner, wondering, hoping, wishing that this woman who echoed the emptiness within her own consciousness would not always travel alone.

❖

Rune Dyre rubbed her eyes and rolled her tight shoulders. The cup of coffee by her right hand had grown cold, but she lifted it and sipped absently, rereading for the fifth time the paragraphs she had written. Frowning, she highlighted a phrase, deleted it, and typed something new.

```
Secret Passions – Scene One

    I had expected the room to be empty,
but it wasn't. She was sitting in a chair
before the desk, one slender leg crossed
over the other. Her skirt had abandoned
decorum unawares, baring pale skin as it
kissed her thighs in a delicate caress.
Without even knowing her name, I wanted to
```

trace my fingers over the landscape of her soul.

As I stepped closer, she looked up, and her very acknowledgment gave me life. Blue eyes, almost green, drifted over my face, leaving heat in their wake. My pulse rose, called forth by her gaze traversing my skin. The breath left my body, my heart pounded. Until the sound of the sea was all I could hear.

She ought to have been surprised at my uninvited entrance, but that wasn't what I saw in her eyes. There was a question. *Who are you?* And without even knowing the answer, there was welcome.

Let me touch you.

If she had held out her hand, I would gladly have taken it and followed. Unto death.

Rune clicked the Save icon, scribbled a note on one of the dozens of Post-its scattered over the surface of her desk, and stood. She winced at a sudden cramp in her back and glanced at the clock.

Two a.m. Another night without sleep.

Her head throbbed, and distantly she felt a faint surge of nausea. Sighing, she walked to the window and looked south toward the river. To her left, a string of blue lights outlined the soaring arch of the Ben Franklin Bridge as it curved against the starlit sky. Below her, the city slept.

She closed her eyes, imaging soft fingers brushing the weariness from her soul.

CHAPTER THREE

It was almost two a.m. before Auden finally fell asleep and four and a half hours later when her alarm jolted her instantly upright in bed. She had an eight o'clock meeting with Haydon Palmer, and the last thing she wanted was to be late. As it was, she probably wouldn't look her best. She usually didn't on less than seven hours of sleep. Despite her lingering fatigue, she was excited, although the rapid beat of her heart and the butterflies in her stomach seemed to be about more than the first day of a new job. Then, Haydon Palmer's dark eyes and fleeting grin flashed through her mind, and she smiled.

An adventure. Yes, I guess that's what this is.

As she stood in the shower, savoring the heat working its way into her tired body, scenes from the book she had fallen asleep with kept replaying in her mind. She wondered why she was surprised at how much she had enjoyed the story of the hard-boiled undercover cop and the emotionally wounded FBI agent.

It's not as if I've never read a romance before. Who hasn't? They're practically the staple of the American reading public, if the stands at the supermarket checkout lines and the piles on the new arrivals table at bookstores are any indication of popularity. They just never appealed to me. Before.

She'd never found much to identify with in any of those stories that she had read as a teenager. Eventually, unable to relate to the recurring theme of the fragile young woman swept off her feet by the domineering, dangerous hero, she had stopped reading romances. She found much more comfort in things that were factual in nature, and the books that she read were grounded and solid—satisfyingly predictable—like her life.

She stepped from the shower and reached for a towel. "Then what in the world am I doing thinking about publishing romances? Not just romances, *lesbian* romances. I really don't know anything about either."

But then she thought of the book that had quickly captured her imagination the night before and realized that wasn't exactly true. The scene of a woman awakening to only memories lingered powerfully in her mind still.

The sound of waves crashing to shore beyond the open window was hypnotic and soon had her reminiscing of lazy mornings lying like this with her lover beside her. They always seemed to waken at almost the same moment. Maybe it was the fact that they were so in tune with one another's mind and body. Whatever it was, they both treasured the rare mornings that they could stay in bed together, watching the sun slowly rise over the horizon, making slow, gentle love until a different hunger drove them from the bed.

She closed her eyes, remembering her lover's touch, feeling again those slow caresses and feather-light kisses as they nearly drove her insane. Remembering how she had begged for release from the sweet torture. Making love had been their way of pushing the darkness and evil from their lives.

Auden had never awakened in the arms of a lover. She'd never had anyone touch her in passion or take her beyond herself to a place of only feeling. She'd read the passage over and over again, and although she had never experienced that connection, the emotions had felt far from foreign. She could see the two lovers, safe and secure in one another's arms, rejoicing in their love. Someday, she imagined that she would have a lover, but she hadn't formed an image of what that joining would be like. Friendship, companionship, affection—these things she could envision.

"...she begged for release from the sweet torture."

Being moved to such heights she had never considered.
But I do know a little bit about loneliness.

Was this romance? If so, then she had been wrong in thinking that she could not relate to it.

Maybe if I'd read this instead of Danielle Steel, Auden mused as she dressed, *I would have changed my mind about reading fiction.*

The fact that the lovers were women hadn't struck her as odd. Quite the contrary, their love had seemed completely natural. Why wouldn't it? Her best friend was a lesbian and never kept her sexual adventures a secret. Gayle didn't share the details, but Auden definitely got the gist. Fleetingly, she wondered why she'd been holding her breath as she'd read, envisioning the lovers' touch.

Startled as she caught sight of the clock and saw that it was later than she'd realized, Auden hastily assembled her coffeemaker and waited impatiently for the brewing to finish. She stood at her open window and watched passersby outside, draining the cup as soon as it was cool enough to drink. At one point, she became aware of the fluttering in her stomach again. *Nerves.* Briefly, she considered calling Gayle for a little moral support, but she remembered that her friend had worked all night at Temple Hospital. The surgical resident was probably just crawling into bed.

I'll just have to do this by instinct. It seemed to work all right yesterday. Let's just hope that Haydon Palmer hasn't had time to regret her decision.

❖

Rune sat in front of her computer with a fresh cup of coffee. After four hours of sleep, the most she ever slept at one time any longer, she felt unusually refreshed. Her dreams had been remarkable, too—leftover images of the scene she had written. Tantalizingly erotic, mercilessly taunting visions of a beautiful woman just beyond her reach. Far from awakening frustrated by the unrequited passion, however, she was invigorated by the lingering arousal. It was good just to have the memory of desire rekindled.

She logged on and checked her mail.

-----Original Message-----

From: [mailto:stargrl@worldlink.net]
Sent: Tuesday March 18, 6:22 AM
To: Rune@HeartLand.com
Subject: Re: Dark Passions

Rune:

Even though *Secret Storm* will ALWAYS be my favorite, I just love your new web story. I thought at first that *Dark Passions* would be too hard to read. It wasn't at all what I expected. Will this be available in print like your others that have come out already?? I hope so!
I'll be first in line to buy one!

A big fan, Star

-----Reply-----
From: Rune@HeartLand.com
Sent: Tuesday March 18, 7:15 AM
To: stargrl@worldlink.net
Subject: About Passion Series

Star:

Glad to hear that you liked the web story *Dark Passions*. Its publication is on hold for now. As you probably noticed on the website, WomenWords has closed and will not be publishing any longer. I'm not sure what will happen with the new publisher, but I'll post any news I have on the site or the news list.

Many Thanks, RD

Rune scrolled through the half-dozen other messages, most from readers, and answered each. When she'd finished, she opened the file she'd been working on last and reread the final passage. Had the face she'd created with barely adequate words been the image in her dream? Sighing, she checked her watch and closed the program. The next scene would have to wait.

❖

"Good morning, Alana," Hays said as she exited the elevator and walked across the spacious reception area toward the hallway leading to her corner office.

"Ms. Palmer," Alana said demurely, her eyes following Hays as she passed.

Hays had only been in her office a few moments when the phone rang. "Yes?"

"A Ms. Frost is here. She tells me that she has an appointment with you." There was a brief pause. "I don't see anything regarding that on the schedule that Mr. Pritchard left with me last evening."

Rubbing her eyes, Hays sighed. Abel Pritchard was indispensable to her. He was an excellent adviser, he kept her business organized, and he kept her on track. However, his obsessive insistence on an immutable schedule sometimes drove her crazy, and his subtle but persistent efforts to see that she wasn't overworked only made her *more* determined to work every available moment.

"That's fine, Alana. I arranged the meeting myself."

"Mr. Pritchard prefers that only appointments on the day's calendar—"

"Yes, I know precisely what Mr. Pritchard prefers." Hays's voice was edged with irritation, and she paused, letting her temper cool. Alana was only doing her job. "Please show Ms. Frost to my office."

A second passed; Hays thought she could feel the receiver freeze in her palm. She grinned. *Alana will be giving Abel an earful momentarily.*

"*Yes*, Ms. Palmer."

"Thank you, Alana," Hays said softly as she lowered the receiver.

When the door to her office opened only seconds later, Hays stood and smiled as Auden entered the room. Her new director looked vibrant. Aware of an unaccustomed surge of anticipatory pleasure at their meeting, Hays wondered when it had happened that the business had become only a responsibility.

"Good morning."

"Yes, isn't it?" Auden smiled, her nerves vanishing at the sight of the warm welcome in Haydon Palmer's eyes.

"Please." Hays gestured to one of the leather sling-back chairs in front of her desk where Auden had sat during the interview. It was amazing that their first acquaintance had been less than twenty-four hours before; Auden Frost had already assumed such a marked presence in her mind.

"Thank you." Auden settled in, crossing one stockinged leg over the other. She wore a navy suit, thinking that it was too soon to dress informally. She noticed that Haydon was dressed much the same as she had been the day before, although this time the charcoal-gray trousers and jacket were cut more casually and she wore a plain open-collared white shirt with them. The publisher looked every bit as attractive as she had the previous day, although the shadows beneath her eyes seemed slightly deeper. Auden felt the smallest jolt of concern.

"Are you still of a mind to take this job?" Hays asked as she resumed her seat.

"Are you still of a mind for me to have it?"

Hays grinned. "I rarely change my mind once I've decided on something."

"And I never give up on a project once I've undertaken it."

"I thought you might reconsider once you had time to reflect on the specifics." Hays watched Auden carefully, wanting very much to see the light of excitement dance in her eyes again. *Such a small thing. And such a pleasure.*

"No," Auden said firmly. "I spent the night planning a crash course to get to know my new field."

"Must make for an interesting syllabus," Hays replied, laughing. She leaned back, aware of her tension only as it left her. Auden would be staying. "You'll probably have some new additions when I give you the names of our recently acquired authors."

"I read quickly." Auden recalled falling asleep with the book on her chest, something she had done countless times in her life. The difference had been that the evening before, she *hadn't* read with her normal efficiency and focus. She'd lingered, savored, reread passages. She hadn't wanted to rush the experience; it was too surprisingly pleasant. "I'll be up to speed before very long."

"I don't doubt it." Hays leaned forward again and placed both hands on the top of her highly polished walnut desk. "Then you and I have a lot of organizing to do. Before we get down to talking about personnel, projections, and deadlines, we need a name." She laughed softly at the quick look of confusion that passed across Auden's face. "For the new division."

"Oh, of course." Auden blushed, aware that Haydon Palmer's gaze had not strayed from her face for an instant since she had walked into the room. The intensity of that scrutiny was both unusual and exhilarating. "What did you have in mind?"

"Uh-uh, not me," Hays said with a shake of her head. "I thought we'd give the honors to the new division director."

"I don't have any idea what might be appropriate," Auden protested. To her surprise, Haydon rose and came around the front of her desk, stopping only a few feet away. She leaned her hips against the front of the desk and tucked her hands into her pants pockets. The jacket flared behind her, drawing the white shirt taut across her chest. Fleetingly, Auden thought that she had described the publisher appropriately to Gayle the day before. *Lean and tight and nearly vibrating with tension.* She caught her breath as she felt the energy pour from the woman in front of her, stirring her own excitement.

"I'll give you an idea of where to start," Hays offered. "Harlequin Publishing recently added a new imprint designed to appeal to the *modern* reader. As you know, Harlequin has been around forever, and they're practically the gold standard in terms of romance fiction—at least if you happen to be straight."

Auden couldn't read a single thing in the other woman's expression that might suggest either a question or a revelation. Gayle's words came back to her. *Is she gay? Does she know you're not?*

Does it matter? Auden realized her attention had drifted, and she quickly refocused, fearing that she had missed something important. *That is so unlike me.*

"In recent years," Hays was saying, "in the heterosexual market, at least, the tone and direction of romance fiction have changed with the evolving role of women in today's world. There are more depictions of career women who marry later or not at all, of single women who are sexually active, and of women who don't think that finding a husband is the most important function of their existence. To highlight these new books, Harlequin started Blaze, their *sexy* division." She grinned. "I wish I could have been in that boardroom when they discussed how they were going to structure *that* new baby."

Auden found herself laughing at the image as well. "All right, I get the point. But let me ask you this—has lesbian romance fiction followed the same trend? Has it changed much in the last twenty or thirty years?"

Hays arched an eyebrow. "Good question. Yes, in some ways I think it certainly has. There are far fewer coming-out stories, and those that are don't tend to spend a lot of time depicting characters who struggle with the idea of being a lesbian. That reflects the greater degree of comfort of many lesbians with their sexuality, I think. There are more stories about having children and dealing with the challenges of being a couple in today's world." She shrugged. "But still, the things that drive romance fiction remain the same, whether it's lesbian or heterosexual, twenty years ago or today."

It was Auden's turn to lean forward, caught in the spell of Hays's deep, smooth voice. "What things?"

"Dramatic tension—emotional resonance, sexual attraction, and the struggle to overcome whatever obstacles prevent the lovers from being together."

"So it's formulaic, you're saying," Auden observed, not critically. She was searching for a point of reference, a yardstick against which to measure her understanding of the form.

Hays lifted a shoulder. "To a certain extent, as much as any one genre is formulaic. There are certain elements most writers and critics consider important in a mystery, for instance. The same could be said for a good romance."

"And a big part of my job is going to be recognizing those elements," Auden mused aloud.

"Exactly. You'll have help, but in many instances, you'll have the first look at a manuscript, and you'll certainly be involved in the final edits."

Auden rose and walked to the expansive wall of windows. Below, traffic moved sluggishly along Walnut Street on the north side of Rittenhouse Square. The four-square-block park was filled with early morning strollers, dog walkers, and people sitting on benches sipping coffee while perusing the morning newspaper. The unseasonable weather continued, and the hint of an early spring had drawn everyone to the streets. Even as her mind unconsciously registered the common sights, Auden was absorbed in thinking about the challenges of her new position. After a moment, she turned, blushing faintly.

"I'm sorry. I was just thinking about...all of this."

"Problem?" Hays's question was quiet, her voice gentle.

"No, not at all," Auden replied hastily. She moved back across the room until she too was standing in front of the desk, within touching distance of the publisher. She rested the fingertips of her left hand against the desktop. "It's just that I've never thought about these things before, not in the context of a work of fiction. I haven't read enough to recognize all the elements, but last night..."

When Auden hesitated, Hays prompted softly, "Last night?"

"I started reading a book—one that was recommended to me by a good friend who has an enormous collection of lesbian fiction. The book captured my attention so quickly that it truly took me by surprise. I wasn't consciously aware of the formal elements, but now, in retrospect, I can recognize the things we've just been discussing in that book." She smiled self-consciously. "Obviously, the author was effective. I'm quite sure she didn't intend for me to be thinking about the mechanics."

"What was the book?"

"Rune Dyre's *Secret Storm*."

Hays blinked, then nodded slightly. "Well, there's nothing that readers like more than a strong woman, wounded by loss, and *another* strong woman to help her heal."

Auden recalled the scenes that had drawn her in so completely. The strength of the characters contrasted so sharply with their obvious emotional pain. Strange, that something like that had captivated her.

"Before yesterday, I would have said that scenario had no particular appeal for me."

"Why not?"

Hays's dark eyes had become opaque, unreadable. Auden felt the sudden distance like a cool wind blowing unexpectedly across her skin, and she fought the urge to shiver. Off balance, she answered without thinking. "I love to read, but it's never been an emotional experience for me. Last night, it was."

"You were moved?" Hays's tone was quiet, probing.

"Yes," Auden replied softly.

For a moment, they were both silent.

"Well, then," Hays finally said, "let's see to the first order of business. What about that name?"

Auden still held Hays's dark eyes, watching the tiny flecks of silver and gold flicker through their onyx depths. Emboldened, she proposed, "How about...Destiny Books, a division of Palmer Publishing?"

"Destiny. Yes," Hays said softly. "That would be at the heart of things, wouldn't it?"

CHAPTER FOUR

Auden smiled, inordinately pleased that Haydon Palmer found her suggestion for the new division name acceptable. As she watched the publisher's eyes grow distant once more, Auden wondered what thought had passed through her mind to draw her away so quickly. Then, seconds later, Haydon seemed to pull herself back to the present with a small shake, and she favored Auden with a fleeting smile.

"Now that the *important* task is finished," Hays said with a wry grin, "we need to get you settled. I hope you don't mind, but at least temporarily, I'd like you to work out of one of the offices on this floor."

"Why would I mind?" Auden hadn't expected to have a choice about her work surroundings. She certainly never had before.

"Well, most of the people with whom you'll eventually be working closely—marketing, graphics, editing—are located several floors down. But until we have the division structured satisfactorily, I think it would be easier if you and I were a bit closer in proximity."

"That sounds reasonable." In fact, it suited her just fine. Auden had expected that after this introductory meeting, she and the publisher would have little contact. She didn't imagine that Haydon Palmer spent much time with the day-to-day dealings of her company. The chance to spend even a few more days working closely with her was very welcome.

"I don't want you to feel isolated up here," Hays continued almost apologetically. "I don't intend for Destiny to be the stepchild in the Palmer family. To date, we have promoted a wide array of publications, including, but certainly not exclusively, fiction. Destiny will have a narrow scope but, I hope, considerable reach."

As she spoke, Hays moved toward the second door that led to the interior hallway. Auden followed her into the maze beyond and found herself immediately in the central core of the top-floor suite. They passed a large conference room and the kitchen, then stopped just three doors down from Haydon Palmer's corner office. Through the open door, Auden saw an expansive office with bookshelves waiting to be filled, a magnificent carved oak desk, and other furnishings similar to those in Haydon's office, including another Oriental rug. Windows on the far side of the desk overlooked the park below, affording the same view as the corner office.

After a quick glance, Auden turned to Haydon with a gasp of surprise. "Surely you can't mean for me to have this?"

"Yes." Hays shrugged. The thought had occurred to her as she had ridden the elevator to the top floor earlier that morning. Creating the lesbian fiction division was her brainchild, and even though she knew she couldn't personally tend to its total growth and development, she wanted to have access to all aspects of its inception. She didn't enjoy riding the elevator up and down, phone conferences frustrated her because she disliked being unable to see the expression of her fellow conversant, and the stairs were out of the question. She needed all her energy to focus on the work ahead. "It's empty, it's conveniently located, and the coffee up here is very good."

Auden laughed. "Believe me, I'd take it even without coffee privileges. I just can't believe no one is using it."

"It used to be my office."

Surprised by the unanticipated revelation, Auden leaned one shoulder against the door frame. Haydon stood a foot away, her back against the opposite side of the opening.

"How long have you run the company?" Auden asked before realizing that that was probably an inappropriate question. "I'm sorry, I—"

"Technically, six years," Hays replied, not entirely certain why she was answering. She was cordial with all her directors, but rarely had the time or inclination for casual conversation. Auden, though, with her quietly searching gaze, inspired confidences. "My father left the company to me when I was fifteen years old. I have a brother, almost twenty years older, who never expressed any interest in it. Until I reached majority, Abel Pritchard was acting CEO. I was always involved in the company, though, in one way or another, even when I was in college. Before I took over, I worked from here."

"And Mr. Pritchard took care of the business for you until you were able to assume control?"

"Yes. He was a good friend of my father's, and he's always been something of a guardian, for both me and the company." Hays brushed an errant lock of hair from her eyes, thinking about the last few years. So much had happened, so much had changed. Suddenly, she realized that Auden was watching her with that intent, questioning gaze, and Hays wondered how much she had seen. "Abel never cared for the administrative aspects, though."

"And you do?"

"Most of the time."

"You're very young for this position."

"Am I?" Hays smiled, but her eyes were remote. "I've never really thought of it that way." Straightening, she said abruptly, "Let me show you the rest of the floor and then I'll leave you to get settled. The computer in your office is already online, and I put you in the system this morning. Your e-mail address is AFrost at PalmPub.net."

"You're very efficient, too," Auden observed with a smile.

"I have to be." Hays's expression was impossible to read. "There'll be a planning meeting this afternoon at three with Abel, myself, and you. We can get a start on our battle plan then. Feel free to knock on my door if anything comes up before then."

"Thank you. I appreciate the guided tour. I'm sure that I won't need to trouble you further."

"It was no trouble," Hays said quietly as she turned away.

Auden watched until Haydon disappeared into her office, recognizing the sudden reserve in the publisher's manner and fearing that she had gone too far with her personal questions. It was unlike her to do that. In the four years that she had worked at Miller, she had maintained friendly relationships with everyone. She'd attended the obligatory luncheons and business functions when she couldn't conjure up a believable excuse not to, but she knew very little about the private lives of her colleagues. Certainly she was not privy to anything about the personal affairs of her employers, nor had she had any wish to be. She had been content with the work, but it did not touch her life in any intimate way. Now, after only twenty-four hours, everything about Palmer Publishing intrigued her, most especially its formidable director.

❖

```
-----Original Message-----
From: thaneCutlass@CutlassFic.com
Sent: Tuesday March 18, 9:33 AM
To: Rune@HeartLand.com
Subject: New Company and Eros Anthology
```

Rune:

   What's the word on the takeover? Has anyone contacted you yet? Should I start looking around for a new home?
   And when am I going to see your submissions for the Eros series? Are you posting it on HeartLand?
   Come on, buddy, keep me in the loop. Show me yours and I'll show you mine <g>.

Thane

Rune smiled at the invitation but had no desire to play. There were too many things she had to do. Deadlines seemed to come so much faster now, even if they *were* only self-imposed ones.

```
-----Reply-----
From: Rune@HeartLand.com
Sent: Tuesday March 18, 11:38 AM
To: thaneCutlass@CutlassFic.com
Subject: re: New Company and Eros
```

Thane:

   No word from the new publisher yet, but you know how slow they are.

I'm working on the material for Eros, but
I'm not sure how I feel about it. It's not
coming out quite as I planned. I'll let you
know what I decide soon.

Rune

"No, not turning out quite as I had planned at all." Rune closed her
eyes, tilted the chair back, and tried to clear her mind. For her, words
had never come from conscious thought or intention; they came from
some deeper place, from the dark well of hidden dreams and secret
desires. They came unbidden, uninvited, demanding to be written, to
be seen, to be heard.

She opened her eyes, leaned forward, and placed slender fingers
on the keyboard. Gaze turned inward, stillness suffusing her being, she
typed.

Secret Passions - Scene Two

It was hard for me to believe that she
didn't know how attractive she was. I got the
sense that she rarely thought about herself.
I knew as we stood together, talking, that
she had no idea the effect she had on me. My
heart raced, my skin tingled, and my palms
grew damp. I struggled not to let her see
the faint trembling in my hands, although
I doubted she would recognize my desire.
Still, I needed to be careful.

It was impossible, this attraction, for
more reasons than I could say. I wasn't
free, even had the possibility of touch
existed between us. I reminded myself of
this even as I raised a hand to brush away
the wisps of hair straying across her cheek.
Her green eyes widened, deepening like the
shoals in shadow, and her full lips parted
as if to bless my coming. I had thought my

touch might startle or surprise, but seeing her expression, some foolish part of me believed that my fingers against her skin would not be unwelcome. She gave me no real reason to believe that, or any indication that it would ever be true. No sign—only the stillness in her face and the trilling beat of blood beneath the alabaster skin of her neck.

She waited as my fingertips hovered above her cheek, her gaze warming mine, and the pleasure of the moment was so acute my breath escaped me on a sigh. She smiled at the sound.

To my amazement, hope rose within me. Such a foreign emotion, so long ago lost. Although I knew it doomed, I allowed the emotion to linger, savoring the swell of heat that followed close upon the dream.

Then I let my arm drop and stepped away.

"I'm sorry. I must go."

The words, or more correctly, the emotions that had inspired them, exhausted her. Rune leaned back in the chair once more, acknowledging fatigue and allowing her lids to close. Lights flickered behind her eyelids, ghostly afterimages of the characters, both real and figurative, that had streamed across the computer monitor, dancing just out of reach. Often, she didn't realize what she had written until she discovered her imaginings captured in the regimented march of sentences down the screen.

She knew what awaited her review this time and realized, too, that what she had written was too close to fact. This anthology was proving more difficult than she had anticipated. The baring of fantasies and dreams and desires was proving far too personal a revelation to make while still hoping to remain unaffected. These snippets of time, moments captured through a glass darkly, had been wrenched from her depths, and left blood streaking the surface of her soul.

She had not yet fully committed to the *Eros* project. It had been Thane's idea and only in the first stages when WomenWords had folded. Now, rereading the last several entries, Rune thought perhaps she might have to abandon it. She hadn't thought her words had the power any longer to draw emotion from those places she had safely locked away. She'd been wrong. But then again, perhaps it was not her *words*, but rather their inspiration, that had turned the key and flung wide the door behind which she had sequestered her longings.

The phone rang. Automatically, she saved the file and closed it.

"Yes? No, I haven't forgotten. Thank you." With a sigh, she stood and let the misgivings along with the once-abandoned dreams slip away.

❖

```
-----Original Message-----
From: HPalmer@PalmPub.net
Sent: Tuesday March 18, 12:05 PM
To: AFrost@PalmPub.net
Subject: Authors-For your review
Attachment: WWauthors.doc 26KB

Ms. Frost:

    These   are   the   authors   currently
under contract to WomenWords, Destiny's
forerunner.
    Email addresses, titles of works currently
in progress, and a list of submissions
pending are attached for your review.

HLP
```

Auden opened the file and perused the eight names. Her eyes stopped on one. Rune Dyre.

"Ah, wonderful." She thought of the half-read book on her bedside table, and suddenly, she couldn't wait to get home to finish it. She hadn't yet figured out what had captivated her so immediately, but the urge to return to the world between those covers was almost addicting. Pleasurable and exhilarating, but dangerous. She smiled to herself. Dangerous, adventurous—those terms had never been applicable to her ordered world before, and yet in a matter of hours, they had begun to feel familiar.

Turning her attention back to the concrete realities of her job, she printed the author list and began making her own lists of what she needed to do, people she needed to contact, and what points she wanted to discuss at the first planning meeting that afternoon. She worked through lunch, stopping only long enough to refill her coffee from the ever-full lunchroom carafe. Each time she stepped out into the hallway, she glanced at the door to Haydon's office. It was ajar, a silent invitation to enter.

Of course, she did not. Haydon Palmer had been generous with her time, and as much as Auden wanted to see her, she hadn't the slightest excuse to do so. She didn't think that curiosity and a strange compulsion to listen to her deep voice were quite enough reason to disturb the obviously busy publisher. It was oddly comforting, though, just thinking about her being so near.

Ten minutes before the conference was scheduled to begin, Auden gathered her notes and started down the hall. She glanced quickly into the conference room and saw that it was empty. The door to Haydon's office remained open, and she moved closer to peer inside. The publisher was not behind her desk. Auden was about to turn away when she heard a soft moan. Startled, she moved a few inches into the room and glanced around.

Haydon Palmer lay on the sofa, her jacket off and discarded on the coffee table beside her, her shirt unbuttoned far enough to reveal the subtle swell of pale breasts. She reclined on her back, one leg partially off the sofa, resting on the floor. An arm dangled freely as well. She appeared to be deeply asleep.

Uncertain as to whether she should leave or wake her, Auden stood rooted to the spot. When the sleeping woman twitched as if an electric current had discharged through her body and moaned once again, Auden forgot about propriety and crossed quickly to her side.

Kneeling next to the sofa, Auden whispered softly, "Ms. Palmer?"

Hays didn't move.

"Excuse me, Ms. Palmer?" Auden gently placed her right hand on the other woman's shoulder and gave her a very tiny shake. Now that she was closer, she could see the sweat beaded on Haydon's ashen forehead and her eyes fluttering rapidly beneath the nearly translucent eyelids. "Haydon?"

Hays's eyes flew open, their dark brilliance eclipsed by the remnants of sleep. She blinked and murmured unbelievingly, "Auden?"

"I'm sorry," Auden said softly, her fingers registering the trembling in the other woman's body. "I wasn't sure if I should wake you."

"Forgive me," Hays whispered, caught between the undertow of dark dreams and the pull of Auden's tender gaze. "I hadn't meant to fall asleep."

"You needn't apologize to me." Auden stifled the urge to stroke her damp cheek. "I thought I heard you...are you all right?"

Hays blushed and sat up quickly, rubbing her face briskly. "Fine. Don't trouble yourself."

Surprised by the rebuke, Auden rose to her feet. She was even more startled when the publisher grasped her hand.

"I'm sorry. I didn't mean to sound so short. I do appreciate the wake-up call." Hays tried to grin, hoping her acute embarrassment didn't show. Then she noticed Auden's concerned expression change swiftly to one of alarm. "What—"

"My God!" Auden exclaimed. "You're bleeding."

Hays could feel it then, the warm trickle from her right nostril. She knew what it was and reached quickly for the clean handkerchief that she kept in her pants pocket. Swiftly, she pressed it to her nose and leaned her head back. "Sorry."

"Can I get you something?"

"No," Hays muttered. "It's nothing. Allergy season."

"It's really no trouble, Ms. Palmer. Some ice, perhaps?"

"No, it'll stop in a second." Hays dabbed at her face, then sat up as the trickle slowed. "And please, call me Hays."

Auden blushed this time, inordinately pleased and having no idea why. Her heart pounded as she searched Hays's face for any sign of lingering problems. She'd been frightened, probably more frightened than the minor incident demanded, but the memory of that soft moan made her heart twist. Quietly, she said, "Then you must call me Auden."

Hays nodded, rising carefully. *So far, so good. Now, if I can just manage not to humiliate myself for another few moments.* "Thank you."

"For what?"

"For waking me."

I couldn't bear that you were in pain. Auden watched as Hays tucked in her shirt and reached for her jacket. Without the blazer, Auden saw that the publisher was thinner than she had realized. Hays wasn't frail by any means, but even now there was a fine tremor in her hands. "Are you sure you're all right?"

"Fine." Without meeting Auden's gaze, Hays shrugged into her jacket and crossed the room to her desk. She collected her laptop and slipped a Waterman pen into her breast pocket. "Shall we get started on our new project, then?"

"Yes," Auden replied, recognizing the shift in tone and assuming a professional one to match. "Let's do."

CHAPTER FIVE

When Auden and Hays reached the conference room, Abel Pritchard was there waiting. He sat on the right side of the long walnut table with several file folders spread out in front of him. Hays took her customary seat at the head of the table, settled in, and opened her laptop. Auden took the place opposite Abel at Hays's left hand.

"Nice to see you again, Mr. Pritchard," Auden said.

"Ms. Frost," Pritchard replied coolly with a barely perceptible nod.

Well, he clearly isn't impressed with me. So I wasn't wrong yesterday when I got the feeling that he didn't think much of my qualifications.

Hays interrupted Auden's introspection. "For the time being, Auden, I thought we could put together a temporary team from Palmer's other divisions until you had a chance to interview and choose your own section heads."

"That sounds fine," Auden agreed. "I assume you have a list of possibles for the various positions so I can set up interviews?"

"Yes," Hays replied. "I'll get that to you today. The only exception is going to be graphics, because they pretty much cover everyone. But if you find an artist who has a particular flair for what you want, I'll assign him or her to your division permanently."

"I'll look over your promos and get acquainted with the various artists' styles."

"Good idea." Hays bent her head to type a note.

"What about marketing?" Pritchard interjected, raising one eyebrow. Hays's use of *Auden* hadn't escaped his notice, nor had the way her voice dropped a register when she spoke to the other young woman. *Lord. Is that what this impetuous hiring is all about? Hormones? That's not like her.*

"That's the next thing I want to address," Hays responded. "Liz Nixon, the former president of WomenWords, has expressed interest in coming over to marketing. It makes sense to me, because she knows her authors so well. What do you think, Auden?"

"On the surface, that sounds reasonable," Auden noted mildly. "She should be able to give us invaluable insight into who's been selling, where, and to whom." She met Hays's penetrating gaze and continued steadily, "But they're not *her* authors anymore. How do you think someone who's been used to running the entire company is going to adjust to a lesser role?"

"I've thought of that." Hays appreciated Auden's quick and accurate appraisal as well as her natural confidence. "And that's why I haven't made her an offer. But I thought you might want to interview her sooner rather than later to see if it seems workable."

At that, Pritchard's usually guarded expression registered frank surprise. "I should imagine *you* would be in a better position to judge that, Hays. Marketing is a key position, after all."

"Ms. Frost will choose her own people," Hays said with a bite to her voice. "A strong director, one who is clearly in charge, is what makes a division work."

Pritchard and Hays locked eyes.

"Besides," Hays assumed a softer tone, "I've talked to Liz, and I don't have any reservations about her qualifications. But whether it would work in practical terms—that ultimately must be for Ms. Frost to determine."

Auden watched the exchange silently. There was some kind of power struggle going on here, and she had no intention of getting in the middle of it. She imagined that Hays's youth and relative inexperience might make her appear less than capable to Pritchard's more seasoned eye. Nevertheless, Hays showed no signs of backing down in the face of Pritchard's disagreement. Auden found that strength of character admirable and was struck with the way that the publisher handled a man who had apparently been something of a father figure to her for much of her life. Hays was respectful but secure in her own position and certain in her decisions. *She's very impressive.*

When there was no further rebuttal from Pritchard, Hays rifled through the papers in front of her, then continued.

"The business division has already gone through the financials for the assimilated company, and there's nothing there that we need to discuss now. That was all handled by the attorneys during the acquisition process. Initially, we need to focus on three main areas: marketing, solidifying our author base, and moving ahead with the works in progress. I want to get those books to press as soon as we can."

"I'll need copies of every manuscript as soon as possible," Auden said. "I'll also need any style sheets and partially edited works from WomenWords' editors...oh, and any formatted files they've already done." She looked at her own list. "Graphics will need to get image files transferred, and I want to see the projected covers."

"I'll have all that for you by the end of business tomorrow." Hays made another entry in her laptop.

"Do you intend to read everything personally?" Pritchard asked. His voice held a note of incredulity that bordered on condescension.

Auden met his eyes, marveling at the cool impersonal gaze. She had no idea what he was thinking. "At this stage, I certainly do. Until I have been able to work with our editors long enough to trust their judgment, I plan on screening every manuscript that's submitted."

"That could turn into a sizable number."

"I definitely hope so," Auden remarked, the corner of her mouth lifting in a faint grin. "The more the better."

Hays grinned as well. "For now, I believe there are only six titles slated for publication. In addition, Liz has informed me that we can anticipate several sequels to works on their current publist."

"Do you have those titles?" Auden asked.

Hays glanced at her computer screen. "Not all of them. I'll look into it."

"That's all right. I can do that," Auden said as she wrote herself a note. Her head was down and she didn't see the quick look of approval that flashed fleetingly across Pritchard's face. "Do the previous contracts specifically mention right of first refusal for sequels?"

"It's vague," Hays remarked.

"Is legal working on new contracts for us?"

"Right here." Pritchard passed a folder to Auden. "For your comments."

She smiled at him. "Thank you. If you've reviewed them, I'm sure they're fine, but I'll look them over before they go out."

"Very well."

Hays opened a new file on her laptop. "There's an anthology of erotica in the early stages, too. Apparently a compilation of new works from several of the authors."

"Until we've established Destiny's presence in the market," Auden said, "we'll need to keep the authors we've inherited, if they're worth keeping. I intend to contact each of them within the next day or so to see what they have in the works. And I want to judge their level of interest in continuing with us."

"Excellent. By the way, until you have a secretary, I'll have Alana work with you to set up interviews for your support staff and section heads."

"I'll want to meet with the authors as well."

Hays looked momentarily surprised, then lifted a shoulder. "That will be up to you. Work it any way you want. There are discretionary funds available if you see the need to woo anyone with complimentary accommodations."

"Fine." Auden was pleasantly surprised by the degree of autonomy she had been given. She was also grateful that she would be working closely with Hays, at least in the short term. She was certain that there would be many issues she would need to discuss as she developed a sense of how her division would interface with the company at large and learned the nuances of her new area of focus.

"Abel?" Hays glanced at her associate. "Anything else at this point?"

"You'll want to inform Ms. Frost of the promotional event."

Hays winced, and Auden shot her a curious glance. "Right."

He stood and collected his papers. "That's all at this point, then. Haydon, don't forget we need to look at the quarterly projections."

"Okay, I'll be by shortly." Hays sighed.

"Very well." He nodded to Auden, murmured nearly inaudibly, "Ms. Frost," and left.

"A promotional event?" Auden asked with interest.

"Yes." Hays leaned her head back, closed her eyes, and groaned. "God, I hate those things."

"What's the program?" Auden regarded Hays, who was still very pale, with veiled concern. She had the strangest desire to brush back an errant lock of dark hair that had fallen across Hays's forehead. She willed herself not to move. "Hays?"

Lids still closed, Hays answered softly. "I thought it would be a good idea to launch the new division with a promotional reception and cocktail party. We've invited our new authors and the staff from WomenWords who are interested in coming on board. Some of the local press, too."

"That sounds like a good idea."

"It sounds like a nightmare." Hays opened her eyes and leaned forward, resting her forearms on the table. She grinned ruefully. "But it's good business. You'll need to be there, of course."

"Of course." Hays's hands rested inches from hers, and Auden stared at the subtle pattern of veins and tendons beneath the delicate skin. The very fine tremor would have been unnoticeable to most, but Auden was now looking for it. *You're not well.* "You should go home," she said without thinking.

Hays stiffened and closed her hands tightly, angry with herself for letting down her guard. How had that happened? "Alana will give you all the necessary details for the event."

"When is it?" Auden tried to pretend she hadn't noticed the sudden change in Hays's tone. *God, that was stupid of me. She's my boss, not a friend. It's none of my business, but she just looks so...drained.*

"This coming Saturday night at the Four Seasons." Hays stood and closed her laptop. "Feel free to bring a guest."

"Thank you." There was nothing more she could say.

Hays nodded once, curtly. "See you tomorrow, then, Ms. Frost."

Once back in her office, Auden couldn't forget the image of Hays lying exhausted on the sofa, obviously in discomfort. Rubbing her temples, she pulled up the list of authors from WomenWords and tried to dispel the disquieting memory.

-----Original Message-----
From: AFrost@PalmPub.net
Sent: Tuesday March 18, 3:59 PM
To: Rune@HeartLand.com
Subject: Palmer Publishing

Ms. Dyre:

I am the director of Destiny Books, the new lesbian fiction imprint of Palmer Publishing. It is my pleasure to welcome you to Palmer.

With regard to your manuscript, *Dark Passions*, it is my understanding that it was accepted for publication by WomenWords at the time of their transition. I am anxious to see the current draft so that we may move ahead.

Please review the enclosed contract, which transfers publication rights of said work to Palmer, and notify me of any concerns or questions you may have as soon as possible.

I hope to meet with you personally at your convenience to discuss future directions, and I look forward to working with you.

Sincerely,
Auden Frost
Director, Destiny Books
A Division of Palmer Publishing

❖

Rune worked without a pause. She'd had glimpses of the scene for hours, images and half fragments of dialogue breaking into her consciousness whenever she let her thoughts stray. The words were like a melody that played over and over in her mind, tantalizingly sweet and just as elusive. She was in a rush to capture them before they slipped away.

Secret Passions - Scene Three

I'm dreaming of her now. Even when I'm awake, I'm still dreaming.

In my sleep, I ache, trapped in an ocean of fear. I cannot find the surface; the light eludes me. There is no air in my lungs, no sound to my cries. Then the distant echo of her voice washes over me. She anchors me, instantly calming the restless uncertainties. I long to float within the circle of her arms, surrounded by her sweet fragrance, soothed by the melody of her touch.

I can't move. The weight of my disbelief drags me down, far beneath the waters of my despair. Just as the welcome blackness claims me, she speaks my name. My name breathed from her lips is like a hand stretched down through the murky depths, beckoning me to follow. My desperately reaching fingers just miss hers. I am losing the battle. I am losing.

Too weary now, my eyes close in surrender, allowing the darkness to enclose me.

She touches me, her skin...her skin warm on mine. Even in my sleep, the light caress infuses me with hope. I cry out for her and, without hesitation, she carries me to shore. Tenderly, she cradles my head in her lap and strokes my forehead, consoling me.

Visible beneath the shell of my body, my heart pounds, and she presses her palm to the place where it is breaking, healing me. I draw a breath, her fingers rising with me, never leaving my skin. Never leaving me. She banishes the pain, and I open my eyes to thank her.

Of course, I am yet dreaming. And I am still alone.

Rune read the passage slowly, an unfamiliar longing twisting through her stomach. Not truly unfamiliar, merely forgotten. She could almost feel the fingers on her face, the tender touch.

"How have you done this?" she whispered aloud.

The words mocked her.

```
"Of course, I am yet dreaming. And I am still
alone."
```

Of course, I am still alone. With a disgusted sigh, she opened her e-mail program and began to scan the messages. Abruptly, she stopped, her eyes lingering on the unexpected name.

❖

As soon as Auden let herself into her apartment, she dropped her briefcase along with the mail she had collected from the shared foyer onto the small telephone table just inside her front door. Then she walked directly to the rear of the apartment and into her bedroom. She undressed quickly, taking time only to hang her suit on the closet door, and pulled on comfortable loose cotton pants and a favorite faded V-neck sweater. She curled up on the bed and reached for *Secret Storm*. Before opening to her place from the previous night, she rifled through to the back and found what she was looking for.

AUTHOR'S BIO

Rune Dyre has published three novels: *Hidden Dreams, Dark Destiny,* and *Secret Storm.*

Lesbian Review stated, "Dyre has a talent for infusing the classic romance with an eroticism rarely seen in a love story. She blends the two effortlessly and promises to satisfy aficionados of either genre."

Dark Passions, a forebodingly captivating romance, will be published by WomenWords in the near future.

Auden was disappointed to discover nothing particularly revealing. She wasn't sure what she had hoped to find or why she should care about information concerning the author. The usual official titles and affiliations that she looked for in a scholarly text would have no meaning here. And personal information about the author was of no consequence. Who Rune Dyre was didn't matter; only what she wrote affected Auden. Her words spoke for themselves.

Impatiently, Auden opened the book, began to read, and as had happened the night before, was soon absorbed. Again, the hours passed unawares.

She could taste herself on her lover's mouth, surprised to feel her own body stir again even as the vestiges of the orgasm that had racked her only moments before lingered. Sliding down her lover's finely muscled form, she paused at the hollow of the arched neck to place a light kiss before continuing the slow descent, savoring every inch along the way. Pushing herself up on one hand, she slowly bit an erect nipple.

"Oh, love," came the quiet sigh.

Smiling, she slowly took the small nipple into her mouth, flicking it with her tongue until it was harder still, and the soft moans became urgent gasps. Her own lids were heavy, her eyes hooded with desire, as she lowered her head to kiss the taut stomach and lick a small circle around the trim navel.

"I want to see your face when you come for me," she murmured, nipping at the soft skin of her lover's inner thigh, then blowing a light breath on the soft curls between taut thighs. As she felt her lover's hand stroke her cheek, she lifted those trembling legs over her own shoulders and bent to drink the sweet nectar that was, and only ever could be, love.

Auden closed the book abruptly and stood, dropping it onto the bed. It wasn't as if she hadn't been expecting the scene. Despite the clear action-oriented plot, *Secret Storm* was just as much a love story as a thriller. She just hadn't expected it to affect her the way it had. She was aroused. Unmistakably and uncomfortably so.

Her heart pounded, and there was an undeniable heaviness in the pit of her stomach. She had become so involved in the love scene that even when she'd felt herself starting to respond physically, she couldn't turn her eyes away. Not until she could no longer bear the urgency in her own flesh.

The physical excitement itself wasn't new, and she was no stranger to the pleasures of satisfaction, either. She'd just never encountered such intense arousal in this way before, never really thought about the *source* of her excitement at all. But considering it now, she supposed that she had always assumed it was simply physiologic. She had a body; it was natural now and then to feel physical arousal. But she'd never before become sexually excited just from reading a book. Sometimes images from a film had lingered in her mind and formed a backdrop for her desire, but never in the true sense of sexual fantasy. Her mind just didn't work that way.

"Well, it seems to be working that way now." She walked rapidly through the apartment to the kitchen and pulled a bottle of pale ale from the refrigerator. She opened the bottle, poured the liquid into a glass, and took a large swallow.

"God, my hands are shaking. I can't believe this."

Alone, she sat at the kitchen table, rubbing the cool glass across her forehead as her body slowly returned to normal. "What have I been missing?"

As the moments ticked by, her thoughts were not on fiction.

❖

"Hey, come on in," Gayle said in surprise as she opened her apartment door at the sound of a quiet knock. "What are you doing up so late?"

"I heard you come home, and I was still awake," Auden explained sheepishly. "I know you're probably beat."

"Nah, I'm wired. I always feel that way at the end of a shift." Gayle grabbed Shylock's leash and said, "I have to run him around the block. Wanna come?"

"Sure. I'll just go downstairs and get a jacket."

"Don't bother. Take one of mine." Gayle gestured to several coats hanging on pegs just inside her door.

Auden pulled down a quilted red and black checked hunting jacket and shrugged it on.

Gayle cocked her head. "You look kinda cute all butched out in that jacket."

"Oh yeah?" Auden blushed furiously. "Is that all it takes—a jacket?"

"No, honey. What it takes is *attitude*." Gayle nudged her playfully with a shoulder. "'Sides, it would take a hell of a lot more than flannel to hide *your* femme power."

"Let's just go walk the dog," Auden said, but she laughed as she felt her spirits lift.

As Shylock pulled her down the sidewalk, Gayle asked, "What are you doing up so late? Aren't you usually in bed by now?"

"I couldn't sleep," Auden confessed. The two friends stopped as Shylock investigated a tree trunk and then left his mark, the first of many on his nightly route. "I've been doing my homework."

"Your homework? Oh...your reading list." Gayle chuckled. "How's it going? Are you suffering from culture shock yet?"

"No, actually, I'm...enjoying it."

Gayle glanced at her sharply, alerted to something amiss by the pensive tone in her friend's voice. "Is something wrong? Bad day at work?"

"No, not at all," Auden said quickly. "It's just..." She paused, frustrated, and shrugged. "I don't know. I just finished the first book a few minutes ago. That's when I heard you come in."

"Which one did you read?"

"*Secret Storm.*"

"Ahh," Gayle said, stopping abruptly to disentangle Shylock's leash from around a fireplug. "Did you like it?"

"Very much."

"It's pretty...racy."

"Yes."

Gayle stopped at the corner of 23rd and Pine and leaned her shoulder against a light pole. After midnight on a weeknight in the residential area, the street was deserted. Shylock busied himself trying to dig out a piece of trash from beneath a parked car. "Okay. What's going on?"

Auden placed her hands in the pockets of the hunting jacket and rocked from foot to foot, searching for the words to explain her strange disquiet. "I really liked the book. I didn't expect to. I mean, I want to go home right now and read it over again."

"You mean, you liked the women?"

Auden stared at her friend. "Yes. I liked the women."

"Uh-huh." Gayle nodded. "Come on, Shylock," she said as she tugged on his leash and resumed walking. "That's what's supposed to happen in these books. The women are supposed to make an impression on you. You're supposed to feel as if you know them or, sometimes, as if you might even *be* them. That's the whole point."

"Well, I guess that's what happened, then."

"It's not so different than any other book, right? Any good writer will do that—draw you in."

"Of course." Auden hesitated. "But it was more than just a transitory sense of connection. It was...recognition." She drew a deep breath and looked into Gayle's eyes. "I saw myself."

"Saw yourself how?" Gayle walked slowly, and, as if sensing the mood, Shylock, for once, trotted obediently by her side. *They're lesbians, Aud. What are you telling me?*

"This is going to sound so dumb," Auden mumbled. "I knew their pain and their loneliness, and in the end, I felt as if their joy was mine."

"Yeah," Gayle said softly. "I know what you mean. I guess that's why I love reading them so much. I don't *think* when I read those books. I just feel."

"I didn't expect it."

"I think it's pretty natural."

"Good," Auden replied pensively.

"So, Aud," Gayle teased gently, "that particular book has some pretty hot stuff in it, too. Did it turn you on?"

"Yes."

"Well, good for you." Gayle laughed in delight. "Did you have to do the old 'substitute a man for one of the women' thing, like I substitute a woman for the guy in straight books?"

"What?" Auden's confusion was plain in her voice. "Why would I...oh. No, I...just enjoyed the two of them together." *They were so beautiful. So right together.*

"Whoa. So did you imagine one of those hot sexy women making love to you?"

"No," Auden said softly. Haydon Palmer's face flashed through her mind. "Not exactly."

For some reason, Gayle didn't ask her anything else. She simply threaded her arm through Auden's and gave her a sympathetic hug. "Don't worry, Aud. It will all work out."

Will it?

❖

Rune reviewed the message just to be sure.

```
-----Reply-----
From: Rune@HeartLand.com
Sent: Wednesday March 19, 2:20 AM
To: AFrost@PalmPub.net
Subject: Manuscript-Dark Passions
Attachment: Dark Passions.doc 858KB


Ms. Frost:

    Attached please find the current draft of
Dark Passions for your review.
    Since there are no substantial changes in
the new contract, I will return my signed
copy to you by mail within the week.
    Thank you for affording me the opportunity
to bring this work to completion.

Sincerely,
Rune Dyre
```

Perfectly businesslike. She clicked Send, logged off, and went to bed. When she finally slept, the dreams returned.

CHAPTER SIX

When she opened her eyes, Auden was stunned to feel the warmth of another body, to find that she was not alone in bed.

Gayle? Did I fall asleep in Gayle's apartment? We were talking and...

She couldn't remember. Her mind was suffused with half images and broken fragments—elusive memories fluttering on the edge of consciousness. Her body was strangely lethargic, too, floating in that indolent plane between sleep and wakefulness.

Despite her confusion, she was quite aware of the firm arm wrapped around her waist, and of the heat of the body pressed to her back as she lay curled on her side. Warm breath blew rhythmically across her neck. Carefully, she inched away, only to be stopped by the hand tightening against her stomach and a soft murmur of protest. Almost at once, that hand, which had been softly stroking her stomach, drifted higher, cupping her bare breast. Sharply, she drew in a breath as a swift shaft of arousal pierced her, her thighs clenching as the muscles deep within contracted. She felt the sudden urge to press her hips back into the heat that flared against her buttocks, but she resisted, lying as still as she possibly could.

Another muted murmur, lips against her skin, and a swell of moisture anointed her thighs.

"Oh," she gasped as a warm mouth explored her neck, then a teasing tongue traced the rim of her ear. This time, she couldn't hide the small jerk of her hips as pleasure seared through her. Rocking back against the soft breasts and firm thighs, she heard an answering moan. Struggling to contain the onslaught of sensation, her vision clouded as other senses burst to life. Her skin tingled, light danced beneath her half-closed lids, and passion beat in her blood.

Fingers explored her breast, then brushed the nipple that was already so hard, already so sensitive. Everything pulsed in a single rhythm now—her body, her blood, the swiftly swelling heart of need between her thighs. Her mind emptied even as her flesh erupted with sensation. Excitement hammered in her depths, and she pulled her bottom lip between her teeth to still her cries.

The mouth on her neck grew more insistent, biting lightly in time with the rhythmic pressure on her nipples. It was more than she had ever imagined, and far less than she required.

"Oh God, I need you to touch me."

Not thinking, not questioning, she turned onto her back, grasping the tormenting hand, drawing it from her breasts, down over her abdomen, finally pressing it between her thighs. Her body was screaming for release, her clitoris stiff and pulsing, achingly hard. The first touch was electric, and she reared up, stomach clenched—desperately watching as the fingers beneath her own stroked her. Her breath left her in a rush; she was dying, poised on the precipice of discovery.

"Please."

Even as the plea escaped her lips, she turned her head, eyes wide, needing the connection as her climax hovered just out of reach. As tender fingers closed along her length, drawing her closer with agonizingly exquisite pressure, she met not Gayle's hazel eyes, but obsidian ones, flecked with silvers and golds. Familiar eyes, deep with desire.

"Oh!" she cried, lost in those dark depths, everything inside of her exploding.

The wrenching climax rocketed Auden from sleep just as the alarm went off.

"Oh God," she sobbed, squeezing with the hand still caught between her thighs, legs jerking as the orgasm raged. "Oh God, oh God…"

When she finally caught her breath, Auden rolled over and shut off the alarm, then lay on her back staring at the ceiling. Chest heaving, she twitched faintly as her muscles struggled to recover.

Well, that's a first. More than a first. I would have thought I was too old for wet dreams, and I've never come in my sleep like that. God, it was so real. I can't believe I dreamed that. What's happening to me?

Beneath her fingers, her clitoris still pulsed. She knew if she lingered much longer, she would need to come again. Reluctantly, but with a sigh of relief as well, she forced herself upright and out of bed. The orgasm had been brilliant, burning through her with terrible urgency. But even as her body welcomed the release, her heart seemed heavier for the coldness of the empty bed beside her.

Her legs were still shaking, and an insistent echo of desire rolled through her. Swiftly, she crossed to the bathroom, leaned into the shower, and turned on the water. The sluice of spray helped restore her body *and* her mind to some sense of normalcy.

Okay. No big deal. You were turned on when you went to sleep. Obviously, your body decided to take care of matters all on its own. Nothing else to read into it.

"Yeah, right." She tried to ignore the memory of looking into all too familiar eyes as she came. "Sure. God."

As she dressed and made coffee, lingering by the window for a few moments to watch the morning, Auden steadfastly refused to think about the dream. Nevertheless, it flitted across the recesses of her memory. She didn't try to deny that she had come while imagining a woman's touch. That didn't bother her.

That could mean anything, probably means nothing. Just one of those dream things where everything gets turned upside down. Jeez, I even dreamed it was Gayle.

Auden turned from the window and busied herself with collecting her keys and briefcase. She didn't need to think about what she refused to put into words. She knew the truth to her core. It wasn't Gayle who had made her come.

❖

When Auden arrived at work, she nodded hello to Alana and started down the hall toward her temporary office.

"Ms. Frost?" the receptionist called.

Auden turned and walked back. "Yes?"

"I have several messages here for you."

"Oh?" She hadn't even had time to check her e-mail before leaving the house. Her morning had been too disjointed, another sign that she was off her stride. She forced herself to concentrate. "What?"

"A Ms. Liz Nixon called to say that she received your e-mail and was available for a meeting."

"Did she say when?"

"At your convenience," Alana said formally.

"Do you know if I'll be getting a temporary secretary today?"

"I wouldn't know." After a beat, Alana's expression softened. "But I'd be happy to set up the appointment for you."

"Thank you. I know you're busy—"

"It's no trouble, Ms. Frost."

"Please. Call me Auden."

Alana smiled fleetingly. "When would you prefer to see Ms. Nixon?"

"As far as I know," Auden replied with a grin, "my schedule is wide open. Any time tomorrow or Friday would be fine."

"I'll see to it then. There's also a message from Ms. Palmer."

"Yes?" Auden's pulse skipped a beat, and she hoped the faint flush she felt rise to her face didn't show.

"She wanted you to know that she would be out of town for several days, and that you could refer any questions to Mr. Pritchard."

"Oh." Auden tried to hide her surprise. *Odd that Hays didn't mention that yesterday. But then again, why should she have?* Auden nodded neutrally. "I see. Thank you."

Still, as Auden walked away, she couldn't ignore the keen sense of disappointment. She had so much work to do, work she was looking forward to, but knowing that Hays would not be right down the hall left her feeling empty in a totally unexpected way.

It's probably for the best if I don't see her for a few days. Clearly, too much has happened too fast. I just need to get my sense of balance back. A few days with nothing to distract me should set that straight.

She entered her office, already thinking of the people she needed to contact and the interviews that needed to be scheduled. Within minutes, she had forgotten all about Haydon Palmer and the strange happenings of the early-morning hours.

❖

-----Original Message-----

From: AFrost@PalmPub.net
Sent: Wednesday March 19, 10:05 AM
To: Rune@HeartLand.com
Subject: Personal Meeting

Ms. Dyre:

Thank you for your prompt response. I received your draft of *Dark Passions* and will review it as soon as possible.

I would like to arrange a meeting here in Philadelphia at your earliest convenience to discuss future projects with you in person.

Palmer Publishing resource personnel are available to assist you with travel and accommodations. Let us know what you may require.

I look forward to hearing from you,

Sincerely,
Auden Frost

Auden sent similar e-mails to the seven other authors she had inherited. She could handle the necessary negotiations by teleconference if she had to, but there was nothing like seeing a person face to face when discussing business. At least at this stage, she thought a personal assessment would be wise, considering that the future of Destiny books might rest with these eight women.

Alana had arranged several in-house interviews for the late morning. By the time Auden realized that she had missed lunch again, it was almost two p.m. She hadn't been out of her office all day.

To her delight, when she approached the lunch room for coffee, she saw that Hays's office door was open and heard voices emanating from within. Her happiness was short-lived, however. In passing, she was surprised to recognize not Hays's deep tones, but Abel Pritchard's distinctive baritone.

"Are you sure you don't need me to come over?...Have you called Rosenberg?"

Something in his tone, a totally uncharacteristic edge of anxiety, brought Auden up short.

"*Damn* it, Hays, this has got to stop. You simply can't keep this up."

Hurriedly, Auden moved away. The conversation was obviously private. But the worry in Pritchard's voice was hard to forget. She poured coffee, still thinking about the odd snippets of conversation. When she turned around, Pritchard was standing in the doorway watching her.

"Good afternoon, Mr. Pritchard," she said calmly.

"Ms. Frost."

They regarded one another silently for a moment.

Pritchard asked, "Are you settling in?"

"Getting there," Auden acknowledged with a weary shrug. "I have a secretary and a copy editor, or I *will* have as soon as the transfers are approved." She hesitated. "Should I send the personnel requests through you?"

"If these are routine matters that don't specifically require Haydon's input, yes, that procedure would be best. She has...enough to do."

"Certainly."

"You have the information about the reception Saturday evening?" His tone was formally cool.

"I do. Thank you."

"Very well, then. I'll be here until eight, if you need anything."

He turned to leave and Auden said suddenly, "Mr. Pritchard?"

"Yes?" His expression was guarded.

"Is she all right?"

"Who?"

Auden smiled thinly. "I don't make a habit of eavesdropping, but the door was open, and I heard a bit of your conversation as I passed. Hays...Ms. Palmer...didn't look well yesterday. I was just wondering—"

"She's fine."

His eyes probed hers, looking for something, but what it might be, Auden had no clue. She had nothing to hide and let him search, waiting quietly.

"A touch of the flu," he said at last.

"I'm glad it's nothing serious."

"No. Good day then, Ms. Frost."

"Good day, Mr. Pritchard."

When she returned to her office, Auden punched in a number from memory, then replaced the receiver. A few moments later, the phone rang. She answered, smiling at the familiar lilting tones.

"Dr. Dunbar."

"Hiya, superdoc."

"Aud!" Gayle exclaimed. "Where are you? I don't recognize this number."

"My office."

"Ooh—sounds so official. What's up?"

"You busy Saturday night?"

"Uh," Gayle muttered. "Let's see. I'm off call, so I had planned to hit all the hot spots. Sisters. Key West. The 2-4. Maybe bring home the love of my life." She laughed. "Make me an offer."

"I have a feeling this won't compare," Auden remarked glumly. "A cocktail party with some people from Palmer. Some of the authors, too."

"Authors?" Gayle asked quickly, her voice rising. "Authors? Like dyke romance writers?"

Auden laughed. "Uh-huh."

"Like who? Who?"

"Well, there's Thane Cutlass and Margo Elliot and Rune—"

"Thane Cutlass? Rune Dyre? You're kidding!"

"Well, I haven't seen the acceptance list, but they've all been invit—"

"What should I wear? Ooh—can I wear a tux?"

"Sweetie, you can wear anything you'd like." Auden couldn't help but smile when she talked to Gayle. Her enthusiasm was contagious.

"Uh...what are you wearing?"

"Me?" Auden mentally reviewed her closet. "Standard cocktail fare. A black, off-the-shoulder—"

Gayle's gulp was audible. "Hey, Aud? Is there something we need to talk about?"

"Huh?"

"'Cause you know I love you, but—"

Auden burst out laughing. "God, Gayle. It's not a date!"

"Well, you know—when a lady invites me out, I think romance."

"I'm not...a lady," Auden said quietly, wondering if Gayle noticed that she hadn't declared "I'm not gay."

"Oh, honey," Gayle crooned, "you have *no* idea."

"So that's a yes?"

"Most definitely."

❖

When Auden was satisfied that she had the next several days' work organized, she checked her e-mail one more time. She opened one new message immediately.

```
-----Reply-----
From: Rune@HeartLand.com
Sent: Wednesday, March 19, 4:52 PM
To: AFrost@PalmPub.net
Subject: Re: Meeting

Ms. Frost:

    I regret that I will not be able to meet
with you in Philadelphia. I will be most
happy to address any issues you may wish to
discuss by email.

Sincerely,
Rune Dyre
```

"Well, that's pretty definite," Auden mused with a mixture of surprise and irritation. In her experience, authors were usually a little more anxious to foster good relationships with their publishers. The response was scrupulously polite but left no room for negotiation. "Not even an offer of a phone call. Let's see what she has to say Saturday night."

Before she gathered up the papers she intended to review over the next few days, Auden printed out a copy of Rune Dyre's manuscript, *Dark Passions.*

"Let's see if she can write another one as good as *Secret Storm.*"

❖

Clad in her pajamas, Auden answered the knock on her door. It was almost one-thirty in the morning. At this hour on Friday night, it could only be Gayle or Mrs. Truman, the octogenarian who occupied the second-floor apartment. After another long day of meetings, a day in which Haydon Palmer had still not made an appearance, Auden decided to indulge herself in a late night of reading and a solitary bottle of wine. She'd finished two more novels and had finally begun what she'd really been thinking about reading for more than a day. She peered out the door and smiled.

"Hello, sweetie."

"Hello, my lady love," Gayle said with a grin. "I saw your lights on."

Auden held the door wide and stepped aside so that Gayle could enter. She caught a whiff of whiskey and smoke. "You strike out tonight?"

"Not really." Gayle flopped into the overstuffed chair in Auden's living room. "I had an offer or two."

"But?" Auden perched on the other chair and settled her bare feet on the coffee table. She studied her friend, who looked chic and sexy in tight black jeans, a black, tight-weave net top that revealed just a suggestion of nipple shadows, and a leather jacket. Auden searched for any hint of sexual response on her part when she looked at Gayle, but her body was quiet. She was happy to see Gayle, but she wasn't excited. Not the way she had been in the dream. *Oh, for Pete's sake. Forget the damn dream!*

"But...I just didn't feel like it." Gayle swung her legs over the arm of the chair and leaned her head back, gazing at Auden out of half-closed lids. "I think I'm getting old."

"Poor baby. You're only twenty-seven."

"I've been dating girls since I was fourteen years old. I've never even come close to being serious about one."

"How come?"

"Don't know. You got any Fresca?"

"Don't I always? Wait a minute." Auden got up and delivered the soda, then poured the last of the wine into her own glass. "You okay?"

"Hmm? Oh, yeah. I didn't have much to drink. Just tired." Gayle took a long swallow. "My mom's divorced. My older sister is a single mom. I haven't exactly been surrounded by examples of happy relationships."

Auden nodded. "Same here. My parents divorced when I was twelve. My mother seems happy with my stepfather though. I just always thought..."

"What?"

"That she married him because it was convenient, or maybe necessary. There doesn't seem to be a lot of...passion between them."

Gayle snorted softly. "I'd take someone who could stand my mood in the morning over hot sex right about now."

"You think the two are mutually exclusive? Love and good sex?" Auden curled up in her chair, running the edge of her soft flannel shirt through her fingers. She thought about the women who had so captivated her in *Secret Storm*. The love and affection and physical passion the two had shared. *That's fiction, Aud. Come on.*

"No, not really. Just rare." Gayle stretched and grinned. "I'm probably just premenstrual. Give me a week, and I'll be dragging home the *next* love of my life."

"Who knows?" Auden smiled. "Maybe you'll meet her tomorrow night at the party."

"Huh. So what are you doin'? Homework still?"

"Work-work, actually. I'm reviewing a manuscript."

"Anyone I know?"

"Uh-huh. Rune Dyre."

"Oh, yeah—she's one of my faves." Gayle sat up and leaned forward, her eyes dancing. "Whatcha reading?"

"*Dark Passions.*"

"Ooh—I *love* that one."

"What do you mean you love it?" Auden's brows rose. "It's not published yet."

"I mean the Web version. It's practically an Internet legend."

"Web version?" Auden felt as if she were suddenly speaking another language. "What are you talking about?"

Gayle sighed, rose, and held out her hand. "Come on, honey. You need some more lessons."

A minute later, they were perched in front of Auden's computer. Gayle typed www.HeartLand.com and clicked Go. Seconds later, the website appeared.

Auden leaned forward and read:

HeartLand
Welcome to Rune Dyre's fiction. Enter, linger, enjoy. These are love stories disguised as fantasies, mysteries, and chance encounters. The lovers are women and their love is physical.
Please send comments to Rune@HeartLand.com

Auden took the mouse from Gayle and followed the links to the stories.

Webversions
Hidden Dreams
Dark Destiny
Secret Storm
Dark Passions

She clicked on the first chapter of *Dark Passions* and began to read. Her visual memory was nearly eidetic. As she scanned the first paragraph, she immediately saw the differences from the manuscript she had just read—there were changes, but in some places they were subtle.

"This is crazy," Auden exclaimed, scanning quickly through several more pages. "This is *my* manuscript."

"Well, actually," Gayle pointed out, "it isn't. It's a beta version. An early draft."

"But it's out here for people to read *free*."

"Uh-huh. Good promo."

"*Promo*?" Auden gaped at her, incensed. "How about lethal

competition? Why buy the book when you can get it here for nothing?"

"Plenty of reasons," Gayle said with an unconcerned shrug. "The print versions are lots more of a good thing—extra scenes, more dialogue, smoother prose—the pleasure of holding the book in your hands and reading it anywhere you want. A lot of authors do it."

"We'll see about that," Auden muttered. "We need a market study to look at this."

Gayle stood and rubbed Auden's shoulders. "Wait a few days before you get yourself in an uproar. I'll show you around the Web. We'll check out some other authors, see what's on other sites. You'll need to get a sense of it anyhow, 'cause this is where you're going to find a lot of your readers."

"More homework, huh?"

"Yeah, but high school English was never like this, honey."

Auden thought about what she had read so far, the physicality and the raw emotions and the sexual passion. And her own unexpected responses. "No, it most certainly was not."

CHAPTER SEVEN

Auden sat curled up in one corner of the plush brocade sofa, her shoes on the floor, her stockinged feet tucked beneath her. Outside the windows, a light snow fell steadily. When she'd walked to the office at a little after seven, the scene that greeted her on the still Saturday morning had been breathtakingly idyllic. Rittenhouse Square lay pristine under a white blanket of fresh snow that covered the central fountain, the stone benches, and the carefully trimmed hedges. Here and there, a daring daffodil pierced the immaculate surface with an unexpected splash of color. The elegant park reminded her poignantly of the history and beauty of the old city.

Now, alone in her office in the Palmer building, she was lost in a scene that contrasted sharply with that quiet tranquility.

The stranger led her up a flight of stairs and into a darkened apartment. "Wait here."

She was aware of lights being turned on in other rooms and of the sound of soft music. She stood and waited, not thinking at all. When at last she heard sure footsteps approaching, her body stirred in anticipation. The effect this woman had on her was inexplicable, and, lost in the moment, she didn't try to understand. She responded purely with her senses, and she reveled in that sense of abandon. She didn't want to think. She wanted to feel.

"This way."

She followed the blond stranger into a bedroom lit solely by soft blue lights in a recessed ceiling track. A small table stood next to a large rectangular bed that dominated the otherwise bare room. When the stranger turned suddenly to face her, she stood absolutely still. In silence, the stranger reached out and loosed the buttons on her shirt, being careful not to touch the skin laid bare as the shirt fell away. Once exposed, her nipples contracted almost painfully, an urgent plea for contact.

"Your boots."

She hesitated only a second and then unbuckled each of her heavy black boots and pulled them off. Naked except for her leather pants, she stood before the stranger, still waiting. A slender hand traced the muscles in her shoulders and arms, and then a palm lay against her chest and pressed, softly massaging the muscles beneath the smooth skin. Eventually, both hands moved down to her abdomen, carefully avoiding her breasts, outlining flickering muscles with deliberate strokes.

The slow, wordless survey set a fire simmering in her belly. She felt her clitoris swell and moisture flow in response to the stimulation. Her chest was covered with a thin film of sweat. She was panting slightly in the still room.

"Lie down on the bed. Face me."

She did as directed, her eyes locked on the stranger's.

"You can say anything you want to me right now, but after this, no more. I won't hurt you, but once I start, I won't stop until I'm done."

Looking back steadily, she searched for a clue as to who this woman was. The face was edgy and strong. The eyes, even in the half-light, were piercing and clear. Inexplicably, she sensed not danger, but honesty. "I'm all right."

The stranger nodded once and then moved purposefully to the side of the bed, reached somewhere beneath the frame, and pulled out soft, padded leather restraints. Deftly, the stranger bound her left hand, then moved to the other side and repeated the actions, leaving her securely but not painfully bound with her arms spread wide.

The stranger stood once again at the foot of the bed, slowly removing her own shirt, methodically baring her upper body. Small high breasts accentuated the finely muscled torso, and a pulse beat close to the surface of a pale throat. Silence enclosed them in the cone of blue light.

She was bombarded by conflicting sensations. The feeling of being helplessly bound was at once frightening and exhilarating. She wanted this woman on top of her, she wanted her inside of her, she wanted more than she could put words to. Her inability to actually seek her own release made her even more acutely aware of her desires. Her clitoris strained against the seam of her pants, threatening to explode just from the constant contact as her hips rocked back and forth. She stifled a groan as she stared transfixed at the stranger's body, so close to her and yet so completely untouchable.

After what seemed like hours, all sense of time lost, the stranger placed both hands firmly on either side of her jaw and moved surprisingly gentle fingers over the flesh and bones of her face. Then, with one hand under her chin, the stranger tilted her head back, exposing her neck to its fullest.

"Close your eyes and keep them closed."

Fingers traced the vulnerable structures of her throat, resting on the fragile windpipe as the blood rippled through the pulsating arteries just below the skin. A tongue ran lightly from her collarbone to her ear.

A voice, barely a whisper. "I don't want you to move. Just remember my hands on your throat while I'm making you come."

The words made her hips jerk, and as her pants were stripped away, she bit her lip to stifle a cry. She had never felt so physically vulnerable in her life. The restraints, on her ankles now as well as her arms, were barely perceptible, yet she was totally immobilized. Now, with her throat exposed, locked in darkness, she felt as if she had lost control of her very life. Despite the helplessness of her position, she was powerfully excited. She feared that the merest touch would set her off.

Dimly, in the last fragment of her thinking mind, she knew she could break the spell of her own bondage by a word to the stranger. But she didn't want to escape. She wanted to feel what the stranger aroused in her. She wanted to know how far into her physical self the stranger could take her.

More than she wanted to come, she wanted to know.

Suddenly, a sharp sensation centered in each breast as hands enclosed them, fingers squeezing the erect nipples hard. She gasped at the unexpected contact, her back arching. The entire surface of her body was sensitized with need. Her clitoris twitched urgently.

Just as suddenly, the small pinpoints of almost-pain disappeared, and a leather belt was placed the length of her abdomen, the buckle resting between her breasts. The soft tongue of leather was pressed into the triangle between her legs. The edges of the belt rode against her distended clitoris, and the roughness against the exposed nerves pushed her close to orgasm. She pulled against her restraints for the first time, wanting connection, needing to feel the heat of a body against her own.

"Please, no more," she groaned. "Please, I have to come."

"I'll decide."

When lips finally claimed hers, their tongues met in a probing duel. When fingers slipped inside her, the belt trapped beneath the palm rubbed the length of her distended flesh, and she moaned frantically. Her inner muscles contracted hard around the hand. When a thumb slipped beside the leather to beat an insistent rhythm against her clitoris, she closed her eyes tightly, jaws clenching, and tried to resist the aching need to come. But she was too far gone; her body arched and bucked as she closed around the fullness within, ripples of sensation flooding into her thighs, coiling through her belly. A strangled cry escaped her lips as the pounding in her head fused with that in her body, and her orgasm crested in one wave of unbound fury.

She was drifting on the edge of consciousness when the stranger straddled her, a leather-clad leg on either side of her thigh. She pushed her hips upward to meet the desperate downward thrusts, all of her energy immediately focused on bringing the same pleasure to the stranger that she had just experienced. The stranger gasped brokenly, jerking erratically, fingers clenched on her upper arms. There would be bruises.

When the stranger stiffened, then climaxed, moaning uncontrollably, she smiled, triumphant.

Auden rested the manuscript in her lap and closed her eyes. She'd read enough of the first draft of *Dark Passions* to know that it wasn't at all what she'd expected. She'd been interested in the story from the first line, just as quickly captivated by the sharply drawn characters with their thinly veiled pain as she had been when reading Dyre's romance, *Secret Storm*. But the tone of this story had taken an unexpected turn into an area she rarely associated with romance fiction. The anonymous liaison between two women, who had met for the first time in a bar where strangers gathered for no other purpose than to explore each other sexually, produced reactions Auden was at a loss to decipher. She'd never before considered sex reduced to only sensation without emotion, the physical with no greater context than sensual satisfaction.

In fact, she'd given very little thought to her own intimate relationships, or lack thereof, physical or otherwise. She'd dated but not seriously, and she'd never suffered from the absence of some deeper connection. At least not in a way that she'd wanted to explore too closely. She had friends, like Gayle, and a life that suited her. If something vital had indeed been missing, its absence had hovered on the edges of her consciousness where she had been able to ignore it by immersing herself in the routine of her daily life.

Now these books, these lives, these *women* had drawn her into worlds she'd never thought to visit. Their dreams and desires left her wondering why she had none of her own. Her reactions to the passion and intimacy she'd discovered in *Secret Storm* had left her in turmoil, but her reaction to this first encounter in *Dark Passions* unsettled her even more. She'd read the scene, in fact *reread* it, several times and was taken aback to find herself stirred both emotionally and physically. Not stimulated to the extent that the love scene in *Secret Storm* had excited her, but there was no question that she had been aroused by some of the images created by Dyre's words. That very fact confused her. If she had been asked, she would've answered categorically that such a scenario—sex without love, surrender without commitment—would never have stimulated her. Now she knew differently, and yet she could not fathom what that meant.

When she had fantasized, she'd imagined a lover's touch, but never a face. She'd envisioned connection, but never the kind of intense union she'd experienced in her dream looking into—

A knock on her open door caused Auden to jump in surprise. She turned, falling unexpectedly into Haydon Palmer's eyes. She caught her breath, her heart racing with sudden pleasure.

"Hello!"

"I'm sorry to disturb you," Hays said quietly. "I saw the light on in here."

"That's no problem," Auden said quickly. Her voice sounded breathless to her own ears. She indicated the sofa with a sweep of her hand. "Please, come in."

Hays carried a cup of coffee in her hand, and after a second of hesitation, she entered. She sat on the opposite end of the sofa, faced Auden, and smiled. "You look right at home."

Auden was suddenly conscious of the fact that she was wearing a faded pair of jeans and a Penn sweatshirt that had seen far better days. When she'd dressed earlier, she hadn't expected to see anyone else in the office. Hays, Auden noticed, was dressed far less formally than during the workweek as well, but even in jeans, a button-down cotton shirt, and low-heeled, square-toed black boots, she looked splendid.

"I feel at home, too," Auden replied, realizing just how much she meant it. She wasn't even certain why she'd come herself, except that she hadn't yet transferred many of her work files to her home computer. Once there, she'd gotten caught up in the manuscript and had forgotten all about work.

"How are things going?" Hays asked, surprised and pleased to see her new director. Three days' absence had not diminished her memory of how attractive Auden was. Seeing her now, relaxed and casually attired, Hays realized that she was truly beautiful.

"Very well, I think," Auden said with a small laugh. "Actually, better than I really expected at this early point." She wanted to ask Hays how she was feeling but was acutely aware that that kind of question was inappropriate. The publisher looked much the same as when Auden had last seen her. Her complexion always had a slight pallor, but the shadows beneath her eyes seemed no deeper. Her dark eyes, too, were lustrous and clear. Auden realized she'd fallen silent and suddenly added, "I met with Liz Nixon yesterday afternoon. I like her. She has some good ideas."

Hays raised her coffee cup and nodded. She regretted having been absent for the interview. One of the most frustrating things about the illness was the inability to concentrate. It stole from her the one thing she valued the most, her ability to work. Frowning slightly, cradling the cup in both hands, she asked, "So, did you offer Liz the position as head of marketing for Destiny?"

"No," Auden said swiftly. "But I want to."

Hays laughed. "Then by all means, go ahead. I've talked with her several times, and if she seems like a good match to you, I'm all for it."

"I'm not entirely certain that Mr. Pritchard—"

"Don't worry about Abel," Hays said. "He has very definite opinions about almost everything, but in the end, the business is mine to run."

"I appreciate that, believe me. Nevertheless, I don't want to create conflict."

"Is there any?" Hays studied Auden's face intently.

"No, but I have a feeling that he isn't entirely pleased with me as your selection to head Destiny."

Hays grinned, an utterly disarming grin. "Abel doesn't see what I see in you."

Completely nonplussed, Auden blushed. "What is that?"

"Enthusiasm. Desire. Drive. The things that we need to make this work. I never wanted an overly experienced director, because too often they come with preconceived notions of problems. You don't have that. You're fresh and optimistic."

Auden wasn't certain how to reply. She certainly had never seen herself that way. *Am I those things?* It pleased her enormously that Hays viewed her so. "Thank you for that. So far, I'm loving every minute of it."

"Yes, I can see that you are," Hays said softly. *And I can feel your enthusiasm. It fills the places that have felt empty for so long.* Hays gestured to the pile of papers in Auden's lap. "What are you reading?"

"Rune Dyre's manuscript."

"*Dark Passions?*"

"Yes."

"How's it going with the pending works from WomenWords?"

"I'm just getting started," Auden confided. "I'm not entirely certain about *this* book, though."

"Why not?" Hays asked neutrally.

"It's not exactly what I expected. I've only had a chance this week to read through a handful of the popular published titles, but this one is...different. Are you familiar with it?"

"I've seen the Web version."

"Then you know that it's a very dark story, rather outside the common experience of sexual expression."

"Auden," Hays said with a short laugh, "we're talking about lesbian love stories. Don't you think *they're* outside the common experience of sexual expression?"

"No, I don't," Auden said with absolute seriousness. "And neither, I'll wager, do ninety-nine percent of the people who will be reading Destiny's publications. But this book is about power relationships, or perhaps I should say, the *imbalance* of power. The very topic is going to prevent some people from reading it."

"And you think that's a reason not to publish it?"

Auden was brought up short by the question. Because that was *exactly* what she had been thinking. "Destiny is a brand-new imprint. I assume our goal is to establish a profitable division. To me, that means that every book needs to be a bestseller. Or at least, we need to believe that it *can* be."

Hays said nothing, waiting, watching Auden's face.

"I'm not sure that this book will ever fall into that category."

"You dislike the book?"

"What?" Auden was momentarily confused by what seemed like a change in the direction of the conversation. "No, actually, it's very well written. Rune Dyre is an excellent author, obviously. That's clear from her previous work. But this is quite a departure from her other works."

"Have you read them all?"

"Yes," Auden said. "*Secret Storm*, for example, is a beautiful book. A glorious romance."

Hays smiled and studied her coffee. "It has done well, according to Liz Nixon."

"According to everything," Auden stated. "But *this* book, however well written, is not standard fare."

"Finish reading *Dark Passions*," Hays suggested. "If you still feel the same after you've read it in its entirety, do whatever you think is best."

"Of course." Auden appreciated that Hays was giving her veto power, and she had every intention of using that power well. "It's not fair to judge a book by...oh God...I was about to say something stupid like 'by its cover.'"

"No, it probably isn't." Hays grinned, and they both laughed. "You're coming this evening?"

"Yes, of course. I'm very much looking forward to it."

Hays stood, placed her cup on the table, and walked to the window. "It's snowing quite heavily now. It's late in the season for this kind of weather, but a spring blizzard is not unheard of." She turned, leaning a shoulder against the window casing. "Are you driving tonight?"

"No," Auden said. "I was going to take a cab."

"I can have a car come around for you."

Surprised, Auden shook head. "No, that's all right. I'm bringing a friend, and I'm not certain precisely when she will be available."

A friend. Of course, she would have a date. Hays pushed away from the window, her expression remote. "I'll e-mail you a list of the attendees, in case there's something you want to review before this evening."

"Thank you," Auden said, watching as Hays crossed the room, leaned down to grasp her empty cup, and swiftly left.

Her departure left Auden once more feeling slightly bewildered and oddly bereft.

CHAPTER EIGHT

Secret Passions – Scene Four

Outside, the snow is falling, but here inside, there is warmth. Not just warmth, but light. It astounds me that I have not noticed before the terminal absence of heat, for I know now that I have grown cold. I realize, too, that shadows have served as the only illumination for so long that I have forgotten the brilliance of the sun.

She has no idea, of course, that I draw close to her warmth like the homeless on a street corner gathered around a dying fire, their hands out-stretched to the guttering flames. Beseeching—hope long gone. The walking dead, unaware that life passes by on the other side of the street. Hours, days, may pass, yet I am unaware of my living presence. My body moves through time, but my mind does not register that the moments of my life are ticking away, unnoticed.

Then, with a word, she stops the clock, and I can almost see the hands turning backward, returning to me what I thought I had lost. I am embarrassed that she might guess how I wait for each smile, hunger for the light that dances in her eyes, thirst for the fire in her voice that makes my heart beat hard enough for me to feel it,

reminding me that blood still flows, that
life resides within me still.

Unaware, she reminds me that it is not
time that we need, but the belief, however
false, that we *have* time. When love is a
distant memory, we cling to the belief that
it exists around the corner—untarnished and
unspoiled—waiting there to save us.

I wonder that she does not see beneath
my charade and recognize that I clutch each
word, grasping each spark with desperate
fingers, happy for the flame that sears my
flesh. I wonder if I were to touch her skin
if it would burn, knowing I would not care,
if only I were to feel—

Hays swiveled away from the monitor toward the sound at the
door, sliding instantly into the blue-green seas of Auden's eyes. She
might have made a sound as she tightened inside, pulled too quickly
from the dimension of sensation and unfettered emotion, unguarded
and undefended. She closed her fingers to hide their trembling, her fists
resting on her desktop.

Auden stood at the door, lips parted, poised to speak, staring into
Hays's face. Hays looked dazed, but her expression was not one of pain
or fatigue, the way it had been that afternoon when she had found her
asleep on the sofa. Now, her dark eyes were filled with longing—and
something else. Something that even from across the room looked to
Auden like desire. Flushing, Auden said hastily, "I'm so sorry. I didn't
realize—"

"No," Hays said quickly, her throat sounding thick to her own
ears. "It's all right. I was just...catching up on some correspondence."

Auden hadn't moved, and neither had Hays. They continued to
look at one another across the office, both barely breathing. The air was
filled with questions.

What do you see in my eyes?
Do you know how you look right now? So beautiful.
Do you sense what I feel?
Why can't I seem to hide from you?

How can you make me feel so much, without a word?

"There's something I want to talk to you about with regard to our new authors," Auden said quietly, forcing out each word with deliberation. What she really wanted to do was run. Because the other thing that she wanted to do was walk across the room and place her palm against Hays's cheek. She'd never wanted to touch another human being as much as she wanted to touch Haydon Palmer in that moment.

"What is it?" Hays asked hoarsely. *What is it in your eyes? Pity? Can you possibly see what no one else can?*

"It seems that some of the authors are posting early drafts on the Internet of works that have been contracted to be published." Auden struggled to remember what had bothered her so much about that. Hays's expression, so penetrating as it settled on her face, caused her thoughts to scatter.

"Beta versions." Hays searched Auden's eyes for the welcome she was coming to count on. Still, neither of them moved.

"Dyre's *Dark Passions* is on her website." She smiled softly, unable to hide her pleasure at being with Hays for any reason.

"That's fairly common," Hays remarked casually, relaxing under the warmth of Auden's smile.

"I understand that. I'm just not entirely certain that's something we should encourage or even permit, contractually."

"Some of these authors were actually discovered from their Internet posts." Hays got to her feet, briefly aware of a surge of dizziness that quickly abated. "Many of their fans evidently follow the progress of a new work by reading the Web posts. It's a new kind of marketing."

"That's just the point," Auden said, her voice stronger now. Her mind was clearing, as if she were breaking free from a dream, her senses slowly returning to normal and her brain beginning to work. She crossed the room to Hays's desk and rested the edge of a hip against the corner, a few feet away from where Hays stood with a hand resting lightly on the back of her chair. "It's not marketing at all. These works are being distributed without charge to anyone who might want to read them."

Startled by Auden's sudden proximity, Hays could only nod as she looked quickly to her right and reached to hit a key on the keyboard. Her screen saver flashed on, obscuring her work. Then she lifted a shoulder insouciantly. "Some of the readers who have access to these Web versions are unable to acquire lesbian fiction any other way, either because of the prohibitive costs of the books or because of the unavailability of the works where they live. I'm sure that many of the authors feel that posting their stories online is a community service."

"Fine. Then let them post the things that they don't intend to publish."

"Most authors probably don't have time to create two bodies of work, one for commercial publication and one for the Internet only."

"Then what do you suggest?" Auden ran her hand through her hair absently, then glanced out the window at the increasingly heavy snowfall. "It runs counter to everything we know about publishing and market sales."

"Well, I think that today's marketplace is different than it was ten or fifteen years ago. These Web versions are akin to the chapters some publishers append to their books to promote forthcoming titles."

"Chapters are one thing—entire stories are something else again." Auden was adamant, but her impatience was tempered by concern. Hays was swaying slightly, and she was very pale. "Hays?"

Hays jerked, realizing that she had been watching Auden's lips but not listening. I wonder if I were to touch her skin if it would burn...

"I'm sorry...what?"

"Are you all right?" Auden lifted her hand but stopped short of touching her.

"Yes. Fine." Hays stepped out from behind the desk and moved closer to the windows. "You'll need to come to a decision about how you want to handle this, because we'll need a uniform policy."

"All right, I'll give it some thought." Auden could see Hays's profile before the window, the snow just beyond seeming to envelop her in its swirling clouds. Hays appeared so isolated against the stark beauty, and so starkly beautiful herself. Auden felt an unfamiliar pang of pleasure so acute it was painful. *What is it that you do to me?*

"Why don't you sit down with Liz next week and talk about it." Hays brought her eyes back to Auden, having finally regained her control. Her expression was calm and businesslike again. "She'll have had experience with these authors and their sales, and perhaps she can give you a better picture of how Web posting actually affects profit margins."

"I think that's an excellent idea."

"I'm not saying you're wrong, Auden," Hays said gently. "But I believe you will get resistance from some of these authors if you ask them to pull their works from their websites."

Auden shrugged, a ghost of a grin curling at the corner of her mouth. "I guess I'll get a chance to see how good a negotiator I am, then, if it comes to that."

"I have no doubt that you'll be superb."

Smiling at the compliment, Auden still shook her head. "I hope that your confidence in me is not unfounded."

"You know it isn't."

"Thank you just the same," Auden replied softly. *For inviting me into this world. For your faith in me.*

❖

-----Original Message-----
From: thaneCutlass@CutlassFic.com
Sent: Saturday March 22, 11:52 AM
To: Rune@HeartLand.com
Subject: Private Pleasures
Attachment: Slow Kisses.doc 56KB

R:
   Here's the first of my Pleasures series. Thought you might like to ride along <g>.
   Are you going to make the Palmer soiree tonight so I can finally meet you ftf? Come on, you've been teasing me long enough.
   Besides, we can compare notes and watch women together. Oops, sorry, there I go being PI again. Be there, huh? Oh—and tell me if this gets you hot. Cause if not, I'll have to retire <g>

   T

Reading the e-mail, Hays grinned to herself. *Thane fancies herself such a player.*

Without much thought, as she had done dozens of times before, she opened the file and began to read.

Private Pleasures — Slow Kisses

I'm a morning person. I'll spare you all the rapturous details of why I love the mornings. Suffice it to say it's quiet, the hours seem longer, and there's a sense of owning everything around me that is at once comforting and inspiring. She's *not* a morning person. Or, perhaps it would be fairer to say, she is not *any* kind of person until after two cups of coffee and a slow perusal of the newspaper.

On this particular Saturday morning, I find her at her usual place, starting on her second cup of coffee, engrossed in the local news, and still looking a bit sleepy. I can tell that she has showered, but I know from the slightly bleary, soft smile she tosses my way that she is not yet truly awake.

There's something about seeing her in her robe, when I am fully dressed, that turns me on. I love to be dressed when she is naked. I especially love to have sex with her when I'm clothed and she is not. I love the damp patches she leaves on the denim on my thighs, the faint reminder of my effect on her. I look at her this morning, and my stomach instantly clenches with want.

She loves to kiss. Me, I enjoy it, but it is usually a warm-up for what I'm really after. The appetizer. For her, it's an entire feast. I've never experienced kissing quite

the way I have with her. I'm in sweatpants
and a tight faded T-shirt, barefoot. I've
been in my office writing for several hours.
I pad across the room and gently lift her by
her elbows. She looks at me, a question in
her eyes. I smile, sit in her seat, and pull
her down onto my lap. She is naked under the
robe. I knew she would be.

She settles into me, the way she does
when she's falling asleep or not yet awake
in the morning. I curve my arm around her
shoulders and with my free hand lift her
chin to kiss her lightly. She murmurs
softly—a happy, contented sound. She brings
one arm around my neck to grasp the hair at
my collar, threading it through her fingers.
Her eyes are almost closed. Then she very
gently takes my lower lip between hers,
sucks it in slowly, running the tip of her
tongue along the sensitive surface.

I feel that soft caress streak through
my entire body, landing like a laser beam
between my thighs. I groan softly, and she
smiles against my mouth.

Taking her time, she moves to my top
lip and explores there, sucking, nibbling,
licking. This makes me crazy. And she knows
it. My mouth opens slightly, my tongue
barely touching hers. I can feel myself
grow hard, the wet heat seeping through
my sweatpants. She shifts a little on my
lap, pressing her weight into my crotch. I
open my legs further, letting the pressure
gently massage my aching flesh.

Her kisses are firmer now, but still
controlled. She strokes the inside of my
lips, the tip of my tongue, the undersurface
of my teeth—slowly claiming every part of
my mouth. Somehow, I've ended up with my

head leaning back from the tug of her fingers
in my hair. Somehow, she is in control, her
other hand under my chin as she kisses me
unhurriedly, deliberately, thoroughly.

I'm way past hot now, swollen, needing
her to touch me so badly. And she knows
it.

She knows if she touches me, strokes me
just a little, I'll come all over her hand.
Maybe even if she doesn't, the pressure of
her hips, the thrust of her tongue, will be
enough. She moves her mouth a breath away.

"Don't you dare."

I close my eyes tightly, concentrate on
her tongue probing me gently, and loosen
the tie on her robe. I cup her breast; she
is warm and soft in my hand. I run my thumb
gently over the nipple, feeling it tense
under my touch.

She gasps, drawing her tongue back for an
instant. Her hips are moving rhythmically
now, rocking in my lap as she works her way
around every corner of my hungry mouth. I
slide my hand to the other breast, finding
the nipple already erect, and pinch it
firmly. She moans, and I catch her sounds in
my throat...

Hays looked away, trembling. She'd read Thane's erotica many
times. They'd critiqued each other's work, traded ideas and plot lines,
and shared vignettes since they'd met online over two years before.
They were friends, not competitors, although they shared the same fan
base. Usually she found Thane's direct, unvarnished style enjoyable
and on occasion stimulating, even though not much had actually stirred
her physically in recent months. Now she was painfully aroused.

She leaned her head back, closed her eyes, and waited for the
urgency to pass. She hadn't anticipated this reaction. Any other time,
she probably would have welcomed the feelings, the unmistakable
testament to the fact that she was still living and breathing. Any other

time, being this excited, she would have gladly surrendered to the rhythm and cadence of the words, allowing the images to stroke her to satisfaction accompanied by her own barely perceptible touch in the background of her consciousness.

She was a writer, and words were as tangible to her as flesh. She might be in one instant an observer, in another a chronicler, in yet another, a participant. This time, she had been only herself, joyously experiencing a gifted moment with a woman she desired. And this time, the woman had a name and a face—and the whisper in her ear was a too-familiar voice. This was far too real to be confined to the margins of a page, the borders of a monitor. This was passion spilling over her in an agony of need.

How can this be happening?

Hays brought trembling fingers to the keyboard and closed the file without looking at it again. Then she typed rapidly, still breathing hard, searching for control. She found it in that part of herself that dwelt closest to her soul.

-----**Original Message**-----
From: Rune@HeartLand.com
Sent: Saturday March 22, 2:47 PM
To: thaneCutlass@CutlassFic.com
Subject: Re: Private Pleasures

T:

Important things first. Great setting, great mood, great sex. Yeah, I got a bit warm <g>. Excellent intro for Eros.

Sorry, friend, but I probably won't be there tonight. Besides, you don't need to see my face. You already know the best part of me.

Stay out of trouble.

R

That sounds okay. Just the right amount of nonchalance.

As to the issue of their meeting—she'd decide what to do about Thane when she had to, if she ever had to. It was going to be much more difficult to face Auden at the party, especially feeling the way she did at the moment. She'd forgotten how alive desire made her feel.

CHAPTER NINE

At six-fifteen that evening, Auden's phone rang. She quickly turned off the shower, wrapped herself in a towel, and crossed her bedroom to the bedside phone. "Hello?"

"Aud?"

"Hey, Gayle. How are things going?"

"I'm just leaving the hospital. I got hung up in the ER seeing a consult, and my night-relief was late getting in. The snow has screwed up all the SEPTA schedules. Hopefully, the subway is running on time. I'll be home as soon as I can make it."

"That's okay. It doesn't matter if we're fashionably late."

"We should probably take a cab."

"I'll call now and tell them eight o'clock."

"Good. Sorry about this," Gayle repeated. "Oh, listen, could you take Shylock out for a walk?"

"Sure." Auden slipped the towel off and dried her hair as she spoke. "I'll go get him in a few minutes."

"Thanks, honey."

Gayle had just arrived home by the time Auden finished walking Shylock around the block, having made all the obligatory stops at his favorite spots. She dropped him off on the third floor and went downstairs to dress. Ready quickly and restless, she returned to Gayle's apartment and knocked on the door.

"I'm in the bedroom," Gayle called. "Come on back."

When Auden entered, her friend was standing by the closet, nude. Gayle was lean and trim, an avid runner, and it showed. Her small breasts were high and firm, with dark chocolate nipples against her slightly paler skin. The muscles in her abdomen and thighs rippled as she leaned into the closet to take something down off a hanger. Auden had seen her friend naked before, but tonight she saw her in a new light.

When Gayle turned, she met Auden's eyes and grinned. "What?"

"You have a beautiful body," Auden said quietly.

"Thanks." Gayle cocked a hip and studied her friend. "What's going on?"

"I don't know." Auden's reply was soft with a hint of uncharacteristic shyness. She sat on the edge of the bed, smoothing the lines of her black dress as she did so. "I've been having the strangest sensations for days."

"Oh yeah?" Gayle crossed to her dresser, sorted through her underwear, and selected black silk bikinis. She stepped into them, then a pair of tailored tuxedo pants, and pulled on a ruffled white shirt. "What do you mean?"

"Maybe it's just the fact that I've been doing nothing except reading lesbian fiction twenty-four hours a day, but I've started paying...God, this is so crazy..."

Gayle paused, her shirt halfway buttoned. "Are you telling me you're getting turned on, for real, by what you've been reading?"

Auden nodded. "What do you think that means?"

"What do *you* think it means?"

"Well, the obvious, I guess," Auden replied, blushing faintly as she remembered the dream about Gayle that *hadn't* been about Gayle. And the very real orgasm attached to it. "That maybe I'm gay?"

"That's a leap."

"Oh? Why?"

"Have you ever thought—before this, I mean—that you might be gay?" Gayle tucked in her shirt and reached for the jacket that went with the trousers. It was a tailored tux cut specifically for a woman, but with traditional lines. It fit her perfectly, accentuating her body in all the right places.

"Not consciously, no," Auden admitted. "I've always thought that I was just not particularly sexual. I enjoy the company of most of the men I date, but I never feel an overwhelming physical attraction for any of them."

"Did you ever think you were in love with any of them?"

"No."

Gayle shrugged. "Well then, maybe that's the answer. If you *had* been in love with them, then you probably would have been more physically attracted as well. Not being turned on by the guys you've dated doesn't mean you're gay."

"I know." Auden hesitated, then said quietly, "How about being turned on by a woman?"

Gayle stopped dead. "You're not talking about a fictional woman in a book, I take it?"

"I'm not sure, really. I might be confusing the two."

"Wait a minute." Gayle crossed the room and sat on the bed beside Auden. "I think you're starting to confuse *me,* honey. What are you trying to tell me?"

"It's just that I seem to be thinking about sex a lot. I thought at first that maybe it was just everything I was reading—the characters, the love, the...sex—I connected with so much of it so strongly." Auden lifted her hands. "You said it yourself the other night—when the story is done well, it makes you want to *be* the characters."

"Yeah," Gayle said doubtfully. "But reading *Gone with the Wind* never made me want to screw Rhett Butler." She laughed. "But it *did* make me want to do unmentionable things to my gym teacher."

"I'm having a similar reaction."

Gayle raised an eyebrow. "Okay. Details, please."

"When I imagine...something physical, I seem to be thinking about a particular woman." Auden sighed. "My new boss."

"Whoa. This *is* news."

"I'm as surprised as you are."

"I don't know what to tell you. It could be just a crush." Gayle took Auden's hand and softly stroked her fingers. "Even straight girls get crushes on other women sometimes. It doesn't necessarily mean you're gay."

"I'm a little worried that I'm confusing what I'm reading with real life. I mean, after all, romances are *fiction.* That's the whole point." Auden studied Gayle's fingers moving on her skin. She found the touch comforting, but not erotic. *That means something, right?*

"Well," Gayle mused, "romances are supposed to be about idealized love. Once in a while, ideals do come true, you know."

"Yes, but..." Auden frowned. "I *know* I love you, and I've never... well..."

"Wanted to jump my bones?" Gayle offered helpfully.

"Uh, right."

Gayle laughed. "Maybe I'm just not your type."

"How would I know?"

"You'll know when someone makes you feel what you need to feel." Gayle gave Auden's shoulder a little nudge. "Like the things that turn you on in your homework."

"You of all people know that fiction is far from real life." Auden stood, shook her head, and smiled ruefully. "I think what I need is to concentrate a little more on real life and accept that fiction is just that. A fantasy." She held out her hand, pulled Gayle to her feet, and gestured with her chin toward the door. "Come on, finish getting dressed and let's go to the party."

"Yeah," Gayle said as she went to her dresser. "I want to get a look at the woman who's turned your head. You *will* see that I meet her, right?"

"Of course."

"Excellent." Gayle dabbed a touch of scent behind her ear. "I can't wait."

Auden didn't reply, but the idea of Gayle anywhere near Hays bothered her unaccountably. Yet another new sensation she wasn't certain how to explain.

❖

When Auden and Gayle stepped out onto the small marble stoop, both of them murmured in dismay at the rapid accumulation of snow on the streets and sidewalk.

"I feel like I should carry you to the cab," Gayle quipped. "You're not going to make it in those heels."

"What we won't sacrifice for fashion," Auden said with a sigh as she followed in the depressions made by Gayle's dress shoes through the snow to the cab that idled, double-parked, in front of their building.

Settled inside, Gayle gave the driver their destination and asked, "How are the roads?"

"Terrible, and getting worse," came the gloomy reply. "Radio says this is going to keep up all night. This city goes to hell with less snow than this."

"Thank God I'm not on call tomorrow." Gayle leaned back in the seat next to Auden. "It's going to be a bitch getting anywhere if this keeps up."

"I hope we'll be able to get home," Auden replied, glancing out the window. The city already seemed eerily deserted. There were no pedestrians and very few vehicles moving in the snow-covered streets.

"Well, at least we'll have four-star accommodations if we can't."

"There is that," Auden agreed.

The trip should have taken ten minutes even at rush hour, but it took nearly forty. The cabbie had to detour down several side streets to avoid cars stuck in the snow or to make room for emergency vehicles working to clear the drifts. When they reached the Four Seasons on Logan Square, it was almost nine p.m.

"Thanks," Auden said as she leaned forward to pay the driver.

"I'd promise to come back for you ladies," the cute young woman in the Phillies baseball cap said, "but I'm not sure I'll be able to make it." She winked. "And I hate to disappoint a lady."

Auden searched for an appropriate comeback but couldn't think of one. She simply smiled and said, "I'm sure you never do."

Beside her, Gayle moaned, "I hope they have food left. I'm starving."

"I have a feeling there'll be plenty," Auden replied as she exited the cab and watched it move carefully off down the street. She turned and took Gayle's arm to steady herself as they crossed the slippery, snow-covered sidewalk. "With this weather, I'd be surprised if everyone who sent an RSVP actually shows up."

They checked the bulletin board in the lobby, verified that the gathering was in the Independence Hall banquet room on the second floor, and rode the escalator upstairs. Upon entering the large room lit by a number of chandeliers in the high vaulted ceiling, Auden was surprised to see the number of people present. Somehow, she had expected a small, intimate business gathering. Instead, there were close to seventy-five people present, a preponderance of women, most in stylish evening clothes. A jazz combo played in one corner.

She recognized almost no one and cast about, searching for a familiar face. She saw Abel Pritchard in conversation with one of the women she had interviewed for the position as her assistant, but she couldn't find Hays anywhere.

Next to her, Gayle stood gracefully, surveying the crowd. "Where's the woman in question?"

"I don't see her," Auden said worriedly. *Maybe Hays is ill. She seemed herself this afternoon, but she did miss the last few days at the office.*

"There are a lot of good-looking women here tonight," Gayle noted with approval. "This should be fun."

Auden laughed; Gayle's enthusiasm was always contagious. At that moment, someone called her name, and she and Gayle turned in the direction of the voice. An attractive, athletic-appearing blond with sparkling blue eyes approached, smiling brilliantly.

"Auden! I'm so glad you made it. I was starting to worry."

"Liz, hello," Auden said, pulling Gayle forward with a hand in hers. "Gayle, this is Liz Nixon. She ran WomenWords and hopefully will be our new head of marketing."

Liz cocked her head, grinning. "Is that a job offer?"

Auden lifted a shoulder. "Let's say it's not quite official but very close to a done deal."

"Just tell me when and where to sign," Liz replied. Then she turned her attention to Gayle, her eyes sweeping from Gayle's striking profile down her tight, compact body. Then she extended her hand. "It's a pleasure."

"Likewise." Gayle took the offered hand and squeezed firmly, noting that the other woman held the handshake just a moment longer than was probably necessary. *Well, here's a lesbian for sure. And she's a knockout.*

"Will you promise to forgive me if I talk business with Auden for just one minute?"

"No problem at all." Gayle leaned close to Auden and murmured, "I'm going to find a waiter. I'll bring you back the fruit of my hunt."

"Thanks." Auden squeezed her friend's forearm gently. "I'd really appreciate it."

As Gayle moved away, Liz followed with her eyes for an instant, then turned back to Auden. "Girlfriend?"

"Friend," Auden said gently.

"Hmm," was all that Liz replied.

❖

From across the room where she was leaning against a pillar and watching the activities, Hays saw Auden and a striking tuxedo-clad woman enter. Her heart leapt at the first sight of Auden, who looked beautiful in an off-the-shoulder black silk dress that subtly draped her figure, accentuating her graceful curves. Auden's companion was cover-model perfect, and she appeared to relate to Auden with the casual comfort of long acquaintance. They made a gorgeous couple. Hays could look nowhere else, noting the small intimate gestures between the two and the way that the woman in the tux leaned into Auden when she spoke close to her ear. Every touch was painful for Hays to observe.

Eventually, she forced herself to look elsewhere and noted the approach of another woman she had been observing from a distance for the last hour. Tall, close to her own height, but more heavily built and ruggedly good-looking, the brown-haired woman approached her with a directness that spoke of utter confidence. When she was within conversational distance, the newcomer extended her hand to Hays.

"Thane Cutlass, Ms. Palmer. One of your new acquisitions."

Hays knew who she was because Thane always put a recent picture on the back cover of her books. She also made frequent public appearances and was a very visible personality in the small lesbian romance-writers community. Hays took her hand. "Haydon Palmer, Thane. Most people call me Hays."

"Thanks. This is a nice shindig."

"I'm happy to see that the snow didn't keep you away."

Thane shrugged. "I live in Wilmington, practically your backyard. I came up last night, before the storm really got going."

"Palmer Publishing has booked rooms here. You'll want to stay tonight, our compliments."

"I won't pass up that offer," Thane said with a wide grin. "It will give me more of a chance to make some connections. I've already talked to several reviewers and scheduled a signing at Giovanni's Room."

"Glad to hear it. I had hoped that, in addition to all of us getting acquainted, this gathering would provide some networking opportunities for the authors."

"It's working." Thane nodded approvingly. "I haven't yet met Auden Frost, the new director, but I'm looking forward to it. Is she here?"

Hays indicated Auden across the room. "She's talking to Liz Nixon. You know Liz, of course."

"Oh yeah. Liz and I go back a ways." There was an unmistakable note of familiarity in her tone. "She's quite a writer in her own stead, you know, but she decided that she prefers business ventures to fictional adventures."

Hays laughed. Thane was every bit as vigorous and direct as Hays had imagined she would be from their e-mail association. In time, probably not long hence, she would need to tell her about Rune. But this was not the place or time.

"So," Thane said appreciatively, "Auden Frost is the blond?"

"Yes." Hays watched Thane study Auden, saw the way her eyes moved slowly over Auden's face, then drifted down her body. She saw the appreciation flare in Thane's dark brown eyes. *Is everyone here tonight going to be attracted to Auden? Well, even if that's true, it has nothing to do with me.*

Abruptly, Thane turned her attention back to Hays. "It was nice meeting you, Hays. I hope that we will be very happy with each other for a long time."

"I have a feeling that we will be."

Watching Thane walk away, Hays recalled the last vignette Thane had sent her—the heat and the lust in the passionate images. Hays wondered, too, if the sensual scenes Thane wrote were a product of her imagination, or her experience. She had a feeling that Thane Cutlass would be an inventive and adventurous lover. That idea bothered her quite a bit as she followed Thane's unerring course directly toward Auden.

CHAPTER TEN

Auden's attention drifted from Liz, who was telling her about an upcoming writers' convention, as she sensed a feather-light touch on her skin. There was no one nearby, but her gaze was drawn across the room to where Hays leaned with a shoulder against an enormous marble pillar—in the crowd, but not part of it. Even from a distance, she was singularly striking. Her black hair was untamed and her pale complexion as flawless and still as the stone at her back. Her dark suit cast her figure in stark relief against the alabaster column. Auden's lips parted in a soundless murmur as their eyes met. A smile twitched at the corner of Hays's mouth and was just as quickly gone. Auden took one step forward, and then, as so often happens in dreams, Hays had vanished.

"Auden?"

Liz's voice beckoned, and Auden, struggling with the lingering sense of unreality, brought her mind back to the blond at her side. "I'm sorry? Where did you say the convention would be held?"

"The next big one's in Manhattan in a few weeks. All the major publishers and most of the popular authors will be in attendance. I think it's essential that Destiny have a presence there."

"I agree. We'll need to start putting something together next week." Auden's eyes flickered back to the spot were Hays had stood. *Where is she? Could I have just imagined her there?*

"Here you go," Gayle said as she rejoined them, handing Auden a champagne flute filled with the golden wine along with a small plate of assorted bite-sized delicacies.

"Thanks," Auden replied, smiling at Gayle. She sipped the champagne and held the plate out in Liz's direction. "Help yourself."

"I've had my fill already. Thanks." Liz turned her attention to Gayle. "Are you a fellow writer?"

"No. Just a rabid fan."

"Ah, even better."

"I thought WomenWords had some of the best authors around," Gayle remarked. "I'd kill for a few autographs."

"Oh, we can't have you committing a felony." Liz laughed. "I'll see if I can help you avoid arrest."

Gayle grinned. "Thanks. I'd appreciate that."

"Anyone in particular you'd like me to rustle up for you?"

"Well, just about any of them—Stevenson, Elliot, Cutlass, Dyre..."

"Margo Elliot is here tonight, and Thane. You can forget Rune, though. She never makes public appearances."

Auden's curiosity was immediately piqued. "Never?"

"Not as long as I've known her." Liz looked past Gayle into the crowd and smiled—a slow, fond smile. "Well, here's one of the infamous crew now."

"Ms. Frost?"

Auden turned at the sound of the deep alto voice and found herself looking into eyes the color of rich, fertile earth. Charmingly tousled dark brown wavy hair, a rakishly arched brow, and a smile to light the darkest night completed the attractive visage. "Yes?"

The full, sensuous lips curved seductively. "Thane Cutlass."

"Hello," Auden said, pleased. She balanced the small plate along with the champagne flute in her left hand and extended her right. "I'm delighted to meet you."

"Believe me, the pleasure's mine." Thane smoothly enfolded Auden's fingers in her palm.

Thane's handshake made Auden's skin tingle. Embarrassed, she pulled her hand back as soon as she could without appearing too obvious. "I'm so happy you could be here."

"I wouldn't miss it." Thane tipped her head in Liz's direction. "Hello, Liz."

Liz moved closer, lifted her face, and kissed Thane fully on the lips. Drawing back, she murmured, "Hello, Thane."

Witnessing that greeting, Auden recognized that the women were more than friends. Or at least, they had been once. When Liz and Thane moved apart, Auden continued the introductions. "Thane, this is my friend, Gayle."

"Gayle," Thane said softly, extending her hand with another penetrating smile.

"A pleasure to meet you," Gayle replied in a tone of voice that Auden had rarely heard. She sounded the way Auden imagined a great jungle cat would sound if it could purr a greeting.

"I promised Gayle an autograph," Liz explained.

"Of course." Thane hadn't taken her eyes from Gayle's.

"Unfortunately," Gayle replied, "I don't have pockets big enough to carry a copy of *Hungry Kisses*, but—"

"Ah, have no fear," Thane said lightly. "I never leave home without a few copies."

"Oh God," Liz interjected with a snort, "don't tell me they're upstairs with your etchings."

"No, actually there's a signing table across the room with some of our titles." Thane managed to look affronted, but she was grinning. "I'd be happy to inscribe one for you, Gayle."

"Wonderful."

For the next few minutes, the four women spoke companionably of the event, new releases, and Destiny's imminent launch. After a polite interval, Auden turned to Gayle and inquired quietly, "Will you be all right for a few minutes here?"

"Go ahead." Gayle gave her a little push, watching Thane intently. "Don't worry about me, Aud. I'm sure I'll find something, or someone, to occupy my time."

❖

Auden worked her way through the crowd, skirting groups of people who were drinking and chatting, heading for the point where she had last seen Hays. Several times along the way, she stopped to greet individuals she recognized from Palmer. When she finally reached her destination, Hays was nowhere to be found. Another familiar face, however, was nearby.

"Good evening, Mr. Pritchard," Auden said with a smile.

The militarily erect man inclined his head infinitesimally in her direction. "Ms. Frost."

She had come to recognize the distant expression and dismissive tone of voice as Pritchard's modus operandi and took no offense at his cool welcome. "From what I can see, this launch party is a great success. So far, I've talked to about half of Destiny's new authors plus any number of retailers and representatives from the media. Destiny won't be an unknown quantity when our first books are released."

"It does seem to be going well." He met her gaze squarely. "How are you doing in terms of filling the positions in your division?"

"Alana has been a great help in setting up interviews. I've met with a number of people in the last several days." She thought he had placed just a little too much emphasis on the term *your* but didn't intend to be baited into a power struggle. She *was* the division head, and that's how she intended to proceed. "I'll have a list of my choices to you by noon on Monday."

For the briefest instant, he looked surprised. "That was fast."

Auden shrugged. "Hays isn't the only one who's efficient."

"Apparently."

"Is she still here?" Auden tilted her head, still meeting his very direct stare. "I saw her earlier."

"I wouldn't know." For the first time he looked away, then, as if catching himself, quickly back. "It's usually her habit to put in an appearance at affairs such as this and then slip away as soon as possible. She has a great deal of work to do."

"Yes, I know." Auden heard just a hint of warning in his voice, as was so often the case when Hays was the subject. He was protecting her, or isolating her, but Auden had yet to understand why. Whatever his motives, she didn't intend to be deterred. If Hays was still there, she wanted to see her.

"The weather outside is deteriorating rapidly," Pritchard informed her. "I'm about to make an announcement that we've reserved a block of rooms here for anyone who wants to spend the night. I've taken the liberty of getting you and your companion a suite."

"Thank you, but that won't be necessary," Auden said quickly. "I'm only a cab ride across town from here."

"Yes, I'm aware of your residence. However, the mayor has

declared a snow emergency and soon only official vehicles will be allowed on the streets."

"For how long?"

"At least the next twelve hours."

"You're kidding."

He shook his head.

"Well, that's going to be interesting." Auden glanced about the room at the people in evening clothes, many of whom had probably arrived by limo or cab. "I doubt that many people here came prepared to spend the night."

"At least those from out of town who booked rooms for the night or weekend will be fine." He smiled briefly. "As for the others, the hotel has graciously offered to provide casual clothes for anyone who requires them."

"Casual clothes?" she asked suspiciously.

Finally, Pritchard smiled. "I believe that would be T-shirts and sweatpants from the Four Seasons health spa."

"Lovely. I can hardly wait." Auden laughed and to her amazement, Pritchard joined in. "It was very thoughtful, nevertheless, Mr. Pritchard."

"Well, we could hardly have our promoters and authors tramping about Philadelphia in knee-deep snowdrifts or spending the weekend here in rumpled eveningwear."

"God, I hope we aren't marooned beyond tomorrow morning." She had visions of trekking across town in heels.

"Apparently, this storm is of blizzard proportions, and if that's the case, I very much doubt that vehicular travel will be possible before Monday."

"Terrific." Auden glanced around the room. "Well, I guess we'll just have to consider this an adventure and make the best of it."

"I do believe that would be the best approach."

She smiled at him once again and moved off into the crowd. After another five minutes of fruitless searching for one particular face, she stood still and surveyed the large ballroom. Most large spaces such as this doubled as convention centers, which meant that the ballrooms and banquet halls were usually connected to smaller adjoining spaces that could be turned into meeting rooms. She made her way around the periphery, checking the adjacent rooms. All were deserted.

In the far northeast corner, she found a door marked "Lounge" and pushed through. Like all the other rooms she had checked, the lights were off and the space was unnaturally quiet, especially in contrast to the continuous low rumble of voices in the ballroom. Opposite the door, large windows admitted a soft silver glow from the streetlights surrounding Logan Square. Outside, the snow continued to fall, a heavy curtain of unbroken white. She was about to step back into the ballroom when she heard the familiar deep voice.

"Are you looking for a little peace and quiet?"

Auden stood still, searching the shadows. A dark figure, backlit by moonlight and snow, rose from one of the sofas near the windows. Auden couldn't see her face, but she didn't need to. She knew the unmistakable profile and the sharp, strong form. "No, actually, I was looking for you."

"Were you?" Hays's voice held a note of surprise. *I would have thought you would be completely occupied once Thane found you.*

"Yes." Auden made her way carefully between the tables, chairs, and sofas until she reached the sofa where Hays leaned with a hip against the broad arm. Closer to her, Auden could make out the publisher's features in the illumination reflected off the snow, but shadows remained. Shadows always seemed to hover in Hays's eyes, no matter how bright the light. "I saw you earlier across the room, and then you disappeared." She laughed softly. "For one second there, I almost thought you were a ghost."

"I'm not." Hays's voice was very still.

"Oh, I know," Auden replied, just as quietly. "But you do have a habit of disappearing."

"I have a relatively low tolerance for gatherings such as these. Every twenty interactions or so, I have to escape for a while."

"Well, Destiny's launch is a tremendous success. Everyone is incredibly enthusiastic—authors, staff, and promoters alike."

"Good. I'm glad that you're happy with the way that things are coming together."

"Yes, I truly am. Of course, I'm a little disappointed that some of the authors couldn't make it, but I know it was unrealistic to expect all of them, especially with the weather." Auden put her hand down on the top of the sofa, leaning close to Hays in the dim light. "I'm especially sorry that Rune Dyre isn't here, though. She's a big seller, and I wanted to meet her."

"Cutlass is here, and she's as popular. Have you met with her?"

"Yes, just a little while ago. Do you know her?"

"We've e-mailed. She's quite charming and very talented."

Charming. Yes, I suppose she is. And suave and very attractive, too. But she doesn't intrigue me. Not like you do. Auden lifted a shoulder. "She's very nice. More importantly, she promised me a look at her new manuscript soon."

"Excellent," Hays said, happy to have diverted Auden's attention from the question of Rune Dyre's absence.

"Now, if I can get a few of the other authors to commit to sending me their current works in progress, we'll have a full schedule for the next eighteen months."

"Eighteen months," Hays repeated. *A lifetime.*

"It would be a good beginning."

"Yes," Hays said quietly, watching the light play across Auden's features, one half of her face outlined in moonlight, the other lost in darkness. "It would be a...start."

"It appears I'll have a bit more time to work on those who are here. Mr. Pritchard tells me that we may *all* be marooned here for the next day or so."

Hays walked to the window and glanced down at the Benjamin Franklin Parkway below. Logan Square, with its large central fountain, empty now save for snowdrifts, was shrouded in white, as pure and untouched as any fantasy world. "I believe he may be right."

Auden joined her at the window. "It's beautiful, isn't it?"

"Yes. Very," Hays said softly, taking advantage of the shadows to drink her fill of Auden's face caught in a halo of light reflected off the snow.

Auden turned slightly, her eyes moving to Hays's face. "Will you be staying, too?"

"Yes."

The room was so very still, and the world so very tranquil, and the beauty of the night—and the woman—so excruciating that Auden hurt in a place she hadn't known existed. *Why do you do this to me? You and no one else?*

For an instant she glimpsed the fragile woman beneath the impenetrable exterior.

"If I'm lucky, sometimes I find a treasure just waiting for someone to look beneath the surface. It doesn't always happen, but when it does, it's like a gift."

"What is it?" Hays's heart beat quickly, her pulse thudding in her ears. Auden had the strangest expression in her eyes. Sad and yet impassioned, all at the same time.

"You'll think I'm being silly." Auden almost touched her, but she held back. *This is not like that. They were lovers.*

"No, I won't."

Auden believed her. "I was thinking about a passage in a book."

"What?"

"In *Dark Passions*..." Uncertain, Auden held Hays's eyes and saw her pupils flicker in the moonlight. "It was a moment like this one—when the silence was filled with secrets."

Hays gasped. *You can't know.*

"You know the story, don't you?" Auden asked softly.

"Yes."

"I don't know what made me think of the characters just now."

She's asking you, but you can't answer. You shouldn't be alone here with her like this. Hays drew a deep breath and lied. "No, neither do I. There is a great deal of pain in that book. Look outside—the night is filled with joy."

"Yes, I know." Auden shook her head, smiling ruefully. "Sorry. I can't seem to keep these things out of my head."

"You needn't tell me," Hays said with a faint laugh. "I'm as attached to those fairy tales as you, I'm sure. But real life is rarely like our fantasies."

"So I've been told." Auden knew that whatever connection had shimmered on the air between them for an instant had vanished. She had ventured too far inside Hays's walls and had been reminded yet again that such intimacy was not welcome.

"I should get back to our guests," Hays said, retreating from the window into the darkness of the room.

"Yes." Auden followed. "So should I."

When they stepped out into the brightly lit ballroom, Auden blinked as if emerging from a deep sleep. Beside her, Hays's expression was friendly but guarded.

"Good night, Auden."

"Good night, Hays."

As Auden watched Hays slip into the crowd, she was aware that Abel Pritchard stood a few feet away, observing her with thinly veiled displeasure. She glanced at him quickly, then turned to look for her friends. Whatever threat he thought she might pose to Hays's controlled world, he was clearly wrong. The only one whose balance was the least bit affected by their relationship was her own. Haydon Palmer was unassailable.

"Hey!" Gayle exclaimed from so close by that Auden jumped. "Where did you disappear to?"

"What? Oh—I was talking to Hays."

"Ah, the mystery woman. Where is she?"

"She just...left." Auden tried to keep her voice light. "Apparently, she isn't big on crowds."

Gayle raised an eyebrow but didn't press. "I hear you and I are going to be roomies tonight. I just called Mrs. T, and she said she'd walk Shylock as far as the sidewalk. If he didn't do his business there, she informed me, he could just hold it."

Auden laughed. "Oh, poor Shy."

"He'll survive." Gayle lowered her voice. "Besides, this could be fun. I told Liz and Thane they could come up for a while after the party is over, and we'd...talk."

"You didn't."

"You mad?"

"No," Auden said with a sigh. "Liz and I have a lot to discuss. If we're going to be stuck here for a while, we might as well work."

"Gee," Gayle remarked with a grin, "it wasn't exactly work I had in mind."

"Which one do you have your eye on?" Auden asked good-naturedly.

"I thought I'd give you first dibs."

Auden blushed. "Gayle. God. I don't...I mean...I'm not...I *work* with these women!"

Gayle cocked her head. "You don't work with Thane, exactly. And you don't officially work with Liz yet. And we're just talking a little fun here."

"No." Auden realized she sounded harsher than she meant to. She forced a smile. "I'm not in the market for a date. You go right ahead."

"Hey, Aud," Gayle said softly. "I was only teasing. They're nice women. It'll just be talking, I promise."

Auden took Gayle's hand. "Sweetie, we're all over twenty-one. If you decide you want to spend a little private time with one of them, we're in a suite. Go ahead."

"I would never want to make you uncomfortable—"

"Oh, for crying out loud. I'm a virgin, not a nun!"

Gayle burst out laughing and slid her arm around Auden's waist.

"Come on then—let's go find the infidels."

CHAPTER ELEVEN

Hays stepped out of her hotel room, still dressed in the white shirt and black trousers she had worn to the cocktail party.

Uncomfortably warm despite the too-cool thermostat setting of the room's ventilation system, she had left the matching jacket on the king-sized bed in her suite. As she pulled the door closed behind her, voices from down the hallway caught her attention, and she looked that way automatically.

Auden stood with the handsome woman in the tuxedo accompanied by Liz and Thane. Auden's date was just unlocking the door to the corner suite, laughingly commenting on the luxurious accommodations. Despite the fact that Hays had made no sound, Auden pivoted in her direction, and their eyes met.

Apparently sensing Auden's hesitation, Thane looked down the hallway as well and, when she saw Hays standing there, tossed her a rakish grin. Hays nodded and walked away. She didn't know that Auden watched her until she stepped into the elevator.

❖

Secret Passions - Scene Five

She came to me out of the darkness, silhouetted in moonlight, as ethereal as a dream. But this night, she was not a mere whisper of longing to disappear on the edge of awakening. She was solid and real, and I could feel her heat so very near on my skin. Together, we watched the world dissolve into pinpoints of starlight reflected off the falling flakes. Outside, the night was untarnished, untouched by disappointment or loss. Inside, with her close by my side, I could not remember why I despaired—my skin was too alive, my heart too full, my mind lost to all save the sense of her. Had I been able to think, I would have realized that I was no longer thinking at all. There was only her.

As she stood facing the snowscape, perfect in the radiance of otherworldly light streaming into the still space, I stepped behind her and rested my fingertips on her bare shoulders, pale above the edge of the dark gown. The strength beneath the smooth skin astounded me. Everything about her was alive. Energy streamed along my fingers into the very marrow of my bones. For one brief instant, I feared that I could somehow steal her life, feared beyond reason that that might be what I truly desired. She was everything I was not—most critically, alive.

But then she turned, and I saw her eyes, and I knew that nothing could diminish what lived within her soul. She could only call forth what had lain buried for so long in my own. I had no words, and she seemed content with none. She merely waited. There were questions in her eyes, yet she did not ask. I could hear her questions thunder in the silent air. She trusted me to answer. Trust such as that is a gift beyond flesh, beyond breathing, beyond existence. She offered me that, a kind of immortality, and I so desperately craved it. But I could not take without giving, and to give, I must confess.

I had lowered my head without realizing

it, until our lips were nearly touching. I
could taste her in the air between us. My
very bones ached to feel her in my arms. But
if I confessed, she would know. And if she
knew, it would change everything.

Sometimes, the price of honesty is loss.
I would rather desire without having than
hold her for an instant, only to lose her
forever upon the next breath.

Hays looked away from the monitor, not needing to read what
she had written. There were times when syntax and grammar were
superfluous. This had been about her heart. She automatically copied
the paragraphs into a blank e-mail and sent it to herself, then deleted
the file from the hard drive. She threaded both hands into her hair and
cradled her face in her palms, breathing shallowly. Her head ached, her
stomach twisted with an urgency that was foreign to her, and beneath it
all was rage. *Why now?*

For the first time in longer than she could remember, she couldn't
assuage her longing by writing away her need. Perhaps it was the
knowledge that Auden was in the same building, only twenty floors
above, which made it so difficult. More likely, it was the belief that
even now, Auden was very possibly with another woman. The very
beautiful African-American woman, or perhaps Thane. *Thane. Yes, I
imagine Thane would be hard to resist.*

Hays and Thane had never spoken directly about anything intimate,
but she didn't need to hear the words to know what would happen.
She knew Thane's secrets, just as Thane knew hers, because they had
exposed them in the volumes that they wrote. She had seen Thane and
Auden together only hours before, and she could imagine them now in
their private moments. *Private Pleasures*—Thane's desires. The images
were so clear to Hays, the edges so sharp, that she bled from them.

Unexpectedly, the door to the business center opened, and Hays
lifted her head. She had been working in semi-darkness, illumed only
by the light of the two computer monitors sitting side by side on the
work counter, but the hallway beyond was brightly lit. Auden's figure
was clearly outlined.

Hays blinked. The apparition remained.

"Oh God," Auden said. "I'm sorry. I always seem to be walking in on you."

She was wearing navy blue sweatpants, a matching T-shirt with the Four Seasons logo, and white crew socks. She was shoeless. As if knowing that Hays was taking stock of her apparel, Auden raised her hands and looked down at herself sheepishly. "I didn't expect anyone to be in here. It's four o'clock in the morning."

"Actually, the outfit is rather fetching." Hays tried but couldn't hide her grin.

"Fetching." Auden's tone suggested she wasn't amused, but she smiled back. "I notice that you're still wearing your evening clothes. No off-the-rack workout apparel for you."

Hays lifted a shoulder. "I thought I'd save that for the morning. Do you plan to walk around in your socks all day tomorrow?"

"Actually, I intend to walk *home* tomorrow...today...later." Auden stepped further into the room as her eyes adjusted to the dimness. "It's only fifteen blocks or so."

Suddenly serious, Hays replied, "If you truly intend to go out in this storm, I'll see that a car comes for you."

"I appreciate that, really, but it won't be necessary."

"Auden, it's a blizzard. You can't walk across town when the streets haven't even been plowed. Especially when it's still snowing."

"Then how do you expect a car to get through?"

As they spoke, Auden crossed and sat on the chair in front of the adjoining computer station. The business center was open twenty-four hours a day for guests who wanted to use the Internet connections and fax machines. She swiveled in the chair to face Hays, curling one leg beneath her opposite thigh and resting an elbow on the desktop.

"I'll manage something," Hays replied quietly. "I don't want you at risk."

Touched, Auden shook her head, smiling faintly. "I'll tell you what. If the streets are clear, I'll go home. If not, I'll wait it out with everyone else."

"Agreed." Hays glanced at the clock on the wall opposite. "It's rather late at night for business, isn't it?"

Auden cocked her head and made a small deprecating sound. "I was about to ask you the same thing."

"I couldn't sleep so I thought I'd work. You, too?"

Auden searched Hays's face, aware of the shadows that rarely left it. She looked tired. More than that, she looked weary in a way that went beyond the physical. *What is it? What is it that plagues you so?* Auden had never wanted to know the answer to a question as much she wanted to know that. Instead, she found herself revealing more than she intended, which often seemed to be the case when Hays was involved. "Actually, I came down here because I wanted to be alone."

Hays stood immediately, steadying herself with a hand on the back of the desk chair. "Then I'll go."

"No," Auden said swiftly, impulsively grasping her hand. "It's not *you* I want to be away from. There's a mini-party going on in my suite, and I just..."

"Just...what?" Hays asked softly, staring at the fingers curled around her own as she sat again. She closed her fingers around the warmth left behind when Auden drew her hand away.

And once again, Auden answered because she trusted Hays without really knowing why. "I felt slightly out of my depth."

"That's hard for me to imagine. I take it the conversation wasn't about publishing?"

Auden smiled faintly. "It started out that way. Actually, Liz and Thane and I had some interesting discussions about the direction of lesbian fiction, with Gayle plugging all her favorite authors. But I don't think anyone really wanted to talk shop."

"What happened?"

"Nothing, really." Auden looked away for a second and then brought her gaze back to Hays's, finding gentle acceptance in her dark eyes. "So much has happened in so short a time. I'm not exactly as I appear to others, I guess."

"Really?" Hays leaned forward, her elbows on her knees, her chin resting in the palms of her hands as she gazed at Auden. "I think you're bright, capable, energetic, and altogether...fascinating."

Auden's lips parted in a soundless *oh.* "I...I don't know what to say."

"You don't need to say anything." Hays regarded her steadily. "Why were you uncomfortable upstairs?"

They were facing one another, bathed by the pale glow from the monitors. Auden was completely unaware of the time, or the strange surroundings, or the unexpected turn in the conversation. Hays had a way of taking her beyond the commonplace to some plane where only what transpired between them had meaning. She had never in her life felt at once so ungrounded or so solidly moored. Leaning toward Hays, drawn into the hypnotic depths of her unflinching gaze, Auden answered in a voice barely above a whisper. "Because the atmosphere was intimate, and I didn't feel that way about anyone."

"Aren't you here with your lover?"

The silence that stretched between them seemed infinite. Auden swallowed and shook her head. "I don't have a lover."

Hays lifted her hand, then slowly traced a finger along the edge of Auden's jaw. "You should have."

Auden trembled, heat instantly suffusing her body. Hays's fingers rested lightly on her chin. All that remained to her was truth. "I think... I'd like to start with something simpler."

"Oh?" Hays's voice was deep; she was vibrating with tension. Leaning forward further still, she slipped her palm down to Auden's neck, her fingers moving into her hair. "Like what?"

"A kiss."

Auden waited, not thinking. Unable to put words to her feelings beyond what she had confessed, not knowing why it seemed right to bare her uncertainties to a woman who had done nothing beyond look at her with the closest thing to raw desire she had ever seen, Auden waited.

Hays watched the emotions swirl in Auden's eyes—vulnerability, strength, trust, longing. Her throat was so tight she couldn't breathe. *Auden.*

```
     I would rather desire without having than
     hold her for an instant, only to lose her
     forever upon the next breath.
```

Hays's own words pealed a silent warning. Perhaps it was the lateness of the hour, or the memory of Thane's grin in the hallway outside Auden's room, or the ache of desire she had felt just minutes before, but Hays drew Auden closer with gentle pressure against the back of her neck.

Against Auden's mouth she whispered, "A kiss can be everything."

And when Auden felt the first brush of Hays's lips, she understood. Every particle of her being coalesced into the singular space where their mouths met, and then she was aware of nothing beyond the silken warmth of the lips moving slowly over hers. The first touch was tender, but not tentative. They came together, flesh on flesh, with a rightness that defied logic, joined by a kiss that was as familiar as a beloved song and as captivating as a new sunrise.

Distantly, Auden was aware of Hays's fingertips resting feather-light against the angles of her jaw, tilting her face as Hays gently ran a questing tongue along the inner surface of her lips. Auden leaned into the kiss, resting both palms on the center of Hays's thighs, needing both the support and the contact. The muscles beneath her hands were as tight as steel wires singing in a high wind. She could feel Hays's heart beat inside her mouth, and the far reaches of her being turned to liquid heat.

Without realizing it, Auden dug her fingers into Hays's legs. It was difficult to breathe around the sudden tension that coiled deep in her chest. A pain, like hunger, but far more critical than any physical need, surged through her. The magnitude of her wanting made her kiss even gentler, care warring with the terrible urgency.

When Hays moaned, a broken sound, Auden slid her hands higher up Hays's thighs until her fingers rested close to Hays's hips, which strained beneath her touch. Auden reveled in the unbidden response.

Hays slid her tongue into Auden's mouth, thirsting for her but fearing that with the first taste, as with the first drop of water in the desert, she might drown from the pleasure. When Auden's tongue welcomed hers with a long slow caress, need hammered through her blood and settled like a fist between her thighs. It had been so long, she had lost the ability to control what she had thought not to experience again. She stiffened, wrestling with the onslaught of sensation that rocketed rapidly toward a peak she dared not crest.

"Auden," Hays gasped, torn between seeking escape and begging for her touch. She moved her mouth a fraction away, instantly aching at the loss.

Breathing unevenly, Auden rested her forehead against Hays's. "There are...so many reasons...why this is a bad idea."

"You can't...possibly imagine...them all," Hays groaned, her eyes closing tightly as she fought back the warning spasms that assaulted her with relentless insistence.

"We should...stop," Auden murmured as every nerve in her body screamed for more. She had never felt anything to equal what this one kiss had done to her. Just the absence of Hays's lips against hers was unbearable. She wanted to feel Hays's mouth, her hands, the hot demands of her flesh—everywhere. She *wanted* with a ferocity that she had never imagined. "Oh God."

"Auden," Hays moaned again, drawing back further still, her fingertips brushing along Auden's face until they broke contact.

Frantically, Auden searched Hays's face, fearful that she would find anger or regret. "I don't...I'm sorr—"

"No," Hays whispered fiercely. "Don't. Let it be as simple and as perfect as it was."

Auden held Hays's eyes and saw the plea in their smoky depths. Finally, she allowed herself to do what she had wanted to do almost every time she had seen Hays since the moment they had met. She placed her palm against Hays's cheek, her fingers gently trailing through the dark hair that fluttered down onto her forehead. Hays closed her eyes, her expression a mixture of intense pleasure and exquisite pain. Auden felt an answering stab of desperate desire pierce her own heart. "Yes. I will."

Then, Auden got to her feet on legs that shook badly and moved around Hays's chair, leaving her still leaning forward, and made her way carefully to the door. There, she turned and looked back. Hays sat with her head slightly bowed and did not turn around. "Good night, Hays."

So softly that Auden almost didn't hear, Hays replied, "Good night, sweet Auden."

Hays couldn't hear Auden disappear down the corridor outside the suddenly still room, but she didn't need to. The air around her emptied of life and grew cool against her skin. When she stood, a wave of dizziness rolled over her, and she was forced to sit again. Grimly, she leaned her head back, but not before she felt the first telltale trickle against her lips. She drew a handkerchief from her trouser pocket and pressed it to the corner of her mouth, watching through half-closed eyes as she caught the bright red drops against the pure white linen.

Blood on the snow. Oh, Auden. What have I done?

CHAPTER TWELVE

A uden let herself quietly into the suite, intent on reaching her room without awakening Gayle. All she wanted was to close her eyes. Perhaps then the swirling storm of emotions that rendered her unable to think clearly or to make much sense of everything that was happening in her body would quiet. Maybe then she could consider the ramifications of what she had just done.

*It wasn't me. I never would have asked...*She remembered the look in Hays's eyes. The tenderness. The wanting. The unguarded need. *Oh God. Yes, I asked her for that kiss. I would ask again, ask for more, ask for everything. How could I not have known, all this time, what I was waiting to see in someone's eyes? How could I not have kno—*

"Aud?" Gayle sat up on the sofa, blinking in the subdued light from the solitary lamp on the opposite side of the room. "Hell, I fell asleep."

"I thought sure you'd already be in bed," Auden said awkwardly, standing in the middle of the room, confused and uncertain. "Is everyone gone?"

"Uh-huh." Gayle shrugged sheepishly. "I think I might have just made one of the dumbest moves of my life."

Auden had the sense that Gayle wanted to talk, and maybe *she* did, too. She wasn't quite sure. In fact, she wasn't sure of anything. But she had a feeling that she wasn't going to get to sleep very quickly, and she suddenly very much did not want to be alone. It was comfortable to curl up on the sofa next to Gayle, her feet tucked under her and one arm stretched out along the top. She rested her cheek against her arm and studied her friend. "What happened?"

Gayle shifted into a similar position with her fingers nearly touching Auden's. She sighed. "I turned down an invitation to go to bed with Liz."

*Liz. I thought it would have been Thane. The way Thane looked at you. It was almost the way Hays...*Auden's stomach clenched, and she realized her thoughts were wandering down a very dangerous path. "How come you said no?"

"I wish I knew." Gayle's tone was thoughtful and at the same time surprised. "It wasn't exactly an explicit invitation, but I could tell that she was interested. I basically sent her on her way with a peck on the cheek."

"Where was Thane?"

Something flickered in Gayle's face that Auden could not decipher. For a second, Gayle looked a little lost. It was an expression that was rare for her confident friend.

"She left right after you did. I guess she's set her sights on you."

"Me?" Auden laughed mirthlessly. "God, I hope not."

"Why not?" Gayle asked swiftly. "She's gorgeous. And she's incredibly talented. And funny."

"I know all that. But I have a *business* relationship with her." She thought of Thane, but all she could feel was Hays.

"Well, it's not as if you couldn't pass her work off to someone else to edit. The contracts are all sewed up, right?" Gayle picked distractedly at the fabric of the sofa, her expression distant. "You said you were feeling attracted to women, and she's...hot, Aud."

"She's very attractive, I agree." Auden fell silent and wondered why finding Thane attractive didn't translate into attraction. The four of them had spent three hours talking together after the party downstairs broke up, and Thane had been everything Gayle had said, and more. But Auden hadn't been drawn to her, hadn't felt a connection, hadn't been pulled into her eyes the way...

"But?"

Auden gave a start, then blushed. "But it's just not a good idea."

"Well, I hope you don't have anything against just socializing with her." Gayle sounded subdued and, uncharacteristically, she wouldn't meet Auden's gaze. "Because I kind of agreed to, um...oh, hell..."

"Gayle!" Auden's tone was threatening. "What did you do?"

"I just said that you and I would meet the two of them at the 2-4 Club next weekend for drinks, and...well, you know..." When she saw

Auden's expression, she rushed on. "Well, it's not exactly a date or anything."

Auden was stunned. She stared at Gayle as if she were speaking another language. Finally, she managed to croak, "You didn't. Tell me you didn't."

Gayle looked slightly panicked. "I did."

"I can't believe it. I cannot believe you would do that without asking me. I can't go out with Thane Cutlass."

"It's not *a date*. It's just a friendly get-together."

"Gayle, the sexual tension was so thick up here it was hard to breathe. I had to leave, for God's sake."

"*That's* why you left?" Gayle gaped at her, then just as quickly looked concerned. "Did Thane say something to you? Did she make you uncomfortable?"

Auden shook her head. "No. Nothing like that. It's just that...it was as if, well, as if everyone was testing, trying to figure out if there was the possibility of something happening. I mean, after all, we're all single..." She hesitated, not sure of exactly what she meant to say. *We're all lesbians? Is that what I was going to say? I know that's what Liz and Thane thought.*

Leaning forward slightly, Gayle rested her fingers on Auden's. "I'm sorry, Aud. I didn't know you felt that way. I...I couldn't tell. I guess I was too busy thinking about..." She looked away for a second and shrugged. "I guess I was just thinking about my own possibilities. Jeez, I'm really sorry."

"There's nothing to be sorry about." Auden smiled faintly. "Nothing happened. It was just...I don't know, I just felt like things were happening that I wasn't ready for."

"But you *are* seriously thinking about being with a woman now," Gayle stated softly. "Aren't you?"

Auden nodded. "Yes."

"Are you okay with that?"

Am I? I've been doing nothing but imagining women together, reading about their lives, reading about their problems, reading about their joys and sorrows and desires and passions. And all of it has seemed so familiar to me, so right. And then tonight... Auden drew a deep breath. "I'm okay...no, more than okay, I'm fine with it. I just need a little time to get used to the idea."

"Well, I should think so." Gayle suddenly shook her head and burst out laughing. "You've spent your whole life thinking you were straight. Now, in a matter of...well, *days* practically, you're realizing something entirely different."

Hesitantly, Auden said softly, "I think I might be doing a little bit more than just thinking about it."

Gayle's eyebrows rose. "Meaning?"

"It's entirely possible that I've done something rather dumb tonight myself."

"Huh?" Now Gayle looked completely confused. "You just went downstairs to use a computer, I thought."

"I did. Except while I was down there, I ended up kissing Haydon Palmer."

"You *what*?" Gayle's jaw dropped. She made a small sound as if she were choking.

"I asked her to kiss me." Thinking about it, Auden began to tremble.

"*You* asked her to kiss you," Gayle said very slowly in a monotone.

"Yes. And...she did."

"Oh my God."

Unconsciously, Auden raised her fingertips to her lips, surprised that they felt normal, half expecting them to be somehow indelibly altered. She stared at Gayle. "It was the most incredible thing I've ever experienced."

"I don't know what to say," Gayle said quietly. "That was it? Just one kiss?"

"Yes, that was it." Auden laughed a bit unsteadily, struck by the understatement. "One simple, perfect kiss."

"And then she stopped?"

Auden shook her head. "No, I think *I* stopped."

"Because you were uncomfortable?"

"No," Auden whispered. "Because I wanted so much more."

"You wanted...you wanted to go to bed with her?" Gayle's voice was flat, uncomprehending. "I mean...you just started thinking about women, and...God. She must be something."

"Time doesn't seem to mean anything when I'm with her." Auden stared into Gayle's kind eyes. "I only know that I...I wanted her."

"Jesus," Gayle murmured reverently. "Auden. What the hell is happening here?"

"I don't know."

Gayle stretched out her hand further and Auden took it, their fingers intertwining. The two friends regarded one another solemnly.

Finally, Auden said quietly, "I think I need to go sleep now."

Gayle nodded. "Yeah. Me, too. There's been something about this night that makes me feel like I'm in another world."

"Yes." Auden felt Hays's mouth on hers again, sensed muscles straining beneath her hands, heard the soft moans of pleasure that were almost pain. "A dream world."

❖

Down the hall, Hays lay on the king-sized bed in the dark, fully clothed, her eyes closed, her mind a confusion of reverie and remembrances. Her body still stirred to the sensation of Auden's lips, Auden's breath, Auden's fingers pressed tightly to her thighs. Desire coursed along the sinews and vessels of her limbs and burned in the core of her, smoldering hot like the embers of a fire long banked, then blown to life on the cold night air. Her palm lay on her abdomen and the muscles twitched under her trembling fingers. Her chest was tight, each breath spun on a thread of pure yearning. Behind closed lids, she saw Auden's face, soft with arousal, and she conjured the feel of Auden's body, warm against her skin. Despite every warning, against all reason, she allowed the essence of that imagined touch to fill the void within her soul.

With a muted cry, she at last turned on her side, curled desperately around the dream, and surrendered to restless sleep.

❖

Thane bent over the laptop centered on the small desk in one corner of the hotel room, her shirt sleeves rolled up, a split of champagne from the mini-bar open by her right hand. A glass of the sparkling wine stood forgotten next to it. The dawn was not far off, but it was impossible to tell through the drapery of snow that fell steadily outside her windows.

She worked without pause, a faint sheen of sweat on her forehead, unaware of the hour or her own weariness. The night had abandoned her to solitude, and she struggled to give form to what she would not have come morning—the touch of a lover's hand, gentle on her skin.

Private Pleasures — Afterglow

I love moments like this, right after you come, when you can't move because the aftershocks are still softly rippling through your muscles, twisting in your depths. I love the way you fall into me, pinning me to the bed with your spent desires.

I reach down and pull a sheet up over us— I don't want you to get chilled. You settle into my arms, heart still pounding, head on my shoulder, one leg over mine. You're trembling with exhaustion; I can taste you on my lips. You murmur, "I love you."

"I know," I whisper back. I did not come when you came, although I grew harder with each pulse of your orgasm in my mouth. When I am inside you, surrounding you with my lips, holding your passion on my tongue, there is only you. My own need is but a distant thunder. Now the urgency has come roaring back, and I ache for relief.

Your hand moves aimlessly over my breasts and belly as you drift near sleep, occasionally rubbing my nipples, tugging for a fleeting second then abandoning them. My clitoris, still rampant, twitches, and I spread my legs just a little. You snuggle closer, wet and hot where your leg straddles my thigh. We are lying so still, I can hear our hearts beating in time.

"I want to come," I whisper hoarsely. "Can I...touch myself?"

"Mmm, no," you mutter, your eyes still closed. "Not yet."

Your hand drifts slowly down the center of my abdomen; I hold my breath. I know you might fall asleep any second, and I start to pray that you will touch me. I glance down. My clitoris is visibly swollen, pushing up, throbbing steadily. If you'll just stroke me, I know I'll come right away. Now all I can feel is the pressure building between my legs. I lift my hips, trying to get you to move your fingers down—you are so close; I am so close. I only need the briefest pressure to push me over. I'm hanging there now, barely breathing, waiting for you to give me what my body is screaming for.

"Touch me, please, baby," I beg. "Just rub your fingers over me. I wanna come so bad."

You don't answer. Jesus, are you asleep?

Your hand is still and I'm in agony, wondering if you're asleep. I shift my hips, trying to press my clitoris up against your fingers. My hand edges forward; I can't help it. It will only take a second, and I am so close alre—

"No."

Ever so slowly, your fingers move lower between my legs, brushing through my wetness. Helplessly, I groan, and I can feel you smiling against my skin. Slowly you fondle me, sliding my lips between your fingers, tugging them apart. My legs are like steel, they're so tight. My hands are digging into your shoulders. I'm whimpering, low constant pleas for you to make me come. I'm so stiff, I hurt. Do you know how this is killing me?

"Baby, make me come, please. I have to come. Please."

"Mmm." Your fingertips rest on the shaft, pressing firmly. Not moving.

My hips are off the bed now. I'm trying desperately to move your fingers where I need them so badly. I can't see. I can't even breathe. You slide down, rubbing the tips of two fingers over the exposed nerve endings. Slow circles, coating the engorged length with my own come.

"You're going to make me come," I moan, my whole body twitching now. I think I hear you laugh, but my mind is turning to heat and color—I have no thoughts, only a desperate need for relief. You're working me between your fingers, and I can feel myself ready to explode. You feel it, too. My insides clench, my clitoris spasms once, hard, and I start coming.

"*Now* touch yourself," you order as you push your fingers into me and start pumping.

I'm shouting, coming hard, my fingers stroking in time to the rhythm of your hands pulling the orgasm from me in long, deep thrusts. I stay on myself until the quivering slows; you cup all of me with your hand, squeezing me gently until you milk the last tremor from my exhausted flesh. I contract around your fingers, gripping you tightly. Muscle by muscle I relax against you, still moaning softly as the last of the orgasm trails through my belly.

You let out a sigh of satisfaction and

fall asleep. I drift off, your hand still
held inside me.

Thane leaned back and blew out a long breath. *At least frustration is good for something.*

She rubbed both hands over her face, stared out the window, and tried not to imagine what Liz and Gayle were doing at that moment. She had no trouble at all envisioning what Liz would look like in the midst of passion—or after, for that matter. They'd been lovers for four frantic months, right after Liz had started the company and Thane had been preparing her first novel for publication with WomenWords. They'd been good in bed together but had spent most of their waking moments arguing over artistic differences.

Liz thought Thane's fiction was too edgy for the romance market. Actually, *crude* had been a term she'd used at one point. Thane had accused Liz of lacking imagination and had suggested that she was a throwback to the days when sex was only alluded to and lovemaking always took place offstage.

"Try reading Rune Dyre, Thane," Liz had snapped at one point. "*She* manages to write romance and sex without offending half the readers."

"*Fuck* Rune Dyre," Thane had shot back.

"I'd love to, actually, but I can't seem to get to her in person."

The two women had stared at one another for long seconds across the desk in Liz's office, and then they had burst out laughing at the same time.

"Yeah, well, I didn't hear you call me crude last night," Thane had said eventually, her trademark grin lighting up her handsome face.

"No," Liz had replied with a smile of her own. "I think I called you God."

"Just let me write it the way I can, Lizzie," Thane had said softly. "Just trust me to tell the story, and it will work."

Liz had sighed, and nodded her head. "Go ahead. They'll either love it or hate it. There are worse fates for a book."

Or for an author, Thane thought. She stared at the computer screen blankly for another second, then shook off the memories. She proofed the vignette, opened her e-mail, and checked her inbox. *Nothing new. Most everyone is here.*

```
-----Original Message-----
From: thaneCutlass@CutlassFic.com
Sent: Sunday March 23, 5:32 AM
To: Rune@HeartLand.com
Subject: Party Update
Attachment: Afterglow.doc 90kb
```

Hey Rune:

   You missed a good time, buddy. Very swanky place, very, very nice guest list. I met Palmer's new director, Auden Frost. Seems on top of things, not to mention she's a knockout. Of course, I was on my best behavior <vbg>. Well, at least for our first meeting. We'll see about the next time.
   Looks like Liz will be coming over to marketing at Palmer. That's a good deal for us, I think. She's got the connections, and she knows us.
   When are you going to send me some of Secret Passions? You've been leaving me high and dry lately, and I could use a good hot distraction. Just to motivate you, I'm sending another of mine. So how about a little something in return - huh?
   Enjoy it.

Thane

"Too bad this one isn't a true life story," Thane muttered as she hit Send. She winced at the cramps in her shoulders as she stood and thought about a shower, just to relax enough to sleep. But the insistent thud of arousal still plagued her, accentuated rather than assuaged by the scene she had written. She decided there were easier and more pleasant ways to put herself to sleep. Swiftly, she closed the drapes, shed her clothes, and slid naked into bed. Then she slipped her hand beneath the sheets.

When I am inside you, surrounding you with my lips, holding your passion on my tongue, there is only you. My own need is but a distant thunder. Now the urgency has come roaring back, and I ache for relief.

CHAPTER THIRTEEN

A ud?"

At the knock on her door, Auden rolled over in bed. She hadn't been asleep. She'd been lying with her eyes closed, picturing Hays's face just before they'd kissed. Remembering her expression, almost feverishly intense, yet her touch so controlled, so careful, and her mouth so impossibly soft. Auden felt a rush of heat. *I know when I see her I'm going to want to—*

"Hey, Aud?"

"Come in," Auden called, struggling to banish the images.

Gayle entered, waving a sheet of pale red stationary. In her tuxedo pants and a white Calvin Klein shirt that showed off her lithe, graceful figure, she looked annoyingly refreshed and attractive. Indicating her shirt, she announced happily, "I went downstairs to raid the hotel shops before everyone else who is marooned along with us got the same idea. Thank God the manager opened the places that are Four Seasons franchises. She's got bellmen and assistant managers running the registers—the regular staff couldn't get in to work because of the storm."

Auden sat up, pulling the sheet with her. She was naked and tired and disturbingly aroused, and she wasn't sure if Gayle would be able to tell. She had no idea anymore what might show in her face. "Please tell me you bought clothes for me, too."

Grinning, Gayle perched on the end of the bed and leaned forward with one arm down on the covers close to Auden's thigh. Seductively, she asked, "What's it worth to you, sweet stuff?"

As Auden's eyes grew wide, Gayle cocked her head and studied Auden's panic-stricken expression. "Hey, what?" Then, as if making a startling discovery, she shot up straight. "Jesus, Aud. You don't think... I didn't mean...I'm not coming on to you."

Her friend's concern was so sharp that Auden immediately felt guilty. "Gayle, sweetie, it's okay. I know you're not."

"I wouldn't do that, cause even if you are gay—"

"Stop. It's not you," Auden said with an embarrassed shake of her head. "I'm just all turned around here. It's as if I suddenly don't have any skin." She leaned back and closed her eyes. Her voice was a whisper. "I hardly recognize myself."

"Oh, Aud." Gayle placed her palm lightly on the sheet covering Auden's calf and squeezed gently. "I think you're beautiful and sexy and smart, but what we have...it's already special."

Smiling softly, Auden opened her eyes. "Yes, to me, too. I'm sorry. I didn't mean to make you worry."

"Does it bother you," Gayle asked carefully, as she studied her hand on Auden's leg, "when we touch?"

"No," Auden said swiftly. "No, never. We're friends, and we've always been demonstrative—physically, I mean. Just because we're both," she took a deep breath, "attracted to women, doesn't mean we can't still be affectionate. Right?"

"Right." Gayle kept the light contact between them. "You're pretty sure about this, aren't you? About being a lesbian, I mean."

"Yeah," Auden replied quietly. "It's kind of hard to deny when I... feel what I feel."

"Just don't rush anything, okay?"

Auden heard Hays's last words, the finality in them. *Good night, sweet Auden.*

"No, I don't think there'll be anything to rush into." Forcing a smile, she asked, "What did you buy me? And what's with the red flag?"

"Oh," Gayle replied. "It's a notice that was under the door." She looked down at the single page and read, "Palmer Publishing invites you to join us...blah blah blah..." She met Auden's inquisitive gaze. "Gee, they're a very sophisticated bunch. They're comping us all to brunch today from ten 'til three."

"What did you buy me to wear?" Auden looked at the clock. It was almost eleven. *Hays will be there.*

"A red Alberta Ferretti blouse cut down to here." She demonstrated, pointing to her own chest someplace south of propriety. "Black Versace jeans—"

"Ouch. I can see I'm going to have a big bill." Auden grinned ruefully, doing the math in her head. "I hadn't planned on spending my first month's salary on clothes."

"Yeah, but you'll look hot. Besides, it's my treat. I get to spend a weekend in this place for free."

"Gayle, no! It's a fortune."

"Not really. I'm a discriminating shopper." She shook Auden's leg. "If it really bothers you, you can take me out to dinner some night. Now—let me finish."

"There's more?" Auden was enjoying herself despite the lingering concern.

"Just the Bally loafers."

"Underwear? Please say underwear."

Gayle shrugged. "Yeah, but they're not designer."

"Somehow, I don't think that will matter." Auden pointed to the door with her index finger. "Bring them, then give me fifteen minutes to shower and get dressed."

"Yes, m'lady."

Auden laughed. "Out. Go. Now."

Gayle just grinned and sauntered out.

❖

```
-----Original Message-----
From: Rune@HeartLand.com
Sent: Sunday March 23, 11:42 AM
To: thaneCutlass@CutlassFic.com
Subject: Comments
Attachment: Afterglow-RDcoms.doc 55kb
```

Thane:

The vignette is good. Better than good. I've attached a few comments, but they're just window dressing.

You've always been able to find the right

balance in erotica – enough anonymity so
that the reader can make of it what she
needs to, while adding that critical human
connection that makes it so much more than
just a sexual exercise.

You've never been given enough credit
for that skill. You don't need me for this
anthology. For some reason, it's just not
coming together for me.

Do it on your own or get Clary or Morgan
to toss in a couple. It will be great.

Best, Rune

Hays hadn't exaggerated; it was very good. Thane had always
been a good writer, and she was getting better. There was something
about this last piece that had even more heart to it than usual. But it was
going to kill Hays to keep reading these fantasy dreams and desires
while she was imagining Thane imagining Auden.

As a reader, she'd always been able to separate herself from the
writer and avoid imagining whatever might have been behind a scene
or a story or an erotic vignette. Even when she'd been stimulated by the
words, it had been her own fantasies come to life that had ultimately
released her. But she'd seen Thane with Auden the night before, and
just that brief glimpse of them together made it impossible to distance
herself from what Thane had written. She wasn't aroused by Thane's
secret desires. She was jealous.

She'd slept very little, and her dreams had all been of passion
hovering just beyond her reach. She'd finally arisen, aching and tired,
to shower and return to the Web—a world where she had always found
escape and with it, peace. But Thane's e-mail had changed that. She
tried for a while just to ignore the vignette, but the presence of the
attachment haunted her. To ignore it was impossible. She and Thane
were friends, and they'd been critiquing each other's work for over
two years. They'd supported, cajoled, and teased one another through
periods of uncertainty and disappointment, and they'd shared success,
as well. In the process, they'd forged a strong personal bond. She

couldn't simply abandon Thane even if Thane *was* developing an interest in Auden.

It's not as if I have a hold on her, or any plans to forge one.

When the door to the business center opened, Hays half expected it to be Auden again. Hoped it would be. She turned at the sound, and her face revealed none of her disappointment.

"Good morning, Abel."

"I had clean clothes sent up to your room," he said by way of greeting. "You weren't in when I rang, so I took the liberty of ordering you a few things."

"Thank you. How are our guests doing?"

Pritchard stood ramrod straight beside the console where Hays was seated. His voice had the neutral tone of a lieutenant reporting to his commander. "I've made arrangements for the brunch, as you requested. I've called Alana at home, and she'll help anyone who needs to change airline reservations or the like from there. A message has been delivered to everyone with that information."

"Excellent," Hays replied, although she was only half listening. She had no doubt that Abel had taken care of everything that could be taken care of. "What about the weather report?"

"Unfortunately, snow is expected to accumulate until late this evening. We're looking at record totals approaching three feet."

Hays groaned. "So the travel prohibitions are still in effect?"

"The hotel manager, Ms. McMichaels, informs me that City Hall has promised that the roads will be open sometime tomorrow."

"Airport?"

"Hour to hour, but certainly not before tomorrow evening."

"All right," Hays said with a sigh. "Please check in with each of Palmer's guests this evening to make sure everyone has what they need."

"What about you?" Pritchard asked evenly. "You look like you have a fever—"

"I'm fine, Abel."

"Are you having any bleeding?"

"No."

His expression did not register his disbelief, but he'd gotten very good at judging her physical state from the degree of pain in her eyes.

"Temple Hospital is out of the question, but the Hahnemann ER is only five blocks away. If you need—"

"Damn it," she whispered lethally. "I'm *fine.*"

He stiffened. "If you do need anything—"

"What I *need* is breakfast," she pronounced, forcing a lighter tone. "How about you?"

"I'll have something in my room. I want to check in with Alana again."

"Abel," Hays said quietly as the tall man turned away. "Thanks."

"Of course," he answered as he slipped out the door.

You can't fix this, Abel. You have to let it go.

Hays shut down the machine she was using and considered brunch. *Auden will be there.*

She had no idea what she would say when she saw her, and she feared that she might see regret in Auden's eyes. But she couldn't deny that the only thing she'd truly wanted since awakening had been to see Auden again.

❖

Auden and Gayle exited the elevator on the mezzanine level where the brunch was set up, joining many of the same people they'd socialized with the previous evening. More than a few were dressed in odd combinations of formal and leisurewear.

"You did good with the shopping, Doc," Auden whispered. "At least I'm not wearing heels with sweatpants."

"Thanks, I had fun," Gayle replied, then tugged on Auden's arm. "There's Liz. Want to sit with her?"

"Sure." Auden followed Gayle's gaze and saw the blond, in a stylish forest green brushed cotton pants suit, gesturing to them with a smile. "She came prepared."

"She lives about an hour outside the city, and she told me she had planned to stay for the weekend anyhow."

"Hey!" Liz called as they approached. "Have you looked outside? It's amazing. Snowdrifts and whiteouts. We might as well be in Alaska."

Gayle and Auden returned the enthusiastic greeting, and the three of them joined the line for the buffet. When they'd completed the circuit and begun the serpentine journey between the tables back to their seats, Auden spied a lone diner and said impulsively, "Do you two mind if I leave you?"

Gayle stopped in surprise, then looked where Auden was staring. A black-haired woman in a dark double-breasted jacket, white shirt, and jeans sat alone with a pile of papers spread out beside her plate. Her face in three-quarter view was sharply etched and perfectly sculpted. She was breathtakingly handsome. In a barely controlled whisper, Gayle asked, "Holy jeez. Is that her?"

"You want to talk shop with the boss?" Liz interjected as Auden merely nodded. "You two are a matched set. Everyone says she does nothing but work."

"It's early in the game," Auden said offhandedly. "I just want to get a jump on things."

Gayle made a small snickering sound, and Auden shot her a mock-threatening look, but Liz didn't notice.

"Go ahead, Aud," Gayle said with a grin. "I'll catch you later."

❖

"Do you mind company?" Auden asked quietly.

Looking up in surprise, Hays smiled and rose halfway. "Good morning. No, not at all. Please, sit down."

Auden settled her tray on the small round tabletop, then sat as Hays took her seat. Reaching for her coffee, Auden remarked, "This is nice of you. This brunch."

"Well, I'm grateful to the people who came last night, despite the bad weather forecasts. And hopefully, they'll all be business associates soon."

"Mm-hmm. Just good business to be so thoughtful, huh?" Auden regarded Hays with a raised eyebrow and a half smile.

Hays blushed, a rare event. "Something like that."

"It's nice," Auden said again softly.

Hays tried but couldn't help letting her gaze drift over Auden's body. The red blouse would have looked good on any woman, but on Auden, complementing the faint hints of red-gold in her blond hair and subtly hugging her breasts, it was gorgeous. With the jeans, the glamour of the top was relegated to casually elegant, and Auden looked understatedly beautiful. "I see you even found shoes."

Smiling, Auden nodded. "Gayle surprised me with an early-morning raid on the shops, and she has excellent taste."

"She knows what looks good on you," Hays murmured. *You share a room, and she buys you clothes that are perfect for you, but you're not lovers?*

Auden saw the question and caught the flicker of retreat in Hays's eyes. "Gayle is my best friend. We've been shopping together dozens of times, and she knows my sizes as well as my tastes."

"I'm sorry." Hays shook her head, discomfited by her transparency. She didn't seem to be able to hide much from Auden, and that was highly unusual.

"No need to be."

"How are you today?" Hays leaned forward slightly as she spoke, her dark eyes searching Auden's.

Spellbound, Auden watched the colors dance in Hays's midnight irises. "Are you asking me about last night?"

"Yes." Hays's voice was deep, husky. "I wasn't going to, but I need...to know."

"I wasn't going to bring it up either," Auden murmured, "but I can't pretend it didn't happen."

"Are you sorry?" Hays drew a breath. "Are you upset? Auden, I never meant to upset you."

"*I* asked you to kiss me," Auden reminded her quietly.

"I..." *couldn't say no.*

"It complicates things just a bit, don't you think?" Auden asked, unable to decipher the hesitation in Hays's voice. "Professionally, I mean?" Her food lay untouched, the coffee forgotten. *Help me understand what happened. Tell me what you feel.*

Hays's chest tightened. "It has nothing to do with work. It never will."

"We'll see each other every day." Auden's gaze held questions that she didn't know how to ask. *What did it mean? Why did you kiss me?*

There was something close to panic in Hays's eyes now. *Christ, she's going to quit.* "It won't happen again. You don't have to worry." She raked a trembling hand through her hair. "Last night...it was, I don't know...I wasn't thinking. You were so..." *beautiful, so alive, and I wanted you so.* "I didn't mean to offend you. If you feel I took advantage of my position—"

"No, of course not." Embarrassed, Auden shook her head. "Please, it's not necessary for you to explain. I'm not upset. I just didn't want there to be an issue between us."

"I want you at Palmer, Auden. I *know* it will work."

"I want to be there." Auden struggled to ignore the swift jolt of disappointment. *She only really cares about the work.*

"Good," Hays said with a sigh of relief. "This has been an unusual weekend, to say the least."

Auden laughed shortly. "A bit of an understatement."

"Any...problems with anyone? Do all the authors seem firmly in our camp?"

"Yes, I think so," Auden replied, trying to focus on business and not the pulse beating in Hays's throat. She wanted to put her fingertips there, to feel Hays's heart beat the way it had inside her mouth hours before. "I feel confident about the ones who are here, at least. I've talked to all of them, and they're eager. Thane was extolling the praises of an erotica series she's working on."

Thane. First name. Cutlass moves fast. Hays reached for her toast and then realized that her hand was shaking badly. *Fatigue.* She pulled it back quickly. "She should be good at it if her novels are any indication."

"She promised me a preview this week."

Hays looked up sharply, but Auden's attention was on her fruit plate. "She's sending you a manuscript?"

"Uh-uh. Just a sample."

"Ah, I see. A dry run to see if you like it."

Their eyes met and they both grinned. "Well, those weren't her precise words."

No, I'll bet they weren't.

"I believe she said she'd send me a taste so that I could see if it met my needs." Auden smiled, remembering the almost self-mocking expression in Thane's eyes as she'd said it. Auden had gotten the impression that the good-looking author wasn't nearly as cocky as she appeared, or as confident as most people probably perceived her.

"What do you think?" Hays asked.

"About the erotica?"

"Yes."

Auden studied Hays's face. "Do you expect me to have an issue with it?"

"It's not romance fiction."

"No, but I wouldn't dismiss it out of hand as having no appeal to our readers, either." Auden speared a melon ball and turned the fork aimlessly as she reflected. "If one judges popularity by what sells, erotica anthologies are hot."

Hays grinned.

"Stop." But Auden was smiling, too.

"I agree, but that doesn't mean our readership will be interested in it," Hays pointed out.

"Is there any way to find out? A market study of some kind?"

Intrigued, Hays straightened, her gaze narrowing in thought. "No one to my knowledge has ever looked at the demographics of the crossover between erotica and romance fiction."

"Could it be done?"

"I don't know—maybe." Hays's eyes glinted and her weariness seemed to drop away. "We could set up polls on the websites and fanfic lists—"

"Which ones?"

"Ours—"

"What? Palmer's?" Auden questioned, confused.

"Uh...no." Hays drew up short and realized that she'd forgotten that Auden didn't know about Rune. Actually, no one other than Abel did. "Well, most of Destiny's authors have websites. We could link a poll to those."

Auden sensed she had missed something, but she wasn't sure what. Hays seemed suddenly subdued. "It bears looking into. I'll talk to Liz about it."

"Good idea."

"In the meantime, I still want to see the manuscript."

"Of course," Hays affirmed, suddenly aware of a faint ringing in her ears "It's your division."

"I'm a bit worried about Rune Dyre."

"Why?" Hays brushed a hand across her forehead, and her fingers came away damp with sweat. She considered taking off her jacket, but didn't want to stand. Her legs felt leaden.

"It bothers me that I can't meet with her. According to Liz, she was WomenWords' biggest seller, but she is reclusive in the extreme."

"That's not so unusual." Hays shrugged, struggling to concentrate on the conversation, but finding her thoughts muddled. "I get the impression that some authors would just rather let their work speak for them."

"And I don't disagree, but with a new venture such as Destiny and with an author whose sales may be critical, I'd like to get a sense of her future plans by speaking with her directly." When Hays didn't reply, Auden glanced up from buttering her bagel. Hays was extraordinarily pale. "Hays?"

"I'm sorry." Hays blinked, but her vision wouldn't clear. "Would you please excuse me?"

As the publisher abruptly rose, Auden caught a glimpse of Thane Cutlass approaching their table. Before Auden could utter a greeting or question Hays's unexpected departure, Hays collapsed to the floor.

CHAPTER FOURTEEN

Distantly, Hays heard voices, but the words were garbled and indistinct, as if she were underwater. When she opened her eyes, she found that she couldn't focus. Light-headed, she was nevertheless aware of a familiar presence and the touch of gentle fingers on her cheek. The warmth of that small point of contact grounded her, tethering her tenderly to the earthbound plane.

"Au...Auden?"

"It's all right." Auden's voice was calm and soothing, despite the fact that she was terrified.

Hays blinked several times, and she managed to make out Auden's worried features as she bent near. "How...what happened?"

"Hays, you fainted. You're going to be all right."

"Oh, Jesus." Hays closed her eyes, struggling to control the nausea and dizziness. When she opened her lids again, her vision was clearer. "Help me get to my room. Please."

"Just lie still." From where she was kneeling by Hays' side, Auden looked up at Thane, who stood above them keeping onlookers away. "Go get Gayle."

"Okay. I'll be right back."

Hays struggled to a seated position and rested her back against a chair to wait for her head to stop spinning. She took a steadying breath and reached behind her, bracing a hand on the seat.

Auden moved quickly, threading her arm around Hays's waist. "Just wait, please? I don't want you to try standing and fainting again."

"I won't. It's passing." Hays met Auden's apprehensive gaze. "Please, Auden. Just help me up. I don't want everyone here to see me like this. Please."

There was something in Hays's eyes, a sheen of desperation that was so out of character for her that Auden's heart turned over. "You're so pale. I'm afraid you'll hurt yourself."

"I'll be okay. Please believe me."

Auden rested her fingers fleetingly on Hays's cheek. Then she tightened her grip around her and murmured, "All right. But hold on to me and go slowly."

Just as they were getting to their feet, Gayle pushed her way through the crowd of curious people who had gathered nearby. Her gaze went immediately to Hays and her eyes narrowed. "What happened?"

"She fainted," Auden said grimly as Hays leaned heavily against her side.

"Sit down here," Gayle instructed, pointing to the nearby chair.

"No." Hays breathed heavily but her voice sounded strong. "I want to go upstairs."

"Gayle is a doctor, Hays," Auden urged. "Let her look at you first."

"Not here."

Gayle held Hays's wrist with two fingers resting over the radial artery, taking her pulse as she scanned Hays's face. "As long as you promise to let me or the hotel doctor examine you once we're in your suite."

"It's not necessary—"

"It is." Gayle's tone was unyielding. "Someone needs to check you over."

Hays looked like she was about to argue when Auden whispered, "Please, Hays."

"All right then," Hays assented reluctantly, too ill to argue. "Please, let's just get out of here."

"Do you need any help?" Thane asked quietly from just behind Gayle.

Gayle turned and smiled appreciatively. "It's okay. But thanks."

Thane nodded, and Auden, Hays, and Gayle made their way to the nearest bank of elevators. Auden kept her arm around Hays's waist, and within five minutes, they were inside Hays's suite.

"Auden, would you wait out here while I take a look at her?" Gayle requested quietly while Hays moved slowly but steadily into the bedroom.

Auden wanted to object, because she desperately wanted to see for herself that Hays was all right. But she respected Hays's privacy and appreciated that Gayle was speaking not as her friend at the moment, but as a physician concerned about her patient.

"Of course." As Gayle turned away, Auden caught her hand. "Can I see her when you're done?"

"If she's up to it," Gayle replied gently. "Do you want to wait for me back in our suite?"

Auden shook her head. She couldn't bear to be that far away. "I'll just wait out here."

Gayle nodded and disappeared inside Hays's bedroom, closing the door behind her. Auden sat on the plush sofa in the well-appointed sitting room, staring at the blank television screen. She had no desire to turn it on. As she gazed fixedly ahead, all she could see was Hays as she slumped to the floor, so unbelievably pale, a fine mist of sweat on her forehead.

In that instant, Auden had felt fear like none she had ever known. Even now, the memory left her feeling at once helpless and bereft. Her thinking mind told her that she was overreacting; Hays had probably picked up a flu bug and would be fine in a day or so. But even as she rationalized, she remembered the way Hays had looked that afternoon in her office when Auden had come upon her sleeping. She had been ill then, too. Most of the time, in fact, she seemed on the edge of exhaustion.

And despite her regard for Hays's privacy, Auden still needed to know what was wrong. She couldn't bear the thought of Hays suffering alone, and yet she knew she did not have the right to intrude. Just because *she* felt a connection to the solitary, private woman did not mean that there was one. As she waited, her anxiety mounted with each passing moment.

Auden watched a light on the multiline phone flicker and then blink steadily. At first, she was surprised that Hays was making a phone call, and then she realized that it could be Gayle. *What if Hays is seriously ill? What if Gayle is calling for an ambulance? Can they even get here in this storm?* That thought made her chest tighten, and she almost got to her feet with the intention of knocking on the bedroom door. Even after the light blinked out, she continued to imagine the worst. She stared at the closed bedroom door, willing it to open.

When the buzzer to the suite sounded, she jumped, her heart suddenly racing. Quickly, she crossed to the door and pulled it open. A woman she did not recognize, dressed in a conservative dark skirt and cream-colored silk blouse, stood in the hall with what resembled a black plastic tackle box in her right hand. "Yes?"

"Dr. Dunbar?"

"No, she's inside."

"She called about medical equipment. I'm sorry," the woman said, indicating the box with a tip of her chin, "but the best we have is the emergency kit from the dispensary. We're not really equipped for anything beyond basic first aid, and I doubt that any of our on-call doctors can get here."

From behind Auden, Gayle spoke, having approached from Hays's room without Auden hearing. "That's fine. If I need medications, do you have any on hand?" Seeing the woman's hesitation, Gayle added, "I'll give you my license number. It won't be for controlled substances."

The woman, who Auden assumed to be one of the assistant managers, nodded. "Call the front desk when you know what you need and ask for Valerie Brown. They'll find me."

"Thank you," Gayle replied as she took the kit and disappeared again before Auden could ask her anything at all.

After another interminable wait, during which time the lights on the phone blinked on and off several more times, Gayle finally reemerged from the bedroom, shutting the door quietly behind her.

"She needs some sleep, Aud, but she wants to see you." Gayle smiled, the kind of smile a doctor uses with worried loved ones. "Don't stay too long, okay?"

"Is she all right?"

"She needs some sleep."

Auden had known Gayle Dunbar for almost seven years. She was closer to Gayle than to anyone in her life, even her family. But in all that time, she had never interacted with her as a physician. For the first time, she realized that there was another Gayle she barely knew. This woman's expression was sympathetic and her tone soothing, but Auden could not see past the barriers in her eyes. "Gayle?"

Gayle shook her head. "Go see her, Auden. She asked for you."

"Thank you," Auden finally said, meaning it. Whatever had happened or would happen, she was grateful that Gayle had been there for Hays.

❖

Auden knocked lightly. When the familiar deep voice answered, she was nearly weak with relief.

"Hi," Auden said softly as she stepped into the bedroom and carefully closed the door. Hays sat propped up on the bed, still fully clothed, but with the top two buttons of her shirt open. As Auden approached, Hays swung her legs to the side as if to rise. Quickly, Auden held up a hand. "No, please, don't get up."

"It's all right."

"I'm sure it is." Auden kept her voice as casual as she could. "But there's no need for formality. You're fine right there. I just wanted to see how you are."

Hays gestured to the side of the bed with her hand and reclined again. "Please, sit down."

Auden sat, her left hand a few inches away from where Hays's lay on top of the covers. "How are you feeling?"

So lightly as to be almost unnoticeable, Hays rested her fingers on Auden's. When she answered, her voice was gentle. "I'm fine. I'm sorry if I worried you."

Without thinking, Auden laced her fingers through Hays's. The small bit of contact was enormously comforting. "I can see that you're better now. That's all that really matters."

"Apparently, I skipped one meal too many yesterday and was so busy talking to you that I forgot breakfast as well." Hays smiled ruefully. "It was just a combination of too little sleep and not enough fuel. Nothing to be concerned about."

"Well. I just needed to see for myself that you're all right." Auden stared at their interlocked fingers, rubbing her thumb softly over the space between Hays's thumb and index finger. The skin was so soft there and the muscle beneath so tender. She'd never noticed before how beautiful a woman's hands could be. Before Hays could reply, Auden lifted her gaze and met the midnight eyes searching her face. "I understand if you don't want to talk about it. But please, I'd rather you didn't lie to me."

Hays drew a swift breath, her grip tightening on Auden's. "Auden—"

"You have no reason to trust me, and I'm not asking you to. Not now. Maybe someday..." Auden looked away, then with a tremulous smile, continued. "I have no idea why I feel so close to you so quickly. It doesn't make any sense, but then not much has for the past week or so. There's something between us, and even if it's simply friendship, it feels special."

"I know." Hays's voice was low, husky, barely audible. "I can't explain it either, but I feel it, too."

"I want you to know something," Auden said with absolute conviction. "*Everything* about last night, not just the kiss, was perfect. And that is something that I'll never forget."

"No, neither will I." Hays smiled faintly, resting her head back on the pillows. She was so very tired, and the touch of Auden's hand made it so difficult to think. But for the first time in longer than she could remember, she felt peaceful, without fear or sadness, and she didn't want to lose that tranquility. She didn't want Auden to go.

Auden saw Hays's eyelids flutter and realized that she was fighting sleep. Although she was loathe to leave her, she remembered Gayle's admonition not to linger. Fleetingly, she wondered if Hays would even remember this conversation, but then realized that didn't matter. *She* would remember. Carefully, she began to withdraw her fingers from Hays's grasp. "You need to rest."

"Could you stay...just another minute?"

There was a look of such unguarded need in Hays's eyes that Auden wasn't sure she could answer. Her throat was suddenly so tight she couldn't swallow. What she wanted to do was take Hays in her arms and shelter her, keep her safe. She leaned forward and with her free hand brushed the hair back from Hays's forehead. "I will if you promise to close your eyes and try to sleep."

For the longest moment, Hays simply stared into Auden's eyes as if she were searching for deliverance. Then she nodded wearily. "I promise."

Auden sat unmoving for a long time, listening until Hays's breathing became slow and regular. Finally, satisfied that the other woman was truly resting comfortably, she extricated her hand from Hays's grip and rose carefully. She hesitated, indulging herself by simply watching Hays sleep, and then she leaned down and kissed Hays's forehead. Ever so softly she whispered, "Sleep well, sweet Hays."

❖

When Auden walked through Hays' sitting room, she noticed a small orange plastic vial in the center of the coffee table with a note beside it. In Gayle's handwriting, she read, *Take these as directed. Call me at x3251 if your fever spikes.* Gayle had underlined *Call me.*

Auden picked up the vial but didn't recognize the name of the medication. Then, mortified to realize that she was prying into Hays's private business, she hurriedly replaced the container next to Gayle's instructions. Without looking back, she crossed to the door, pulled it open, and stepped into the hall.

Abel Pritchard, looking more disturbed and angry than she had ever seen him, stood just outside. "Why didn't you call—"

"Shh!" Auden said forcefully, pulling the door nearly closed. "She's asleep."

He looked past her into the suite as if expecting to see Hays standing there. Then, he made an almost visible effort to compose himself. When he spoke again, his voice was once again dispassionate.

"What happened?"

"She fainted downstairs."

Pritchard regarded Auden intently. "Describe for me exactly what occurred."

For a second, Auden returned his stare. She didn't want to talk about Hays without her knowledge, especially remembering how desperately Hays had not wanted people to see her incapacitated. "Hays can tell you when she wak—"

"She may not remember everything, Ms. Frost." His blue eyes were nearly purple with the effort to contain his emotions. A soft sigh escaped him. "Please. It's important—for her."

There was something about the sadness in his voice that made

Auden's stomach twist. She was frightened—no, more than frightened. Thinking about Hays being ill, she was sick at heart. Straightening her shoulders, she cleared her throat and quietly told him everything she could recall, which wasn't much because it had been over so fast.

"Did she regain consciousness immediately?"

"Yes, very nearly so. She was out for a minute, no more," Auden answered, sorting through the jumble of memories, colored now by her own growing alarm. *He seems far more upset than a simple fainting spell warrants.*

"And when she awoke—she knew you?"

Auden? Auden's voice was tight. "Yes. She was a little confused at first, but that passed quickly."

"Did she strike her head when she fell?"

"No, I don't think so. No. She just went down." Auden's heart was pounding now. "Mr. Pritchard, what—"

"Did she complain about anything at all? Chest pain?"

"God, no. It was just a few seconds, and then she seemed to recover." Auden steadied herself with a hand on the door. "Gayle checked her right away, and she didn't seem too worried."

"Gayle?"

"I'm sorry. My friend, Gayle—Dr. Dunbar. She examined Hays up here."

Pritchard's eyebrows rose in surprise. "Your doing?"

"Yes." Auden blushed. "I asked Gayle to check her."

"And Hays complied?"

"She resisted a bit," Auden replied with a fond smile, "but Gayle insisted."

"Yeess," Pritchard said slowly. "I'm sure it was your doctor friend who persuaded her." He drew himself up, his eyes having regained their glacial clarity. "I appreciate your assistance, Ms. Frost. Please forgive my earlier outburst."

"No need for apologies, Mr. Pritchard. We were all a bit worried."

He nodded, then stepped through the door into Hays' suite. The door swung closed, leaving Auden alone in the hallway.

❖

Auden returned to her suite and found Gayle waiting in the sitting room. It was hard for Auden to believe that, only hours before, they had been curled up on the sofa, talking about their love lives. Now, it seemed as if everything had changed.

"Hi," Auden said quietly as she walked to the large double windows and pulled back the drapes to look out. "It's still snowing."

"Yeah." Gayle joined her at the window. "Fox Weather said it would let up sometime near dawn tomorrow."

"Another night here, then."

"Uh-huh. Mrs. T says Shy prefers his kibble with warm gravy. By the time I get home, he's going to look like a little brown and white bowling ball." Gayle laughed softly.

"Is everything okay there?" Auden watched the snow fall and thought about standing in the moonlight with Hays. Remembered looking down on the square, warmed by Hays's voice in the still night and stirred by the feel of her in the dark, even though they had not touched.

"The college kid next door has been keeping the walks clear. They're fine."

"Good."

"Liz called. She said she and Thane want to come by and play cards. You up for that?"

"I don't know, Gayle." Auden sighed. "I'm not feeling like I'd be very good company."

Gayle slid her arm around Auden's waist. "It'll pass the time."

"Is she in any danger?" The question was quiet, wistful.

"Aud, I can't." Gayle held her closer. "I'm sorry."

"You don't have to tell me anything confidential," Auden said, finally meeting Gayle's gaze. "Just...for tonight? Will she be all right?"

"Oh, honey," Gayle murmured, brushing her fingers over Auden's cheek. "What's that I see in your eyes?"

Auden knew, but just shook her head.

"Yes," Gayle said at last. "For tonight, she's all right."

Auden turned back to the storm, finding comfort in the memories swirling in the snow. "Thank you."

CHAPTER FIFTEEN

"G od damn it, Teddy," Liz complained as she pushed her last two quarters into the pile of change in the center of the coffee table. "You've *got* to be bluffing. Nobody could win five hands in a row."

The foursome was sitting on the floor around the coffee table in the sitting room of Auden and Gayle's suite. They'd been playing cards and talking for several hours. Gayle looked across the table at Thane, who had a satisfied smile on her face.

"Teddy?" Gayle asked, an eyebrow raised and a grin quirking the corner of her mouth.

Thane met Gayle's eyes and shrugged. "Theodora."

"Nice."

Gayle's voice was soft, almost sensuous, and Thane blushed. "Thanks."

"Which do you prefer? Thane or Teddy?"

"Whichever you like," Thane replied, her own voice susurrant. "So much of my day is spent writing and corresponding as Thane, I answer to it as naturally as to anything else."

"I guess it would depend on the circumstances then, wouldn't it," Gayle remarked, her eyes dropping for an instant to Thane's expressive mouth.

"I guess it would."

Liz coughed. "Any chance you could see my bet, *Teddy?*"

Without taking her eyes from Gayle's face, Thane picked up a dollar bill from her winnings and deposited it on the money in the middle of the table. "See you and double the raise."

"Pretty confident, aren't you?" Liz leaned forward to slide her wallet from the pocket of her slacks. A moment later, she placed a bill on top of Thane's. "I'm calling your bluff this time."

Thane finally looked from Gayle to Liz, her grin widening. She fanned her cards and put them down. "Full house. Aces over eights."

Gayle laughed as Liz muttered, "Son of a bitch."

Throughout the exchange, Auden sat quietly, observing with only half a mind the interplay between the three women. She couldn't think of anything except Hays, knowing she was right down the hall, but not knowing how she was. Not knowing if she was resting peacefully, or if she was caught in the throes of a nightmare, or worse, if she was even more ill than earlier. A dozen times, she'd thought of calling Abel Pritchard, just to ask for an update. She hadn't, not because it would've embarrassed her for him to know of her concern, but because she did not want to invade the privacy that Hays obviously guarded so closely. The hours had passed incredibly slowly. She had truly tried to immerse herself in the good-natured repartee, but the ache in her chest made it impossible.

When the phone rang, Auden jumped. She and Gayle looked at each other, and Auden said quickly, "I'll get it." She crossed rapidly to the writing desk in the corner and snatched up the receiver. "Hello?"

She could see Gayle watching her from across the room, and she quickly shook her head, indicating it was not for Gayle. Turning her back slightly to the group, she murmured, "Are you all right? Do you need to speak to Gayle?...Are you sure?...What, tonight?...No, no, I wouldn't mind at all."

When Auden hung up the phone, she found that the other women were all watching her expectantly. She was sure they were curious about what had happened earlier, but after she'd said that Hays was fine, neither Liz nor Thane had asked for further details. "Would it ruin your game if I dropped out? That was Hays. She wants to talk to me about...work."

"No problem."

"Sure."

"Go ahead."

Gayle got to her feet and crossed to Auden. In a voice too low to be heard clearly by the others, she asked, "Is she all right?"

"She says that she is." Auden's discomfort was clear. "I'm not sure I believe that."

"You can always call me if you think there's a problem. We'll probably all still be hanging out here. You don't mind that, do you?"

"No, of course not. Will you be okay? I don't mean to—"

"Hey," Gayle said with a laugh, placing her fingers lightly on Auden's wrist. "Everything is fine. I've got a little more than twenty-four hours before I have to be at the hospital for another twenty-four-hour shift. Believe me, there are worse ways to spend it than trapped in a hotel room with a couple of good-looking women."

Auden studied Gayle intently. "Just be careful, okay?"

"What do you mean?"

"You know, I've never seen you when you've been...trying to make a connection with a woman."

Gayle lowered her voice even more, although Thane and Liz were bickering over who had lost more times at poker and were not listening. "You mean *cruising?* Is it that obvious?"

"If you're trying to hit on Thane, then it is. If not, then I'm worse at this than I thought."

"You're not wrong." Gayle sighed. "But she's such a player, I can't read her at all. She probably flirts with everyone, and besides, I still think she's hot for you."

"I am *not* interested in Thane Cutlass," Auden whispered vehemently. "And she does not look at me the way she looks at you."

"Yes, she does. You just haven't been paying any attention." Gayle stroked her hand. "Worried about Hays?"

Auden nodded, slid her fingers up, and squeezed Gayle's. "You're my best friend. I only ever want you to be happy."

"Oh, Aud." Gayle leaned forward and kissed her quickly on the cheek. "Why in hell I didn't fall for you long ago, I'll never know. Don't worry, honey, my heart is too cynical to get broken."

Auden knew that wasn't true, but she sensed that Gayle needed to believe it. "Well, be careful anyhow. I don't know when I'll be back."

"If there's a towel on my bedroom door, you'll know I got lucky."

"A towel?"

Gayle grinned. "Old sorority signal to tell your roommate to sleep somewhere else."

"You have got to tell me those stories," Auden replied. "Later."

"Uh-huh. Go on. Go see her."

A minute later, Auden was finally headed where she had wanted to be all evening.

❖

Auden rang the buzzer by the suite door and waited with a flurry of anxious anticipation in the pit of her stomach. Less than a minute passed before the door swung open, but it seemed like a lifetime. Then Hays stood before her in a black T-shirt and the blue jeans she had worn earlier, and the world seemed to right itself for the first time in hours. Hays's hair was wet from the shower, and her eyes were clear and bright.

"Hi," Hays said softly. She stepped back so that Auden could enter.

"Hi."

For long seconds, they merely stood and gazed at one another. The lights in the suite were muted and the curtains open. The world beyond appeared much as it had the previous evening, though the falling snow had lightened to just a dusting of white against the black night. Auden's heart hammered in her chest, and she suddenly found it difficult to swallow. Her gaze kept returning to Hays's lips, which were parted slightly, as if words had been spoken that she had not heard.

"You said...business," Auden finally managed. "You needed to talk to me about business."

"Yes." Hays hadn't moved. Was afraid to move. Because she was in danger of taking that one small step forward and pulling Auden into her arms. *God, I want to hold her.* She wanted desperately to recapture that dizzying feeling she had experienced the night before, of being so lost in that kiss, of being so *alive*. Which was why she stood rooted to the spot, the breath burning in her chest, her stomach seething with urgency. "I..." She forced herself to think. "Would you like dinner?"

"Dinner?" Auden hesitated, trying to get her mind to function and her attention away from the idea of threading her fingers into Hays's thick, wet hair. She hadn't had lunch, and the chips and beer while playing cards didn't exactly count as a meal. "Yes. All right. Here?"

"Mmm," Hays murmured, mesmerized by the way Auden's eyes

drifted over her own face, as languorous as a caress. "I'll order room service and we can...talk."

Auden drew a long breath and stepped around Hays toward the sofa. *If I don't get out of touching range, I'm going to do something to embarrass us both.*

Hays could think a little more clearly with Auden on the other side of the room, but the sudden distance produced an unexpected ache, as if some part of her had been abruptly severed. To distract herself from the way Auden looked in the tight black jeans, she walked to the desk phone and opened the room service menu that stood beside it. Eyes on the print, not seeing a thing, she asked, "Requests?"

"Ah...salad and whatever pasta entrée they have."

"Do you drink wine?"

For the first time, it occurred to Auden that she was alone in a hotel room with a woman. Not just *any* woman. A woman whom she had kissed. A woman she still *wanted* to kiss. And she had no earthly idea how she was supposed to behave. She wasn't certain she would be able to tell if Hays wanted something to happen between them. She wasn't certain how much she *herself* wanted to happen between them. A kiss was one thing, but from the way she had felt when they had kissed last night, she wasn't sure that a kiss was all she wanted. And wanting more just might be crazy.

Hays was her new boss. Hays had been the one who had said, just that morning, that the kiss wouldn't be repeated. Hays was ill, and Auden was supposed to be there to talk abou—

"Auden?"

Auden jumped. Hays smiled at her—a kind, gentle smile—and Auden's tension immediately eased. No matter what happened between them, of one thing she was suddenly very certain. It couldn't be wrong. "Yes, wine would be wonderful."

"Anything special?"

"A white burgundy if they have one."

"Done," Hays said firmly. She pressed several buttons and, after a moment, gave their order. Then she crossed the room and sat next to Auden on the sofa. "I'm going to be away from the office for a week or so."

Auden's stomach clenched. Hays looked a hundred times better than she had six hours before, but she still didn't look well. There were smudges under her eyes and the faintest of tremors in her hands. "Are you all right?"

Hays surprised herself and answered truthfully. With part of the truth, at least. "No, not quite. I've got a bit of a bug, apparently. Nothing all that serious, but it's kicked the hell out of me the last few days." She looked away for a second, then smiled softly. "I suppose Gayle told you."

"No. She wouldn't do that."

Hays nodded, relieved and at the same time a bit embarrassed. "I'm sorry, of course she wouldn't. She was great. She got the hotel manager to let me have some antibiotics from their emergency dispensary. I'm sure that will take care of it—that and a few days' rest."

"Yes," Auden agreed, knowing there was more, and knowing she was not going to learn what it was. Not that night—perhaps never. And that thought saddened her. "I'm glad you're taking a little time off. You should...take care of yourself."

Hays grimaced. "The timing is bad, what with all we have going on now with Destiny. I'm sorry about that. I won't be gone long, and you can e-mail me or call me if there's a problem."

"I'm sure there won't be any problems," Auden said, thinking that the last thing Hays needed was to be bothered with work when she obviously needed to rest. But the thought of not seeing her, even for a little while, was more distressing than Auden could have imagined. The thought of going to work and not seeing Hays's door open, knowing she wasn't just down the hall, missing the cadence of her deep voice, left Auden feeling empty. "Besides, Mr. Pritchard will be there if I have any questions."

"You can e-mail me or call me...for any reason," Hays repeated quietly.

Auden flushed, wondering how transparent her feelings really were. "I've got plenty of reading piled up, and Mr. Pritchard and I need to finalize the new appointments. Liz will be—"

"Auden," Hays murmured gently, leaning toward her but managing, just barely, to resist touching her, "I *want* to hear from you."

Remember it's the job. It's all about the job. Auden nodded briskly. "Of course. I'll be sure to keep you apprised."

"Thank you." For one insane moment, Hays wanted to tell her everything. About Rune and the illness and what she felt every time they were together. Everything. All of it. She wanted so terribly not to be alone with the pain tearing at her, but still she held back. *Tell her and everything will change. She'll never look at me the same again. And the way she looks at me is the best part of my life.*

"Hays," Auden said carefully, resting her hand on Hays's where it lay palm down on her thigh. "You're shaking."

"It's nothing." Hays's voice was gravelly, strained with the effort to sustain her silence.

"Maybe you should lie down."

"The food will be here soon."

"Just until then."

"My entertainment choices are limited," Hays warned, grinning with a semblance of her usual charm. "Can I tempt you with cable?"

"Only if it's not sports."

"Ahh, a lady with discerning tastes."

Auden smiled and took Hays's hand. "Come on. Let's watch it in the bedroom, just in case you fall asleep."

Hays's eyes widened momentarily before she caught herself, covering her surprise with a bland expression. *She's just being friendly; she's not making a pass. Still, last night...* "Okay. Sure."

They propped pillows against the headboard and reclined side by side on top of the covers in the center of the king-sized bed. Hays worked the remote until she found a classic movie channel where a black and white film was just starting. "Ah—*Rebecca*. Is this okay?"

Auden peered at the screen. "The 1940s version?"

"Yep."

"Oh, yes. I love this film. And the book."

"Me, too," Hays said as the music rose and the credits rolled. She leaned her head back and dimmed the room lights. "Your romantic side is showing, Auden."

"Didn't you think I had one?" Her tone was teasing.

"Oh, no," Hays said softly, completely serious. "I knew right away that you did."

"Did you?" Auden was captivated by the patterns of light from the screen playing over the sharp planes and angles of Hays's face.

"Uh-huh. So," Hays asked, as she settled into the pillows, "who did you want to be?"

"What?" Auden enjoyed the way Hays's profile softened as she began to relax. *You're so beautiful. Do you know?*

"When you watched this." Hays turned her head, meeting Auden's eyes. "Who did you want to be?"

"Oh, Joan Fontaine. The young Mrs. de Winter. You?"

Hays grinned. "Maxim de Winter, of course."

"Ah, the suave mysterious lover."

"Oh yeah," Hays murmured, her lids suddenly heavy. "That's me."

As Auden watched, spellbound, Hays slipped into sleep. She debated leaving, but when she started to move, Hays's eyes flickered open for an instant.

"Auden?"

"I'm right here."

Hays smiled and closed her eyes again, and when Auden got up to answer the buzz at the door, she didn't move.

Auden took care of the room-service bill and had the attendant leave the food covered on the cart in the sitting room. She stood for a long time in the doorway of the bedroom watching Hays sleep. Then she carefully covered her with a corner of the bedspread. It was close to midnight when she left.

❖

Auden returned to her suite and entered the sitting room just in time to see George Clooney shoot what looked like a harpoon into Cheech Marin's chest. She stopped dead and stared at the television, unable to make sense of what she saw. "What in God's name are you watching?"

Gayle looked over from where she was curled up on the sofa with a bag of potato chips in her lap. "*From Dusk Till Dawn.* It's this really great vampire cops and robbers movie."

"Looks disgusting."

"Yeah." Gayle grinned, her eyes dancing. "I've seen it four times."

"Doctors. Strange bunch." Auden collapsed with a sigh next to Gayle and put her hand into the bag of potato chips. "No towel on the doorknob?"

"Nope. Another night flying solo."

"Should I ask what happened?"

"No big deal." Gayle stared straight ahead. "Thane left a few minutes after you did—again. That's a pretty clear message, I guess." She sighed and reached for the bottle of beer beside her on the end table. "Liz and I hung out for a while, talking and watching the tube. Then we got to the point where we were either going to have to go to bed together or call it a night. We called it a night."

"I'm curious," Auden said as she watched Harvey Keitel morph into some sort of drooling monster, "as to why you're turning Liz down. She's really good looking, and she's smart, and I get the sense that she's really attracted to you."

"I don't know, exactly," Gayle replied pensively. "She's terrific. And she's hot. And I like her. I just don't want to sleep with her."

"Is it because you don't have an emotional connection with her?"

"Have you forgotten who you're talking to?" Gayle gave Auden a quick glance and grinned unself-consciously. "You've seen me drag home enough near-strangers over the last seven years to know that sometimes the only thing it's about is sex."

"But not this time."

"No," Gayle said softly. "Not this time. I guess maybe it's because Thane and Liz are friends. And if I sleep with Liz, I'll never be able to have anything with Thane. Even I'm not that incestuous."

"Why Thane and not Liz?"

Gayle shrugged her shoulders. "I don't know, Aud. I really don't. Do you think anyone does, really? We give all kinds of reasons why we want one person and not another, and why we're attracted to someone. But maybe in the end, it's just a matter of timing and circumstances. Or hell, I don't know, maybe fate."

"Maybe," Auden said, as she leaned her head back against the sofa to watch the vampires surround George Clooney and Juliette Lewis, thinking that perhaps destiny was the answer, after all.

CHAPTER SIXTEEN

Hays woke a little after five a.m. She lay on her side, still in her clothes. Before anything else, she reached out a hand, but the bed beside her was empty. She had known it would be, but for just an instant, she had hoped.

The room was dark, the day not yet dawned. She ran her fingers lightly over the pillow next to her, trying to feel the depression where Auden's head had rested. The crisp cotton was cool, and there was no trace of her that lingered, not even the subtle scent of her. That absence struck Hays as crueler than anything she could remember feeling since she had learned almost eight months before that she was very likely dying.

Such a simple thing to miss—the sense of a woman next to you in the night. She hadn't realized just how much she had missed it until she had fallen asleep with the comfort of Auden by her side. Being near Auden reminded her of many things that she missed and had not thought to experience again.

Hays rolled onto her back and stared at the ceiling. Their kiss felt like an isolated moment out of time, born of unusual circumstances during a fairy-tale weekend when reason had been suspended. It had been perfect, and perhaps that was the most it could ever be. Even had she been less uncertain of her future, it was possible, even likely, that Auden's interests lay elsewhere. And common sense told her that any kind of involvement with Auden was impossible, even if Auden *was* interested.

"And it really doesn't matter, because I can't get involved. Not now." She swung her legs off the side of the bed and waited for the inevitable dizziness to pass. Then she made her way to the bathroom and stripped off her clothes, all the while trying to put the memory of Auden's soft voice, reassuring her as she fell asleep, from her mind. She couldn't remember Auden's soothing words, only the sense of rightness she had experienced stretching out next to Auden on the bed. Auden. Auden's voice in the dark, Auden's hand on hers, Auden's mouth—

"Stop it, for Christ's sake." Her voice bounced harshly off the tile walls.

To prevent further reminiscences, she concentrated on the arrangements that needed to be made. A car—she needed to make sure Abel had arranged for a car. Frowning, she examined the trousers she had hung over a hanger on the shower door the night before. Good. Most of the wrinkles appeared to have worked their way out. She had another clean T-shirt that Abel had purchased for her, so she'd have reasonably fresh clothes for the morning.

No matter how she tried to distract herself with the details of the day, as she turned on the shower and waited for the water to get hot, she was still thinking about Auden—about her smile, her gentle strength, her tender comfort. When she stepped into the heat, she was imagining what it would have been like had they truly slept together and awakened side by side. They would be together now.

The water sluicing over her body brought the blood coursing to the surface of her skin, and she felt the rush of stimulation as her capillaries opened, her skin tingling as from a caress. In her mind, she saw Auden reach out to stroke her, and she gasped as her nipples hardened under the needles of heat dancing down her body. Eyes closed, she leaned her shoulders against the wall as the fine spray beat against her breasts and abdomen, heightening the need that had never quite left her since the moment she and Auden had kissed. She remembered the pressure of Auden's palms on her thighs as they'd leaned into one another, and, pressing her palms flat against the wall, she tilted her hips forward enough to allow the fingers of water to stoke her arousal as they struck rhythmically between her legs.

She was back in that still room, Auden's lips against her mouth. She could taste her now, in her mouth, as the blood and vessels in her thighs tightened under the relentless beat of the pulsing spray. Her stomach tensed, the muscles contracting as the excitement feathered down her spine and coiled deep inside. Moaning softly, she arched her neck, arms braced by her sides, feeling the touch of knowing hands claim her turgid flesh.

Yes, there. Touch me there, like that. Don't be gentle, not now. I want to feel you everywhere...yes, yes, there...

Seconds from climaxing, Hays forced her lids open, blinking into the streaming water, needing to see those tender eyes as she came. For an instant, as she trembled with the first wave of orgasm, she did.

"Oh God, Auden."

Strength fading, she slid down the wall, shuddering as the final spasms rocketed through her. She wrapped her arms around her bent legs and rested her head on her knees, gasping. The moisture on her face was not from the water that continued to beat on her head and back.

Oh God, Auden.

❖

Thirty minutes later, dressed and once more in control, Hays used her room card to let herself into the business center. As she had expected, she was alone. Within seconds, she was logged on and checking her e-mail.

```
-----Original Message-----
From: thaneCutlass@CutlassFic.com
Sent: Monday March 24, 12:33 AM
To: Rune@HeartLand.com
Subject: Weekend Update and Business
```

Rune:

You've been quiet this weekend, friend. I know you're in the Northeast, so you're probably getting hammered by the same storm that has me snowed in here in Philadelphia. You probably aren't enjoying the kind of weekend I've had, though. Palmer put us all up at the Four Seasons, and it's been one hell of a fun time.

Unfortunately, I haven't had time to write much. I've been too busy socializing

with Destiny's new director along with Liz
and another friend. Pretty tough being
snowbound with beautiful women <g>. Don't
worry, though, I've definitely been inspired
by the last few days, and I should have
something new soon. Nothing like unrequited
lust to stoke the fires.

I'll be back in Philadelphia next weekend,
because I've got a date to go dancing with
Auden, her friend Gayle, and Liz. Rough
duty, huh? What I won't do to further our
cause <g>

Seriously now, friend, when can I expect
to see something from you for Eros? I know
what you said, but I know what you're like
when you're first getting into something new.
You never think anything you're writing is
decent. So send it to me. You know I'll tell
you the truth.

Thane

Hays reread the message, focusing on one line.

I'll be back in Philadelphia next weekend,
because I've got a date to go dancing with
Auden, her friend Gayle, and Liz.

Auden. First-name basis. Well, it's not like that's a surprise.
Hays almost didn't reply. But she had to. What had happened the
morning before was a warning she couldn't deny. She might be out of
time, and there were things left undone.

-----Reply-----
From: Rune@HeartLand.com
Sent: Monday March 24, 6:38 AM
To: thaneCutlass@CutlassFic.com
Subject: re: Business

Thane-

I'll send what I've done so far for Eros
later today. I'm not promising I'll let it
stand for the anthology, but you should
have a look at it.
There are some things we need to discuss
face-to-face. I'll email you later this week,
and maybe we can get together on Saturday
in Philadelphia. I'm not completely certain
I'll be able to make it next weekend, but
I'll try.
I'll be off-line intermittently during the
week, so don't worry if it takes me a while
to get back to you.

Rune

Hays clicked Send before she could change her mind. She had tried for so long to keep her writing, that most private part of her life—of herself—untouched by the vagaries and inconsistencies and small betrayals of daily life. But she couldn't any longer. Thane deserved to know, after all they had been to one another. *And if Thane is dating Auden, she'll find out soon anyway...Thane and Auden...*

She couldn't deal with that thought, not today, not after the previous evening with Auden, or the morning. But there were truths she had to face now—her world was getting smaller and her secrets too difficult to keep.

❖

Auden picked up the receiver on the first ring. "Hello?...Hi." She turned her back to Gayle, who was stretched out on the sofa cradling a cup that held the last of their morning coffee. "How are you? Good, that's good...We're waiting to see if we can get a cab...No, that's not necessary. Really...I...all right, of course. Thank you."

When she put down the phone, she found Gayle regarding her

with a questioning look. "That was Hays. She said there'll be a limo here in an hour to take us home."

"Ooh, I do like that woman. Besides being drop-dead gorgeous, she makes things happen."

"Yes," Auden replied, thinking that Hays had sounded even more reserved than usual.

"Speaking of making things happen," Gayle continued as she sat up and put her coffee cup down on the room-service cart, "what's going on with you and her?"

"Nothing is going on," Auden replied, leaning against the desk.

"Huh. Do you want it to?" Gayle's voice was soft, her eyes kind.

Auden hesitated for a moment, then nodded. "Yes, I do. Very much."

"Does she know?"

Auden shook her head.

"Letting a woman know you're interested is generally a good first step, Aud."

As they spoke, they both gathered the odds and ends of their personal belongings scattered about the room.

"How?" Auden asked. "How do I do that?"

Gayle laughed. "It's a matter of style, I guess."

"I don't *have* any kind of style."

"Oh yes, you do." Gayle took Auden's arm and turned her friend to face her. "You're honest and straightforward and sincere."

"Wonderful." Auden made a face. "I sound like a Girl Scout."

"So?"

"Not very sexy."

"You really don't know, do you?" Gayle commented with a note of awe in her voice.

"What?" Auden placed her folded clothes into a plastic bag with the hotel logo on it.

How goddamned sexy you are. Gayle sighed. "How sexy trust can be. Listen, honey, when the time is right, and you'll *know* when that is, just tell her how you feel."

"You make it sound so easy," Auden said wistfully.

"Uh-uh. It isn't. It's the hardest thing in the world, laying yourself open like that, but I can't see you doing it any other way."

Auden pictured Hays falling asleep beside her and felt again how right that moment had seemed. She wondered if she'd really be brave enough to take the chance, if ever the right time came.

❖

Abel Pritchard, Auden, Gayle, and Hays sat in uneasy silence throughout the fifteen-block ride from the hotel to Auden and Gayle's street. Even in a Hummer limo, a ridiculous lumbering monstrosity of urban chic transportation, it had taken forty-five minutes to navigate the narrow unplowed streets, many of which were blocked by abandoned cars or impassable drifts. The vehicle couldn't maneuver down the single lane of St. James Place, so it just stopped in the middle of the cross street to allow Auden and Gayle to climb out.

"Can you make it?" Hays asked with a frown, stepping out into the snow with no concern for her dress shoes. Auden and Gayle had purchased rain covers from the hotel gift shop in some hopes of protecting theirs.

"We'll be fine," Auden assured her. It was clear from the look on Hays's face that she intended to come with them. Although Hays seemed fine, Auden found her a little too flushed. *She has a fever.*

Gayle plowed a few feet ahead, purposely leaving Auden and Hays alone.

"Will you call?" Auden hadn't intended to ask, but suddenly faced with the prospect of not seeing Hays for days, she couldn't stop herself.

"If I can," Hays murmured. "You'll e-mail or leave a message, if you need...anything?"

"Yes, all right." Auden knew she had to go. Hays wore only her suit jacket, and she was starting to shiver. "Please, take care of yourself."

A simple request. One she'd heard so many times in the last months. For the first time, Hays considered it seriously. "Yes. I'll do that."

They regarded one another silently for another moment, gusts of snow swirling from the drifts around them.

"You should go, Hays."

"I know." She didn't move.

Auden smiled softly, touched Hays's uncovered hand with her own bare fingers, then turned resolutely away. When she joined Gayle and looked back, the oversized vehicle had already started off down the street.

"You okay?" Gayle linked her arm through Auden's.

"Just sad."

"How come?"

Together, they forged a narrow path through the three feet of untouched snow.

"I feel as if I'll never see her again."

Gayle was quiet for a long time. Finally, she said, "Sure you will."

Auden glanced at her, struck by something she'd never heard in Gayle's voice before. Uncertainty. She didn't ask about its source, because she had a feeling it was a question that Gayle would not be able to answer.

❖

Gayle stopped by Auden's apartment at five p.m. before leaving for her shift. "God, what I wouldn't give to have that Hummer right now."

"How are you going to get to the hospital?"

"I'm walking to the Market Street El, and then I'll catch the Broad Street subway to Temple. The stop is right in front of the hospital. It should be okay."

"Call me later?" Auden had changed into a flannel shirt and baggy, threadbare jeans. "I'll be up. I've got plenty to read."

Gayle, in jeans and work boots, leaned against the doorway with her hands in the pockets of her leather jacket. "Anything good?"

"I think so. Different anyway. I'm still working on Rune Dyre's *Dark Passions.*"

"Ooh, that is so hot. I wish I were staying home all nice and cozy reading that, instead of shlepping off into the snow. Of course, after meeting Thane, I think I might reread one of hers." Gayle grinned. "Spending time with her puts a whole new light on the subject."

"You think so?" Auden asked, intrigued.

"Oh yeah. Now when I read one of her books, I'll be able to imagine her in the characters."

"In the characters? Or in bed?"

"Jeez, that's kinda personal, Aud." When Auden merely snorted, Gayle said, "It would be hard *not* to see her in the story, don't you think?"

"Do you think she's writing herself then?"

Gayle looked pensive. "Maybe not entirely. She *is* as smooth and sexy as any of her characters, but in the flesh, she's a little more... sensitive. In fact, she has a shy streak I never would have expected. That's pretty sexy in itself."

"You think pretty much *everything* about Thane is sexy," Auden jibed.

"Yeah, well. Maybe." Gayle shrugged good-naturedly. "Ah well, enjoy *Dark Passions* while I'm off working away. I'll talk to you later."

"Night. Be careful."

❖

Alone in her living room, Auden started a log burning in the fireplace and curled up in the old leather armchair with a glass of wine. She wasn't sure she'd be able to read. Her thoughts kept drifting back to Hays. How Hays's mouth had felt when they'd kissed, how Hays had looked falling asleep, how Hays had sounded when they'd said goodbye.

Auden's eyes turned to the pages, and as she read, she fell prey to the power of Rune Dyre's magic.

She got the fire going easily and settled herself into a comfortable leather chair. She was amazed at how relaxed she felt, and how unconcerned she was at being there. For once, she didn't have to do anything. She liked the change.

Kyle came in quietly and handed her a glass. "Brandy okay?"

Nodding silently, Dane took the heavy glass filled with dark, swirling liquid. Kyle settled herself in front of Dane on a large cushion on the floor, her back lightly resting against Dane's knee.

Auden looked up automatically at the sound of a log falling in the fireplace, absently watching the sparks dance to their death. Barely aware of the interruption, she shifted, curled her legs closer beneath her, and returned to read from the beginning of the scene.

> Auden got the fire going easily and settled herself into a comfortable leather chair. She was amazed at how relaxed she felt, and how unconcerned she was at being there. For once, she didn't have to do anything. She liked the change.
>
> Hays came in quietly and handed her a glass. "Brandy okay?"
>
> Nodding silently, Auden took the heavy glass filled with dark, swirling liquid. Hays settled in front of her on a large cushion on the floor, her back lightly resting against Auden's knee.
>
> "As soon as I unwind a little, I'll fix us some food. Hope you like simple cooking," Hays said as she stretched her legs toward the warmth of the fire.
>
> "No rush." Auden looked down at Hays's face in profile. The dancing flames made little changing patterns of shadow across her boldly planed face, blending softly into the waves of her tousled hair. "I like the fire."
>
> Hays nodded and settled a little more firmly against Auden's leg. "I'm glad you came."
>
> "Are you?" Auden murmured, mesmerized by the reddish glow of the fire and the warmth of Hays's back against her leg.
>
> "Uh-huh." Hays reached up and curled an arm softly over Auden's thigh.
>
> Auden stretched her legs a little and Hays pushed closer, her head coming to rest gently against Auden's inner thigh. Auden reached down almost without thinking and curled her fingers softly into Hays's thick hair, then leaned her head back against the worn leather and closed her eyes. She might have drifted for a while in the soothing heat from the fire and the

warmth of Hays's body against her. She was startled to feel a soft caress on her neck, and when she opened her eyes, she found Hays kneeling upright between her legs, looking down at her.

"Did I wake you?"

Auden smiled, not moving. "Wasn't sleeping. Just drifting."

"Good." Hays smiled gently then also. "Close your eyes again."

Auden did as Hays requested, feeling as if she were hypnotized. Hays's hands gently traced her face and throat, warming her wherever they touched. When Hays leaned forward as she stroked Auden's face, the heat from Hays's body penetrated the denim covering Auden's thighs. Auden stopped herself from reaching out to draw Hays closer. So exquisite was the slow rise of her desire, she didn't want to hurry. Still, when Hays tugged Auden's shirt free and gently loosened the buttons over her breasts, Auden couldn't prevent herself from sliding her hands along Hays's hips to pull her near. Auden wanted, needed, more of her. She opened her eyes to see Hays's gaze upon her, cloudy with desire.

Smiling slightly, Hays shook her head. "Uh-uh. Keep your eyes closed."

Auden stared at her for an instant, knowing her need must show clearly in her face. Not caring that Hays could see how much she wanted her, she did as she was bidden. She wouldn't have done it for anyone else. There was no one she trusted that much.

Gently, Hays pushed the shirt down Auden's shoulders, tethering her arms in the tightly stretched sleeves. Auden knew she could free herself if she tried, but the effect of being restrained was not unwelcome. She wanted to be hers.

"Ohh." Auden moaned as Hays brought her lips softly to an exposed breast. Auden's head grew light as Hays's tongue ignited the sensitive skin of her nipple. She arched her back as she tried to push more of herself against the warm mouth. Even as Hays's lips worked her nipples, Auden felt a hand pull open the buttons on her jeans. She lay quiet, holding her breath, as Hays slipped an arm under her to push down her clothing. The warmth of the fire caressed Auden's bare thighs as Hays once again lay gently down upon her.

The denim of Hays's jeans was rough against Auden's skin, and as Hays insinuated herself more firmly between Auden's legs, Auden gasped at the contact of the material against her swollen flesh. She couldn't prevent herself from pressing closer, seeking even more contact. A cry escaped her, and Hays quickly pulled away, breaking the exquisitely tormenting pressure.

"What is it?" Hays gasped.

"Oh God, Hays, don't stop." She needed Hays's touch; more, she needed Hays to release her. When she started to lift her head, Hays held her back with one hand firmly in the hair at the base of her neck.

"Wait, Auden—wait," Hays whispered as she carefully slipped her free hand between Auden's legs.

Auden cried out again, strangling on her own desire, as Hays's fingers, feather light, stroked her, drawing Auden's passion forth in a flood upon her hand.

"I can't. Oh, please, I can't." Auden moaned, her hips writhing, urgently seeking to bring Hays inside. Auden's breath caught in her throat as Hays entered her fully, the weight of Hays's body bearing down upon her. She sought Hays's kiss hungrily, and Hays filled her mouth as deeply as she filled her body. Auden clung to her as both mind and body exploded.

When Auden's breathing quieted and her body ceased to quiver, Hays gently slipped free, drawing forth another soft moan. She rested her head on Auden's chest and sighed contentedly. Auden pulled her arms free of the shirt sleeves and held Hays tightly, keeping her warm, keeping her safe. They lay together wordlessly until long after the fire had burned down.

With a start, Auden blinked unfocused eyes and looked around in confusion, stunned to find herself alone. She stared in confusion at the book in her hands, expecting the warmth of a woman. Gasping, she fixed on what she had just read. *Kyle and Dane. Kyle and Dane. Not Hays and...*

Shivering, she stared across the room at the dying embers. She was chilled, but her skin was hot, her blood racing. She held the pages in trembling hands. It had been so very real, and it was so very clear what she wanted. What she needed.

"Oh my God," she whispered. "Hays."

❖

Gayle climbed the stairs out of the subway tunnel and made her way toward the emergency room entrance of Temple University Hospital. There were few people out and even fewer vehicles. The Hummer limo that slid to a stop across the street in the emergency room turnaround would have been impossible to miss, even if she hadn't recognized it. Gayle stopped and watched as the rear door opened and two people stepped out. Abel Pritchard carried a suitcase. Haydon Palmer had a slim briefcase in her right hand. Gayle waited until they made their way inside the hospital. Hays deserved her privacy.

"Oh, Auden. Honey. Please don't fall for her."

As she made her way through the snow, Gayle tried to pretend it was possible to dictate matters of the heart.

CHAPTER SEVENTEEN

The first few days of the workweek were hectic, and Auden was grateful for the distraction. It was impossible for her not to wonder where Hays was and if she was all right. Still, her schedule was crowded with last-minute interviews for Destiny's few unfilled positions, meetings with new division members, and manuscript reviews. She had only intermittent moments free to worry.

Late Thursday morning, Liz Nixon appeared at her open office door, a big grin on her face. "Reporting for duty, ma'am."

Smiling as well, Auden got up from behind her desk and came around to greet Liz. She gestured to the sitting area off to one side. "Sit down. It's great to see you."

"It's great to get started. I've got some ideas."

"I certainly hoped that you would." Auden reached for one of the pads of paper lying on the coffee table in front of them, settled it on her knees, and took the pen from her shirt pocket. "Is it something you want to get into now, or would you rather wait for a time when I can get the other members of the division together?"

"Some of it should wait until we can talk to everyone, including Hays, I would imagine. For now, though, I wanted to remind you that the next big convention is coming up in just a little over two weeks."

"Yes, I know. The one in New York."

"And we're going to be there, right?"

"Yes. Once you're fairly settled, I thought I'd let you and your people handle the promotional aspects. I want to be there, of course." She hesitated. "I'm not sure if Hays or Pritchard will be interested. I'll check on that."

"I think we need to do more than just hand out media packets. I think we need to show up with a new Destiny publication."

Auden laughed out loud. "I think you're absolutely right. And it's absolutely impossible. There's no way."

"What about Margo Elliot's *Pale Imitations*? That was almost completely edited when we cut back on production at WomenWords. It shouldn't take much to get it ready for typesetting."

"Even if I pressed Margo for final edits, we don't have a cover. I might be able to pull one of the graphic artists to work on that, but it's pretty short notice." Auden ran rapidly through the list of things to be done in order to get the first title out. "I haven't even seen the production specs yet. I don't know if anyone's available to typeset, or how much lead time I need."

Silent, Liz waited, a faint smile on her face as she watched Auden check off points on the pad. Auden's eyes were bright, her expression intense.

"Besides, we haven't done any advance promos. We'd be walking into the convention cold."

"We don't need a national launch campaign at this point, although I'll have something cooking on that soon, too." Liz appeared confident and unruffled. "I've got connections with half a dozen Internet groups that would have the word out in less than twenty-four hours that Margo's new release will be available at the convention. We don't have to worry about promoting to retailers yet, because we'll be hitting a key segment of the grass-roots buying population directly via the Internet. We can worry about mass marketing later."

"I'm worried we might be a bit premature." Auden's tone was contemplative as she studied her list yet again. "There are other conventions later in the year, and by then, we'll have had an opportunity to advertise."

"Margo Elliot has a solid following. Her name is known. We can capitalize on that at this convention to introduce ourselves. After all, at this point in time, it's the author recognition that's going to carry us."

Auden stood, pacing quietly. Finally, she turned to Liz. "You're the marketing director. If you think it's that advantageous, I'll go e-mail Hays right now."

Liz quirked an eyebrow. "Have you heard anything from her?"

"No." She hadn't wanted to intrude on Hays's personal time. Nevertheless, she was grateful for a legitimate reason to contact her.

Any kind of communication would set her mind at ease. "I'll get back to you just as soon as I can."

"Thanks. I'll be in my office, as soon as the lovely Alana shows me where it is."

Auden smiled, but her mind was already on her e-mail.

❖

Hays awoke from an unplanned nap feeling refreshed. She hadn't meant to fall asleep in the middle of the day, but she had to admit she felt better. In fact, her headache had finally resolved, and she could read without any blurred vision. She felt terrific and she wanted to go home. She wanted to make the weekend meeting with Thane, and more than that, she wanted to get back to work. Mostly, she wanted to see Auden.

And none of those things was going to happen unless she could talk her hematologist into discharging her. And knowing Paul Rosenberg as she did, she wasn't counting on it.

The doctor's words from just that morning still rang in her mind.

"Out of the question."

"Paul, I feel fine. Let me out of here."

"You need a full course of antibiotics. Your white count is still well above normal."

"But the temp is down."

He ignored her. "And you still might need another transfusion."

"No more blood." She was adamant. "We agreed we'd keep that to a minimum. Emergencies only."

"This was an emergency. Hays, you were so anemic you could have had a stroke or an MI. If you'd been older, you probably would have."

"Yeah, well, getting someone else's blood is a risk, too."

He shook his head, clearly aggravated. "The risk of contamination is practically nil, and the likelihood of blood-borne infection is one in 60,000 or better. A hell of a lot lower than the risk you're running every time you let things get this out of hand."

"And there's going to come a time when I can't tolerate the

transfusions without liver damage." She looked away. There's going to be a time when I don't have any choices left.

"You're nowhere near that point. But this infection could have killed you in the state you were in."

"But it didn't."

"You almost waited too long this time. You've been playing the odds far longer than anyone should. You'll lose one of these days." His irritation, as well as his affection, was clear in his tone.

"Everything about this goddamned disease is odds. Odds and percentages, risk versus benefits."

"I agree. And I've agreed to be conservative with your treatment for as long as I can. But you're making this harder than it has to be."

She laughed hollowly. *"Do you really think that's possible?"*

"No," he sighed. *"I'm sorry. But I can't let you go yet."*

"The weekend?"

"If your temp is normal and your hemoglobin holds up."

"Deal."

Sighing with helplessness and frustration, she swung the bedside table into place, opened the laptop that sat on the narrow surface, and plugged a line into the bedside phone. Then she dialed up an Internet server, opened her e-mail program, and quickly scanned the messages. She stopped at one, her heart pounding.

God, how can just seeing her name do this to me?

It was the one thing in her life she couldn't deny. She liked the feeling—the quick surge of excitement, the expectation, the edgy pleasure in her stomach. Even her skin was tingling. Hands shaking, she clicked on the message.

```
-----Original Message-----
From: AFrost@PalmPub.net
Sent: Thursday March 27, 2:05 PM
To: HPalmer@PalmPub.net
Subject: Publication Prospectus: Pale
Imitations
Attachment: Datelines - PI 21kb
```

Hays:

I hope this finds you well. Forgive me for bringing up business, but I don't want to go ahead with this without your okay.

Liz feels strongly that Destiny should promote its first title at the Manhattan book convention April 11th. Pale Imitations is in final edits (I'm waiting on Margo's last review) and should be ready to typeset soon.

I'd like to try to get it out if you think it's doable. What do you think?

I've enclosed a production schedule if it's a go. I'll be here until 9 or so tonight.

Auden

Hays grinned as she opened the attachment and scanned the file. She made a few comments, then returned to her mail program. *Abel is going to have a heart attack.*

-----Reply-----
From: HPalmer@PalmPub.net
Sent: Thursday March 27, 4:55 PM
To: AFrost@PalmPub.net
Subject: re: Publication Prospectus: Pale Imitations
Attachment: Revised Dateline - PI 22kb

Auden:

Liz has good instincts. I'd go with them.

I made a few changes on your preliminary schedule. You'll probably need another day at least for binding, but you can make up some time if you get the covers run ASAP.

Pull Nancy Baker from graphics and tell her
what you need. I'd like to see the image
before you give final approval.

Set Liz up with Ralph Aiello, who's
been doing the media promos for the other
divisions. She'll need him to get plugged
into our advertising accounts.

Best talk to Abel soon - there's going to
be overtime involved.

I'll be back Monday. Let me know how
things are going.

Hays

Leaning back against the pillows, Hays closed her eyes. *Rosenberg's
worries be damned. I'm out of here this weekend.*

❖

Auden smiled as she read the e-mail for the third time.
I'll be back Monday.
Suddenly energized despite the fact that it was after ten and she'd
been in the office since seven that morning, Auden began jotting notes
about the things she needed to discuss with Liz, thankful that her new
administrative assistant was starting in the morning. *I'll need to call—*
"Ms. Frost?"
Auden jumped in surprise and looked toward her open door. "Mr.
Pritchard!"
"Working late." It was a statement.
"Yes. Come in, please."
He walked a few feet into the room and regarded her thoughtfully.
"Getting Elliot's book ready to go?"
"Ah, news travels quickly. I'm sorry, I should have called you
earlier today, but by the time I got to it, it was later than I—"
He held up a hand, and he actually seemed to smile, for perhaps a
second. "I understand. Hays filled me in."
"You've seen her?" Auden asked before she could stop herself.
Again the contemplative look. "Yes."

Auden blushed. *Is she all right?*

Pritchard continued smoothly, "She said you had a workable production schedule. It's an ambitious undertaking at this stage, as I'm sure you must realize."

"The worst that can happen is that we won't make the deadline," she pointed out mildly. *And I'll be guilty of making a disastrous decision my first month out.*

"No," he countered quietly, "the worst that can happen is that you'll cut corners to make the deadline and produce an inferior product."

Auden leaned forward, her eyes on his. "That will not happen, Mr. Pritchard. I will not sacrifice Destiny's reputation for the sake of my own."

He was silent, as if weighing her words, then nodded. "You should call me Abel."

A smile flickered on Auden's lips. "Thank you."

"I've had some practice at this, so if you need help..."

"You'll be the first to know."

He nodded again, then turned to go.

"Mr. Pritchard...Abel?"

He looked back.

"How is she?"

For a long moment, she thought that he would not answer. He studied her, as he did so often, and she waited, unflinching under his steely gaze.

"She's better."

Auden relaxed, the tension ebbing from her body. "Good."

"Yes," he whispered as he turned to go. "Yes, it is."

Smiling, Auden swiveled to her computer, planning to shut it down for the night. She saw the mail icon on the task bar and checked her e-mail.

```
-----Original Message-----
From: HPalmer@PalmPub.net
Sent: Thursday March 27, 9:35 PM
To: AFrost@PalmPub.net
Subject: Warning—Incoming

Auden:
```

    You might want to take cover. Abel is
headed your way with fire in his eyes <g>
    Seriously, he'll want to go over things
with you soon, so I thought you'd want to
be prepared.
Good luck.

Hays

Auden hit Reply.

❖

```
-----Reply-----
From: AFrost@PalmPub.net
Sent: Thursday March 27, 10:55 PM
To: HPalmer@PalmPub.net
Subject: Status report
```

Hays:

    All is well. No shots fired. Truce
declared.

    See you soon.

A.

In a private room on the upper floor of Temple University Hospital, Hays read the message by the dim light of the computer screen and laughed out loud. *Yes, soon.*

Across town, Auden extinguished the lights in her office and walked down the silent corridor toward the elevators. *Good night, Hays. Sweet dreams.*

CHAPTER EIGHTEEN

I'd really rather pass," Auden repeated, a hint of desperation in her voice.

"You can't back out now." Gayle applied a dab of scent to the hollow at the base of her throat and regarded her friend's reflection in the mirror. She'd bet Auden had no idea how hot she looked in black pants and a close-fitting, pale green sweater a shade lighter than her eyes. "I can't handle both of them."

"Sure you could."

Gayle turned, hands on her hips. "Okay, let's get something straight. I definitely kiss on the first date. I even occasionally screw on the first date. I do *not* do threesomes." She paused, looked thoughtful. "Although with Thane and Liz..."

"I didn't mean in bed!" Auden laughed. "I just meant, you know, entertaining them."

"You're coming with me."

"I'm nervous," Auden said quietly.

Gayle stopped in mid-motion, her leather jacket in her hand. "About what?"

"I don't know." Auden shrugged. "Of what...people...are thinking about me."

"You mean Thane and Liz?" Gayle crossed to Auden and put her hand on her friend's arm. "What do you think they're thinking?"

"They expect me to know things." Auden looked away, embarrassed. "About being a lesbian. About...sex."

"Ah." Gayle slipped her arm around Auden's waist and hugged her. "It's hardly mysterious. And nothing you don't already know about."

"In theory."

"So that's it. It's the inexperience part you're feeling shy about?"

Auden made a wry face. "You said yourself that no one my age—"

"Oh, honey. You don't really *listen* to me when I'm teasing you, do you?" Gayle rested her forehead on Auden's. "It's fine that you've waited. In fact, it's beautiful. And no one needs to know, except maybe Ms. Right. And not even her, if you don't want to tell her."

"Still," Auden protested, "they must assume—"

"That you're a lesbian because you and I are friends?"

"No," Auden said with a hint of asperity. "That I'm a lesbian and I've probably been on at least *one* date."

Gayle laughed. "Okay, yes, most likely they do. So let them. You weren't uncomfortable with them when we played cards, were you?"

"No."

"This won't be any different. You don't have to do a damn thing you don't want to do. And if either of them pressures you—about anything—I'll make them pay."

Auden relaxed infinitesimally. "I'm sort of looking forward to it, but I'm not—you know—interested in anything else with either of them. I don't want to give the wrong impression."

"You're sure?" Gayle quirked a brow. "If, say...Thane were to ask you..." She fell silent as Auden shook her head, and Gayle found herself conflicted. As much as she was attracted to Thane herself, she almost wished that Auden were, too. She couldn't help but remember Hays walking into the hospital earlier in the week. Although she hadn't checked the publisher's hospital records, honestly couldn't bring herself to pry, she knew that Hays was still an inpatient as of that morning. And she knew what was wrong; Hays had told her about it after she'd collapsed in the hotel. "Is it because of Hays?"

"Yes."

"You're sure?"

Auden nodded.

"Well, then," Gayle said brightly, "I'm going to make a play for Lothario Cutlass tonight."

"What about Liz?" Auden was relieved to have Gayle focus on someone other than Hays. She didn't want to talk about Hays when just *thinking* about her brought up all sorts of unanswered questions and fears.

"Liz and I already crossed that bridge." Gayle shrugged into her leathers. "Friends, not lovers. Now come on, let's go meet those good-looking women and have some fun."

As Auden followed Gayle downstairs, she thought longingly of her comfortable chair, a warm fire, a glass of wine, a good book filled with good-looking women, and a chance to dream. She thought, too, that in a day and half, she'd see Hays.

❖

Thane worked by the light of the small desk lamp in the unfamiliar living room. She'd lain awake for a long time, and finally, she'd risen and made her way carefully to the computer tucked into the corner. It had been running and connected to the Internet. She'd written steadily for over an hour, then checked her e-mail. There was a new message from Rune that had come in at just after two a.m.

Guess I'm not the only one who can't sleep. She scanned the message and felt a thrill of excitement.

        -----Original Message-----
From: Rune@HeartLand.com
Sent: Sunday March 30, 2:12 AM
To: thaneCutlass@CutlassFic.com
Subject: Possible Meeting

Thane-

    If you're free today, how about I buy you
lunch at the Striped Bass at 11:30?
    We have a lot to talk about,

Rune

Thane typed her response, and, after a second's hesitation, added an attachment.

"Everything okay?"

The soft voice from behind her and the gentle fingers on her neck made her smile. Looking over her shoulder at the beautiful woman,

Thane was uncharacteristically at a loss for the words to describe just how good she felt. "Everything is...great." She gestured to the computer. "Sorry. Do you mind? I swear I wasn't snooping."

"Not at all. And you don't need to ask to use the telephone either."

"Okay." Thane was having trouble thinking about much except the way those liquid eyes drifted slowly over her face. The promise of a touch. Better, almost, than a caress. Swiveling suddenly on the chair, she reached out and took the woman, who was clad only in a long T-shirt, into her arms, settling her onto her lap. "I didn't mean to wake you. I just couldn't sleep."

"Couch too lumpy?"

"Soft as a cloud."

"Liar. You must write fiction." She laughed and threaded her arms around Thane's neck. "You *could* come sleep with me."

"I wouldn't sleep."

"That would be okay."

"That would be better than okay," Thane murmured, rubbing her cheek against the hard nipple beneath the thin cotton. "But maybe not just yet."

"Why not?" Unerring fingers slid into Thane's hair and massaged the sensitive places at the base of her neck. "We're adults. And just in case you hadn't noticed, we're both...interested."

"Oh, believe me. I noticed." Thane drew a shaky breath, her insides flooding with instant desire. "You said something last night... while we were...kissing."

"Did I?" Warm lips moved over Thane's ear, a tongue slipped along the inner rim, making her groan. "I can't remember *saying* much of anything."

"You said—oh, Christ...that feels good."

Laughter again, throaty and low.

"You said," Thane tried again despite the fact that her head was swimming, "that you wanted to have more than a one-nighter."

"Mmm. And?" Lips brushed Thane's mouth, sucked on her lower lip lightly.

"I want..." Thane pulled her head back, barely able to focus, and cleared her throat. "You have to stop that."

"Why?" Curious, concerned eyes searched hers. "What's wrong?"

"You're going to make me...embarrass myself here." Thane's chest was heaving. "I'm too ready...already...for this kind of teasing."

"God." A soft moan. "You are so, so sexy. Just knowing you're that close makes me crazy."

"I don't want to ruin my reputation by firing off too fast." Thane tightened her hold, brushed a kiss along the undersurface of the most beautiful jaw she'd ever seen. "At least not the first time."

"Ah, but who's to know? And trust me—" The kiss was deep, demanding. "*I* won't mind a bit."

Finally, Thane drew away and ran a finger over the sensuous mouth, swollen now with arousal. "I want to start this off right. Slow."

"You're serious?" Surprise now, and wonder.

"Yes," Thane whispered. "I want you to have what you want."

❖

```
-----Reply-----
From: thaneCutlass@CutlassFic.com
Sent: Sunday March 30, 5:03 AM
To: Rune@HeartLand.com
Subject: Re: Possible Meeting
Attachment: Obsess.doc 128KB
```

Rune:

Yes, I'm still in town and will be here until at least tomorrow afternoon. Definitely free to meet today. I'll see you at eleven-thirty at the Striped Bass. Looking forward to it.

As to last night, in case you were wondering <g> -- Let's just say that it was everything I expected and more.

There is only one thing that inspires better than unrequited lust, don't you think? Requited lust <g>

```
     Fact  or  fiction?  Grin  -  you  decide,  or
just enjoy imagining.

Later, Thane
```

Oh, Christ. Hays knew just where Thane had been the night before, and with whom. All week, she'd been trying not to think about Auden's planned outing with Thane, Gayle, and Liz. Only the receipt of Auden's frequent e-mails outlining the progress on their first publication had enabled her to put Thane's date with Auden from her mind the last few days. Now, confronted with the reality of it, the last thing she wanted was to share Thane's experiences, even if they were filtered through the artist's lens and changed by the process itself. The words, if not the facts, would still hold the image of Auden.

Auden and Thane. God.

```
Private Pleasures - Obsession

    I'm not counting on anything, just hoping,
as I shower slowly, covering every part of
my body with thick, scented suds. I can't
help imagining it is your hands sliding over
my sensitized skin, and just the thought of
your fingers smoothing along the edges of my
desire makes me throb.
    I dry off, careful not to linger near
responsive areas. When I'm this ready, the
merest touch will make me wet. Still, as
I pull the soft, well-broken-in leather
pants over my naked legs, I know I will
be soaked before I get the zipper closed.
The ridged seam presses against me. I'm
stone hard. I'll be harder still before the
night is over, and I might very possibly
end the night alone. Again. With nothing
for comfort but this anticipation and the
lingering memory of you.
    I was wrong. So wrong. And so happy to
be wrong.
```

I don't know how it happened, what turn of events led me away from the noise and the crowd and the uncertainty back to your apartment, but here I stand.

Ready. So very, very ready.

I stand, my butt resting against the rounded back of the sofa, waiting as you watch me from just inside the door. Part of me is praying. Can you feel my need in the dark, hear my desire in the silence?

You turn on one dim light, then step to me silently, taking me in—not brazenly, not boldly, but through still, calm, steady eyes. I look back, trying to give nothing away. But it's hard to be cool when my bones are melting. My trembling hands rest on the leather sofa back as I present myself, expose my need, bare not just my body, but also my soul. The air between us crackles with currents of unspoken desire.

You flicker a smile, then lower your gaze—down the plane of my chest, over my belly, to my crotch. Your finger follows your glance, tracing the center of my body lightly, lingering on the space between my thighs. I make a sound—a moan, I think. Before I can draw another breath, you kneel between my parted legs and press a palm to each black-clad thigh. The muscles in my belly clench at the first faint touch.

Then your face is against the leather covering me, pressing hard enough for me to feel the ache in my clitoris, and a warning tingle ripples down my legs. I swallow the next moan, trying not to pump against you. I want it to last. I want to come so very badly. I look down, watching you through the haze of need as you slowly touch me. I want it to be what you want it to be.

Your hands come to my fly; you slide the zipper down, spread the material, grip the waistband and pull hard, almost but not quite exposing me. The leather rides against my swollen flesh and the sudden pressure almost makes me come. My arms shake with the effort of keeping myself upright. I am barely breathing, struggling not to move. Your arms circle behind me, hands kneading my buttocks, pulling me hard against your face. Your chin striking my rigid clitoris, trapped by soft leather, sends fire along my spine. I am dying; I am silent. I want you to have what you want.

The tip of your tongue flicks at me, toying with me, making me twitch, the pleasure unbearable. I think I might fall. I grip the edges of the sofa harder, straight-arming it, determined to take it for as long as I can. My head is already swimming, my stomach in knots. As you slowly draw down the leather pants, you press your tongue lower, running along each side of the shaft, then rocking it back and forth. I bite my lip. I taste blood. I am poised to come, have been for hours, but I will wait until you have taken what you want.

You tug my clothes to the floor, press your shoulders between my legs, parting them, opening me. Your tongue slides between slick folds, releasing a flood of passion onto your lips. You lick it greedily, bring your thumb to spread me wide, and dive deep inside with your mouth. It hurts to breathe; my thighs are shaking, muscles cramping. I choke on a groan that threatens to become a wail. I won't last.

You suck my arousal into your mouth, pulling gently, tormenting me. I'm whimpering—I can't help it. You hear it, but you have the decency not to laugh. You allow me to believe that I am still in control as you enter me. The sudden pressure hits my clitoris, a swift spiral of pleasure shoots through me—I didn't think I could get any harder, but I do. I'm so ready now it hurts. Gasping, hips jerking, I keep my eyes open, focus on you watching me, and will myself to hold on. The entire surface of my body is electrified. I'm suspended by a thread on the edge of orgasm, painfully swollen, inner muscles contracting spasmodically around your fingers. I want you to take what is yours.

"Please, let me come." The first words spoken.

Mercifully, blessedly, you take pity on me. Thrusting into me, you pull all of me into your mouth, sucking hard, tongue working over the shaft, across the exposed tip. My head snaps back, a strangled cry escapes me, and—oh God! Finally, I start to come. Wave upon wave, pulsing, mind wrenching, consuming. I'm sobbing, falling; you hold me up, strong arms wrapped around my thighs.

"God, don't stop," I plead, still coming so hard.

You lift your lips from me for an instant. "Not until I have it all," you whisper, before you suck me into your mouth again.

All of me. I want you to have what you want.

Hays stared at the screen, not certain what she'd just read. Well, she *knew* what she'd read. Christ, Thane wrote the kind of sex she could taste. But there was something else going on, both in this segment and the last, that she sensed but couldn't quite grasp. If she didn't know better, she'd almost think that Thane was in love.

The thought made her stomach twist. She closed her eyes and the words, the images, scrolled across her mind in vivid detail. And beneath it all was Auden.

God, don't let that be true. Don't let this be real.

Chapter Nineteen

Thane nodded a greeting to the receptionist at the trendy upscale restaurant on Walnut Street and asked for Rune Dyre.

"Right this way, please."

Thane followed across the large open room sectioned off by imposing columns toward a corner table set slightly apart from those of surrounding patrons. A dark-haired woman with her back to the other diners was already seated there.

"Here we are," the hostess said with a pleasant smile and turned away.

Thane started toward the empty seat and then stopped in surprise when the woman looked up. "Ms. Palmer?"

"Hays, remember?" Hays stood, smiling, and extended her hand. "And Rune Dyre as well. Hello, Thane."

"Holy hell," Thane said softly, taking Hays's hand. After she shook it firmly, she said with a wry grin, "I'm standing here trying to figure out if I've said anything imprudent about you to Rune."

Hays laughed and gestured to the seat opposite. "I can assure you that you haven't, but I thought we'd best meet before things got much more complicated."

She had been out of the hospital for exactly three hours. She'd had just enough time to get home, shower and change, and make it to the restaurant in time for her meeting with Thane. Fortunately, she hadn't had too much opportunity to ruminate on Thane's latest vignette, or on what it meant. Sitting across from Thane now, Hays thought again how impossible it was not to like her. The other author exuded confidence and a roguish charm. At the moment, however, there was astonishment in Thane's warm brown eyes, and she appeared to be speechless.

"I've enjoyed our correspondence these last couple of years," Hays confided, hoping to set her at ease.

"So have I. You're a hell of a writer, and it's been a privilege to share that with you." Thane leaned back in her chair, shaking her head, a grin lifting one corner of her mouth. "You've done one impressive job of keeping your identity a secret."

"I didn't set out to create a mystery around Rune's identity. At first, it was simply a matter of personal privacy," Hays said reflectively. "Then Rune just became who I was when I was writing—not just to associates or readers, but to myself as well. It didn't feel like a secret identity; it just felt natural—another part of me."

"I know what you mean." Thane paused a moment while a waiter advised them of the luncheon specials and took their drink orders. "I spend a lot of my life writing or working on some aspect of getting my writing published. I have long-term relationships with people, people I think of as friends, and they know me only as Thane."

"Well, you are, aren't you?'

"Pretty much. Most of me, at least."

"By the way," Hays asked, "what would you prefer I call you? I'm afraid you're always going to be Thane to me, but I can adapt."

"Thane is fine. Teddy is okay, too, although usually just my girlfriends call me that." Thane grinned when Hays laughed. "You?"

"However it is that you see me." Hays shrugged. "I can't imagine being anyone other than Rune when we're working. I answer to it as quickly as Hays."

"Agreed."

"I hope our collaboration continues. Writing can get lonely sometimes."

Thane toyed with a roll, trying to get her head around the fact that Rune was not only her confidant and co-author, but suddenly her publisher also. "So you plan to keep on writing, now that your company has our books?"

"There are going to be some challenges now that Palmer has acquired WomenWords, and, if I have to, I'll take my own work elsewhere. But I can't imagine not writing." Hays studied Thane's handsome face. "Can you?"

"No." Thane fell silent for a few moments as she sampled her appetizer, then she asked, "Do you plan to tell Auden?"

The ease with which Thane said Auden's name caused Hays'

stomach to lurch. Until then, she'd been able to avoid thinking about Thane and Auden and what might have transpired between them. It was a moment before she was certain that her voice would be steady. "I haven't decided. Probably. Eventually, I'm sure she would find out, and I don't want her to feel compromised by working with me as Rune and not knowing."

"It's more likely she'll view your work impartially if she doesn't know."

"Yes, that's occurred to me. In many ways that would be best." Hays found it increasingly difficult to discuss Auden with Thane, because images of the two of them together at the party, and worse, flashes of Thane's *Eros* fantasies, kept intruding. "I'll have to make a decision about that soon."

"Well, for the moment, it sounds like she's pretty involved just getting things off the ground with Destiny. She won't get to your book or *Eros* for a while."

"Yes, but she's incredibly efficient. It won't take long."

"Yeah. She's amazing. Smart *and* beautiful." Thane's admiration was obvious.

Hays could only nod, studying Thane's face, searching for hidden meanings.

Oblivious to Hays' silence, Thane continued, "Have you made a decision about the *Eros* anthology? Are you going to let me use those vignettes?"

"I'm not certain."

"Why not? They're fabulous."

Hays glanced away. "They're...personal."

"Jesus, do you think mine aren't?" Thane laughed. "Christ, I'm practically writing my wet dreams these days."

"I—"

"The one I sent you this morning was written after—"

"Look, Thane—" Hays's heart pounded rapidly and her head felt light. And it wasn't because her blood count was in the cellar. She couldn't hear this.

"If Gayle hadn't come out—"

"Gayle?"

Thane paused, her expression quizzical. "You remember her,

don't you? She was there when you..." The word *collapsed* died on her tongue, and she dropped her gaze awkwardly.

"Yes," Hays said, finding her voice. "Of course. She's terrific."

"Terrific?" Thane looked up again. "Jesus, I'll say. She's got me tied up in knots. Anyhow, every time I think of her I want to write something else, and every time I do...my insides come pouring out. So I know about *personal*."

Hays was so relieved she couldn't concentrate, could barely breathe. "Well, good luck. With Gayle, I mean. I hope it works out."

"Yeah, me too," Thane said seriously, all semblance of bravado gone. Then, she smiled ruefully. "So how about you? Those new vignettes are powerful. More than that. They're..." *Heartbreaking* was the word she wanted but couldn't bring herself to say. "...hot in the extreme. Is there a woman behind those scenes?"

"No," Hays said softly. "Just dreams."

❖

Auden sat on her couch wearing what she had slept in—a pair of scrubs that Gayle had given her—and cradled a cup of coffee in her hands. Her eyes were open, but she wasn't really seeing anything. She was thinking about the previous night.

"They look like they're having a good time," Liz said as she slid over one seat to be closer to Auden at the table.

"Yes," Auden said, watching Thane and Gayle dance. They looked so right together, Thane with her cheek against Gayle's hair and Gayle's fingers stroking the back of Thane's neck.

"Are you okay?"

Auden smiled. "Yes, I'm fine."

"I just wondered, because you seem a little distracted. Are you upset that Thane can't take her eyes off Gayle?"

"No." Auden laughed. "Not in the least." Then she gave Liz a kind glance. "Are you?"

Liz shook her head. "No. I'll admit I wouldn't have minded a chance to date Gayle, but it just didn't happen. Thane's an old friend, and I'd love to see her happy. I thought maybe you had designs on Thane, though."

"Ah, no."

"Good. So, then, would you like to dance?"

Auden hesitated.

"Just a friendly dance," Liz qualified quickly. "I'm not crazy about relationships in the workplace." She sighed. "God, I seem to be talking myself out of dates these days faster than I can get one."

"I'd love to dance," Auden said. "And friendly seems just right."

As they reached the dance floor, another slow song started, and before she realized it, Auden found herself in Liz's arms. It happened so suddenly that she didn't have time to be anxious. In fact, within seconds she realized that there was nothing to be anxious about. The subtle pressure of Liz's body felt entirely natural. The soft swell of Liz's breasts and the firm plane of her abdomen and thighs against hers were pleasant. The hand resting gently in the hollow of her back was warm and comfortable. She felt herself relaxing, enjoying the music and the moment.

A knock on the door brought Auden back to the present. Barefoot, she padded over and called, "Yes?"

"It's me."

Auden opened the door and smiled at Gayle. "Somehow, I didn't expect to see you today."

"Teddy had an appointment." Gayle grinned sheepishly. "Have you got more of that coffee?"

"In the kitchen."

A moment later, Gayle returned with her own mug, kicked off her shoes, and curled up in one corner of the sofa facing Auden. "You okay?"

"Sure," Auden replied, a hint of surprise in her voice. "Why?"

"I don't know. You look kind of...sad. You're not mad about me bringing Teddy home, are you?"

"No, of course not. I was just thinking about last night."

Gayle looked concerned. "Did something happen that I missed?"

"Not really." Auden gave a small self-conscious shrug. "I danced with Liz a few times. It was the first time I've ever danced with a woman."

"And?"

"And I enjoyed it. But I didn't feel anything...well, sexual. I guess I was wondering if I should have."

"It depends on how you're wired. I get turned on being that close to a woman even if I'm *not* interested in anything happening between us."

Auden gave her friend's shoulder a shove. "Gayle, sweetie, you get turned on just *talking* about it."

"I tell you too many secrets." Gayle extended one leg and slid her foot beneath Auden's thigh, wiggling her toes teasingly. "I've got a feeling you might need a little bit more of a connection to get you going, though. I wouldn't worry about it."

"Probably. It *was* nice." Auden grinned. "Speaking of getting turned on, should I even ask how *your* evening went?"

Gayle studied her coffee cup for a moment, then met Auden's inquisitive gaze. "We didn't sleep together."

"You didn't?" Auden's eyes widened.

"No. She didn't want to." Then she smiled, a pleased smile. "Well, that's not exactly true. She *wanted* to. I'm pretty certain of that from the way she—"

"Stop." Auden quickly held up her hand. "I don't want *all* the details."

"There aren't any details. She wanted to wait."

"You okay with that?"

"Yeah," Gayle said slowly. "It surprised me. It's not like I have anything against being physical *any* time, but it was awfully...sweet."

"It is." Auden reached down and squeezed Gayle's calf. "So what are your plans for the rest of the day?"

"Teddy is coming back here after her meeting, and I intend to jump her bones."

Auden laughed out loud. "That sounds like a plan."

"What about you?"

"I'm going in to the office for a while."

"You're kidding. It's Sunday afternoon."

"I know," Auden said softly. "But I don't have anything else to do, and I enjoy the work."

"You need more than work, Aud."

"I know." She met Gayle's eyes. "Hays is coming back to work tomorrow."

"Aud..." For a heartbeat, Gayle considered telling her about Hays's condition. But she couldn't, and not just for professional reasons. She knew that Auden would not want to learn something that private from anyone except Hays. She took a deep breath. "I'm glad."

"Me, too," Auden confided. *So very, very glad.*

❖

Auden walked quietly through the deserted hallways, heading directly for the coffee room. To her surprise, a pot sat on the warmer and when she lifted it and sniffed, it smelled remarkably fresh. She set it down, walked to the doorway, and peered up and down the hall. Her heart leapt when she realized that the door opposite was standing open. Wanting to run, she forced herself to walk slowly. Almost afraid when she looked in, she expected to be disappointed.

"You're here." Her voice was less surprised than grateful.

Hays glanced up from the papers in her hand, her eyes sparkling, unable to suppress a wide smile. "Yes, I am. And so are you."

They looked at one another across the room, both of them grinning foolishly.

"You look rested." Auden was amazed at the difference a week had made. It was the first time she'd ever seen Hays when she didn't look tired. Although naturally pale, now her skin was lustrous, with a healthy sheen. She had always appeared sure and certain, but now there was an aura of vigor about her that was nearly palpable. *You look wonderful.*

"I suppose I should take a vacation more often," Hays agreed, staring at Auden as if to memorize each detail. "But I hate to be away." She gestured at her desktop, which was covered with piles of correspondence and reports. "There's just more work to do when I get back."

Auden scanned the desk, looking for a mug among the disarray. "There's coffee. Do you want some?"

"Oh, yeah. I made it when I came in, and then I forgot all about it." Hays rose. "You don't need to get it for me, though."

Auden gestured her down with one hand. "Don't be silly. I'm up and I was about to get some for myself. I'll be right back. That is, if you don't mind."

"No, not at all. Please, join me."

When Auden returned a few moments later, Hays was waiting on the sofa. Auden sat beside her and put the two cups down on the low table in front of them. Hays reached for hers at the same time, and their hands briefly touched. Hays caught her breath sharply at the contact, and Auden gave a small start. They both drew back, careful not to look at one another.

"So," Hays asked in what she hoped was a conversational tone, "how are you progressing with Destiny's debut publication?"

"Well, I've contacted everyone involved, and we're geared up to start tomorrow." She wondered if her voice was shaking. She found it difficult to concentrate on anything except the subtle hint of Hays's cologne.

"I'd say you've definitely gotten your feet wet in a hurry, Ms. Frost."

The way Hays said her name was like a caress. Auden forced herself to focus. "I'd say I'm about hip deep at this point."

"I stand corrected." Hays laughed as she stretched one arm out on the sofa behind Auden's back. God, it felt so good to be back. She couldn't think of anything she'd rather be doing at that moment than sitting here with this woman. "Seriously, I'm very impressed with how quickly you've grasped the critical issues. Have you handed off the manuscripts to your editors yet?"

Auden shook her head. "I know I'm probably being too controlling, and I'll need to learn to delegate, but I really want to review these first works myself before they go to anyone else."

"It's up to you." Hays lifted a shoulder. "The timetable can be flexible, although some time this week I'd like to draw up a tentative publication schedule for the upcoming year. Will you have gone through all the manuscripts by then?"

"Definitely. And I have a pretty good idea how much work needs to be done on each so we can at least rank them in terms of potential release dates."

"Sounds fine." Hays phrased her next question cautiously. "Any problems or reservations in regards to any of them?"

Auden's reply was just as careful. "I wouldn't say problems, no. I think that Silverman's manuscript is a little rough and is probably going to take more editing than she might expect. I got the sense from my meeting with her that she wasn't used to much critical input."

"She's a popular author. Popularity tends to produce a fair amount of...confidence."

"That's a nice way of phrasing it," Auden said with a smile. "Thane Cutlass is enormously popular, and *she* didn't blink an eye when I asked her if she could expand the plot line in *Midnight Rendezvous*."

Hays raised an eyebrow. She'd critiqued that manuscript as Thane had written it and thought the book was a clear winner. "You thought the plot was light?"

"No, I thought the sex was heavy."

"Thanc Cutlass is known for that."

"Yes, and from what I can see, she's very good at it. I'm not suggesting she change that." Auden was mentally reviewing the work again and didn't notice Hays's intent expression. "I just think she needs to balance the two a little bit more."

"Why?" Hays asked, genuinely curious.

"I read some of the posts to her discussion group, and it seems that all of her fans love her style. But a few of the readers wanted more of the emotional interaction to complement the physical relationships."

"You've been trolling the websites? When have you had time to do *that* in addition to reviewing all the manuscripts, hiring a staff, and launching our first publication?"

Auden blushed, suddenly self-conscious. "I'm a fast reader."

Concerned, Hays said seriously, "No one expects you to become familiar with every aspect of the business overnight, Auden. It won't help if you burn out from overwork."

"I'm not overworked," Auden protested. "I love it."

"Still," Hays continued, leaning forward to rest her hand on Auden's arm, "it's Sunday afternoon and here you are."

"You're here, too," Auden pointed out quietly. She stared at the fingers, strong and steady, on her arm. When she raised her eyes, Hays's face was very near. Auden couldn't take her eyes from Hays's mouth. Her lips were parted slightly, and Auden felt again their softness, felt the gentle press of a tongue along the sensitive inner surface...

"Auden?" Hays's voice was low, husky.

"Yes?" Just a breath of a word.

"I think your phone is ringing."

Auden blinked, sat back. "Oh...I should get that."

Hays nodded as Auden bolted from the room, then collapsed back against the cushions. She was shaking, her hands were trembling, and for the first time in months, it had nothing whatsoever to do with being ill. It had everything to do with being alive. It felt wonderful—and terrifying.

CHAPTER TWENTY

Auden lunged across her desk and snatched up the receiver on the fifth ring. Panting slightly, she announced, "Auden Frost."

"Aud?" Gayle asked. "What are you doing? It sounds like you're running a race."

"Trying to beat the voicemail—I was in the other room. What's up?" Auden settled her hip onto the corner of her desk and struggled to concentrate. All she could think about was how much she had wanted to kiss Hays a minute ago. *Correction—still wanted to.* Her heart was hammering and every nerve fiber in her body jangled. She realized that Gayle had been speaking and that she hadn't heard a word. "What? I'm sorry."

"Hey, are you sure you're okay?"

"Yes. Fine."

"I said that Teddy called a little while ago from her hotel. She's checking out and, well, staying here tonight."

"Congratulations."

There was a moment's silence. "Last night she slept on the couch and that might be where she's sleeping tonight, too. It's up to her. I don't intend to rush her."

Auden shook her head, smiling faintly. "I'm afraid you two have been taken over by aliens. I'm not sure any of your friends would recognize either one of you."

"I tend to agree with you." Gayle laughed with her friend. "At any rate, the reason I'm calling is to share a little gossip."

"Oh? By all means."

"Guess who Teddy had lunch with?"

"Uh...God, Gayle, you know I hate guessing. Who?"

"Rune Dyre."

Auden drew a swift breath. "You're kidding? Someone finally got her to come out in the light of day?"

"Yep. You know Teddy and she are working on something together, don't you?"

"I do, although I haven't seen any of it yet. Thane promised to send it to me." She walked around behind her desk and booted up her computer.

"Well, apparently, Dyre wanted to talk about it, and she contacted Teddy for a meeting."

"She's in town then?"

"Well, she was a few hours ago."

"I have to go, sweetie," Auden said, her mind working furiously. "Good luck tonight, no matter who sleeps where."

"Don't worry. I'll give you a complete report."

"Not too complete," Auden said with a laugh. "Call me later."

As soon as Gayle hung up, Auden opened her e-mail program.

-----Original Message-----
From: AFrost@PalmPub.net
Sent: Sunday March 30, 3:30 PM
To: Rune@HeartLand.com
Subject: Re: Appointment
Priority: High

Ms. Dyre:

Please forgive the reliance on hearsay, but I chanced to learn that you were in Philadelphia earlier today. I realize that this is very short notice, but if you have remained in town and are available when you receive this message, I am still very anxious to meet with you to discuss the plans for both your current works and future endeavors.

I believe that this would be to the mutual benefit of you and Palmer Publishing. I am free to meet with you this afternoon or

```
tomorrow. I'll be happy to accommodate your
schedule in any way that I can.
     Please call me at 215-555-8950 or email
me here with your itinerary. I look forward
to meeting with you soon.

Auden Frost
Director, Destiny Books
Palmer Publishing, Inc.
```

Auden sent the message and leaned back in her chair. What she wanted to do was go back to Hays's office. She knew she couldn't, because Hays had come to the office to work and so had she. Plus, she had no reasonable excuse to see her again. And most importantly, what she was feeling had nothing to do with her job. She glanced at the papers and manuscripts heaped on her desk, desperately searching for something to occupy her mind. Despite the fact that she had hours of work in front of her, she couldn't settle on a single thing. Fortunately, her computer made the familiar sound that announced incoming mail, and she quickly turned to look at her inbox. To her surprise, she had a return message from Rune Dyre.

She opened it, scanned it, and frowned. She read it again, but the message still said the same thing. Slowly, she got to her feet and walked out into the hallway. A moment later she knocked on Hays's partially open door.

"Come in," Hays responded immediately.

When Auden entered, Hays was standing at the window, facing the square.

"The snow is melting so quickly," Hays observed musingly. "It's hard to believe that just a week ago we were in the middle of a blizzard."

"It's the season for rapid changes," Auden commented as she crossed to Hays' side.

"Yes, you're right," Hays murmured. "I guess that it is."

"I just got a very strange e-mail from Rune Dyre." When Hays failed to answer, Auden continued. "I had heard that she was in town, and I contacted her again about a meeting. In her e-mail reply, she suggested that I talk to you."

Hays turned away from the window, meeting the question in Auden's eyes. In a voice that was faintly apologetic, she said, "I'm Rune Dyre."

It took a moment for the meaning of Hays's words to register. Then Auden was bombarded with a plethora of images from Dyre's works—words and phrases and scenes she practically knew by heart. Lonely, desolate women—betrayed by lovers, abandoned by love—often too wounded to be healed, even by the touch of their beloved. Interspersed were vivid visions of passion—tender, gentle caresses; wild, magical moments of abandon; dark needs and desperate joinings. *You wrote all those things? Are those women you? Are those your needs, your fears, your desires? Do you hurt that way inside?*

"Auden?" Hays had expected that Auden might be angry that she had not told her right away, but she hadn't anticipated the distant, almost pained expression in Auden's eyes. "Auden, are you angry?"

"Angry?" Auden shook her head, feeling slightly dazed. "No...I... I'm just surprised. I've read everything she's...*you've* written." Senses on overload, she tried desperately to make the connection between the woman she knew and the works that had moved her so much, and she was having a hard time assimilating it. There was one thing of which she was certain, though. "Oh, Hays—you're very good."

Despite herself, Hays was pleased. "It means a lot to me that you think so. I'm not sure why I didn't tell you sooner. It's just that for me, writing is such a private thing."

"Who else knows?"

"Just Abel and Thane."

"Thane," Auden repeated, taken aback. "She never let on."

Hays shook her head. "She didn't know. Not until today."

"It's been a day of revelations for you, then."

"Yes, it has." Hays reached for Auden's hand, grasped it very lightly, her fingers just curling over the edge of Auden's palm. "Are you sure you're not angry?"

"I'm certain. It's just going to take me a little while to get used to the idea. When I think of Rune Dyre, I have this image of her that I've... constructed, I guess, from reading her...*your*...books. Now I wonder, are any of the things I've unconsciously assumed really true?" She shook her head, laughing faintly. "I must sound a little crazy, don't I?"

"No, not at all," Hays replied softly. "I think part of the reason that I've kept Rune's identity a secret is that I wanted my work to be the focus, uncontaminated by my presence. I like being the anonymous voice behind the words."

"You're not interested in celebrity?" Auden asked with a hint of levity. She was aware that their hands were still linked, their fingers lightly clasped now. She liked the contact, but she liked the warmth in Hays's eyes even more.

Hays laughed. "I don't think there's any real danger of that, although I suppose I wouldn't mind. But I've always been very private about the things that matter most to me."

"I think I understand that."

As they talked, they drifted even closer together, until their bodies were almost touching. Hays, slightly taller, inclined her head to hear Auden's soft words, and she felt Auden's breath flutter against her cheek. "I knew somehow that you would."

Auden raised her head, inadvertently bringing their lips a whisper apart.

She's going to kiss me.

I want to kiss her.

God, I want her to...

God, I have to...

Desire shimmered in the air. Breath hung suspended. Hearts beat wildly.

Auden stepped back.

"I...I'm sorry. I'm still a little stunned..." Auden knew she wasn't making any sense. Her head was filled with a roaring sound that made it impossible for her to concentrate. Her legs were shaking, and she was so aroused, she knew it must show in her face. She had no idea what Hays was feeling at the moment, but she'd asked once to be kissed, and she couldn't ask again. "Hays, I..." *want you and I don't know how to tell you.*

Hays gently placed her fingers against Auden's mouth. She felt her tremble, saw the desire in her hazy eyes. *We can't do this here, not in the office, not in a place where our relationship is defined by the professional. Because if we kiss, I won't stop, and I don't want to make love with you here, not this way—even if you want to.*

"Shh, you don't need to say anything. I'm the one who should apologize for springing this on you. I just don't want it to..." *come between us* "be a problem for us working together."

"No. It won't." Auden wondered if only she felt the desire. The expression in Hays's eyes—so intense, so serious—was so hard to read. "I should...get back to work."

"Yes. So should I." Hays hesitated for a moment. "I'm very glad you're here, Auden."

"So am I." Finally in control again, Auden smiled wistfully. "A few days from now, when I've turned the whole place upside down trying to get this book out, you might think differently."

"I can't imagine that anything would ever make me change my mind."

Auden sat for a long time in her office, reading things she knew she wouldn't remember the next day. She wondered what Hays was doing, what she was thinking. She wondered if Hays was writing. Finally, she picked up the manuscript of *Dark Passions* and started reading again from the beginning. She looked for Hays in Rune's words and thought she saw the loneliness and sadness that so often seemed to shimmer beneath the surface of Hays's dark eyes. She reread love scenes, imagining Hays writing them, wondering if Hays was writing her desires or only her dreams. When she finished, she had even more questions about the enigmatic author than before. She also felt closer to Hays in a way that she couldn't define, but she knew that she had glimpsed a very special part of her, and she cherished that.

When Auden finally left her office that evening, the light shone from beneath Hays's office door, but the door itself was closed. She did not pause as she walked quietly by.

❖

Gayle opened her apartment door and smiled up at the woman standing in the hallway. "Hi."

Thane put her overnight bag on the floor, lifted her wrist, and studied her watch. "It's been nine hours, five minutes, and...twenty-two seconds since I've kissed you. Does that count as taking it slow?"

Gayle reached out, gripped Thane's jacket in her fist, and pulled her through the doorway, barely giving the taller woman a chance to grab her overnight bag and drag it in with her before Gayle slammed the door.

"I'd say you've shown remarkable restraint," Gayle muttered as she pressed Thane to the door and then pressed her mouth to Thane's. She kept Thane pinned with the weight of her body as she kissed her hard, pulled her shirt from her pants, and slid her hands over bare skin all in one movement.

Never taking her lips from Gayle's mouth, Thane shrugged out of her jacket and then tugged at the snap on Gayle's jeans. She stopped herself just as she was about to slide her hand down the front and pulled her head away, banging it against the door, never even feeling the pain. Gasping, she said, "Say no now, if you want—"

"I want. I *want*," Gayle growled, pushing her hips hard into Thane. She found a nipple beneath the silk shirt, captured it between thumb and forefinger, and tugged on it as she squeezed.

Thane's knees buckled. Gayle laughed.

"Oh God..." Thane's neck was arched, her lids almost closed.

"Do you want to say no?" Gayle teased, her mouth on Thane's throat, biting gently.

"No...oh, yeah...no. Jesus, I haven't thought of anything else...all day."

Chest heaving, Gayle stepped back, grasping Thane's hand. "Come into the bedroom."

They moved quickly, shedding clothes along the way. By the time they reached the side of the bed, they were both shirtless and without shoes. Gayle sat down and reached for the buckle on Thane's belt.

Thane stepped away and opened her pants herself, not trusting what would happen if Gayle touched her just then. "You, too," she urged.

Gayle smiled as she watched Thane bare herself. "You're gorgeous." She lay back on the bed, lifted her hips, and pushed off her jeans.

One leg still in her trousers, Thane met Gayle's eyes and grinned. "You're crazy, Dr. Dunbar. But I'm glad you think so."

One small lamp glowed on the far side of the bed, and they looked at one another almost shyly in the muted light. Gayle held out her hand and Thane took it slowly.

"Come lie down on top of me," Gayle whispered.

Gently, Thane settled herself between Gayle's thighs, her arms on either side of Gayle's shoulders with her fingers resting against Gayle's jaw. Gayle's leg was hard and smooth as it slid against her own heated flesh. "Ah, God, you feel so good. Everywhere...so good."

"Mmm." Gayle wrapped her arms around Thane's shoulders and pushed her thigh upward, drawing a gasp from the woman above her. "Oh, baby, you're still ready, aren't you?"

"All day." Thane's voice was husky, her eyes unfocused. When Gayle brushed a hand down her back, gripped her hips, and started to rock into her, Thane groaned again. "I won't be responsible for what happens if you keep that up."

"I've wanted to make you come all day."

"You're going to get your wish." Thane trembled and pressed her face against Gayle's shoulder. "Soon, if you're not careful."

"Do you want to?" Gayle pressed her lips to Thane's ear, finding a spot just inside the rim that made Thane twitch when she licked it.

"Oh Christ, yes." She pushed her clitoris, wet and hard and close to bursting, along the length of Gayle's thigh.

"How do you want it, baby?" Gayle bit the soft earlobe, tugging it between her teeth. Her voice was low, barely more than a growl. "Do you want to come in my hand, or in my mouth...or with me inside you?"

Thane jerked and arched her back, giving a small cry as she edged close to climaxing. She couldn't keep her eyes open, could barely manage sounds. "I want you...to have...what you want."

It was Gayle's turn to utter a cry, and she quickly put both hands on Thane's shoulders, pushed her over onto her back, and rose above her in one smooth motion. "Look at me. Baby, look at me now."

Thane, breath coming in sobs, fixed on Gayle's face as Gayle reached between her legs and slid into her. When Gayle's palm brushed over her clitoris, Thane came instantly. As Gayle's mouth covered hers, swallowing her cries, Thane clenched around Gayle's fingers, heaving with each wracking spasm.

When Thane finally opened her eyes, she was lying in Gayle's arms, her cheek cradled on Gayle's chest, one leg over Gayle's thigh. She felt as if she'd been hit by a truck. Her muscles were rubbery and her head was fuzzy. There was a faint buzzing sound in her ears. She couldn't remember ever having felt so good in her life. "Christ, I'm wrecked."

"Good." Gayle kissed the top of Thane's head and stroked her shoulders and back. She felt a faint aftershock ripple through Thane's body, heard her gasp, and she smiled. She loved the way Thane's body felt, pinning her to the bed with the weight of spent desire.

She reached with one hand to pull up the sheet, not wanting Thane to get chilled. Thane's hand lay on her stomach, making small aimless movements. It was driving her crazy. She hadn't come, but she'd grown harder, wetter, with each pulse of Thane's orgasm around her fingers. She hadn't felt her own need then, only Thane's pleasure, but now the urgency came roaring back. She ached for relief.

When Thane, drifting near sleep, found Gayle's breast and lightly rubbed her nipple, Gayle closed her eyes and bit her lip. Her clitoris, still rampant, twitched steadily, and she couldn't stop a moan. She slid her hand toward the pounding need between her thighs.

"How you doin'?" Thane murmured drowsily.

"I want to come," Gayle whisper hoarsely. "You okay if I...touch myself?"

"Mmm, yeah. Not yet, though."

Gayle trembled as Thane's hand wandered slowly down the center of her abdomen, and she began to fervently pray for just one brief touch. Just one touch and she'd come. "Oh God, I am so hot."

"Uh-huh." Thane laughed softly. "I noticed."

Breathless, heart pounding, every muscle tense, Gayle moaned. "Touch me, please, baby. I want to come so bad."

When Thane didn't move, didn't answer, Gayle wondered if she'd fallen asleep. Desperate, she moved her hand lower again.

"No."

Ever so slowly, Thane brushed her fingertips through the hair at the base of Gayle's belly, then pressed lower, a torturous fraction of an inch at a time, until she had parted the swollen folds below. Gayle whimpered, her legs like steel bands. Thane fondled her lightly, stroking near her clitoris but not touching it. Not yet.

Gayle's whimpers became a litany of pleas. "Please, make me come. Please. I have to come. Please."

"Mmm." Thane pressed the shaft, firmly, once. And stopped. When Gayle's hips rose from the bed and she made a choking sound, Thane started again—slow circles, coating the engorged length with Gayle's arousal.

"You're going to make me come," Gayle moaned, her whole body twitching now. She was gasping, her fingers digging into Thane's shoulders. "Oh God, oh God—"

"Now touch yourself." Thane pushed into her, pulled out, and thrust again.

Gayle shouted, coming hard, her fingers stroking her clitoris in time to the rhythm of Thane's long, deep thrusts. When she was too weak to continue, Thane took over, milking the last tremor from her exhausted flesh.

As Gayle moaned softly, the last of the orgasm trailing through her depths, Thane sighed, infinitely satisfied, and closed her eyes. Gayle followed her into sleep, Thane's hand still held within.

CHAPTER TWENTY-ONE

Thane pulled on her trousers and shirt, then sat on the side of the bed and watched Gayle get ready for work. It was still dark outside. The bedside clock read 5:45. Earlier, she'd lain awake listening to Gayle shower, thinking about the night before. It hadn't been what she had expected. She'd barely recognized herself. She was used to being in control, used to being the aggressor. It was an image she was comfortable with, and most of her lovers had been, too. With Gayle, though, everything had shifted—perceptions had blurred—and parts of herself that she hadn't even realized existed suddenly emerged.

"I'm sorry about getting you up so early." Gayle wore faded green scrub pants and nothing else as she searched in her dresser drawers for a clean scrub shirt. "I've got rounds at 6:30."

Thane crossed the room and slid her arms around Gayle's waist from the back, resting her chin on Gayle's shoulder. "I'm sorry about last night."

"Oh?" Gayle stiffened almost imperceptibly. "Why is that?"

"I'm usually not so much of a dud in bed." Thane sighed, one hand smoothing the taut skin over Gayle's abdomen. She met Gayle's eyes in the mirror above the dresser. Hers were unusually soft; Gayle's were wary. "I don't think anyone has ever been able to knock me out the way you did. I hope you're not going to judge my performance—"

"You're joking, right?" Gayle turned in the circle of Thane's arms, an incredulous look on her face as she placed her hands flat against Thane's chest.

Cradling Gayle's hips, Thane shook her head. "I feel like a novice. Christ, I practically left you high and dry."

"Okay, I'm going to say this once. Listen very carefully." Gayle rested a palm against Thane's cheek to soften her words. "I know you weren't firing on all cylinders there at the end, but surely you remember the fact that I begged you to let me come. *Begged.*" Just thinking about it, she shivered. "No one does that to me. No one controls me that way. No one."

Thane grinned with a combination of pleasure and humility, and seeing it, Gayle wrapped both arms around Thane's neck. Pressing close, with her lips against Thane's ear, she murmured, "It was wonderful. *You* were wonderful. And, if you ever tell anyone that I let you top me on our first night together, I will make you suffer for all eternity."

"That sounds almost tempting." Thane dipped her head for a kiss, lingering a moment too long on Gayle's soft lips. Heat flared in her depths and she almost gasped. "I just want to be sure you know..." For one of the few times in her life, when it mattered so much, she couldn't find words. "Jesus, I—"

"I know." Gayle's voice was tender. "I felt it. I felt you; I felt me. I know how special it was."

Thane could only nod and hold her more tightly. "When can I see you again?"

"I'm working tonight and next Saturday night. Friday night?" She was unusually hesitant, uncertain, wondering if she was expecting too much. She'd said that she'd wanted more than a night, but Thane had never answered. *I never gave her time to say what she wanted; I looked at her standing outside in the hall, all sexy charm and deep brown eyes, and the only thing I wanted was to get my hands on her. Well, I had that. Now what?* "Teddy?"

"God, Friday seems like forever."

Gayle smiled against Thane's neck, enormously relieved. "Then you'll be nice and ready for me."

"Are you kidding? I'm ready now."

Gayle found Thane's unguarded emotional honesty stunning. It was one of the most wonderful things about her, as if her good looks and charisma and quick intelligence weren't enough. Gayle's head was spinning, and most other places had already left orbit. She groaned faintly. "God, I want you again, too. And I have to go to work."

"Listen," Thane murmured, her cheek resting against the top of Gayle's head, hands softly stroking her back. "I know it's kind of soon to ask, but I'll be going to New York for a book convention the weekend after next. Would you...come with me?"

"I'd love to."

Thane sighed contentedly and kissed her again. "Good. Now I'm going to go back and sit down on the bed while you finish getting ready for work. Because if I keep touching you, you *are* going to be late."

"Yeah, I know." Reluctantly, Gayle let Thane go, but as she continued her preparations, she was smiling.

❖

Hays knocked on Auden's half-open door, saying at the same time, "Auden?" Looking in, she realized that Auden was not alone. Liz stood beside Auden's desk, leaning over, smiling down at her. "Oh, sorry."

"Hays," Auden said brightly, "come in."

Hays dipped her hands into her pockets, looking uncertainly from Liz to Auden, wondering if she had interrupted something personal. "No, that's okay, I can come back."

"I was just leaving," Liz offered as she walked toward Hays. She held out her hand. "Good to see you again. I came on board last week while you were away."

"I'm glad you're here. It sounds like the two of you have gotten things off to a running start." Hays shook Liz's hand warmly.

"Not me—Auden." Liz looked over her shoulder, smiling back at Auden. "I'm just following her lead. She's amazing."

"Yes, so everyone says," Hays murmured, her gaze on Auden, who blushed from the compliments.

When Liz left, Hays asked, "Are you busy?"

"Enormously." Auden stood up. "But never too busy for you. Liz and I were just talking about the timing for the media releases for *Pale Imitations*." She ran a hand through her hair and shrugged ruefully. "It's rather hard to make that sort of decision when I don't know yet how things are going to go. We just sent the manuscript off to the compositor for copy fitting."

"Who have you got doing that for you?"

"Abel suggested Martin Jones. What do you think?"

Hays nodded. "Martin is good. He's very fast and very thorough."

"I hope to get a castoff on the page numbers today or tomorrow so graphics can size the cover." She looked at a list of notes she'd made on a yellow legal pad. "I'm not sure where we'll be in the print queue, which is the one thing that may sink us in terms of the convention."

"I should think if you get a galley approved by the end of the week, we'd be able to get a first run done in time for New York. It wouldn't be the first time we've had to send a van to pick up books because of a close deadline." Hays leaned against the door. "You're doing great, Auden."

Auden met her eyes. "Thanks." She hesitated. "Was there something you needed me for?"

"No, I just wanted to say hello." Hays stepped into the room and closed the door. "And I wanted to see if everything was okay, after yesterday."

Auden came around her desk. "You mean about Rune?"

"Yes."

"At first I was a little, well, disoriented, I guess. I needed to find a way to connect the two of you." She lifted a shoulder, frustrated. "Does that make sense?"

"Completely," Hays replied. "Were you able to?"

"A little." Auden smiled. "I'm getting used to the idea."

"How did you manage that so quickly?" Hays smiled, too.

"I read some of *Dark Passions* again last night."

"Really?" Hays was having trouble following the conversation because she was watching the way Auden's lips moved as she spoke, the way the color of her eyes shimmered from blue to green, the way she tilted her head when she concentrated on a thought. "Why that one?"

"Because it's so intense, so...filled with feeling." Auden took a breath and took a chance. There was just so much she needed to say. "There's so much passion, of every kind, in that book. I wanted to see if I could recognize you there."

Heart hammering, Hays tried to focus. "And can you?"

"In some ways." Auden's voice was gentle, her gaze tender. "But there are so many secrets hidden inside, it will take more than one reading to learn them all."

"Have you decided what to do with it?" Hays wondered if Auden was still talking about the book, then thought it must be only her own desires projected. She couldn't seem to be anywhere near Auden without wanting to touch her, without wanting Auden to feel the same compelling connection. *This is getting to be an impossible situation. As if it could* be *any more impossible.*

"I want to keep it."

"Good." Hays trembled slightly, then let out a breath. *Business. Talk about business.* "You'll publish it, then?"

"I definitely think we should, but I'm going to have to give it to someone else to edit." At the slight frown line that developed between Hays's eyes, Auden hurried to explain. "I can't read it and not...lose myself...thinking of you."

They weren't close enough to touch, and Hays was glad, because she wanted to, so much so she ached. "Is that bad?"

"No, but it makes working efficiently almost impossible." Auden held Hays's gaze. "You seem to have that effect on me."

"It's mutual," Hays replied, her voice a husky whisper.

"I'm glad." Auden's smile was just a bit tremulous, and she was almost shaking with the effort it took not to take the last step forward. She was going to have to touch Hays now or find some neutral ground. Thinking about the book, remembering the need and the desire she'd witnessed and experienced, she was losing sense of everything except Hays. "Speaking of work...I need to make about a hundred phone calls."

"Me, too." Hays reached behind her for the doorknob, still looking at Auden. "I'll talk to you later?"

"Yes," Auden said quickly. "How long you will be here?"

"I'll be here until you're done."

Hays quickly slipped out of the room. It was a minute before Auden could make herself move back to her desk. Fortunately, she had so much to do that she managed to concentrate on work and not on how badly she had wanted to walk into Hays's arms the instant they'd been alone. The next time she checked her watch it was close to seven p.m. After pushing aside the checklist she'd been methodically going though, she turned to her computer to read her recent mail.

```
-----Original Message-----
From: thaneCutlass@CutlassFic.com
Sent: Monday March 31, 5:20 PM
```

To: AFrost@PalmPub.net
Subject: Anthology
Attachment: ErosFiles.zip 536KB

Auden:

   Sorry it's taken me so long to get this
to you. I'm sending you the raw material,
hot off the press as it were <g>
   Rune is still on the fence about this, but
I think it's terrific (especially hers—she's
gone somewhere in these vignettes that I
can't quite describe. Somewhere...well, to
quote her..."deeper than desire") Anyhow,
our styles are different but they balance
well, IMHO. I guess that will be up to you
to decide <g>.
   If you like the idea, let me know what I
can do to make this happen.

Regards, Thane

Auden unzipped the attachment and scanned the files.

Private Pleasures—Cutlass.
Secret Passions—Dyre.

After a moment's hesitation, she opened the second and started
to read.

Secret Passions - Scene Six

   As we talked, we moved closer, not just
in body, but in spirit. In that subtle
communication of the soul that needs no
words. It happens every time we're together,
and I knew that this time, I must touch her.
I have been so lost, so far from light and
air and the beat of my own heart—so long a

stranger to all that spoke of life—that I
was not certain I could find my way back.
Then she pointed the way with the hand she
offered.

"Take it. Come with me."

She raised her head, inadvertently
bringing her lips very close to mine. I
felt her breath against my cheek, felt her
fingers graze my hand, felt my blood rise to
her call, rushing as rain through long-arid
plains.

I wanted to kiss her.

Her eyes welcomed me, her parted lips
offered me salvation.

"Take it. Come with me."

Shaking, Auden stopped reading. Then she went back to the first
vignette, clicked properties, and jotted down the date and time the file
was initiated. She did the same for each scene Rune had written. When
she finished, she reached for her desk calendar, but she didn't really
need to check. She knew before looking. She knew where and when
every scene had taken place. She'd known almost from the first words
she'd read.

She closed her eyes. *She's bleeding to death, and she won't tell
me why.*

"Auden?"

Without opening her eyes, she asked, "Have you been writing just
now?"

"What?" Hays crossed the room and stopped in front of Auden's
desk, her stomach roiling. Auden was pale and so frighteningly still. "I
don't know what you mean."

Auden passed a hand over her face, then sighed. She sat forward
and met Hays's worried gaze. "*Secret Passions.* Those scenes are about
us, aren't they?"

Hays was quiet for a long moment. Where she'd just been warm,
she was suddenly cold. "Thane sent them to you."

"Yes." Auden stood and walked to the coat rack beside her door.
She pulled on her overcoat and then looked at Hays. "*Rune Dyre*—I

looked up the etymology last night, after you told me. It means *beloved secrets*. Close enough?"

"Yes. Auden—"

"You didn't mean for me to read those. I'm sorry." She shook her head, and when she spoke again, her tone was hushed. "You are so beautiful, Hays."

Hays moved to intercept Auden as she walked into the hall. "Where are you going?"

"I'm going home." She couldn't be anywhere near Hays right now. She hurt, having glimpsed the terrible sadness the passages had revealed. And despite that, or perhaps because of it, she wanted desperately to have that fierce intensity focused on her. She wanted to share Hays's passion *and* her pain. She wanted her, now more than ever.

"Let me walk you. It's late." Hays sounded frantic. She was. "Auden, please."

Auden stopped and looked at her. "Were you ever going to tell me?"

"I don't know," Hays whispered.

The silence stretched forever as they searched each other's eyes.

"Get your coat."

It was less than a ten minute walk to Auden's building, and they said nothing until they were out on the street. Then, Auden reached down and took Hays's ungloved hand in her own, clasped her fingers, and pulled their joined hands inside her own coat pocket. "You're going to get sick again."

"What?" Hays looked at her sharply.

"No gloves, no scarf, and nothing but a raincoat. It's thirty degrees out here. You just got over the flu, remember?"

Tell her now. It's not fair—she has to know. Before anything happens. Hays was silent, afraid. Afraid if she told her, she would never again be certain that the look in Auden's eyes wasn't pity. *God, I don't want that. Not from her.*

They turned the corner onto Auden's street, climbed the steps to the tiny landing, and faced one another in the dim glow from the sconce above the door.

"Come in," Auden said quietly. "Stay with me tonight."

Hays tensed, torn between wanting Auden and wanting not to hurt her. "There's something you need to know."

Auden unlocked the door and pulled Hays into the foyer, out of the cold, then looked into her eyes. "Do you have a lover?"

"No," Hays said quickly. "But—"

"Is there something we need to be careful about?"

Hays shook her head. "No."

"Then I don't want to know anything else tonight. Only that you want me." She lifted her hand, stroked Hays's cheek. "Tomorrow, tomorrow we'll talk."

And because Hays wanted, so desperately needed, one night of untarnished joy, she turned her face into the warm palm and kissed the tender flesh. *Forgive me, Auden.*

"I want you more than words can say."

Auden took Hays's hand, turned, and led the way to her apartment.

CHAPTER TWENTY-TWO

Hays stopped just inside the apartment door. "Auden—"
"Shh." Auden turned to face her, reached past Hays's right
shoulder, and flipped a wall switch that lit a table lamp on the far side of
the living room. Then she lifted the lapels of Hays's raincoat and gently
pushed the garment off her shoulders. "Let me take this for you."

"Thank you." Hays stood still, watching as Auden hung their
coats in a small closet nearby. She was terrified and so terribly in need.
Arousal was only part of it—it was true that she wanted Auden's hands
on her; it was true that she wanted to feel Auden's body next to hers.
But more than that, she wanted the heat of passion to burn away the
loneliness and horror of the last eight months. Yet even as she hungered
for that moment, she questioned the rightness of claiming it. It felt like
a lifeline, and she feared to grasp it under false pretenses.

Auden turned back with a small smile. "I think that's about as far
as I can get without help for the rest of the night."

There was something so vulnerable in Auden's eyes that Hays's
uncertainty vanished like mist in the sunrise. She reached out and took
Auden's hand, pulling her closer until their bodies nearly touched. Then
she rested her fingers beneath Auden's chin and tilted her head up until
their eyes met. "I think I can assist some with that part."

Like the first time, this kiss began gently, a fragile meeting of
lips that whispered a greeting. Auden placed her palms against Hays's
chest, softly stroking just below her collarbones as they leaned into one
another, bodies slowly joining. Hays lifted her hands to cover Auden's,
and their fingers entwined. As the kiss deepened, they tenderly opened
to one another. Auden moaned softly as Hays's tongue slipped delicately
into her mouth. She loved the firmness, the fullness of having Hays
inside of her that way, and that image, that thought, summoned her
desire with unexpected ferocity.

Gasping, Auden brought her hands into Hays's hair and kissed her hard, their tongues quickly matching stroke for stroke. When she drew away, her voice was husky. "I want to be in bed with you."

"Yes. God, yes."

Auden led the way, her hand in Hays's. She stopped by the side of the bed, the light slanting in from the other room their only illumination. It was enough to see Hays's face, and that was enough to diminish her nervousness. "There's something you need to know."

"Only if you want to tell me." Hays lifted the hand she held to her lips and kissed each finger, saying quietly as she did, "You have filled my thoughts for endless hours. Your face, your voice, your tenderness. I have dreamed of your touch, ached to touch you." She met Auden's gaze, then kissed her lightly on the lips. "That's all I need to know."

"I want you so much," Auden murmured, wrapping her arms around Hays' shoulders, trembling against Hays's body. Quietly, she confided, "I've never done this before."

"Oh, sweet Auden." Hays drew her gently closer, both hands resting in the hollow above Auden's hips. With her lips pressed to Auden's forehead, she said hesitantly, "I don't know if I'm worthy."

Auden sighed softly, aware of Hays's heart beating rapidly against her own breast. She was enormously aroused and yet inexplicably peaceful. "You feel so good, so right." She kissed the tip of Hays's chin. "I haven't been saving myself, Hays. There has just never been anyone who's moved me enough to want this. I want this with you."

"And I want this with you." Hays slid a hand beneath the edge of Auden's sweater, circled her fingers over the smooth back. The heat of Auden's skin made her insides clench. "I want you, so very much."

Auden found Hays's mouth, kissed her again, exploring her deeply, then eased back to run her tongue lightly over the surface of Hays's lips. Hays groaned, and Auden smiled. "You're so beautiful. I want to see you."

Hays nodded, pierced by the aching sweetness of Auden's request. "Anything you want."

"What do you want?" Auden waited, searching Hays's eyes. "What do *you* want?"

"I want to feel you in the farthest reaches of my soul."

With trembling hands, Auden carefully unbuttoned Hays' shirt, drew the bottom from her trousers, and slowly slid the garment from her arms. Her gaze still fixed on Hays's, she lifted off her own sweater and undergarments in one motion. As she brought her hands to Hays's breasts, she whispered, "Touch me back."

Hays shuddered at the first light brush of fingertips on her skin, and her vision momentarily dimmed. Struggling for control, she watched Auden's lips part in wonder as Auden caressed her. Then she lifted Auden's breasts in her palms and rubbed her thumbs across the hard points of her nipples, feeling them harden even more.

Auden's lids flickered, and she arched her neck in supplication. "Oh God."

"Auden," Hays moaned. Her thighs shook as she pressed into Auden's hands, wanting more of her touch. "We'll go as slowly as you like...stop whenever...oh God..." Auden had begun to squeeze her nipples, drawing them firmly, rhythmically, between her fingers. The surge of excitement that shot through her almost dropped her to her knees. "Wait..."

"Did I hurt you?" Auden asked, her voice foreign to her own ears. Her eyes were riveted to Hays's breasts in her hands, *in her hands.* Firm and perfect and incredibly beautiful. The small hard nipples tightened as she stroked them again, and distantly she heard Hays gasp. She looked up, worried. "Hays?"

"It's been...a very long time," Hays confessed. "You're making me a little crazy."

"Oh." Auden smiled, a very satisfied smile.

Hays pulled Auden close, their bare breasts pressing together, drawing small cries from them both. She brought her lips to Auden's ear. "I want to touch you everywhere. I want you to touch me. Let's lie down and make love."

"Yes," Auden murmured against Hays's neck.

They stretched out facing one another, shoeless but still partially clothed. With Auden's fingers softly tracing her face, Hays kissed the side of Auden's neck, then her throat, then the ridge of her collarbones. With one hand, she cupped Auden's breast and caressed it with her mouth, circling a nipple with her tongue.

"Oh my dear God," Auden gasped. Without conscious thought, she shifted closer, pressing her breast to Hays's face, arching her hips into Hays's body. She was aching for more contact, everywhere, but the urgency between her thighs was almost painful. Fitfully, she stroked Hays's back, kneading the taut muscles, urging her with soundless pleas to take more. "So good...you feel so good."

With her mouth still on Auden's breast, Hays smoothed her palm down Auden's abdomen, gasping as the muscles flickered and clenched beneath her fingers. Auden moaned and pushed harder, sliding a leg between Hays's thighs. The pressure against her fiercely ready flesh made Hays's head go light. "Oh yes," she cried, her eyes shut tightly, struggling to ignore the warning pulsations beginning in her depths. Forcing herself to stay still, to let Auden set the pace, she whispered, "Let me undress you?"

"Yes, please." Auden drew back, her fingers coming to Hays's waist. "And you."

They kissed, needing contact, as together they opened buttons and slid zippers and freed themselves of the last barriers. When at last they were naked, only a whisper of space between them, they were both breathing heavily.

"Is this all right?" Auden searched Hays's eyes, finding the reflection of her own gripping need in their obsidian depths.

Hays leaned forward, bringing their bodies together along their entire lengths. The first complete touch was excruciatingly exciting. She groaned, unable to stop her hips from jerking once before she reined in her desire. "It's perfect."

"It never occurred to me that being this excited could make you kind of crazy," Auden murmured, stroking her fingers down the center of Hays's abdomen.

"Crazy...how?" Hays's breath was coming faster. The caress was making her harder, and the aching need to ease the pressure was escalating.

"I can't touch you enough." Auden rested her forehead against Hays's and looked down the length of their bodies, marveling at Hays's exquisite beauty. She traced a hipbone, following the hollow across the top of Hays's thigh to the space high up inside her leg. Then she caressed the soft skin there, the backs of her fingers brushing the fine hair between Hays's legs, damp now with arousal.

"Auden," Hays's voice held a desperate warning. "Not there...not yet."

"No?" Auden's voice was choked, desire heavy in her blood. "Can I...look?"

"Anything," Hays sighed, surrendering without regret. She settled onto her back, resting on her elbows to watch, awestruck, as Auden, the blond hair falling delicately across one elegant cheek, bent over her body. *Take anything. Everything.*

Then all thought fled as Auden touched her. Falling back helplessly, Hays clutched the sheets in her fists, legs stretched tight, as gentle fingers opened her. It wasn't a caress meant to make her come but simply to expose her—to reveal her need and her longing—yet the faint current of Auden's breath so close was magic. Trembling, she cried out softly.

"What is it?" Auden asked, hearing the quiet moan, feeling the muscles in Hays's thighs spasm beneath her breast.

"I'm so close...to coming. I don't know...how long I can wait."

Auden's heart beat wildly and her vision narrowed to the point where she could barely see. Quickly, she moved back up to Hays' side, her palm once again on Hays's abdomen, her lips on Hays's mouth.

"Why should we wait?"

"Just a little longer." Hays stopped the hand that was moving lower on her belly, then ran her fingers along the curve of Auden's hip, over her thigh, and up the inside on her leg. "Let me bring you with me."

Auden shivered. "I'm not sure...I don't know..."

"Auden," Hays murmured, her fingers dancing higher, "you don't need to do anything. I just want to touch you."

"Yes." She found Hays's eyes and clung to the intense gaze, needing the tenderness to hold her safe. "Yes. Please."

For an instant, Hays stopped breathing as she crossed the last boundary, reverently seeking Auden's passion. She found her full and hard, warm and so very wet. "Beautiful," she whispered.

Auden lifted her hips, inflamed by the light caress. "I want...oh, I..." Beyond words already, she slid her fingers between Hays's thighs, stroked the length of Hays's clitoris, and felt Hays answer with an echoing caress. "I'm going to die."

"No," Hays gasped, hanging on to sanity by a thread. "No, not from this." She circled and pressed and teased until Auden whimpered, ignoring the tug of Auden's fingers on her own turgid flesh. She knew when Auden grew harder still that her orgasm was near, and then she eased a finger inside her.

"Hays," Auden cried, the new sensation jolting her from the cloud of her approaching climax. "Oh, that feels...more, oh God...more."

Hays held back, stroking Auden's clitoris gently, waiting for the pleasure to open her further. Then, shaking with the effort to be careful, Hays entered her again, first one, then two fingers, filling her completely just as she felt Auden peak. Auden came with a sharp cry, closing around Hays's fingers, rocking into her palm.

The incredible beauty of Auden's climax was enough to drive Hays to the edge. When in the midst of her own release, Auden pressed inside her, Hays shuddered and tumbled after her into orgasm.

❖

"Hays?"

"Hmm?"

Auden was curled up in Hays's arms, her cheek nestled against Hays's neck. "I'm...speechless."

"Me, too." Hays laughed softly, running her hand down Auden's arm. "You are so amazing."

"Really?" Auden asked, inordinately pleased.

"Mm-hmm."

"So, it's okay that I can't begin to tell you how wonderful I feel?"

"It's not easy to describe." Hays kissed the top of Auden's head, nuzzling her face in the fragrant softness, wondering how one put joy into words. "I know *I* can't."

"As I recall, Rune manages to describe it pretty well," Auden teased, kissing the tender skin beneath Hays's ear. "*She* has quite a way with words."

"Yeah, well, Rune isn't usually writing in a post-orgasmic daze." Hays thought of the solitary hours in the middle of the night, of the silent yearnings and the distant dreams. She drew Auden closer. "Besides, being with you is more than Rune has ever managed to capture with mere words."

"I don't know about that." Auden laid her palm over Hays's heart, reveling in the steady beat. "I love the way you write. I love the way you touch me—with your words, with your body."

Hays pressed her lips to Auden's temple. "I'll never be able to tell you what this has meant to me. Maybe when I can think again, I'll find a phrase or two that comes close, but there is no way to describe the places inside me that you have blessed."

Auden slid on top of Hays, cradling her head in her hands, stroking her damp hair back from her face. Their legs entwined naturally as the planes of their bodies melded. "You don't have to search for words. I heard you just now. You told me with your hands, and with your mouth, and with the beat of your heart around my fingers."

Hays gasped as a wave of excitement crested in her depths, swamping her unexpectedly. She was too raw, too open, physically and emotionally, to contain her response. "Auden," she murmured brokenly as she trembled with the gently rippling orgasm.

"Oh my God," Auden whispered in astonishment, watching the pleasure course across Hays's beautiful face. "Is that...are you...oh, you are too gorgeous."

Closing her eyes, she was aware of Hays's erratic heartbeat and ragged breathing. She had never realized how vulnerable, and how majestic, a woman could be at the moment of orgasm; witnessing it, she felt both powerful and eternally humbled. Turning onto her side, she gathered Hays into her arms and curled around her, protecting and shielding her until she returned to herself. Lips against her lover's ear, she whispered, "Thank you."

❖

When Hays awoke, it was morning. Auden was asleep with her head on Hays's chest, and the room was suffused with the bright glow of early-spring sunlight. She didn't remember drifting off, only the supreme lassitude after climaxing in Auden's embrace and the peace that had followed while being held in Auden's arms. As she stared at the ceiling, watching the patterns of light chase across the pale surface, she tried to remember when she had ever felt so content. She couldn't recall a time.

Oh Auden, why now? She'd asked the question once before, but then she had been filled with rage. Rage at the injustice and fickleness of a fate she had long given up trying to change. Now she asked out of helplessness and despair, because she so very much wanted this moment not to end. Turning her cheek to Auden's hair, she wept silent tears.

Auden lay motionless, feeling the faint tremors in Hays's body, watching through half-open lids Hays's hand trembling against her arm. There were bruises on the inside of Hays's forearm that she had not seen in the dim light the night before. Her heart twisted at the sight, and she tightened her hold around Hays's waist.

"Are you awake?" Hays's voice was muffled, her face shrouded in Auden's blond hair.

"Yes." Auden turned her cheek, kissed the soft skin of Hays's breast. "You're not thinking of leaving, are you?"

"What?" Hays stiffened. "Why would you think that?"

"Because," Auden said carefully, "in almost everything you've written about us, you only come so close. And then you leave."

"Those are just stories. Just fiction."

"Are they? And is Rune just a fiction? Or is she you?"

Hays was quiet, trying to distinguish her feelings from her fears. "Auden, I'm not sure I can stay."

The words were not wholly unexpected, not after the tears Auden had just felt dampen her hair. But still they struck deeply, terrifyingly close to the heart of her own insecurities and doubts. "Last night...if I wasn't—"

"Last night was *wonderful*." Hays brought her hand to Auden's chin, lifted her face to look deeply into her eyes. The hurt she saw there stabbed at her heart. "It was *everything* I have ever dreamed of. You were perfect."

"All right then," Auden said, drawing a shaky breath. "If you don't have a lover, and we were good together—what could be wrong? Something I've done?"

"It's me, Auden. It's my problem."

Auden took Hays's wrist in her hand and turned her arm up to the light. There were puncture marks in the center of the bruises. "Is this the problem? Are these from drugs?"

Hays laughed hollowly. "Christ, it would be better if they were."

CHAPTER TWENTY-THREE

"Did you think all this time I didn't know something was wrong?" Auden asked quietly, still lying in Hays's arms. "Do you think I can't see it in your face, recognize it in the things that you write?" She stroked the arm that was curled around her middle, then grasped the fingers, drawing them to her lips for a kiss. "Do you think I can't see how much pain you're in?"

"You see too much, Auden," Hays whispered, her face against the top of Auden's head. "You have since the first day we met. When you look at me, I feel as if every secret I ever had is exposed."

"Not true. I can't see this one." Auden smoothed her hand over Hays's chest and pressed as close to her as she could. "And you have to tell me."

Hays was silent, struggling between the need to share her burden and her desperate desire to go back to the moment before Auden had awakened. Back to that moment of pure and simple joy. But she couldn't go back, any more than she could change what would happen. And Auden deserved to know, had to know. Now, before it was too late.

"I just got out of the hospital two days ago. The bruises and puncture marks are from the intravenous catheters."

Hospital. The word clamored in Auden's brain—a frightening word under any circumstances. But it wasn't just the ominous word that struck terror to her heart—it was all the things she had seen but had never put together, now suddenly coalesced into a single horrifying picture. She saw the trickle of blood on Hays's face, saw her collapse at the hotel, saw her pale and weak and exhausted. Auden's first instinct was to banish the images, obliterate the words. But she couldn't. Because she was lying in Hays's arms, and Hays's heart was beating so rapidly beneath her cheek.

"What's wrong?"

"I have a...condition." Hays wasn't sure she could go through with this. Auden was trembling. "Auden—"

"Tell me." Auden pushed herself up on the bed, Hays's arm still around her shoulders. She looked into Hays's eyes, saw her anguish. "Oh, sweetheart." She caressed her cheek. "Tell me."

"It's called myelodysplastic syndrome."

"What is that? I've never heard of it."

"Not many people have. It's rare." Hays laughed hollowly. "Before eight months ago, I'd never heard of it either—it's a blood thing."

"How serious is it?" Auden was having a hard time getting her breath. *I will not scream. I will hear this.*

Hays looked away. Auden drew her face back with a hand on her jaw. "Hays?"

"Most people eventually die."

Auden gasped; she couldn't help it. "Oh my God."

"Auden, I'm sorry. I should have told you before last night." Hays tried to move away. "I just wanted you so mu—"

"Most people. You said *most* people." Auden felt the room tilt and realized she wasn't breathing. She forced herself to take a slow breath. "So there's...treatment?"

"After a fashion. I get blood transfusions when I become too anemic, like last week. Antibiotics—other drugs to build up my immune system." Hays ran a hand through her hair, uncertain whether to continue. Auden was so pale, her eyes wide, tormented. "Jesus, this is wrong. I shouldn't be doing this to you." She broke Auden's hold, pushed back the covers, and swung her legs to the floor. "Look, I'm sorry. I shouldn't have slept with you last night. I have to go."

"Don't you even try," Auden said sharply, grabbing Hays's hand. "Do you think I'll just let you walk away?" She sat up, wrapped her arms around Hays, and pressed her chest to Hays's back. She nestled her face against the side of Hays's neck, her lips close to Hays's ear. Tenderly, she asked, "How can you imagine I'd let you go after last night?"

"You have to," Hays said quietly. "There's no future with me."

"I'm not going to debate that with you," Auden said simply. "I just want you to tell me what this is all about."

Hays turned her head, met Auden's gaze. "It's a problem with the bone marrow. I don't make blood cells, or the ones I make aren't normal. That leads to the recurrent anemia and infections. Eventually, the bone marrow will quit working altogether, or it will start making malignant cells, or I'll get an infection the antibiotics can't cure. No matter what, the bottom line is—I die."

"How long can you live with this?" Auden felt numb and was glad for it. It enabled her to ask the questions she needed to ask.

"Months. A few years, with luck." Hays looked away.

Auden closed her eyes. To her horror, she felt tears coursing down her cheeks, but she didn't think she could stop them. She wasn't crying for herself; she was crying for how alone and frightened she imagined Hays must feel.

"I never meant to hurt you," Hays whispered.

Auden pulled Hays back onto the bed, into her arms, and drew the covers around them. "You haven't hurt me. I...I'm all right."

Wearily, Hays rested her head on Auden's shoulder. "I'm so sorry."

"Stop saying that." Auden stroked her hair. "For God's sake, it's not your fault."

"I shouldn't have slept with you."

"And stop saying that, too!" Auden's tone was sharp. "Last night was beautiful, and it always will be. Don't you ever think differently."

Despite herself, Hays grinned. "You are a most remarkable woman."

Auden threaded her hands in Hays's hair and pulled her head up. "You need to call Alana and tell her you'll be late."

"Why?"

"Because you aren't going anywhere until I have the whole story. And I don't intend to let go of you anytime soon." She couldn't bear the thought of letting Hays out of her arms. She needed to hold her, to feel her body, warm and solid. Alive and so very precious.

"Auden," Hays said tenderly, "you can't change this just because you want to. I know. I've tried."

"So what was your plan, Hays? Just to say goodbye?"

"I didn't have a plan. I shouldn't have come here, but I couldn't help myself. I haven't been able to stay away from you." She moved far enough away so that she could look into Auden's eyes. "You pretty much took me by storm."

"Sweet talker," Auden murmured. With one arm still firmly around Hays's waist, she leaned over and fumbled for the phone. "Here. Make the call."

❖

"Auden Frost."

"I love your official 'I'm at work' phone voice," Gayle said. "Did you page me a few minutes ago?"

"Yes," Auden said, pushing aside the reports she hadn't really been reading. "I'm sorry. Are you busy?"

"Nope. Just got off call. I'm heading home soon. Boy, have I got news—"

"Are you too tired to meet me somewhere?"

"I'm fine. It was quiet last night and I slept some. What's wrong? You sound sorta weird."

"I'm okay." Auden felt tears threatening again. *God damn it. This has got to stop. If Hays sees—*

"Uh, honey? I always know when you're lying to me, remember?"

Auden smiled wanly. "I just need to see you."

"Where and when?"

"Can you meet me at the deli at 19th and Sansom?"

"Sure. Forty minutes?"

"I'll get us a booth." When she replaced the receiver, Auden looked at the work piled on her desk. She'd been in the office for an hour and had accomplished exactly nothing. Fleetingly, she wondered how Hays had managed to run a company and write amazing fiction at an astounding rate while dealing with the horror of having her life suddenly derailed. Resolutely, Auden picked up the completed manuscript she had just printed out and reached for a pencil. If Hays could work despite all the stress, she couldn't do less.

Half an hour later, she was surprised to find that she'd actually gotten a few pages edited. When she stepped out into the hall, she automatically glanced toward Hays's office. She wanted to see her. Just to see her. *She's working, Auden, like you're supposed to be.*

Turning away from that open door was one of the hardest things she'd ever done.

Ten minutes later, Auden sat with a cup of coffee in a back booth at R&W deli and prayed that Gayle wouldn't be late. She was so desperately lonely, she didn't think she could stand it.

The previous night with Hays had been the single most expansive moment of her life. Entire worlds had opened for her, emotionally and physically. Hopes and dreams had sprung from the carefully guarded recesses of her unconscious to flower under the gentle hands of a tender lover. She had learned things about herself she'd never imagined, awakened to passions she'd never before conceived. Hays had brought her pleasure beyond description, but it was her own consuming need to pleasure in return that had astounded her. She wanted to touch Hays everywhere, again and again. She wanted to explore her, caress her, inflame her. She wanted to feel Hays's body convulse beneath her hands and watch her face dissolve into orgasm. She wanted her. She wanted *her.*

"Auden?"

Auden raised stricken eyes to her best friend and could only nod.

"Jesus, honey, what is it?" Gayle slid into the booth across from Auden and took her hand. "Your hands are freezing. Are you sick?"

"No." Her voice was a harsh rasp. Auden cleared her throat as she drew her hand away, fearing that the sympathy would make her cry. "I'm okay. You want coffee? Something to eat?"

The waitress approached, and Gayle ordered her standard deli fare without taking her worried eyes off Auden. "Reuben and fries, extra Russian. Large Coke. Thanks."

"I don't know how you stay so thin." Auden tried to smile as she said what she always said when they ate out together.

"Genetics," Gayle replied, just as she always did. "What the hell is going on? You're scaring the bejesus out of me."

"I want to talk to you about myelodysplastic syndrome." She'd been saying it over and over in her mind all morning, and it came out surprisingly easily. She didn't even want to scream this time.

Gayle drew a sharp breath and scrutinized Auden's face. "What happened?"

"You know about it, don't you?"

"Some. I'm a surgeon, not a hematologist." Gayle answered carefully, trying to judge the direction of the conversation. "Auden, you have to help me out here. Tell me what's going on."

"You know about Hays, don't you?"

Gayle sighed. "She told you?"

"More or less." Auden struggled to gather her thoughts. She was so scattered. She wasn't normally like this. "We slept together last night."

"Oh, fuck." The word was out before she could stop it. All she could see was the pain ahead.

"What's the matter?" Auden's tone was sharp as a rush of anger hit her. "You don't approve?"

"What? Approve?" Gayle looked confused. "No, I—"

"You've been hammering at me about it for months. I thought you wanted me to get some experience, throw off the bonds of chastity, join the twenty-first century—"

"Whoa, hey. Take it easy," Gayle said gently, resting her hand on Auden's. "Slow down a minute."

Auden blinked, realizing that she'd practically been shouting. She didn't know why. "I'm sorry. I can't seem to think clearly."

"Okay. Let's do this a step at a time." Gayle fell silent as the waitress deposited her food. As she waited, she reminded herself that the past could not be undone, the future could not be predicted, and only the reality of the moment was of consequence. Auden, and what she felt, was what mattered. "You and Hays were together last night."

Auden nodded.

"Okay." Gayle felt as if she were navigating a minefield. She'd never seen her normally controlled, even-tempered friend like this. It hurt to see Auden suffering. "And how was that? Good?"

"Very."

Gayle grinned. "I love you. Only you could describe your first sexual encounter in one word."

Finally, Auden smiled, the wonder of those moments eclipsing the fear. In that instant, when all she could see—all she could feel—was

Hays, she was blazingly happy. "Amazing. Breathtaking. Beautiful. Earth shattering. Okay?"

"Mmm. For now." Gayle took a small, relieved breath. "But later, I want details."

"I'll never be able to tell you," Auden said softly. "She's so incredible, so special."

"I know, honey." Gayle's voice was very gentle. "I know."

Auden's smile wavered, and she shuddered faintly. "This morning she told me about her condition."

"I'm so unbelievably sorry, Aud."

"I can't remember everything," Auden confessed. "I can't remember what she said about...about her chance of survival." Her eyes were wounded, vulnerable, as she looked into Gayle's. "I can't remember, and I can't make her go through that again."

Gayle didn't want to be the one to tell her. What she wanted was to make the pain go away, not add to it. But what she really, *really,* wanted to do was to tell Auden to run.

Don't do this to yourself, honey. Get out now. There are so many women out there. You can have anyone. You have your whole life ahead of you. Don't make it a lifetime filled with the memory of this kind of pain.

"How do you feel about her?" Gayle asked quietly.

Auden answered without the slightest hesitation. "I'm in love with her."

"I knew that." Gayle touched Auden's cheek gently. "You wouldn't have slept with her otherwise."

"I might have." Auden shook her head. "I don't know. It doesn't matter. I feel what I feel." She regarded her friend intently. "So, will you help me? Will you please tell me what we're facing?"

There was nowhere to go but forward, because Auden wasn't turning back. "I'm gonna have to be a doctor here, okay? It might be rough."

"That's okay. I want the truth."

Gayle nodded. "Hays told me about the MDS at the hotel, and I did some research after that. How much did she tell you?"

"I know the basics." Auden was surprised at how calm she felt now. She wasn't alone anymore. "I know what it is, and I know that most people with it...die. She said there was treatment, but I'm not clear on that. For some reason, she wouldn't go into it."

"Probably because the *real* treatment is risky. It kills almost as many people as the disease."

Auden paled, but she held Gayle's gaze. "Why?"

"You can treat the symptoms for a while. She told you that, right? Transfusions, antibiotics, clotting factors if she's bleeding. Supportive care."

"Yes." Auden's voice was a whisper, but steady.

"Those things are temporary. Eventually, they aren't enough. What she needs is new bone marrow. She needs a bone marrow transplant, but you can't do that unless you destroy all of her own bone marrow first." Gayle fell silent, waiting for Auden to digest the information. *Jesus, I hate this.*

"Okay," Auden said at length. "Okay. So—if you destroy her bone marrow, and the *new* bone marrow lives, she'll be okay?"

Gayle nodded. "Probably, yes."

Auden's voice trembled. "There must be an awfully big *but* coming."

"There is. Once her bone marrow has been ablated—wiped out— she's defenseless. She'll have no clotting factors, no immunoglobulins, no way to resist infection. A...fair number...of people die in the peritransplant period."

"A fair number? How many?"

"Thirty percent."

"My God," Auden breathed.

"She's young, and that's in her favor. But you can see why her docs are probably delaying, especially if she's been reasonably stable."

"And if the transplant works? What then?"

"There's a decent chance of cure." Seeing hope flare in Auden's eyes, Gayle hurried to add, "But it's not a guarantee."

"Is anything?"

Gayle shook her head. "There are a million things that could go wrong along the way, Aud."

"Yes, but there's a chance. Right? That's what you're saying."

"A coin toss. Maybe not even that."

Auden smiled, and this time it reached her eyes. "Those sound like decent odds to me."

CHAPTER TWENTY-FOUR

```
-----Original Message-----
From: Rune@HeartLand.com
Sent: Tuesday April 1, 5:35 PM
To: AFrost@PalmPub.net
Subject: Meeting
```

Ms. Frost:

 I apologize for the delay in getting back to you regarding your request for a meeting. I was unavoidably, but most pleasantly, diverted by a pressing personal matter.
 Although I realize this is short notice, if you are free this evening, I would be delighted if you would join me for dinner.
 I've taken the liberty of sending a car to your home at 7:30pm. If you are otherwise engaged, I hope that we can reschedule for a more convenient time.

Yours very truly,
Rune Dyre

Auden looked at her watch. *Oh my God. Six-fifteen.*

```
-----Reply-----
From: AFrost@PalmPub.net
Sent: Tuesday April 1, 6:16 PM
```

To: Rune@HeartLand.com
Subject: Re: Meeting

Rune:

   Thank you for the gracious invitation. I am very much looking forward to seeing you this evening.

Most sincerely,
Auden Frost

Then she jumped up, pushed papers into her briefcase, and rushed to the door. She was a block from her house when she ran into Gayle, who was walking Shylock.

"Hi, honey," Gayle called, falling into step. "Where's the fire?"

"I'm in a rush. I've got a date with Rune."

"You're seeing someone else?" Gale stopped dead in the middle of the sidewalk. "Wait a minute. Rune? Rune Dyre? You're seeing *Rune Dyre?*"

Auden took Gayle by the arm and tugged her along. "No, *Hays.* Come in with me while I get ready."

"I'm so confused," Gayle grumbled as she followed Auden inside and through to the bedroom, Shylock padding along behind. "*Who* do you have a date with?"

"Hays," Auden said. "Who else?"

"But you said Rune."

"Oh, sorry—Thane didn't tell you? Hays *is* Rune." Auden began to rapidly undress. "I have to shower. Come into the bathroom and talk to me."

"I can't believe it. Hays is Rune? Oh my God, that's amazing." Gayle leaned against the sink as Auden jumped into the shower. Raising her voice to be heard above the running water, she shouted, "Teddy never said a word. I'm going to kill her. Right after I throw her down and ravish her."

"I take it she didn't sleep on the couch?"

"You got that right, but we barely made it to the bedroom."

"Why doesn't that surprise me?" Auden's voice was muffled for a moment, and then she said, "Who jumped whom?"

"Who do you think?"

Auden stepped out and extended her hand. "Towel. Thanks." She wrapped it around her hair and pulled another one from a nearby rack, covering her body. "You."

"Did you say that just because you know me better than Teddy?" Gayle asked with true curiosity.

"Not really. When I watched the two of you dancing together at the 2-4, it struck me how tender Thane seemed with you. I just had the feeling she'd let you make the decision as to when."

"So she's all Ms. Sensitive and I'm just a sex fiend?" Gayle bounced on the bed, looking anxious, an expression that was foreign for her. "Maybe I've forgotten how to do anything with a woman except have sex."

"That's not true." Auden tilted her head as she slipped in an earring, regarding her friend affectionately, aware of the hint of hurt in Gayle's voice. "I happen to know for a fact that you're incredibly sensitive. I also know how attracted you are to her. I don't think there's anything wrong with sleeping with her."

"*Before* the wedding?"

Auden laughed. "I'm willing to bet you didn't have to drag her into the bedroom. Why are you beating yourself up about this?"

"Sorry." Gayle shrugged sheepishly. "It's just that I...I don't want to mess up with this one, Aud."

"You mean she's more than just a pretty face?"

"Not to mention a fabulous body, but, yeah—she's special."

"I can't imagine you have to worry. I don't think I've seen her look at anyone else since the moment you were introduced to her at the Four Seasons. She certainly didn't look at anyone else the other night at the club." She shook out her hair and reached for the blow dryer, giving her hair a quick once over. "Do I need to ask if it was outstanding?"

"The sex was mind blowing." Gayle followed Auden back into the bedroom. Shylock had curled up on the foot of the bed, trying his best to be invisible. She sat down next to him and absently petted his head. In an unaccustomedly small voice, she said, "But that wasn't the best part."

Auden turned from her closet, her expression quizzical. "What do you mean?"

"I think I liked holding her and waking up with her as much as the unbelievable sex."

"Uh-oh. That sounds serious. Are you smitten?"

Gayle nodded forlornly. "Looks like it."

"That's wonderful. I mean it." Auden pulled out a dress and a pair of black silk trousers, and held up one in each hand. "Help me."

"Where are you going?"

"I don't know. Rune—Hays—is sending a car."

"Ooh, sending a car. One of these days you're going to have to tell me what it's like sleeping with one of the goddesses of romance."

"Maybe." Auden blushed, but she smiled with delight. "Besides, you've got a love goddess all your own. Thane Cutlass is known for her hot love scenes. And believe me, when *Eros* hits the shelves, she'll be famous."

"*Eros*?"

"It's an anthology that Thane and Rune are doing. Erotica—you know, sex and love and stuff."

"And you've read it?"

Gayle sounded jealous, and Auden thought sure she could detect a slight pout. Grinning, she nodded. "Well, yeah. I'm their editor."

"I hate you. Are the stories good? Are Teddy's really, really hot?"

"Buy the book." Auden ducked as Gayle threw a pillow, then gestured to the clothes again. "Come on...so what do you think?"

"If you don't know the agenda, I'd wear the pants with a slinky top. That will dress up or down depending on the occasion." Gale nodded her approval at a burgundy silk blouse that Auden held up for her inspection. "Perfect. So, Auden, tell me—is Hays anything like Rune...in bed?"

"Gayle, sweetie. Rune doesn't exist."

"Of course she does." Gayle was adamant and absolutely serious. "She writes books, she has hundreds of fans, she answers e-mail, she writes articles and essays. Of course she exists."

"Hays is passionate and intense and incredibly sensitive, exactly as Rune's writing would suggest her to be. I didn't compare the sex point for point." Auden smiled shyly. "That would require more mental power than I'm capable of when she's touching me."

"Jesus." Gayle flopped back on the bed, arms outspread, groaning. "Auden, cut it out. I'm not going to see Teddy for three more days."

"You asked."

"Yeah, but I didn't expect you to get that really sexy tone in your voice when you answered. Jesus."

"Well, you've never heard me talk about sex before. Come to think of it, I never have." Auden reached down and grabbed her friend's hand, pulling her to an upright position. Then she turned in a circle. "What do you think?"

"I think you look gorgeous." Tenderly, she said, "I hope you have the most wonderful evening."

"I can't wait to see her." A shadow passed across Auden's face. "Sometimes, I forget all the rest of it. Sometimes for a minute or two at a time."

"That's how it's supposed to work. You're supposed to exult in the joy and hold on to every second of happiness you find." Gayle stood and put her hands lightly on Auden's shoulders. "Both of you need to celebrate this new love. It will make you strong."

She didn't say, *For when the hard times come.* But the words hung in the air between them.

"That sounds like a plan." Auden's voice was thick and tears shimmered on her lashes, but they did not fall. "Thank you. For today."

Gayle took Auden into her arms, resting her cheek against Auden's. "I'm going to be with you every step of the way." She kissed her lightly on the forehead. "And tonight, try to pay a little bit more attention during the good parts. I'm dying to know if she makes love the way she writes it."

❖

Auden slid into the back of the chauffeur-driven black Town Car, self-conscious and charmed at the same time. A small cream-colored envelope lay on the seat next to a single red rose. Her name in bold script was written on the front. She carefully opened it, not wanting to crease the flap or damage it in any way. *Silly. But I don't care.*

> *Auden,*
> *Last night was the most beautiful evening of my life. I doubt that I will ever be able to show you how much it meant to me, but I'd like to try.*
> *Thank you so much for gracing me with your presence this evening.*
> *Yours most truly, Hays*

Auden's eyes filled with tears and she quickly looked out the window, trying to distract herself by guessing her destination. The car was headed east on Pine Street into the heart of Society Hill, an enclave of historic brownstones lining narrow cobblestone streets. Blindly, she reached for the rose and cradled it in her lap between her clasped fingers. *What am I going to do if I lose you now?*

"Here we are, Ms. Frost," the driver announced as the car slid to a stop in front of a four-story brownstone separated from the street by a low wrought-iron fence and box hedges. Two sconces on either side of a massive wooden door lit the short walk to the marble steps.

"Thank you," she said as she stepped from the vehicle. She'd tucked the envelope into her coat pocket and held the rose carefully in her right hand. As she walked up the sidewalk, the front door opened. Hays stood backlit by the soft glow from a chandelier in the foyer beyond.

"Hello, Hays," Auden said softly as she stepped close to her.

"Hello." Hays leaned forward and kissed Auden gently, taking her free hand. "Please come in."

Behind them the car slipped away.

Following into the wide foyer, Auden scarcely noted the polished antique furnishings and deep, rich carpets. All she could see was Hays, who wore simple black trousers and a black silk shirt, open at the throat; her sleeves bloused slightly as they tapered to broad French cuffs. Gold links sparkled at her wrists. Auden watched her move, and, for a fleeting instant, felt her stretched along the length of her own body. She gasped.

Hays stopped to search Auden's face, her dark eyes luminous. "All right?"

"Oh, yes," Auden breathed. "Perfect."

"Let me take your coat...and do something with that rose."

"Be careful with it," Auden murmured, as she handed over the stem and slid the coat from her shoulders. "It's very special."

Hays smiled. "I shall handle it gently."

"I know you will."

For an instant they stood close together, their eyes holding, the air about them growing still and thick with silence. A pulse beat steadily in Hays's neck, full and strong. Gently, Auden rested her fingers there. Hays closed her eyes.

"I'm sorry," Auden whispered as she pressed closer, bringing her other hand to rest against the back of Hays's neck, fingers trailing into soft hair. "But I've wanted to do this all day."

Auden's kiss was slow and light, the merest brush of lips over Hays's, a gentle exploration of the very inner surface of her lips. All she wanted, *everything* she wanted at that moment, was to feel the warmth and tenderness of Hays's body as the blood flowed vigorously beneath her fingers with each beat of Hays's heart. When Auden drew her mouth away, Hays's eyes were open, the pupils wide and flickering faintly. She was breathing shallowly.

"No need to apologize...for that," Hays managed around a throat choked with desire. "I...uh...where was I?"

"Coat," Auden murmured, stroking Hays's cheek and moving back a step. "Rose."

"Oh. Yes." Hays blinked and her vision cleared a little. Then she grinned. "Rune would have a sexy line right about now."

"You don't need one."

"Maybe later."

"Mmm," Auden acknowledged, unable to take her eyes from Hays's face.

"The living room is just up the hall to your right. Let me do something with these." Hays indicated the things she still held in her hands.

"All right." What Auden really wanted to do was follow her around the house. She didn't want Hays out of her sight. Wondering if this feeling was normal or merely a result of fear, she forced herself to smile. "Go ahead. I'll find it."

Auden stood in front of the fireplace, watching the burning logs, when Hays returned. Smiling softly, she said, "Your home is beautiful."

"Thanks." Hays stopped a few feet away. "Would you like a tour now or after dinner?"

"Dinner first, I think."

Hays held out her hand and Auden took it, following into the dining room. The room was high-ceilinged and lit with another chandelier that cast warm shadows over the space. The formal table had been laid with two settings, one at the end and the other immediately beside it. Silver covered serving dishes sat on adjacent warmers. Very elegant. Very intimate.

"This is wonderful," Auden breathed.

"Rune's idea."

Auden laughed out loud. "Of course. She lives here, too, I take it?"

Hays grinned. "Mostly upstairs in the study."

"Will you show me later? I'd like to see where you work."

"Anything you like." Hays pulled out Auden's chair for her, then took the adjoining seat. She leaned over to lift a bottle of wine from a standing wine cooler, then held it up for Auden's inspection. "May I?"

"Yes, please." Auden indicated the serving dishes as Hays poured. "Shall I get us started?"

Hays nodded, and they passed plates back and forth in silence for a moment. After the first few bites, Auden closed her eyes and moaned softly. "Tell me you cooked this."

"Uh...no." Hays sighed loudly. "Damn, and I so wanted to impress you."

Smiling, Auden shook her head. "I'm actually glad that you didn't. I'm not sure I could ever match this as it is."

"You don't need to," Hays said seriously, taking Auden's hand and raising it to her lips. She kissed her palm. "This is to say thank you."

"Don't," Auden whispered, the meal forgotten as she watched Hays's mouth lightly touch her skin. "Don't ever say thank you to me for loving you."

Hays stiffened, her eyes growing opaque. "Auden, no."

"Oh God, I really said that, didn't I?" Auden closed her fingers around Hays's hand, sensing that she was about to draw away. "Well, it's true. I won't take it back."

"You can't," Hays said quietly. "*We* can't."

"Why not?"

Hays lowered their joined hands to the table and stared at them, hers so much paler than Auden's even now, when she was about as healthy as she ever could be. "You know why not."

"No, I don't," Auden said clearly. "I know you're ill. That doesn't mean we can't have something together."

"We can date." Hays didn't look at her.

"Fine. I'd like that. My turn to surprise you next time." Auden watched Hays carefully. It was the first time she could ever recall that Hays wouldn't meet her eyes.

"It can't be serious."

"It already is." Auden shifted her chair and put her free hand under Hays's jaw, very gently turning her head. When Hays finally looked into her eyes, she demanded, "Tell me it isn't."

Hays was silent for a long moment, then shook her head. "I can't let you do this."

"Which part would you like to stop? The part where we talk, or the part where we work together, or the part where we touch?" Auden took a steadying breath. "It's all part of what we have, and I don't want to give any of it up. I want more, not less."

"Is six months, a year, going to be enough?" Hays's voice was harsh, heavy with anger and frustration.

"No, it isn't," Auden said softly. "Not nearly enough. But it's a start."

"You know—"

"What about the bone marrow transplant?"

"Jesus..." Hays rocked back in her seat. "How do you know about *that*?"

"Gayle."

Hays closed her eyes. "It's not that simple."

"Yes, I got that much from what Gayle told me, and I'll admit I don't understand it all. So help me."

"This was supposed to be a romantic evening and look what's happened to it." Hays sat forward, her expression intent. "Is this what you want your life to be about? Talking about my illness? Thinking about my future, what there is of it?"

"No, it isn't. But this is part of being with you, so I'd like to talk about it now." Auden leaned forward and kissed the tip of Hays's chin. "And then I'd like to spend the rest of the evening thinking about how much I love the way you look at me."

Hays groaned. "You aren't going to be reasonable, are you?"

"I'll try to be," Auden replied, completely serious. "Explain to me why you haven't had the transplant."

"Because the quality of my life has been decent, and I have things to do with the time I have left." Hays's voice was low, heavy with resignation and the finality of acceptance. "I don't want to waste any of it, and the transplant might not work." Hays looked into Auden's eyes. "Six months is precious if you only have twelve."

Auden was suddenly very cold, and she tried not to shiver. She put her hands in her lap and clasped her fingers together. The room was pleasantly warm, but her body was ice. "But you'll do it, if...there's no other choice?"

"I don't know," Hays said quietly. "I hate the idea of being helpless, of letting them kill off what's left of my defenses. Of dying without even being able to fight."

Auden couldn't stand it. She couldn't have this conversation while being this far away from Hays. There was so much more they had to discuss, but she needed surcease, just for a little while, from the pain. "Do you think we could cover the food and sit by the fire for a minute? I'm freezing."

"Of course." Hays stood, her expression instantly concerned. "Don't you feel well?"

"No, I'm fine. Just a chill." She stood, taking Hays's hand, and nodded toward the living room. "How about sitting next to me and sharing a little body heat?"

Hays slid her arm around Auden's waist, instantly comforted by the embrace. She grabbed the wine bottle with her free hand. "Get the glasses. I think we can take care of this."

Five minutes later, they were curled up on the sofa facing the fire, which Hays had stoked with several more logs. Auden reclined in the curve of Hays's body, her feet tucked beneath her, her shoes abandoned on the floor. Hays had covered them with a knitted afghan and had one arm around Auden's shoulders, her cheek resting against Auden's temple. "Better?"

"Mmm," Auden sighed. "Wonderful."

Hays kissed her temple, then the angle of her jaw. "You're very beautiful."

"Thank you." Auden nestled against Hays's chest and watched the flames dance, listening to the steady beat of Hays's heart. Such an incredible, miraculous thing—this woman, this life. She thought of Rune's scene of two uncertain lovers seated before a fire and how they had eventually surrendered to desire. She remembered the passion and the tenderness and the sweet, sweet longing as if those feelings had been her own. Suddenly, she wanted to live, not just dream, that moment with Hays. "I want to make love with you tonight."

"I want you, too," Hays breathed against her ear. "So much I can't think of anything else."

"Is there anything we need to be careful about?" Auden tilted her head, searched Hays's face. "Could I hurt you somehow?"

"No." Hays kissed Auden's forehead. "No."

"You're sure? The...bleeding?"

Hays shook her head. "I've just been transfused. I can tell when my counts are dropping. Headaches, bruises, and then the bleeding starts. I'm okay now."

Auden turned so that she was lying in Hays's lap, her breasts against Hays's, her arms around Hays's neck. "Good. Because I have this terrible, terrible need to touch you everywhere, and I can't guarantee your safety."

Hays laughed, her heart lifting at the teasing note in Auden's voice. "How come I'm not scared?"

"I don't know," Auden murmured, working on the buttons of Hays' shirt with one hand. "You should be."

CHAPTER TWENTY-FIVE

Hays looked down and watched the delicate fingers open her shirt. Her entire body tensed, anticipating their touch. The room was cast in shadows, red tinged with bursts of orange reflected from the fire. Auden's face was part in shadow, part illuminated by firelight. It reminded Hays of the night in the hotel, only then, the reflections on the exquisite planes of Auden's face had been from moonlight on the snow. That night had been mystical; tonight was breathtakingly real. Both were magic.

"Are you still cold?" Hays whispered.

"No." Auden's voice was hoarse and low. She was intent on removing the barriers between them, swamped with the sudden need to feel the heat of Hays' skin.

Hays pushed the afghan aside, then drew a sharp breath as Auden's fingers slid beneath her shirt and over her breast. Her nipples contracted sharply and an answering twinge echoed between her thighs. She yearned for Auden's touch, but even more, she was desperate to touch her.

"Straddle me," Hays murmured as she reached to undo Auden's blouse.

Auden shifted until she was on her knees above Hays's lap, her hands moving automatically to Hays' shoulders for support. When Hays opened the last button, slid the silk from Auden's shoulders and, with one hand, released the clasp on the sheer lace brassiere, Auden's bare breasts were a breath away from Hays's lips.

"You're perfect," Hays said softly as she let the garments fall. Cradling both breasts in her palms, she pressed them together and lowered her head.

"Oh yes." Auden arched her back, her lids closing, as she felt her nipple drawn into the warmth of Hays's mouth. The sensation was at once soothing and stimulating. She felt cherished even as her body ignited with arousal. Threading her fingers into Hays's hair, she drew her lover's face more closely to her flesh. "Harder," she whispered. "Take me harder."

Groaning, Hays softly licked first one nipple, then the other, until they hardened and contracted with the merest brush of her tongue. She sucked them between her lips, tormented them with her tongue, teased them with her teeth until Auden made small mewling sounds and rocked her hips urgently in Hays's lap.

"Can you come like this?" Hays asked, her mouth still on Auden's breasts, her chest heaving. The intensity of Auden's response was breathtaking, and Hays's head was light with excitement.

"I...I don't know. God, it's wonderful." Auden pulled Hays's head back and searched her face, her vision so clouded with need that it was difficult for her to focus. Despite the demanding pulsations that hammered through her depths with each heartbeat, it was the fierce lust in Hays's expression that sent her soaring. "If you...keep doing that...I think I will. I...want to."

"I love to feel you come."

"Make me."

"Soon." Hays kept one breast in her hand, lightly biting the nipple, as she slid her palm down Auden's bare abdomen and loosened the waistband on her slacks. She felt Auden tense and drew her mouth away for an instant. "It's all right. Just let me have you."

"Yes. Yes." Auden closed her eyes again and lowered her head until her forehead rested against Hays's hair. She wrapped her arms around Hays' shoulders, keeping her lover close in the circle of her embrace. Her thighs quivered continuously as the pressure built. Her breath made a small sobbing sound as she gasped with each pinpoint of pleasure streaking from her breast. She ached to come, but she did not want the ecstasy to end. "Go slow. Oh please, go slow."

Hays continued to caress one nipple as she pressed a hand inside Auden's slacks, between her legs, and gently enclosed her tense clitoris between her fingers. At the measured, torturous caress, Auden gave a small cry and thrust spasmodically into Hays's palm.

"Easy, darling," Hays soothed, her lips on Auden's neck. "Easy."

"You'll make me come," Auden cried desperately, her head thrown back, her fingers gripping Hays's back. "Oh, you will."

Hays stilled her movements, but kept her fingers resting lightly between Auden's thighs. Incredibly aroused herself, Hays was gasping for breath, her heart pounding erratically. She wanted to pleasure Auden, but she wanted to claim her as well. It took every ounce of willpower she had not to push inside her, to possess her immediately. When Auden's frantic motion slowed, Hays began again, sliding her fingers between swollen folds, drawing moisture from Auden's depths, steadily stroking her clitoris. With her ear now pressed to Auden's heart, Hays led her close to orgasm and then backed off, time and again.

"Oh please," Auden choked, grasping Hays's wrist in one hand then forcing the tormenting fingers inside the places that screamed to be filled, "let me come now."

Wrapping an arm around Auden's waist, Hays braced her legs and pushed deeper. The sudden pressure caused Auden to rear back as she cried out her pleasure. "I've got you," Hays groaned, unable to temper her own rampant need. She pressed her palm hard against Auden's clitoris with each forceful stroke, her pace escalating until Auden stiffened and jerked once, violently, in her arms.

"Oh Hays," Auden cried, clutching Hays's arms as she bent double under the force of the raging orgasm. Then she collapsed, burying her tear-streaked face in Hays's neck. "Unbelievable...oh God..."

Hays stilled her motions but remained inside, marveling at the small contractions that rippled around her fingers. Stroking Auden's hair with her free hand, she kissed the damp skin of Auden's temple. "You are so incredible."

"I love you," Auden sighed, unable to move a single muscle.

God help me, I want it. Hays closed her eyes tightly, pressing her cheek to the top of Auden's head. Gently, she leaned to the side and stretched out on the couch, cradling Auden against her until they were lying side by side. Blindly, she groped around, found the afghan, and pulled it over them. With Auden's head pillowed on her shoulder, she was supremely satisfied.

"Hays?" Auden's voice was somnolent and a bit slurred.

"Hmm?"

"Aren't you...shouldn't I...?"

Hays laughed. "Am I turned on? Christ, yes. Like exploding head kind of turned on, and no, you don't need to do anything right now. It's fun to wait sometimes." She kissed Auden, enjoying the way her lips felt, soft and swollen with sex. "And I love holding you, feeling your body relax, knowing I've satisfied you."

"Satisfied me," Auden mumbled, burrowing closer, one leg resting between Hays's. "Ha."

As Auden's breathing eased into the cadence of sleep, Hays watched the fire slowly burn to flickering embers. She kissed the corner of Auden's mouth and saw the ghost of a smile. Her heart was so full, she ached.

Very softly she breathed, "I love you, sweet Auden."

❖

Auden awoke in the darkened room. The fire had long since burned out, and the house was completely still. She lay against Hays' side, her cheek on Hays's chest. It amazed her how normal it felt to wake up in Hays's arms when it was, in fact, such a new experience.

Everything about being with Hays had that strange duality, of being at once something so familiar and, at the same time, so wholly foreign. Hays's hands on her skin, inside her body, was an entirely new sensation, and yet, the joining was so completely right that it felt natural. Giving herself to Hays physically, being claimed by her, was exhilarating and so much more satisfying than she had imagined sex would be. She had anticipated pleasure, but she had expected something similar to the release she had enjoyed by her own hand. She'd been wrong. What she experienced when Hays touched her—when she surrendered all control, loosed all restraints, bared all of her defenses— went far beyond the physical. As she climaxed in Hays's arms, she was no longer alone. That primal connection was more powerful than anything she had ever dreamed, and she knew, without doubt, that she never wanted to lose it. She tightened her hold on the woman in her arms. *I never want to lose you.*

Eventually, Auden lifted her head and kissed the side of Hays's neck. "Sweetheart?"

"Hmm?" Hays's voice was drowsy.

"We should put the food away and go to bed."

"You uncomfortable? It's so peaceful here."

"It is." Auden ran her hand down Hays' stomach and along one lean thigh. "It's wonderful. But I want very much to be close to you with nothing separating us, not even clothes...and if we get naked here, we'll freeze."

Hays felt a stirring in her stomach at the light caresses. "Well, since you put it that way." She pushed back the cover and slowly sat up. "I'll show you the bedroom and then come down and put the food away."

"Thanks. I'd love to jump into the shower before bed."

"No problem." Hays stood and extended her hand. "Time for that tour."

It was hard for Auden to pay attention to the house, although it was beautiful. The problem was, Hays was even more arresting. Her dark hair was disheveled from their lovemaking and fell onto her face in a distractingly charming way, her shirttail hung loosely outside her trousers, and the top two buttons of her shirt were open enough to afford Auden a tantalizing glimpse of her breasts from time to time. Apparently, being in love caused the majority of brain cells to malfunction, because all Auden could think about was being in bed with Hays and pleasing her the way she herself had been pleased.

"Here's the bedroom," Hays said as she indicated the room beyond the open doorway. "The bath is inside to the right." She reached inside, flipped a switch which lit a bedside lamp, then turned and caught Auden around the waist, pulling her into an embrace. The kiss lasted longer than Hays had intended. Auden's mouth was so warm, so soft, that she was immediately lost in the sweetness. It wasn't until she realized that they were both panting slightly and that Auden's hand was under her shirt, stroking her abdomen and sending delicious tremors down her thighs, that she drew back. "Just something to remember me by while you shower."

"Oh," Auden breathed in a throaty whisper. "Believe me, I won't forget. Hurry back."

"You won't even know I'm gone." Hays kissed her again, then, with one last smile, turned and headed quickly to the staircase and out of sight.

Auden was astounded to discover that it actually hurt to watch Hays walk away. The desire she had felt only seconds before coalesced into a hard ache in the pit of her stomach, and she wasn't sure if it was merely the flush of arousal denied or another newly found emotion—the fear of losing Hays. The arrival of love had opened vistas of possibility and delivered a gemini of inextricably bound sentiments—joy and terror. Auden was at a loss to tell, sometimes, which one it was she felt. Pleasure and pain so often, it appeared, hurt the same.

Moments later, Auden emerged from the bathroom after a hurried shower, a towel wrapped around her body, to discover Hays sitting on the side of the bed, barefoot but still in her clothes. She'd started another fire in the bedroom fireplace and turned out the lights. The room was warm, the air shimmering with firelight and promise.

"Hello again," Auden said as she approached. Now that they were there, in the bedroom, in the undeniably beautiful and intimate surroundings, she felt both shy and excited. *Another first time. Another memory to be cherished.*

In an unusually hesitant voice, Hays said, "I didn't get undressed. I thought maybe you'd want to do that."

Auden caught her breath, her legs suddenly so weak she had to fight to stay upright. "Oh, yes. Yes, I would."

Slowly, Hays stood and stepped forward until she was inches from Auden. "Is here okay?"

"Perfect." Auden found it difficult to speak, her throat was so filled with emotion. Desire, gratitude, wonder. Slowly, she opened the last buttons on Hays' shirt, spreading the material as she moved down her body. As Hays stood facing the fire, the flames' reflection danced along the surface of her skin like otherworldly fingers. "I love the way you look."

"I'm glad." Hays shivered lightly as Auden bent to kiss the inner surface of her breast. Her need, ignited by their earlier lovemaking, had never abated but had merely steeped, like embers beneath ashes, while they had slept. The merest brush of Auden's gaze inflamed her.

"I'm sorry I'm not as practiced at this as you," Auden murmured, releasing the button on Hays's waistband.

"Oh no," Hays whispered, at once cupping her palm beneath

Auden's chin and staring intently into her eyes. "You're exactly what I need. Take your time—I want every touch to last...a lifetime."

Auden's eyes filled with tears.

"Don't." Hays's voice was tender. "Keep going. You make me feel wonderful. Please."

Smiling tremulously, Auden nodded. Then, as her hands grazed the skin of Hays's abdomen and the muscles tensed at her touch, she forgot her grief, lost in the splendor of the moment. She slipped the shirt from Hays' shoulders and let it fall onto a nearby chair. Hays's nipples were hard, enticingly erect, and Auden couldn't resist fondling them, gently squeezing until Hays softly groaned. Emboldened, Auden brought her mouth to Hays's while sliding her hands into Hays's trousers and pushing them down over her hips. They kissed, their lips the only point of contact as Hays stepped free of the pants.

Releasing the towel, Auden let it drop to join the trousers on the floor, pressed against Hays, and wrapped her arms around her waist. She was naked, and Hays's briefs were all that remained between them now.

"Auden," Hays gasped, as she felt Auden's hands caress the length of her back. "I've never...felt like this before."

"Like how?" Auden pressed her mouth to the hollow below Hays's collarbone and sucked lightly on the soft skin. "Hmm?"

"Like...oh..." Hays swayed and had to steady herself by gripping Auden's hips. "Like I could stay in this one spot forever and never want for anything else."

Auden slowly traced a finger along the inside band of Hays's briefs, running along her hip, then over the crest of bone, and dipping low over her belly. Hays's hips lifted as her legs tensed. "We *can* stay here forever," Auden promised as she worked her palm beneath the material and pressed lower, her fingers threading through soft curls. "But I want...everything."

Hays closed her eyes, her attention riveted on the single focal point of arousal millimeters away from Auden's fingertips. All thought, every sensation, each iota of awareness was fixed on the instant when flesh answered need.

"Let's lie down," Auden whispered, withdrawing her hand. "So I can touch you."

"Oh, Jesus, yes."

Taking Hays by the hand, Auden stepped to the bed and drew the covers down. Then she reached for Hays's briefs. "One last item."

An instant later, they were in bed, Hays half sitting, propped up against the pillows, Auden reclining next to her, supported on a bent elbow so that she could look down the length of Hays's body and touch her anywhere. Everywhere.

"Teach me what you like," Auden said softly, smoothing her palm down the center of Hays's body, then resting a cupped hand between her thighs.

Hays stroked the back of Auden's neck with trembling fingers, staring at the delicate hand lightly holding her. "I like everything you do. I like..." Her throat closed off with a choked whimper as Auden slid one finger along the side of her clitoris.

"That?" Auden's voice was hoarse. A huge fist had closed around her heart, and it was hard for her to breathe. She had never been so excited in her life. She moved her finger, felt the stiff shaft pulse. "Do you like that?"

"Oh, yes. Yes." Hays pressed her left hand hard against the bed, the other clutching Auden's shoulder. She watched Auden stroke her slowly, the twin sensations of sight and touch almost too much to bear. It was so exquisite, her stomach cramped with pleasure.

"You're so wet." Auden smoothed her fingertips through the evidence of Hays's passion, astounded at the rush of warmth between her own thighs. She drew her fingers upward, felt the echoing pulsation in her own engorged flesh. "So hard."

Hays fought to keep her eyes open, but her mind was dissolving into heat and color. Her vision dimmed as Auden's caress became firmer, faster.

"Will this make you come?"

"Uh...huh," Hays managed, staring through half-closed lids at the hand circling between her thighs, every muscle clenched, her hips rocking, nerve endings on the brink of going off in Auden's hand.

Auden wasn't sure which was more beautiful, the way Hays felt thrusting beneath her fingers, or the way she looked, poised to orgasm. She drew a surprised breath, her eyes locking with Hays. "Oh my God." Hays's pupils dilated, flickering wildly. "I can feel you coming."

Legs tightening around Auden's hand, Hays tensed, gave a small cry, and shuddered into orgasm. As the pleasure jolted through her, she pulled Auden into her arms, needing as much contact as possible. The weight of Auden's body bearing down on her, the hand still massaging her exploding flesh, set off another round of spasms, and she cried out again.

"Oh, sweetheart," Auden moaned, her face buried in Hays's neck. It was all too much—the wonder, the excitement, the heart-wrenching beauty of the woman in her arms. Tears flooded her eyes, wet her cheeks, even as she felt her own body soar to a climax.

It was impossible to tell who sheltered whom as they rocked together in the aftermath of passion, each murmuring assurances and tenderly stroking away their mingled tears. Facing one another, arms and legs entwined, their smiles were twin reflections of vulnerability and awe.

"I don't—"

"I've never—"

They both laughed.

"You leave me unable to say what I want to with frightening regularity," Hays confessed. "For an author, that's rare."

"Margo wrote something that I think of every time I look at you," Auden whispered.

"Oh, really?" Hays raised an eyebrow, then traced a finger over Auden's mouth, smiling when she received a kiss. "What?"

"'After being with you, any other love would be but a pale imitation.'"

"Oh, sweet Auden." Hays's heart nearly broke to see the tears shimmer again on Auden's lids. "No."

"Promise me you won't give up, Hays." Auden threaded trembling fingers into Hays's hair, forcing Hays to look at her. "Promise me you'll fight."

Hays answered the only way she dared. With a kiss.

CHAPTER TWENTY-SIX

I guess it would be a problem if we both showed up late for work again, huh?" Auden lay in Hays's arms, her head nestled in the crook of her lover's neck.

"Mmm." Hays made lazy circles on Auden's back, unable to think of another thing she would rather be doing. "Would it bother you if people knew?"

"About us?" Auden kissed Hays's jaw. "God, no. It's going to be all I can do not to put a big sign on you at the convention in New York saying *don't touch, she's mine.*"

I'd like to be yours. I'd like to be yours forever and beyond. Hays pressed her lips to Auden's hair, unable to answer. She hadn't been so close to tears so often since the day that Paul Rosenberg had explained to her why she was too tired to work a full day and why the smallest cut bled for hours. Auden was the answer to every dream she had ever dreamed, the embodiment of every love story she had ever written, and now that she'd found her, it was too late.

"Hays?" Auden felt the sudden tension. "Too soon? I didn't mean to sound so possessive—"

"No." Hays's voice was hoarse with the struggle to hold back the tears. "Not too soon at all." *Too late. Can't you see that it's already too late?* She cupped Auden's cheek and kissed her mouth softly, a lingering kiss that spoke of cherishing and devotion. "It's not necessary, but I'd wear a sandwich board saying *Property of Auden Frost* if it would make you happy."

Auden leaned up on her elbow and searched Hays's face. "Then what is it? What hurts you?"

Hays looked away. Auden drew her face back with a finger against her chin. "What is it, sweetheart? Please tell me."

"I want you so much," Hays whispered.

"Believe me, you have me." Auden kissed her lightly, then drew away, studying her eyes. And waited.

"I don't want to die."

Auden bit the inside of her lip, determined not to cry. She nodded, praying that the moisture pooling on her lashes would not fall.

"But I'm afraid that I will," Hays admitted, "and I'm afraid it's wrong to let you love me."

"I already do love you." Auden stilled the protest she knew was coming with a finger against Hays's mouth. "I do. Accept it or don't accept it, but let it be because of what you want, not because of what you fear."

"I want it. God, I want you, but—"

"No buts." Auden rested her hand on Hays's abdomen, tenderly stroking her. She loved the way Hays' skin felt, so soft and so different from the firm muscles beneath. She loved touching her and couldn't imagine a day without being able to. If she thought about that possibility, she knew she would scream. "Tell me about the bone marrow transplant."

Hays closed her eyes, and for a moment, Auden thought she wouldn't answer. It took everything she had not to push. She just continued her gentle caresses, letting Hays know she was not alone.

"My brother Christopher has offered to donate, if I decide..." *To take the chance.* "That improves my odds."

Odds. The word, the *concept,* when applied to Hays's life, was indescribably terrifying. Auden took her time, making sure her voice was steady. "That's good then, right?"

"Paul—Paul Rosenberg, my hematologist—wants to try something new. There's a procedure called a *mini* bone marrow transplant." Hays grimaced. "It's complicated."

"What an understatement." Auden laughed harshly. "Tell me the best you can."

"Well, the process is simpler in some ways than traditional bone marrow transplants. It's a lot shorter, which means that I wouldn't have to stay in the hospital for weeks. They use less chemotherapy and radiation before the transplant, which means that I'm not likely to have the really bad side effects—hair loss, intestinal bleeding, nausea and vomiting—the list goes on." She swallowed hard, threading her fingers through Auden's. "That's the good part."

Auden kissed her forehead. "Okay so far. What else?"

"The theory is that the cells from the donor are healthier than my own bone marrow, and they will attack my sick cells and kill them, then repopulate my bone marrow with all new healthy cells." Hays smiled, but her eyes were damp. "If that happens, there's a better chance of cure than with any other treatment."

"What's the downside?" Auden knew there had to be a reason that Hays hadn't done this already. She understood that part of Hays's reluctance was the fact that there was no guarantee that it would work, that it was the choice of last resort. *But God, just hearing about it gives me hope.*

Hays tried to sound nonchalant, but her entire body was rigid. "This process, where the healthy cells kill the bad cells, can get out of hand, apparently. The reaction can end up involving healthy tissues, and there's a chance that I could have other organs fail. Then..." She gave a small laugh. "There's always the chance that it won't work quite right, and the healthy cells will kill off my bone marrow but not repopulate, leaving me with nothing at all. So, the downside is the same as what we're looking at now—I die."

"Okay, what are the chances?" Auden was nauseous and hoped it didn't show. She wanted someone to be angry with; she wanted someone, something, *anything,* to blame; she wanted a weapon with which to fight back. Having none of those things left her feeling helpless and grief stricken and, unless she fought it, defeated. If she felt that way, she could only imagine what it must be like for Hays.

"A little bit better than a coin toss."

Auden remembered what Gayle had told her about the conventional methods. "That sounds decent. Will you do it?"

"I think so," Hays said softly, touching the corner of Auden's mouth with one finger. "If I do, we won't know for a while if it works. Until then, you and I should put this...us...on hold."

Auden gasped. "You can't be serious."

"I don't want you to be hurt by all of this, Auden. I don't want you to suffer through the treatments, and even then—"

"Stop, Hays. Just...stop." Auden spoke quietly, tenderly. "You don't get it, do you? I love you. It isn't conditional. If we waited for guarantees, we could wait a lifetime. I want every minute that I can have with you."

Auden wouldn't have cried if Hays hadn't—she was certain of that. But the sight of Hays's tears was her undoing. With a small cry, Auden gathered Hays into her arms and pressed her lover's face to her breasts. She didn't tell her not to cry, but merely held her as tightly as she possibly could. As Hays sobbed, great bone-wracking, shattering sobs, Auden's tears ran silently down her cheeks. She threaded her fingers in Hays's hair, caressed her, wrapped arms and legs about her, offering a physical shield with the curve of her own body, as if that would ever be enough. She had never felt so powerless in her life.

After a while, Hays quieted. She pressed a kiss to Auden's breast, then lifted her face until she could meet Auden's concerned gaze. "Auden, I'm sorry. I've never done that before."

"Well then, I'm glad you did it now." Auden kissed her and brushed the last of her tears away with a thumb. "Are you all right?"

"Better." Hays managed to grin, a fairly good rendition of her usual one. "We're going to have to hurry if we're going to keep our reputations intact at the office."

"Well, we should certainly keep our priorities straight." Auden moved to sit up, but Hays restrained her with a hand on her arm. "What, sweetheart?"

"There's something I need to ask you."

"What is it?" *What more could there be?*

"It's about the fact that you quoted Margo Elliot last night."

"Surely you can't be jealous." Auden's expression was incredulous.

"I'm not, but Rune might be."

Auden laughed out loud and pushed Hays onto her back. Then she climbed on top of her, slid a thigh between Hays's, and framed her face with her palms. "Rune Dyre has absolutely nothing to worry about. She is, without question, the sexiest, most romantic writer I have ever encountered. And just to be certain there's no confusion, I'll send her an e-mail later and tell her so."

"She'll be very happy to hear that, I'm sure." Hays's voice had gotten husky. "Now you really *do* need to get up."

"Am I too heavy?"

"Not at all, my love." Hays ran her fingertips down either side of Auden's spine, then cupped her buttocks and pulled her closer. "You're too exciting." She shifted her hips slightly, moving against Auden's skin. "Can you feel what you've done to me?"

"Oh...God," Auden breathed, instantly aroused. "You're so wet."

"Mmm," Hays agreed, running her tongue up Auden's neck. "In another ten seconds, I'm not going to be able to let you up."

Auden didn't want to go, but some part of her insisted that they should. As much as she wanted every second of Hays's time, together, like this, she knew that they needed a semblance of normality as well. "Do I get a rain check?"

"As many as you want."

With more willpower than she thought she possessed, Auden moved away. She regretted it immediately as her body screamed in protest and her heart joined in. "One at a time will do nicely."

"There's an endless supply, all with your name on them. Every rainy day, you'll get a make-up day in the sun."

"I'll love you no matter what the weather." Auden kissed her, then jumped from the bed.

Hays lingered a moment as she watched Auden leave the bed and start for the bathroom. It was such a small thing, but she cherished how simple, how normal, the moment felt. Auden had a way of making her life seem both ordinary and enchanted at the same time. Auden made anything seem possible.

"Hays? Come shower with me?"

Hays followed the sound of her lover's voice, a line Rune had written playing through her mind.

"If she had held out her hand, I would gladly have taken it and followed, unto death."

❖

-----Original Message-----
From: AFrost@PalmPub.net
Sent: Wednesday April 2, 9:59 AM

From: Rune@HeartLand.com
Subject: Dark Passions
Attachments: DarPas-EditOneAF.doc 858KB

Ms. Dyre:

  I've enclosed the first edits of *Dark Passions*. Please return with your revisions.
  If you have any problems or concerns, feel free to contact me at any time.

Yours truly,
Auden Frost

p.s.: BTW - no one else writes like you do. You make me weak with wanting. Weather report says no rain tonight. AF

Hays was smiling at the message on the monitor, no doubt looking like a lunatic, when Abel knocked on the door, entered the room, and walked toward her desk.

"Morning, Abel."

"Hays." He regarded her with an expression of cautious concern. "I'm used to you being here by seven. Are you all right?"

Hays reached for her coffee cup. "I'm fi—"

"Good God, Hays!" he blurted, all vestiges of restraint gone. "You've just been transfused. That shouldn't be happening now. You *are* ill."

"What the hell are you talking about?" She followed his gaze and, for the first time, noticed the bruise on her wrist. She remembered Auden grabbing her hand when they'd been making love, forcing her fingers inside. She blushed as a wave of arousal followed fast on the memory. Clearing her throat, she added, "That's not what you think."

"You can't lie to me." His fear came out as anger. "I *know* what happens when your counts drop."

"It's just an ordinary bruise," she insisted. She saw the hurt he tried to hide. "Christ. It's from sex, Abel."

His mouth formed a perfect O, and on him, it was so incongruous that Hays laughed out loud. "You do realize that once in a while I—"

"That's quite all right. I don't require an explanation." He looked at the door, and then back at her. "I just didn't realize there was... someone."

"It's Auden, Abel," she said quietly. She didn't tell him because she felt obliged to tell him, but because she simply wanted to say the words out loud. Auden had said she didn't mind who knew, and just thinking about being with Auden made Hays's heart lift in a way she had forgotten. She couldn't help but smile.

Abel Pritchard seemed a little less than overjoyed. "You think that's wise?"

"Why not?"

"Well, I can think of any number of reasons. You haven't known each other very long, she works here, and—"

"I'm dying and have no business being involved with anyone?"

He looked as if she had slapped him. "No. God, no."

She regarded him thoughtfully and saw the moment he realized the truth about what he really felt.

"I'm sorry, Hays," he said and turned away.

She got up quickly and intercepted him before he reached the door. Closing it quietly, she then turned and placed her hand on his arm. "No, *I'm* sorry, Abel. You didn't deserve that."

"Actually, I did." She was right about what he felt, and he hated that she knew.

"Okay. So we're even."

He smiled infinitesimally. "Does she know?"

"Yes."

"What does she say?"

Hays was silent for a few seconds, thinking of everything that she and Auden had discussed. She thought about the things that Auden said to her without words, but with her touch. "She says that forever is only a series of moments, and that I should fight for every one."

Abel Pritchard did something extraordinary then. He touched her cheek in the faintest of caresses. "Ms. Frost is a very astute woman."

"Yes, she most certainly is," Hays said softly as she opened the door and watched Abel walk away.

```
-----Reply-----
From: Rune@HeartLand.com
To: AFrost@PalmPub.net
Sent: Wednesday April 2, 10:23 AM
Subject: Re: Dark Passions
```

I'll review your comments regarding *Dark Passions* as soon as possible. I look forward to working with you on this manuscript.

Sincerely, RD

p.s.: The weather report shows clear skies every day this week. Rune

❖

Two nights later, Gayle hurried down the stairs to unlock the front door. She'd been watching the clock for the last hour. Through the frosted glass, she could barely discern the outline of a figure standing on the porch, but it was enough to make her heart race. She disengaged the deadbolt and pulled open the door, wondering for the tenth time in as many minutes if everything had changed during the time they'd been apart. Maybe it had all been just a weekend fling. Then she looked up into the softest brown eyes she had ever seen and watched the grin break out on Thane's face. Friday night had never held such promise.

"Hiya, sexy."

"Hey," Thane said, leaning forward to kiss Gayle on the mouth. "I missed you like hell."

"Well, that was the perfect thing to say. You're scary, how good you are." Gayle put her arms around Thane, kissed her again, then took her hand and led her inside. "Then again, you are a writer."

"That wasn't a line," Thane said quickly, stopping Gayle at the bottom of the stairs with a hand on her arm. Her expression was very serious. "I meant it."

Gayle paused at the hurt in Thane's eyes. Gently, she rested her palm against Thane's cheek. "I'm sorry. That was me being tough. I was worried all week that you might change your mind about wanting... me."

"No," Thane said softly, turning her head to place a kiss in the center of Gayle's palm. "I want you. I want us."

"Jesus, you have to stop saying everything I need to hear," Gayle admonished, but her tone belied her words.

"Sorry," Thane replied, her eyes dancing. "Can't help it. I write romances."

Laughing softly, Gayle threaded her arm around Thane's waist and started up the stairs. "Then write us one."

"We'll collaborate," Thane whispered.

As they climbed to her apartment, Gayle said, "I sent Shylock off to camp again. Mrs. T likes to have him, and I figured there wouldn't be enough room for all of us in bed tonight."

Thane smiled as she waited for Gayle to open the door. "Well, we can visit him, right?"

"If I ever let you out of this apartment, sure." Gayle closed the door and turned to study her visitor. "I didn't make dinner reservations anywhere. I wasn't sure what you would want to do. I can call somewhere or..."

Thane dropped her overnight bag, put an arm around Gayle's waist, and led her to the sofa where she pulled her down on her lap. "You know what I'd really like?"

"What?" Gayle kissed Thane's lips, her cheek, then nuzzled her neck, biting lightly. "What would you *really* like, huh?"

"Ah...that would definitely be one thing." Thane smoothed her hand down Gayle's arm, then along her thigh, pulling her tighter into her lap. "Christ, you feel good."

"If you make *me* feel any better, you're not getting any dinner." Gayle couldn't believe how quickly Thane could make her hot.

"What I'd like to do," Thane murmured, drawing her fingers up the inside of Gayle's leg, stopping just short of the vee between her thighs, "is watch a video, eat pizza, and make love to you until you scream."

Gayle moaned softly, pressed Thane's hand against the heat between her legs, and moved her lips softly over Thane's ear. "Would you mind very much if we reversed the order?"

Thane shifted until Gayle was beneath her on the couch and deftly opened the button on Gayle's jeans. "Not in the least."

CHAPTER TWENTY-SEVEN

Gayle opened her eyes and realized that she was alone. For one heart-stopping instant, she thought that Teddy had left her in the night. The aching disappointment was frightening, because she couldn't remember ever having cared that much about a woman before. She took a deep breath to steady herself and peered at the bedside clock, amazed to see that it was almost eight. Sitting up, she took rapid stock of her surroundings. Teddy's pants were lying over the arm of a chair across the room, and her overnight bag was standing open on the floor. *She's still here.*

Quickly, she climbed from the bed and pulled on the first thing she found, an oversized flannel shirt. She didn't bother with anything else. Dashing into the living room, she became aware of several things at once—the enticing smell of coffee emanating from the kitchen and, even better than that, the sight of Teddy, wearing a T-shirt, sweatpants, and no shoes, sitting in front of the computer. The simplicity of the moment was exquisitely sweet. Plus, just seeing Teddy the first thing in the morning was enormously exciting.

"Hey, baby. What are you up to?"

Thane turned from the computer, blushing. "I'm sorry. I usually wake up really early, and I knew I'd probably disturb you if I tossed and turned. I didn't think you'd mind if I—"

Gayle stopped her with a kiss. "I don't mind. Well, I missed you when I woke up, but I forgive you because you made coffee."

"Good," Thane said as she stood, threading her arms around Gayle's waist and pulling her close. "Because I certainly don't want you to be upset with me." She slid her hands down Gayle's back, over her buttocks, and underneath the tail of the shirt. When her palms met flesh, she drew a sharp breath. "Oh, man. Jesus...the minute I touch you, all I can think about is getting naked with you."

"You'll get no complaints from me," Gayle replied, pressing against Thane as she nuzzled her ear. "Are you working?"

"Uh-huh." Thane's attention at that moment, however, was totally focused on the subtle contractions of the muscles under her hands as Gayle gently thrust her hips. The combination of Gayle's body moving slowly along the length of her own and the heat of Gayle's skin against her fingers was intensely arousing. "Writing."

"I like that. I think it's sexy that you're writing here."

"Sexy, huh? How about we get *sexy* in the bedroom?" Thane was breathing heavily and caressing the back of Gayle's leg. She moved around to the front, intent on drawing her fingers up the inside of Gayle's thigh.

Gayle worked her hands under Thane's T-shirt, then upward to her breasts. As she rubbed her palms over the instantly hardening nipples, she groaned softly. "Oh yeah. Good idea."

Before they could reach the bedroom, a knock sounded on Gayle's door. Gayle groaned again, this time with frustration. "It's either Mrs. T about Shylock or it's Auden. Do you mind?"

"No," Thane said hoarsely, although already her body was pulsating with need. "Go ahead." She settled her hips against the back of the couch as Gayle went to the door. Watching Gayle walk, enjoying the line of her long legs and the incredibly rich color of her coffee and cream skin, was almost as good as touching her.

When Gayle pulled open the door, Auden took a step inside, saying "Hi," then stopped abruptly when she saw Thane. "Oh, I'm so sorry. I completely forgot—"

"It's okay," Gayle said. "We were just on our way back to the bedroom."

Thane laughed, and Auden blushed.

"Sorry, sorry to both of you. Gayle, call me...later...or sometime."

As Auden started to back out the door, Gayle caught her hand. "Hey, no you don't. I haven't seen you all week." She turned and looked at Thane over her shoulder. "Do you think you can keep things warm for a while?"

"I'll just set the burner to simmer." Then Thane grinned her enchanting grin. "Go ahead. I've got some things to work on."

"Let me put some sweatpants on and then we'll go down to your apartment, okay?" Gayle was already heading to her bedroom closet.

Auden nodded, and five minutes later she was pouring coffee for them in her kitchen. "I'm really sorry about interrupting you two. I've totally lost track of time."

"I've been looking for you all week, but your apartment has always been dark." Gayle reached for the coffee Auden offered. "Thanks."

"Things have been really hectic at work," Auden explained. "I think I told you that we're pushing to get Margo Elliot's book published for the convention next weekend. And of course, we're doing it with an entirely new team of people, not to mention that a lot of this is new to me as well."

"Mmm, you mentioned it." Gayle observed her friend intently, wondering at Auden's faint agitation. "Problems?"

"Nothing that doesn't happen fairly routinely, apparently." Auden crossed her legs beneath her on the chair and rested her elbows on the kitchen table, her chin in her hand. "I think we broke some kind of speed record getting the galleys back, but when I overnighted them to Margo Wednesday, she decided that she hated the cover. Now, mind you, this was a cover based on the design that *she* sent us from an artist *she's* been working with. And suddenly, at the eleventh hour, she decides it doesn't fit the tone of the book."

"Can't you just tell her she has to accept the cover?" Gayle pulled a banana out of a basket on the table and started to peel it. "After all, you are the big boss now."

Auden lifted a shoulder and made a face. "I could. But it would piss Margo off, and since I'm the one who stepped up the timetable and put a rush on things, I'm trying not to be too much of a dictator at this point."

"So what's going to happen?"

"I spent most of Thursday night and yesterday baby-sitting graphics and making sure that they were getting the revisions to her for her input. Somewhere around midnight last night, we finally got a consensus."

"So the book will be ready?"

Auden blew out a breath. "Well, assuming that Margo doesn't want any substantial changes to the text after she reviews the galleys this weekend, and assuming there are no delays with the printers, it should be a go."

"Cool. This is so exciting. I'm really looking forward to the convention."

"I imagine your excitement has a bit more to do with the fact that you'll be spending the weekend with Thane as opposed to looking at books for three days."

"Well, there is that." Gayle grinned, then eyed Auden speculatively, wondering what had really prompted the early-morning visit. "And what about you? I suppose you've been doing nothing all week except working? Which is why you're never here?"

Smiling softly, Auden ran a finger around the rim of her coffee cup, unused to talking about something so intimate. *Because I never had anything to talk about before.* "I've been at Hays's every night this week."

"Now, why aren't I surprised?" Gayle reached across the table and took Auden's hand. "Is it fabulous? Are you happy?"

Auden met Gayle's eyes, and she didn't even try to hide the tears. "It's...she's...everything is incredibly wonderful. It's just that..."

"What, honey? What?"

"Is it normal that I can't stand to be away from her? I'm not sure if I feel this way because that's what being in love feels like, or if it's because I'm afraid..." Her voice broke and she looked away. After a few seconds she finished, "Or if I'm just afraid of losing her."

"Oh, Aud. Sweetie. No." Gayle felt like weeping. It was unbearable to think that something which should be so joyous could be accompanied by such pain. "What you're feeling for her is absolutely, perfectly normal. At this point, you shouldn't be able to think of much more than getting her clothes off every time you see her. In a few weeks, you'll probably be able to have a conversation. It will take at least a few months before you can actually make it through dinner and a movie without wanting to rush home early and jump into bed." Gayle squeezed Auden's hand. "What you're experiencing is the good stuff, honey."

"Listening to you, I feel tired already." But Auden laughed, and her heart lifted. She refused to think about time and whether she and Hays would have enough of it for Gayle's predictions to come true.

"So how's Hays?" Gayle hoped that her tone sounded normal. Just an ordinary question.

"She's good. She's...unbelievable." Gayle smirked and Auden smacked her on the arm. "Stop."

"Sorry."

Auden drew a long breath, knowing what the real question was. "Her health seems fine. Her color is good, she doesn't appear to get fatigued, and there's been no bleeding."

"That's great."

Frowning, Auden confessed, "But I'm afraid that she won't tell me if she doesn't feel well."

"It's probably going to take a while for her to be able to do that, Aud," Gayle suggested carefully. "I'm sure that she wants to have as normal a relationship with you as possible and not dwell on her disease. Conditions like hers often lead to secrecy and poor communication. Just make sure she knows that you can handle the truth. Then you've got to give her some time."

"I never used to think about the future much before this. Now it seems to be all I think about."

"You've got to give *yourself* some time, too."

Auden sighed. "I'm trying."

"I think you're doing great. I'm so proud of you." Gayle made a conscious effort to lighten the conversation. "So, when are you heading up to New York?"

"The convention officially starts on Friday. Destiny is going to have a booth, and I plan on going up Thursday to make sure everything is in order."

"Are you staying with Hays?"

"Hays isn't going."

"What?"

Auden shook her head, grinning. "Rune Dyre is going to be there, though."

"Oh my God. That's like—*big* news."

"Believe me, I know. Rune—Hays—announced it on her website three days ago, and the e-mail response has been astonishing. I think a lot of people are coming because she's going to be there."

"You jealous?"

"A little," Auden admitted. "I'm not even used to the fact that we're...together yet, and I'm definitely not ready to share her. Still, her personal appearance is good marketing. She's going to do a book signing, even though her published books aren't Palmer's. But it's a great opportunity to push the release of *Dark Passions*, and I think I've talked her into doing a reading."

"Holy God! If she reads anything from that, you're going to have to put a bodyguard on your hotel room door."

"I suggested that we stay in separate rooms." Auden looked troubled. "It's a business trip, and the first time that Rune will be making a public appearance. I just thought it would be better."

"Is she okay with that?"

"I think so. It just seemed better for Rune to be Rune and not confuse the issue."

"Who's confused? Haydon Palmer is this gorgeous young publisher and Rune Dyre is probably the sexiest, most romantic lesbian author on the planet—with the exception of Thane Cutlass, of course—and you're sleeping with both of them. It's perfectly clear to me."

"That's kind of how I think of it, too," Auden agreed, smiling. "Now I need to shower, change, and meet one of them at the office."

"Actually, I've got an author of my own upstairs who needs some tending."

"That's right. You're in that 'can't get out of bed' stage, too. You have to tell me all about *that* next time we get together." Auden stood, her expression affectionate. "Things okay there, though?"

"If they were any better, I'd run screaming." Gayle grinned sheepishly. "She's too good to be true."

"No, she's just what you deserve. If I don't catch up with you again in the next few days, I'll see you in New York."

Gayle stood as well and put an arm around her friend's shoulders. "You can count on it. And until then, don't do anything except enjoy her."

❖

When Gayle let herself into the apartment, Thane was still at the computer. Quietly, Gayle headed for the kitchen and another cup of coffee. She stopped at the sound of the voice behind her.

"I missed you."

Gayle's heart swelled. Turning, she raised an eyebrow. "Oh yeah? I thought you were working."

"I was. But I was thinking about you."

"Oh." For a moment, Gayle wasn't certain what to say. She wasn't exactly sure what the ground rules were, or where the boundaries lay. She adored Thane's fiction, but it was Teddy she was sleeping with. She wasn't entirely certain if Thane Cutlass's writing was part of their new relationship.

"What?" Thane noted the small line that creased the smooth skin between Gayle's brows. Worriedly, she asked, "Does it bother you that I was working during our time together?"

"No, of course not. I think your work is amazing. I'm really happy that you were able to do it here. It's just..."

"What?" Thane rose and crossed the room. Leaning close, she rested her hands on Gayle's hips.

Gayle sighed and shrugged shyly. "I'm curious."

"Ah." Thane kissed her. "Wanna read it?"

"Oh, yeah. Big time." She hesitated. "You sure you don't mind?"

"Gayle, babe, I'm a writer. I want everyone to read what I write." Laughing, Thane took Gayle's hand and led the way to the computer. Then she sat and patted her lap. "Sit here and have a look."

Private Pleasures – Innocence Abounds

It's not what you think. I'm innocent. I swear.

At least, a minute ago, I was. We started out naked together, turning about each other in the warm spray—fighting over who would get the shampoo first. I hadn't intended anything—really—I just wanted to run my soapy hands over your body, to wash your back. Ten seconds ago, even, I was innocent. Then...I reached around you for the bath gel and our bodies collided.

Now, maybe I'm not so innocent.

Thane was very still, her cheek pressed against Gayle's breast, her eyes closed. She could hear Gayle's heart beating. In her mind, she saw the words she had written and waited for judgment.

Absently, Gayle stroked Thane's arm as she read, settling her hips more comfortably between Thane's spread legs, one arm around her lover's shoulder, toying with her hair. With the other hand, she scrolled.

> Our skin touches lightly, belly to belly, thigh to thigh, the silken hair between our legs blending gently in the warm streams of water coursing over our bodies. When I slip my arms around you to reach your back, our breasts meet. My nipples, instantly erect, slide over yours, sending pulsating shocks of pleasure straight down my spine. The flickering contact teases me, starts a tingling between my legs, but the fleeting pressure on the aching tips of my breasts is not hard enough, not long enough, for what I need.

Gayle's nipples tightened and the muscles in her thighs clenched. She was very aware of Thane's mouth a breath away from her skin. She threaded her fingers into Thane's hair more tightly and unconsciously pressed her breast against her lover's face.

> I secret a hand between us, find your nipple and squeeze—once, twice—before circling your breasts with my soapy fingers. The soft weight of you in my palm is an invitation to feast. My mouth is watering. Lifting both breasts so the warm cascade rinses the soap away, I bend my head, lick the clear drops from the tight, hard tips, and drink your passion.

You close your eyes and grasp my hips, pulling me tighter. Moaning, you push a muscled thigh between mine, arching your back as my teeth claim flesh. We reach for one another at the same time; I find your clitoris just as you touch mine. You stroke...

"I don't think I can read this with you so close to me," Gayle said, her voice husky and low. "It's wonderful, but all I can feel is you."

Eyes closed, Thane nuzzled a nipple, found it hard and tight, and sucked on it through the soft, worn flannel. "Too late. Keep going."

Struggling to focus, Gayle tried to follow the words.

You stroke me steadily as I roll the length of you lightly between my thumb and finger. Legs spread, hips pushing slowly forward, our soft sighs mingle. We mirror one another's movements, speeding up, pressing harder—each bringing the other closer with every stroke, moaning now on trembling legs. I search for your lips, clinging to you, and our mouths meet, tongues joining, sucking hard on swollen lips. I'm so hard now...

Gayle moaned and fumbled for Thane's hand, drawing it beneath the waistband of her sweatpants, pushing it between her thighs. "Feel what you've done to me."

Very lightly, Thane ran a single finger over Gayle's clitoris. Gayle gave a strangled cry and pressed her own hand over Thane's. "Oh, don't stop."

With her free hand, Thane opened a button on the flannel shirt, then two, then drew a nipple between her lips. Her mouth to Gayle's breast, Thane whispered, "Don't come until the end."

I'm circling my hips on your hand—it feels...

"So good."

   ...I can't bear it. You turn me away
from the stream of water, kneeling quickly,
both hands opening me for your lips. I'm
so full, so hard, so close to exploding—so
ready to come. Your tongue presses into me,
warm and sweet...

"Oh, yes, right there. Yes. That's so good."

   ...pulling the pleasure from me on a flood
of arousal. My back is against the shower
wall as you lean into me, sweeping your
tongue up the length of my clitoris...

"I'll come if you keep touching me there."

   ...making my head light and my stomach
twist. I can feel you moving against my
leg, wet and hard, and you make me want...

"Oh baby, I want..."

   ...to come. You are rocking against me as
you suck me now, both of us moaning.

"I'm so close, so close now."

   Your fingers are inside me, your lips
tugging at my clitoris...

"I need to come. I need..."

   ...your tongue working me back and forth.
I'm going to come soon. I won't come until

you say—but oh, God—I need to. Tell me when
I can come, tell me when...

"I'm coming...coming..."

   ...soon, soon, please tell me, tell me,
tell me...

"Oh God, Teddy...please, hold me."

"I'm right here. I won't let go."

Gayle clung to Thane, pressed her face to Thane's neck, trembling and shivering. "Oh, Jesus. I can't believe you."

"What?" Thane whispered, smoothing Gayle's hair, kissing her temple gently. "What, babe?"

"Everything," Gayle said with a sigh, overcome with the pleasant torpor. "You are so fucking talented, and so beautiful, and so...good."

"I guess you liked it, huh?" Thane chuckled, supremely satisfied.

"Nah, not really." Gayle bit Thane's ear weakly. "But I *would* like to try reenacting that shower scene."

"Now there's an idea."

"Is that by any chance what you had in mind when you let me read that?" Gayle met Thane's gaze and arched a brow. "Hmm?"

"Who, me?" Thane smiled, her eyes dancing. "No way. *I'm innocent.*"

CHAPTER TWENTY-EIGHT

Hays woke early even though they hadn't set the alarm. It was a little before seven, Friday morning. She gently fondled Auden's hair, letting the silken strands slide slowly through her fingers. She thought, as she lay in the utter stillness, feeling Auden's heart beat against her chest and sensing her own answering rhythm, that this might be the finest moment of her life. When a breath of warmth against her neck became a kiss, she knew that the woman curled in her arms was awake.

"Good morning."

"Mmm," Auden sighed, stretching indolently, nestling closer to Hays. "God, you feel incredible."

"Yeah, I do." Smiling, Hays turned her head on the pillow and kissed the corner of Auden's mouth. She smiled again when Auden gave a small, satisfied moan. Steadfastly, Hays ignored the faint pounding behind her eyes. Headache. It had been lingering just beyond the edges of her awareness for several days. It hadn't made itself completely known until last night. She'd felt it first when they'd reached the hotel after a full day at work and the usual aggravating drive to New York City. When they'd made love, the pleasure had nearly been eclipsed by the escalating pain deep in her skull—almost, but not quite. Nothing could obliterate the joy of being with Auden.

"You ready for today?" Auden shifted until she was lying on top of Hays, her head propped on one hand, one leg between Hays's. The room was brightening quickly. Hays looked so beautiful, with her dark hair framing her face and a smile lifting one corner of her wide, full mouth. As always happened when Auden looked at her lover, her heart gave a small jump.

"Sure," Hays replied. "I can handle two hours of social interaction."

"It'll be more than two hours," Auden pointed out. She ran her finger along the edge of Hays's jaw, then tapped her chin affectionately. "An hour signing this morning, then one this afternoon. And you're not going to be able to just disappear in between. Rune is popular. She has devoted fans. They want to meet her."

"Anything anyone needs to know about me is right there in my books," Hays insisted. "You know—art for art's sake, uncontaminated by the artist's presence."

"That's a point we could argue forever. Art historians certainly would disagree, I imagine." Auden leaned down and kissed the small frown on the enticing lips. "But I can tell you this. Public appearances are appreciated by readers, and it's a way of saying thank you to them for their support."

"Yeah, I know that," Hays grumbled good-naturedly. "Which is the real reason I agreed to come. Other than it makes Liz happy, and she's so hard to deal with when she's cranky."

Auden laughed. "Well, yes. We can't ignore the fact that it helps sales."

"At least I'm sharing a table with Thane. She can entertain everyone."

"She is unbelievably charming," Auden agreed.

"Hey—watch it."

"Ah," Auden crooned, fitting herself still closer to the curves and planes of Hays's body. "You have nothing to worry about. Ever."

Hays caught the back of Auden's head in her hand and pulled her down, kissing her with unexpected fierceness. She slid her other hand to the hollow at the base of Auden's spine, holding her firmly as she pressed her leg more tightly between Auden's thighs. Auden moaned softly and Hays felt herself grow hard against Auden's skin. As they explored one another's mouths, small teasing touches became hungry thrusts, and Hays's desire stirred urgently. Along with the rising arousal, her headache unexpectedly ratcheted up a notch, and she bit back a gasp of surprise.

"You make me so excited so quickly," Auden murmured when Hays broke the kiss. She rocked her hips, her lids heavy with desire. "Do we have time?"

"Time enough." Hays read the need in her lover's eyes. No amount of discomfort could distract her from this moment. Auden was wet against her leg and breathing heavily, hips rolling insistently. "I love how you get—so passionate, so ready."

"You..." Auden arched her back, moving in short hard jerks now. "You do this...to me." She gave a small cry and grew still, her body rigid. "I have to stop. It's...too much."

"No, keep going." Hays's voice was hoarse, her vision wavering with the pain. "I want to see you come."

Auden bit her lip, her stomach muscles quivering as she fought the need to orgasm. "It's all right?"

"It's wonderful." Hays brought her hands to Auden's breasts, cradling them as she grasped her nipples. "Just watch my face. See how you please me."

Auden braced herself with her hands on either side of Hays' shoulders and stared into the gold- and silver-shot depths of her lover's eyes. She wasn't aware of moving, of moaning, of twisting beneath the tormenting fingers that drove her ever higher. All she knew was Hays— her tenderness, her patience, her passion. The steady pressure on her nipples merged with the pounding pulse of blood between her thighs and the first ripples of orgasm whispered along her spine. "Oh!"

"Yes." Hays's heart beat frantically and she was faintly dizzy, but all she cared about was the beauty of watching Auden approach her climax. *I love you.*

In the final instant as her muscles clenched, then shattered, Auden closed her eyes, the image of Hays's face, alight with love, emblazed on her soul. Still coming, she collapsed into Hays's waiting arms and held on tightly.

"Thank you," Hays murmured, treasuring the gift.

"I feel..." Auden struggled to catch her breath and tried again. "I feel a little selfish."

Hays pushed the damp hair back from Auden's face and kissed her. "Oh, no, darling. You've given me something so special." She drew a long breath, pulling Auden even closer. "You've given me your trust."

"I love you, Hays. I'd give you anything." Auden slid a hand down Hays's belly, but Hays stopped her with a gentle grip on her wrist. Auden tensed at the unexpected restraint. "What?"

"Can I take a rain check?" The headache had turned brutal, and Hays knew the nausea was coming next.

Auden half sat up, her expression questioning. "Yeah?"

"I'm a tiny bit preoccupied." Hays managed a grin. "Thinking about the convention."

"Ah. Rune's debut." Auden laughed and stroked Hays's face. "Sure. I'll collect from you tonight." She leaned over, kissed Hays's breast once, then bounded from bed. "Let's shower and get dressed, and I'll treat you to breakfast."

Hays nodded. "You go ahead. I'll be right there."

When Auden disappeared into the bathroom, Hays switched on the bedside light and sat on the edge of the bed. She examined her arms and looked down at her thighs, her heart plummeting. There were bruises where Auden had pressed her hands when they'd made love the night before. Bruises that shouldn't be there, not so soon. *Oh, sweet Auden. I am so sorry.*

❖

"Here's my card," Auden said to the middle-aged woman in the windbreaker and jeans. "It sounds like a great story line. Send me the manuscript when you have it ready, and I'd be happy to take a look at it."

"Great. Thanks!"

As the woman turned away, Gayle edged through the small group of people until she reached Auden's side. "Hey. How's it going?"

"Terrific. This is so much fun. I've been talking to writers, other publishers, artists, and of course, readers. It's amazing." Auden took in her best friend at a glance. As usual, Gayle looked hot in skin-tight hip-hugger jeans and a painted-on black top that stopped somewhere in the vicinity of her navel. When she stretched, Auden glimpsed a hint of gold against her slightly darker skin. "Hey," she said, lifting the bottom edge of Gayle's top. "What have we here?"

Gayle grinned. "Piercing."

"Ooh, I like." Auden raised an eyebrow. "Is there a story behind this new acquisition?"

"Well, let's say Teddy supervised, and it was...fun." Gayle

remembered how carefully they'd had to make love the night they'd had it done, and how damned horny it had made her when Teddy had told the young woman doing the piercing just where she wanted it on Gayle's body—and then demonstrated, drawing her finger lightly over Gayle's navel.

"I'll *bet* it was fun if Thane was helping." Auden looked over her shoulder toward the table on the far side of the conference room where Thane and Hays sat signing books. "They're attracting a lot of attention."

"I can't believe I let Teddy out of the room in those leather pants."

"Uh, Gayle, sweetie, I don't think it's the pants—I think it's the leather vest with nothing under it. I just about died when she walked out of the elevator."

Gayle groaned. "When I saw her upstairs, I was too pheromonally impaired to censor the outfit. All I could think was yummy, yummy, yummy."

"Delightfully descriptive, Dr. Dunbar," Auden commented wryly.

"And now look," Gayle wailed. "Other women are drooling on her."

Auden laughed. "Well, I don't believe you have to worry. She's too busy working to get into trouble. Margo has a good crowd, too. We've sold a goodly number of *Pale Imitations* already. Our debut release is a hit."

Gayle watched the line moving slowly toward the authors. "Hays looks mighty tasty, too. Who would have thought that stonewashed jeans and a white shirt could look so appetizing?"

"Depends on who you put them on," Auden murmured, watching Hays return a book to a woman waiting at the head of the line. When Hays smiled, Auden's heart did a flip. "God, she's gorgeous."

"Mmm, like I said...yu—"

"Enough," Auden hissed. "No more culinary commentary on my girlfriend, if you please."

"So, how does it feel being Rune Dyre's honey?"

Auden blushed. "It feels...odd, and exciting, too. I think about people wanting to meet her or buy her books, and I'm proud and jealous at the same time."

Gayle nodded. "I know what you mean. Teddy writes stuff that makes me want to pull her clothes off and crawl all—"

"Uh, I got it. I got it." Auden laughed.

"Yeah, well, I don't like thinking some other woman might be feeling the same way."

"Sometimes, I'll look over when Hays is writing, and I'll see Rune. Really see her, as if I know her, too."

"You do, don't you?"

Auden followed the author's hands as she opened a book, carefully held it flat, and signed with a flourish. "Yes. There are times, like now, when Rune is as real to me as Hays."

Gayle grinned. "So, does it feel good?"

"What?"

"The girlfriend thing."

"Better than good," Auden said contemplatively, her eyes still on the dark head bent over another book. "Better than anything."

"Life is good, huh?" Gayle said quietly, not a hint of levity in her voice now.

Auden slid an arm around her friend's waist and squeezed. "Life is grand."

❖

Thane pushed her chair back and stretched. "I want a drink. How about you, buddy?"

Hays shook her head. She could barely focus, and she was afraid that if Auden saw her right now, she'd be able to tell something was wrong. "I'm going to find someplace quiet and decompress for a few minutes. I think Auden wants us at the opening reception at six."

"Where are they?" Thane asked, scanning the room. "I saw Gayle and Auden talking a while ago, but I don't see them now."

"I lost track of them. Auden and Liz are probably off in a corner somewhere with their heads together discussing marketing strategies."

"Gayle said she might sneak off to the gym," Thane mused. "I can't believe I miss her this much after just a few hours."

"Sounds pretty serious."

"Yeah. Well, I *am* serious." Thane was uncharacteristically quiet for a long moment. "I'm not so sure Gayle believes me, though."

"Why do you say that?"

"I think maybe Liz gave her the idea that I was a big player."

"And...you're not?"

"Well, I've been around." Thane shrugged. "Not as much as people think. Not *everything* I write is autobiographical." She laughed. "But this is different—it's not just good fun and sex. Gayle is like no one I've ever met; it's like she knows me, or at least sees me, and...she seems to like what she finds." Thane grimaced. "Jesus, that didn't make any sense, did it."

"Not true," Hays replied, thinking of Auden and all the things she'd never needed to explain. "It makes perfect sense."

"Man. Listen to us. A couple of gon—Christ, Rune. You're bleeding!"

Hays felt it at the same moment. She fumbled for her handkerchief, but Thane pressed a couple of paper napkins from a nearby tray into her hand. After a minute, Hays muttered, "Thanks."

"You okay?"

"Yeah." Hays's voice was muffled. "Look, I'm going to go upstairs and get cleaned up. I might be late for the reception. If you see Auden..." Her voice trembled, and she almost lost it. Everything was coming apart so fast, she could barely think what to do next. "If you see Auden, just tell her I got held up. Don't mention this, okay?"

"Okay, sure. Look—do you need me to come with you?"

"No. I'm fine. It's stopped." Hays shook her head carefully. "I've got to go. Listen, Thane. About *Eros*—go ahead and use my stuff if you want."

Thane stared at her, startled by the sudden turn of the conversation. "Great. Excellent. We'll have to get together and decide which ones we want and how to order them. Maybe talk to Paula Young about tossing in a couple. She's popular with the soft-romance set."

"Anything you want." Hays held out her hand. "Thanks, Thane."

Thane shook it, still confused. "I'll see you later, then?"

"Sure."

Two minutes later, Hays was upstairs in her room. The first thing she did was make a series of phone calls. Then she sat down at the desk and booted up her laptop. As she typed, her hands shook.

❖

Forty-five minutes into the reception, Auden was starting to worry. Neither Hays, nor Thane, nor Gayle had appeared. It wasn't absolutely obligatory that the authors attend the opening reception, but most did. And she and Hays had agreed earlier that Rune would go.

With a quick surge of relief, she saw Thane and Gayle enter hand in hand. They'd both changed clothes and both looked a bit sheepish as they approached her through the crowd. Thane turned aside a few feet from Auden to speak to a woman who asked her a question.

"Sorry we're late, Aud," Gayle said, genuinely contrite. "We lost track of time."

"It's okay. I'm not going to penalize you." Auden was too concerned about Hays to care that her friends had apparently taken some time out to make love. "Have you seen Hays?"

"No." Gayle frowned. "Isn't she here with you?"

"No, she's not. I haven't seen her for hours. By the time Liz and I finished talking to the people from *Lambda Book Review*, Thane and Hays had finished with their signings. *I* thought the two of them were off doing author stuff or just hanging out." She tried not to sound as panicked as she felt. "I went up to my room for a few minutes and called hers, but there was no answer. I just assumed we'd meet here, so I came back down to network some more."

"Where's Rune?" Thane asked as she joined them. "I'll kill her if she backs out on this little get-together."

"I guess you don't know?"

"Know what?"

"Where she is?" Gayle and Auden said in unison.

"Should I?" Thane was beginning to feel as if she had tripped down the rabbit hole. "You mean where she is *now?* The last time I saw her, she said she was going upstairs to—uh, she said she'd see me here."

"She went to her room?" Auden studied Thane's face intently. "When?"

"Right after the signing. I'm sure she'll be here. She said—"

"Was she all right?" Auden asked sharply, aware that Thane was uncomfortable about something.

If you see Auden, just tell her I got held up. Don't mention this, okay? Thane hesitated.

"It's important, Teddy," Gayle said gently.

"She was fine. She just had a little nosebleed, but—"

"Oh my God." Auden started toward the exit.

"Where are you going?" Gayle asked urgently, hurrying along beside Auden with Thane following on her heels.

"To her room."

"I'll come, just in case there's a problem."

Once in the elevator, Thane looked from Gayle to Auden. "What's going on? Does this have something to do with her collapsing at the Four Seasons?"

Gayle took Thane's hand. "We can't talk about the details, okay, baby?"

"Sure." Thane rested her hand on the back of Gayle's neck, stroking her softly. "Okay."

The instant the elevator doors slid open, Auden rushed down the hall and knocked on Hays's door. "Hays? Sweetheart? It's Auden."

When she'd tried three times to no avail, Auden turned to Gayle, desperate. "What should we do? What if she's lying in there and needs help? What if...oh God, what if she hit her head or—"

"I'll call the hotel manager and play the doctor card," Gayle said quietly. "I'll ask him to send someone to check, okay?" When Auden nodded mutely, Gayle added, "Come on, our room is down the hall."

Auden paced the room while Gayle placed the call and asked for the manager. She wanted to scream as she listened to Gayle explain that she was a doctor and that she was concerned about a guest with a life-threatening illness. *Life-threatening. No. Oh, no. Not now. Not so soon.*

When Gayle hung up and looked at Auden with a stunned expression on her face, Auden almost *did* scream. "What? What did he say? What is it?"

"She checked out. A couple of hours ago."

"No. She wouldn't, not without—"

"Hang on," Thane muttered from across the room. "I've got an e-mail from Rune. From this afternoon."

Auden spun around to stare at her. "Read it...please."

"It's another *Eros* submission. Probably just something she's been meaning to se—"

"Read it, baby," Gayle said gently.

"Okay," Thane said slowly. "Come read it with me, then."

Auden and Gayle looked over Thane's shoulder as she opened the attachment.

```
Secret Passions - Final Scene

    Time  is  so  subjective,  its  measure
totally  dependent  upon  the  means  by  which
we  mark  its  passage.  When  we  follow  the
conventional  milestones,  meting  out  our
lives  with  birthdays  and  graduations  and
anniversaries  and  funerals,  we  are  left
with  voids  along  the  way—vast  stretches  of
empty  space  lost  forever,  never  to  be  filled.
As  time  grows  short,  the  significance  of
each  moment  increases,  until  finally  every
heartbeat  is  of  monumental  importance.  Or
so  it  seems  at  first.
    I  have  discovered,  almost  too  late,  that
time  is  not  just  arbitrary,  but  of  no  great
consequence  after  all.  She  has  taught  me
that  a  touch  is  a  lifetime,  a  kiss  forever,
and  that  our  passion  will  transcend  the
limitations  of  fragile  existence  to  span
eternity.
    I  no  longer  worry  about  the  beat  of  my
heart—I  need  only  the  memory  of  her  to  live
on.  My  soul,  my  very  being,  pulses  with
wonder  at  the  places  within  me  that  she  has
filled,  with  gratitude  for  the  wounds  she
has  healed,  and  with  everlasting  devotion
for  the  love  she  has  given.  In  her  arms,
```

I found passion and peace and a place to rest.

No matter where I travel or what road I take to reach my destination, I will always have the comfort of her hand in mine and the soft whisper of her voice reminding me that I do not need to be afraid. This, this has always been my secret desire, and now I need search no further.

I am loved, and I am content.

* * *

Thane: Please see that *Secret Passions* is dedicated to Auden, with all my heart. Rune

Auden was shaking, tears streaming unheeded down her face.

Thane's voice was a hoarse whisper. "Will somebody please tell me what the hell is going on?"

"Hays and Auden are lovers," Gayle said gently, her arm around Auden's waist and her free hand on Thane's shoulder. "I forgot that you didn't know."

"I figured that out, love," Thane said softly. She looked up at Auden, wincing to see her undisguised anguish. "This message—how sick is she?"

"Very." Auden suddenly raced for the door. "She must have left me a note."

A few seconds later, she fumbled her key card into her door and rushed into her room. A folded sheet of notepaper lay just inside on the floor. With trembling hands, she reached for it.

> *Sweet Auden:*
> *I've never had the words for what you mean to me.*
> *There is one thing, though, that you should know.*
> *I love you.*
> *Hays*

Auden spun around, the note held out in her trembling hand. "I have to find her."

Gayle took the note and stared at it for a long time. She thought of her oath, she thought of her best friend's agony, and she thought of a woman facing her greatest challenge alone. She thought, too, of one critical thing she had learned as a physician—love has the power to work miracles. She met Auden's frantic gaze.

"I know where she is."

CHAPTER TWENTY-NINE

Thane insisted that Gayle and Auden hire a car to drive them back to Philadelphia, while she agreed, reluctantly, to stay in New York City at least through midday on Saturday. Auden wanted Liz Nixon and Thane, along with the other authors, to maintain Destiny's presence at the convention.

"All right," Thane muttered as she helped them carry luggage to the car, "but no one is going to be able to make up for Rune not being here."

Auden began to cry, and Gayle looked helplessly from her friend to her lover, who looked suddenly miserable.

"Jesus, I'm sorry, Auden," Thane said quickly. "So sorry. It's just... damn, I can't quite believe this is happening."

"I don't want to believe it either," Auden replied, angrily swiping at her tears. "But Gayle called the hospital, and Hays has been admitted. So now I don't have any choice *but* to believe it."

Gayle and Thane embraced, Thane kissed Auden's cheek, and the two friends were on their way home. Most of the ride passed in silence. A few miles from Philadelphia, Auden turned from the window and the night. "I can't believe she did this. I am so angry with her."

"You know why she left, don't you?" Gayle took Auden's hand, rubbed her thumb over the back. Her voice was gentle. "Aud?"

"I can guess some of it." Auden was having a hard time keeping her mind from fragmenting. In one instant she was angry, the next terrified, and the next panicked. Right now, Hays was somewhere alone—and in pain—and Auden wasn't with her. She'd begun the day in Hays's arms, and now she wasn't sure that she would ever touch her again. *Stop. You don't even know what has happened. You won't be any good to her this way. She mustn't see you cry.*

Auden closed her eyes and imagined Hays's face as she'd looked down on her at the instant of orgasm, tender and loving and strong. The anger slipped away. Auden met Gayle's anxious gaze. "She has never wanted me to be hurt because of her illness or to suffer through the trials of the treatment. If she's sick, really sick now, she'll want to spare me."

"Yes."

"She's wrong."

"Of course she is, and I'm not trying to defend her." Gayle slid closer, wrapping her arm around Auden's shoulders. "But she's probably as scared and confused as you are right now." Auden tensed and Gayle hugged her. "I'm sorry, honey—God, I—"

"No," Auden interrupted. "You're right. I'm sure she is frightened, which is why I need to be with her. She thinks she's protecting me, and when I'm not so furious with her, I love her for it."

"Auden," Gayle said seriously. "This could get rough."

"I already know she might die." Auden's strangled laughter was tinged with wild pain. "Anything worse than that you want to add?"

"Ah, fuck." Gayle squeezed the bridge of her nose and tried to sort out her desire to prepare Auden for what might be coming from her wish to protect her friend from as much pain as possible. "If she's doing what I suspect she's doing—"

"Getting the bone marrow transplant?"

Gayle nodded. "That's my guess. It's going to be dicey for a while—she could get...really sick."

"I know. She's told me." Auden felt steadier the longer they talked. It helped to deal with facts and not uncertain fears. "Do you think they'll start tonight?"

"I don't know—maybe. If she's..." Gayle stumbled for the right words. It was hard to keep her doctor shield in place. Auden was her family.

"Gayle, just talk doctor talk. I can take it. Please. Just tell me."

Gayle set her jaw. "If she's deteriorating, and she might be, since she was just treated a few weeks ago and is symptomatic again already, her doctors will jump on this. I imagine they'll start the chemotherapy as soon as they can."

"Will that make her sicker?"

"Not right away—maybe not at all. It depends on the regimen they're using to prepare her for the transplant."

"Will I be able to see her tonight?"

"I don't know. It sucks, Auden, but you're not legally Hays's family." Gayle balled her fists, because it killed her to say that, knowing that Auden probably meant more to Hays than anyone in the world. "I'm going to have to call her hematologist to clear it. I know him by sight, but he probably doesn't know me. I'll do what I can."

Auden thought for a moment, then dug in her briefcase for her phone. After a moment, she punched in a number and waited, holding her breath. "Abel? It's Auden Frost. Are you with her?" She expected him to hesitate or hedge, and his prompt reply surprised her.

"I just left the hospital," he answered with what almost sounded like relief. "Where are you?"

"On I-95, about fifteen minutes from there. How is she?"

"Right now, all right. They're giving her some more blood."

His voice was eerily flat. It was frightening to hear Abel sound overwhelmed. "What about the transplant?"

"Christopher is catching the redeye from Los Angeles, and they've started the drugs. It could be as soon as tomorrow."

Auden gasped. "I need to see her tonight. Can you arrange that?"

"She didn't want you to know about this."

"I don't care, Abel. I...we're lovers and—"

"I know. And I'm glad."

Auden's voice grew stronger. "If there's some list of priority visitors or something, I want on it. I need to be able to see her."

"I'll make some calls."

"You have my cell phone number, in case...you need to reach me for any reason?"

"Yes."

"Thank you for this."

"No, Auden. Don't thank me. Just...please help her get through this."

"I will," she said softly. "Goodbye."

Gayle said, "We'll be there in another five minutes."

"Tell me what to expect."

"If they're treating her on an investigational study, they'll be pretty strict about the protocols, even if all the precautions are not absolutely necessary. She might be in an isolation room already."

"Meaning?"

"Gowns, maybe gloves and masks—everything possible to keep her from getting infected while her immune system is knocked down from the chemo."

"Will I be able to touch her?"

"I'm not sure, Aud," Gayle said softly. It hurt so much to hear Auden's anguish, Gayle wondered if *she* was going to be able to stand this. She wished then that she'd asked Thane to come with them instead of encouraging her to remain at the convention. Suddenly, she longed for the solace of Thane's presence and understood poignantly how much Auden must want to be with Hays. "We'll find out soon. We're here."

While Gayle leaned forward to instruct the driver on where to wait for them, Auden glanced at her watch. Ten-thirty. She squared her shoulders and pushed open the car door. "Okay. Let's go."

Ten minutes later, they were standing at the nurse's station while Gayle spoke to the head nurse. "I'm Dr. Dunbar and this is Auden Frost. We'd like to see one of your patients—Haydon Palmer."

"Oh, the new admission."

Auden hated the place for no good reason at all. The halls were clean, bright, and cheerily painted in pastel tones. And there was a nice big sign saying *Oncology*, and Hays was the "new admission." She wanted to find Hays and take her away. Take her home. She wanted to light the logs in the fireplace and hold her beneath the soft afghan that had sheltered them as they'd made love and make sure that nothing ever hurt her ever again. Auden bit her lip and closed her fists so tightly that her nails nearly pierced her palms.

"Yes," Gayle was saying. "I can call her attending if you li—"

"No, that won't be necessary. Dr. Rosenberg just this minute called and said it was fine that Ms. Frost see the patient at any time. Just be sure to follow the posted instructions. Room 651."

"Got it. Thanks."

Auden followed Gayle to the end of the hall where two rooms opened off a small anteroom with scrub sinks and cabinets which held cover gowns, shoe covers, disposable surgical gloves, and surgical masks. A prominent yellow sign stated *Isolation* above a list of rules. Both doors to the patient rooms were closed.

"Just put on those booties and a yellow gown," Gayle instructed. "Then take off any jewelry and scrub your hands in the sink with the surgical soap from the dispenser for two minutes."

"Good?" Auden asked when she'd finished.

"Yep. Fine. They're not requiring a mask or gloves, so you're set." Gayle gave Auden's arm a squeeze. "I'll wait out here."

Carefully, Auden opened the door and stepped into the patient room. There was a single bed lit by an overhead light fixture turned down to its lowest setting. "Hays?"

"You're unstoppable." She sounded weary but alert. "How did you find me so quickly?"

"I had help." Auden walked to the side of the bed. An IV pole stood on one side of the head of the bed, and blood flowed from a bag connected to an intravenous line that went into a vein in Hays's left arm. There was another intravenous line taped to her right arm, and clear fluids from several smaller intravenous bags were infusing into that one. "How do you feel?"

"Depends. How angry are you with me?"

Auden desperately wanted to touch her, but she wasn't certain it was safe. She curled her fingers around the steel railing that separated her from her lover. "I asked you first."

Silence ensued, but Hays quickly relented. She was so very glad to see Auden that she couldn't bear to keep fighting her. "I had a monster headache a few hours ago, but the blood has helped a lot. I can't feel anything from the chemotherapy yet." She lifted her right hand and placed it over Auden's on the rail. "There's a good chance I'll be out of here in a day or two. I don't suppose I can talk you into leaving and then waiting for me to call you?"

"When will that be, do you think, when you would call?" Unable to stop herself, Auden entwined her fingers with Hays's. "Will it be when you come home in a day or two? Or will it be after all of the treatment is over? Or will it be in six months...or six years...when you've decided that it's safe for me to love you?"

"Oh, Auden," Hays sighed. "Can't you take the easy way out?"

"The only easy way is for me to be with you." Auden brushed her free hand through Hays's hair. "And to answer your question, I was really pissed at you for a while, but I'm mostly over it now. I only have to see you, and I forget how mad you make me."

"Thank God for that."

"I want to kiss you so badly. I hate not being able to touch you as much as I want."

For the first time, Hays smiled. "We made love last night and again this morning. I don't think there's anything remotely contagious about you, and if there were, I've already been exposed." She tugged on Auden's hand. "I would like it very much if you would kiss me."

Auden leaned over the rail and placed a soft, lingering kiss on Hays's mouth. "Will we have to stop this for a while?"

"I think kisses will still be allowed. Chances are I won't be much good for anything else in the beginning." Hays looked away. When she spoke again, her voice was low, tormented. "I'm so sorry about this. Jesus, you deserve so much more."

"You know what almost broke my heart, Hays?" Auden asked softly.

Slowly, Hays turned her head back and met Auden's steady gaze. "What?"

"That you would leave me without saying goodbye."

Tears trembled on Hays's lashes. "I thought it would hurt you less than if something...something went wrong here."

"Well, you were mistaken. But I forgive you because I know you did it out of love." Auden caressed the top of Hays's hand with her fingers, wanting so much more but settling for this small contact. "I can wait to make love with you again, but I can't wait in limbo somewhere not knowing what's happening to you."

"I love you so much," Hays murmured. "I don't want anything to hurt you."

"One of these days, I want you to say *I love you* without sounding sorry." Auden gripped the rail tightly. "That's what *I* want."

"Oh, sweet Auden." Tears trickled softly down Hays's cheeks, unheeded now. "I'm not sorry that I love you. I'm not sorry that you love me—never that—it's the most precious thing that's ever happened to me in my life."

"Then why are you so sad, sweetheart?"

"Because I want you to be happy."

Auden smiled, a sure, certain smile. "You, Haydon Palmer, have *already* made me the happiest woman in the world."

Hays brushed at the tears on her face and heaved a great sigh. "I believe I'm going to have to concede this argument. You're indefatigable."

"Thank you. It's about time you admitted that." Suddenly serious once again, Auden urged, "Tell me what's going to happen in the next few days."

"Tomorrow morning I get a low dose of full-body radiation. Tomorrow afternoon or Sunday morning, I get the stem cell transplant from my brother."

Auden blinked. "So soon?"

"The sooner the better, apparently." Hays held Auden's gaze unflinchingly. "My counts are in the basement. Paul is worried that I won't bounce back again. He thinks we should push ahead before I get...too weak."

"I see." Auden's voice was a whisper. "Is Abel taking care of the arrangements for your brother?"

"All bases covered." Hays shifted restlessly under the thin hospital blanket.

"Does your brother know you're a lesbian?"

Hays nodded. "Yes. And I'll tell him about you tomorrow. You won't need to feel awkward with him."

"What do you intend to tell him?"

"That you're the love of my life."

"No wonder I fell in love with you." Auden smiled faintly. "You really are the most romantic woman on the planet."

"There's something you should know," Hays said quietly. "Abel has medical power of attorney for me and he knows my wishes. If anything happens, he'll take care of things with the doctors. You can trust him."

"Is there anything you want me to know? About that?" Auden's heart was in her throat. This was not a conversation she had expected to have at this point with the woman who had walked into her life and not only captured her heart, but also claimed her soul. Not now. Not yet. But here they were.

Hays shook her head. "I promised you I'd fight. I will, I swear. But if I can't anymore, then I want you to know..." Her voice broke. "Just know it's all right...to let go."

"I'm sorry," Auden whispered. Tears slowly trickled unchecked. "I swore I wouldn't do this."

"It's okay." Hays's voice was gentle, her fingers softly caressing Auden's arm. She was crying, too, but didn't notice. "You're perfect. You're everything. I love you."

"God," Auden gasped, fumbling with one hand to pull Kleenex from a dispenser on the bedside table. She could barely reach, but she wouldn't let go of Hays's hand. Finally, she managed it and wiped her eyes. "I adore you."

Hays grinned. "You know, I look sicker than I am at the moment."

Auden smiled tremulously. "You *can't* be trying to seduce me."

"You can be pretty sure that's one thing I'll never stop doing."

"Well, I'll hold you to that. And just as a reminder..." Auden looked around the room. "Do you happen to have a pen and paper in here?"

"My briefcase is in the closet. Why?"

Reluctantly, Auden released Hays's hand, went to the closet, and pulled out the briefcase. In a second, she returned to the bedside with a pen and note card. She wrote for a moment, then asked, "Can you write?"

"Sure. But wha—"

"Sign this." Auden handed Hays the index card.

Hays read: *I owe you -- the next sunny day*.

Laughing, she signed her name and handed it back. "Rain check?"

"Uh-huh. They're starting to add up, Palmer."

"You charging interest?"

Auden slid the card into her pocket, leaned over, and kissed Hays again. "Mmm. Two for one."

"I love you." Hays loved saying it.

"I love you." Auden forced herself to release Hays's hand. "What time is your treatment?"

"Nine."

With difficulty, Auden forced a smile. "You should get some rest. I'll come back in the morning."

Hays felt as if a huge lead weight had settled in her stomach. She wanted to beg Auden to stay. She wanted to climb out of the bed and go with her. She glanced up. The second unit of blood was almost in. She'd feel better now. They could go home, make love, wake up together. "Auden," she whispered. *Don't leave me.*

"I'll be here first thing." Auden's voice shook. She took a step backward in the direction of the door. *I will not cry again.*

"Okay. Sure." Hays tried out a smile. It wavered. "Is Gayle with you?"

"Right outside." Auden's heart was breaking. Hays looked so alone, and the thought of leaving her even for an hour was painful beyond imagination. She wouldn't even have considered going except that it seemed Hays needed to rest. "Try to sleep."

Hays nodded. "You rest, too, okay?"

Auden was almost at the door, but she wasn't certain she could go through. "I will. I love you."

"'Night," Hays called, her left hand wrapped tightly around the rail. As the door slowly swung closed, she shut her eyes, the better to remember Auden's face through the long night ahead.

Outside, Gayle pushed away from the wall where she had been leaning as she waited. "You okay?"

Auden shook her head, not trusting her voice, and leaned into Gayle for support.

"Okay, sweetie," Gayle said gently, threading her arm around Auden's waist. "Let's get you home."

CHAPTER THIRTY

A uden and Gayle were halfway down to the lobby in the
elevator before Auden spoke.

"I can't do this."

Gayle quickly hid her surprise. She hadn't expected this reaction from Auden, but she understood it. This kind of illness was hell on couples, even when they'd been together for years. Tenderly, she took her friend's hand.

"It's hard, honey, I know. You've had a lot thrown at you in a short time. First, you come out, then you discover that your new lover is terribly ill. No one would fault you for needing to step back."

Auden raised anguished eyes to Gayle's. "Step back?"

"Hays loves you—she'll understand. Take a few days off from work, maybe even get away for a little while—give yourself some time to absorb what's happened." Gayle's expression was compassionate. "I'll talk to Hays if you want and explain why you're not here. I know she'll be glad that you're taking care of yourself. She'll want that."

"You're the best friend I could ever have," Auden murmured.

"I love you," Gayle said softly as the elevator doors slid open on the first floor, and she walked out. She stopped, turned, and looked back in surprise at Auden, who was still in the elevator car. "Aud?"

"I can't leave her." Auden smiled faintly. "That's what I meant. I'm going back upstairs, and I'm staying with her until someone tells me it's not safe for her if I'm there. Otherwise, they'll need dynamite to get me away from her."

Gayle grinned, a wave of relief passing over her face. "Ah—all's right with the world again."

"Yes," Auden agreed, feeling the pain in her heart lessen. "It is."

"You go back—I'll take care of getting your luggage home. Call and tell me if you need anything."

Auden held the door open with her hand. "Go back to New York. Spend the rest of the weekend with Thane."

"You sure?" Gayle asked dubiously, although her eyes lit up just thinking about her girlfriend.

"Yes, I'm sure. I'll be fine." Auden let the doors close as she said, "Go to her. Don't let this chance get away."

Once back on the oncology floor, Auden repeated the washing and gowning routine, then quietly opened Hays's door. If Hays was sleeping, she didn't want to wake her. There was no movement from the still figure in the bed. Stepping carefully, Auden lifted the one upholstered armchair and moved it closer to the bed.

Hays turned her head and opened her eyes. "Auden?"

"Hello, sweetheart."

"I'm so glad you're here," Hays whispered, raising a hand above the rail.

Throat tight, Auden touched her fingers to Hays's. "I need to be with you."

"I..." Hays's voice was thick with tears. "I need you so much."

"That's good, because..." Auden struggled with her own tears of fatigue and fear. "I love you."

"Did I fall asleep? It's not morning, is it?"

"No, honey. It's just before midnight." Auden shook the bedrail slightly. "Will you promise not to fall out if I put this thing down?"

Hays laughed weakly. "Promise."

Carefully, Auden lowered the rail on the right side of the bed and pulled her chair as close as she could. Hays edged to the side of the bed, and they linked hands below the intravenous line taped just above Hays's right wrist. Then Auden leaned down, stretched out an arm on the bed behind Hays's head, and snuggled her face close to Hays's on the pillow.

"Thank you for coming back." Hays's voice was worn thin with exhaustion.

"You never have to thank me for loving you," Auden said quietly before she kissed the corner of Hays's mouth. "I promise that you will always have the comfort of my hand in yours." She smoothed Hays's hair. "And that I will always be here so that you won't be afraid."

"Sweet Auden." Hays looked into Auden's eyes, soothed by the tender gaze. "I love you."

Very softly, Auden kissed her forehead. "And I love you...forever and always."

As Hays drifted off to sleep, she felt no fear.

❖

Auden was awakened by a muted cough. She jumped slightly, turned her head, and almost cried out at the cramp in her shoulder. She'd finally fallen asleep curled up in the chair. Hays's hand was still in hers.

Rubbing her stiff muscles, she regarded the middle-aged man with dark curly hair and the bluest eyes she'd ever seen, who stood just inside the door. She glanced at Hays, who seemed to be still asleep. The fact that she hadn't yet awakened was unusual, and she was very pale, almost colorless. Heart twisting, Auden placed her hand protectively on Hays' shoulder as she looked questioningly at the newcomer.

"The nurses can move a lounge chair in here for you," he said quietly. "They have some sort of cot, too, if you'd rather."

"Will I be able to stay?"

"Unless she shows signs of infection or her white count drops dangerously low, yes." He stepped closer, and Auden saw that he carried a clipboard under his right arm. Flashes of navy blue chinos and hiking boots showed beneath the yellow gown. "I'm Paul Rosenberg, Hays's hematologist." He extended his hand.

"Hello. I'm Auden Frost, Hays's..." Auden glanced at Hays, wondering if there was one word to encompass everything that Hays meant to her. *How is it that when it matters the most, words fail?*

She met his gaze as she returned his handshake. "I'm her lover."

"Pleased to meet you."

Hays stirred, moaned softly, and opened her eyes. Immediately, she looked for Auden, smiling in relief when she saw her. "Hi."

"Hi." Auden lifted Hays's hand and brushed it against her cheek before lightly kissing her fingertips. "How are you?"

"That's my question," Rosenberg said with affection as he stepped up to the bed. "Morning, Hays."

"Hi, Paul." Hays slowly pushed herself up and blinked several times. "Okay, let's see. My head feels a little fuzzy but no pain anywhere." She gave Rosenberg a hopeful glance. "Any chance we can hold off?"

"I'm afraid not." His eyes were soft with kindness, but his tone unyielding. "The red cell transfusion you got last night will mask your symptoms for a while, but the medications just aren't stimulating your bone marrow any longer. You need viable cells before a complication develops. You need the transplant now."

Hays's hand shook in Auden's, and Auden squeezed gently.

"Okay," Hays said steadily after a second. "Radiation this morning and then...?"

"We'll do the transplant later this afternoon. Your brother called me from the airport. I reviewed things with him, and he's ready to go. He'll be here by eleven so we can harvest his bone marrow and prepare the material for transplantation."

"Is it painful?" Auden asked, feeling as if she had sawdust in her throat. *It's really going to happen.*

Rosenberg turned to her. "Not really. Christopher will be sedated for the harvest, and his back will be a bit sore for a few days. Once the marrow is processed, Hays will get something that looks like a blood transfusion through the large vein in her neck."

"It'll be okay," Hays said reassuringly, having heard the infinitesimal tremor in Auden's voice.

Auden smiled at her. "I know." Then she fixed Rosenberg with a steady gaze. "And after that?"

"If there's no temp spike, which might indicate an acute transfusion reaction or some kind of infection, home tomorrow, two days of outpatient chemo, and then...we wait."

"For what?"

"Evidence of engraftment—uh, signs that the transplanted cells have survived—a rising white count, healthy cells on a blood smear, and eventually a bone marrow biopsy to check for repopulation of Hays's marrow with normal cells." He spoke matter-of-factly, watching both Hays and Auden as he spoke.

Hays laughed shortly. "Sounds simple enough."

"Sometimes it is." The doctor shrugged.

Auden asked, "When will we know?"

"Two to four weeks."

"So soon?" Hope resounded in Auden's voice, and she glanced quickly at Hays, whose expression was guarded.

Rosenberg continued, "For the initial take...success...of the graft, yes. Then, of course, we'll have to monitor for graft rejection or host reactions or a flare of the original disease."

Hays turned to Auden. "It will be months, maybe longer, before we really know anything."

"That's okay." Auden brushed her fingers lightly down Hays's arm. "I can handle the uncertainty, as long as I have you."

"Well," Rosenberg said briskly, "the nurses will be in shortly to get some blood for the baseline values, and then you'll go down for the radiation. I'll see you both later." With that, he left.

"Are you really feeling better?" Auden asked as soon as they were alone.

"Pretty much." Hays swung her legs over the side of the bed and sat up. "I'm tired as hell, but I'm used to that. Nothing hurts." She stood slowly. "I'd better get cleaned up."

Auden slipped her arm around Hays's waist. "Need help?"

"Can you help me get these IVs organized so I don't hang myself?"

"Sure." Auden transferred the remaining bags to a wheeled pole next to the bed. "Okay?"

Hays grabbed the pole with one hand and leaned to kiss Auden's cheek. "Yeah, thanks. I got it. You can shower in there if you want."

"Hmm." Auden stroked Hays's back as they made their way to the adjoining bathroom. "I guess you can't join me with those lines taped all over you, can you?"

"No," Hays said with a very healthy grin. "But I can watch."

❖

Three hours later, Hays was back in bed, asleep, after having spent two hours in Radiology receiving a single dose of total-body radiation. While she'd been gone, Auden had taken a cab home, packed an overnight bag, and returned. She'd also picked up some work—final edits on *Dark Passions,* the next book she intended to publish. She sat in a chair by the bedside, the manuscript propped on her knee, a pen in one hand and the other resting on Hays's head.

> The woman pushed the door all the way open and approached the bed. She looked down at her lover for a long time. The bleeding had stopped, leaving the sinewy planes of her perfect body obscured by fluid pooled in the injured tissue. She sank slowly down on the floor beside the bed, pushed her back up against the wall, and reached her hand up into the hair framing the beautiful face. She closed her eyes and gently let the strands fall through her fingers.

As she read, Auden fingered sweat-dampened locks, her breath stumbling on the jagged edge of pain. Images overlapped, fused, and re-emerged so much sharper as her hand moved over fragile flesh. The damage was so terrible, and now the anguish was palpable, so real—so close.

> She thought about the satin-soft skin in the firelight and how it had glowed with perspiration as they made love. She thought about the sharply etched muscles in the sculpted back as she rose above her in ecstasy.

Gently, Auden...

> ...traced the fine planes of the striking face, remembering how her lover looked just before orgasm.

Her eyes blurred and she...

> ...sat still for a long time, listening to the quiet breathing.

The words disappeared as the...

> ...anger flooded her heart.

I will not let you go.

When the door opened, Auden looked up vaguely, still lost somewhere between Rune Dyre's fiction and Haydon Palmer's life. A man with Hays's obsidian eyes, dark hair silvered at the temples, and aristocratic features regarded her with interest.

"Ms. Frost?"

"Christopher?" Auden stood, glancing once at Hays, assuring herself that she was resting comfortably. *She's not bleeding. She's safe here with me.*

He nodded and beckoned with his head to the anteroom outside. Auden followed.

"I'm Auden," she said when they were alone. "You're probably wondering what I'm doing here."

"I hope you don't mind. Abel mentioned you when he picked me up at the airport," he said as they faced each other in the small space. "Things are moving so quickly, he was just trying to bring me up to date."

"He told you about Hays and me?"

"Yes. It's good to meet you." Christopher looked toward the closed door. "How is she?"

"Worn out, but otherwise all right. I'm so glad you were able to get here so quickly."

"I've been waiting—hoping—for the call. I'm glad it finally came." He smiled faintly. "We hardly knew each other when she was growing up. There are a lot of years between us, but she's my sister. Besides, someone has to keep Palmer Publishing going, and it's always been her baby."

Auden smiled. "Where's Abel?"

"Parking. I wanted to see Hays before the procedure. I only have a few minutes, but if she's asleep—"

"No, go in. I'm sure she wants to see you. And Christopher...thank you."

He met her eyes, and his held the same intensity she often saw in Hays's. "I'll do it a dozen times if we have to."

"Let's hope that isn't necessary," Auden whispered as he disappeared into Hays's room.

❖

Hays was sitting upright in bed, a new intravenous catheter taped to her chest, when Paul Rosenberg walked into her room five hours later. The large line ran into the subclavian vein just below her collarbone and from there, directly into her heart.

"You ready?" He held up a plastic bag filled with viscous red material.

Hays looked at Auden, and they both looked at him. "Yes," they said in unison.

He fussed with the line and the bags for a moment and then stepped back, observing the flow of harvested cells into Hays's bloodstream. "They'll float around for a while and eventually find their way into your bone marrow. Then they'll set up housekeeping and get busy reproducing. Smart little buggers."

"Let's hope so," Hays said fervently, watching the slow migration of life into her body. "How's Christopher?"

"Fine. He's sore but out of recovery already. Mr. Pritchard took him to your place."

"Good."

"I'll be back in a few hours to check on you," Rosenberg said as he left.

As soon as he was gone, Hays pushed to the far side of the bed and said to Auden, "Come lie here next to me."

Carefully, Auden settled beside Hays, taking her lover's hand and leaning her head on Hays' shoulder. "Can you feel anything at all?"

"I can feel you," Hays whispered into her hair, unexpectedly calm and content. "That's all I need to feel."

Auden turned her head and kissed the corner of Hays's mouth. "*I* can feel something."

"What?"

"The future."

"Are we together?" Hays's voice trembled.

"Oh, yes." Auden held her lover more tightly. "Forever and beyond."

❖

Three weeks later, Auden steadfastly clung to that belief because she had no other choice. Hope seemed to be all there was left.

"I'm going to admit her for observation," Paul Rosenberg said quietly. A few feet away, an emergency room technician bent over Hays, drawing yet another blood sample. "She should be showing signs of repopulation by now."

"And she isn't?" Auden was amazed at how calm she sounded. Inside, she was screaming. Hays looked terrible. Her color was beyond pale now; her eyes, always so intense, were dim with pain and exhaustion. She'd lost weight in the weeks since the transplant, and, for the past twenty-four hours, had been too weak to leave the house. Now she had a fever, and Auden feared that an infection at this point might be more than Hays could fight.

"Not yet. The chemo and radiation have worked—*her* bone marrow has shut down, and her own counts are low. That's the good part. The problem is, Christopher's cells don't seem to be flourishing."

He looked worried, and that frightened Auden more than anything had thus far.

"What are we looking at here?" The question terrified her, but she had to know. She wanted to be ready. Hays would need that.

"If her counts don't rise soon, she'll be at risk for hemorrhage and widespread infection. I'll transfuse her tonight, and we'll keep a close eye on her temperature." He gave Auden an encouraging smile. "This may just be a bump in the road. In a week, we could all be celebrating."

"Isn't there something else you can do?"

"I'm sorry." His frustration was evident. "I'll talk to her."

"No," Auden said quickly, grasping his arm. "I'll tell her."

As the technician left with her tray of blood samples, Auden crossed to the stretcher and leaned down to kiss Hays's forehead. Hays's eyes were closed and her breathing shallow. "Darling?"

Hays's eyes flickered opened, and she smiled weakly. "I think I fell asleep."

"That's all right." Auden stroked her cheek and managed a smile of her own. "Paul wants to keep you here for a bit."

"That bad, huh?"

"Your blood counts are low. He wants to be careful."

"What about the results of the bone marrow tests?"

"The transplant hasn't kicked in yet."

Hays studied Auden's eyes and saw the fear she tried so hard to hide. "Call Gayle, okay? I don't want you to be alone."

"I'm not alone," Auden replied softly, her throat thick with tears she would not shed. "I'm with you."

"Auden, please call her." Hays's voice was weary but insistent. "I need to know that you're okay."

"I'm all right." Auden bent near and kissed Hays's cheek again. With her lips close to her lover's ear, she whispered, "I have you, and that's all I'll ever need. I want you to remember that no matter what comes, I'll be with you."

"I love you," Hays murmured. "But I'm so tired."

"Then you should sleep." Auden was grateful that Hays had closed her eyes again and could not see her face. She bit her lip and steadied her voice. "I'll be right here when you wake up."

Already drifting away, Hays clung to those words and the image of Auden's smile.

❖

"Any change?" Gayle asked softly.

Auden shook her head. Hays was asleep, her face a wash of sweat. The light sheet covering her chest barely seemed to move with each shallow breath. *She's so still. Almost as if...* Auden shuddered, the pain so swift she couldn't breathe.

"Have you had dinner?"

"I...I'm not sure." Auden tried to think. It had been three days since Hays had been admitted, and Auden had spent almost every minute in the hospital, sitting by her bedside, talking with her when she was awake, holding her hand or stroking her hair as she'd slept. Sleep, however, was something that had eluded Auden. She was afraid to be away from Hays' side. Desperately, she hoped that her constant presence would lend Hays strength and prayed that her love would ease Hays's pain.

"Come on," Gayle whispered, resting her hand gently on Auden's shoulder. "Thane is coming by to have dinner with me in the hospital cafeteria. You're joining us."

"No," Auden replied quietly. "I can't."

"You have to." Gayle's voice was fierce, but her touch tender as she brushed her fingers over Auden's hair. "You need to take care of yourself. You know Hays will never forgive herself if you get sick. Is that what you want, to add to her pain?"

Auden glanced up into her friend's concerned eyes. "You don't play fair."

"Never said I did." Gayle shrugged. "I love you, and she'll need you more than ever now."

"All right," Auden agreed with a sigh, rising unsteadily. She *was* hungry, and so very tired. "Just for a little while."

As they stepped out into the hall, Paul Rosenberg unexpectedly appeared around the corner. He was in street clothes and without his usual clipboard.

Auden's heart rose in her throat, and she grasped Gayle's hand automatically. *It's after seven on a weeknight. Why is he here?*

"Is something wrong?" Auden asked anxiously before he even had time to greet them.

"No," he exclaimed, a huge smile breaking over his face. "Something is finally right. I just looked at the results of Hays's latest bone marrow biopsy. She's finally chimeric..." At Auden's uncertain look, he clarified. "There are definite signs of transplanted cells growing in her marrow. We're getting a response."

"It's working?" Auden whispered, almost afraid to believe she'd heard correctly.

When he nodded, Auden suddenly felt dizzy. Had Gayle not slipped an arm around her waist, she might have fallen. Instead, she turned her face into Gayle's neck and let the tears come.

❖

"Auden?" Hays's throat was dry and her head pounded with the dull ache that seemed to be her constant companion whenever she was awake.

"I'm here, darling."

Hays frowned at the dark circles under Auden's normally vibrant eyes. "What time is it?"

"Eleven."

"At night?"

"Yes." Auden slid the chair forward and tilted the water cup with its straw toward Hays's lips. "Here. You must be thirsty."

After Hays managed a few sips, she said, "Thanks. You look tired, sweetheart."

"Mmm, a bit." Auden smiled. "I have news."

"Good news?"

"The best." Auden couldn't hide the tears, but for the first time in a long time, she didn't try. "Paul says the latest bone marrow biopsy shows sign of take. The transplant is working."

Hays's eyes grew wide, and then she gasped, a small choked sound. "Oh God. Auden." She reached for Auden's hand and held on tightly. "Oh God, I love you."

And then they were both crying and laughing and daring to dream once more.

EPILOGUE

```
-----Original Message-----
```
From: Rune@HeartLand.com
Sent: Friday November 26, 2:40PM
To: AFrost@PalmPub.net
Subject: Dark Passions-Frontmatter
Attachment: DP-ded.doc 26KB

Ms. Frost:

   I've attached the information you requested for Dark Passions. I am delighted to hear that it is on schedule for the planned release in two weeks. Thank you for all you have done to make that a reality. Need I say that I could never have done it without you?

   I look forward to seeing you at the convention in Washington next month. I do hope that you save an evening there for me.

Yours most truly,
Rune Dyre

Auden smiled and hit Reply.

```
----Reply----
```
From: AFrost@PalmPub.net
Sent: Friday November 26, 2:48PM
To: Rune@HeartLand.com
Subject: Re: DarkPassions-Frontmatter

Ms. Dyre:

It was my great pleasure to assist you in completing this work. You may be sure that we will meet in DC. My calendar is always free for you—name the time.

Yours most sincerely,
Auden Frost

Then she opened the attachment.

Acknowledgment

Thane Cutlass said write it, and she never stopped believing. She was there in the uncertain hours of its inception, weathering all my doubts and misgivings — reading, critiquing, and encouraging. This is as much hers as mine.

Most importantly, Thane and her lover, Gayle, remained steadfast friends to me during my own dark hours, lending strength not only to me but also to the woman I love. For that, I am more grateful than I can say.

This book embodies my darkest dreams, my brightest hopes, and my greatest passions. To my everlasting joy, it has all come true.

RD

Dedication

To Auden
My Passion, My Love

With trembling hands, Auden picked up the phone and dialed an extension.

"Hello?"

"Have I ever told you how much I love you?" Auden asked.

"Every day for the last eight months."

"Some things bear repeating."

"Good," Hays whispered. "Because I'll never tire of hearing it."

"That's *very* good, then," Auden said softly. "Because forever is a long, long time."

The End

About the Author

Radclyffe is the author of numerous lesbian romances (*Safe Harbor* and its sequels *Beyond the Breakwater* and *Distant Shores, Silent Thunder*; *Innocent Hearts, Love's Melody Lost, Love's Tender Warriors, Tomorrow's Promise, Passion's Bright Fury, Love's Masquerade, shadowland,* and *Fated Love*), as well as two romance/intrigue series: the Honor series (*Above All, Honor*; *Honor Bound, Love & Honor, Honor Guards*) and the Justice series (*Shield of Justice*, the prequel *A Matter of Trust, In Pursuit of Justice,* and *Justice in the Shadows*).

A 2003/2004 recipient of the Alice B. award for her body of work as well as a member of the Golden Crown Literary Society, Pink Ink, and the Romance Writers of America, she lives with her partner, Lee, in Philadelphia, PA, where she both writes and heads Bold Strokes Books, a lesbian publishing company. She states, "As an author, I know how much more it takes to 'make a book' than just adding a cover to a manuscript. Done with respect and love for the craft, creating a book is a never-ending joy. As a publisher, my mission is to provide that experience to every author at Bold Strokes Books."

Her upcoming works include selections in *Stolen Moments: Erotic Interludes 2* from Bold Strokes Books, *After Dark* from Bella Books, *Hot Lesbian Erotica* from Cleis, the next novel in the Honor series, *Honor Reclaimed* (Dec. 2005), and the romance *Turn Back Time* (Feb. 2006).

Look for information about these works at www.boldstrokesbooks. com.

Other Books Available From Bold Strokes Books

Course of Action by Gun Brooke. Actress Carolyn Black desperately wants the starring role in an upcoming film produced by Annelie Peterson, a wealthy publisher with a mysterious past. How far is Carolyn prepared to go for the dream part of a lifetime? And just how far will Annelie bend her principles in the name of desire? (1-933110-22-8)

Justice Served by Radclyffe. The hunt for an informant in the ranks draws Lieutenant Rebecca Frye, her lover Dr. Catherine Rawlings, and Officer Dellon Mitchell into a deadly game of hide-and-seek with an underworld kingpin who traffics in human souls. (1-933110-15-5)

Rangers at Roadsend by Jane Fletcher. After nine years in the Rangers, dealing with thugs and wild predators, Sergeant Chip Coppelli has learned to spot trouble coming, and that is exactly what she sees in her new recruit, Katryn Nagata. But even so, Chip was not expecting murder. The Celaeno series. (1-933110-28-7)

Distant Shores, Silent Thunder by Radclyffe. Ex-lovers, would-be lovers, and old rivals find their paths unwillingly entwined when Drs. KT O'Bannon and Tory King—and the women who love them—are forced to examine the boundaries of love, friendship, and the ties that transcend time. (1-933110-08-2)

Hunter's Pursuit by Kim Baldwin. A raging blizzard, a remote mountain hideaway, and more than one killer for hire set a scene for disaster—or desire—when reluctant assassin Katarzyna Demetrious rescues a stranger and unwittingly exposes her heart. (1-933110-09-0)

The Walls of Westernfort by Jane Fletcher. All Temple Guard Natasha Ionadis wants is to serve the Goddess, and she volunteers eagerly for a dangerous mission to infiltrate a band of rebels. But once she is away from the temple, the issues are no longer so simple, especially in light of her attraction to one of the rebels. Is it too late to work out what she really wants from life? (1-933110-24-4)

Change Of Pace: *Erotic Interludes* by Radclyffe. Twenty-five hot-wired encounters guaranteed to spark more than just your imagination. Erotica as you've always dreamed of it. (1-933110-07-4)

Fated Love by Radclyffe. Amidst the chaos and drama of a busy emergency room, two women must contend not only with the fragile nature of life, but also with the mysteries of the heart and the irresistible forces of fate. (1-933110-05-8)

Justice in the Shadows by Radclyffe. In a shadow world of secrets, lies, and hidden agendas, Detective Sergeant Rebecca Frye and her lover, Dr. Catherine Rawlings, join forces once again in the elusive search for justice. (1-933110-03-1)

shadowland by Radclyffe. In a world on the far edge of desire, two women are drawn together by power, passion, and dark pleasures. An erotic romance. (1-933110-11-2)

Love's Masquerade by Radclyffe. Plunged into the often indistinguishable realms of fiction, fantasy, and hidden desires, Auden Frost discovers a shifting landscape that will force her to question everything she has believed to be true about herself and the nature of love. (1-933110-14-7)

Beyond the Breakwater by Radclyffe. One Provincetown summer three women learn the true meaning of love, friendship, and family. Second in the Provincetown Tales. (1-933110-06-6)

Tomorrow's Promise by Radclyffe. One timeless summer, two very different women discover the power of passion to heal and the promise of hope that only love can bestow. (1-933110-12-0)

Love's Tender Warriors by Radclyffe. Two women who have accepted loneliness as a way of life learn that love is worth fighting for and a battle they cannot afford to lose. (1-933110-02-3)

Love's Melody Lost by Radclyffe. A secretive artist with a haunted past and a young woman escaping a life that proved to be a lie find their destinies entwined. (1-933110-00-7)

Safe Harbor by Radclyffe. A mysterious newcomer, a reclusive doctor, and a troubled gay teenager learn about love, friendship, and trust during one tumultuous summer in Provincetown. First in the Provincetown Tales. (1-933110-13-9)

Above All, Honor by Radclyffe. The first in the Honor series introduces single-minded Secret Service Agent Cameron Roberts and the woman she is sworn to protect—Blair Powell, the daughter of the president of the United States. First in the Honor series.
(1-933110-04-X)

Love & Honor by Radclyffe. The president's daughter and her security chief are faced with difficult choices as they battle a tangled web of Washington intrigue for...love and honor. Third in the Honor series.
(1-933110-10-4)

Honor Guards by Radclyffe. In a journey that begins on the streets of Paris's Left Bank and culminates in a wild flight for their lives, the president's daughter and those who are sworn to protect her wage a desperate struggle for survival. Fourth in the Honor series.
(1-933110-01-5)

BOLD STROKES BOOKS